Robert Williams Buchanan

**Rachel Dene**

A tale of the Deepdale mills

Robert Williams Buchanan

**Rachel Dene**
*A tale of the Deepdale mills*

ISBN/EAN: 9783337174088

Printed in Europe, USA, Canada, Australia, Japan

Cover: Foto ©Andreas Hilbeck / pixelio.de

More available books at **www.hansebooks.com**

# RACHEL DENE

## A TALE OF THE DEEPDALE MILLS

BY

## ROBERT BUCHANAN

AUTHOR OF

"GOD AND THE MAN," "THE SHADOW OF THE SWORD," ETC.

*A NEW EDITION*

LONDON

CHATTO & WINDUS, PICCADILLY

1895

# CONTENTS.

# CONTENTS.

# RACHEL DENE.

## CHAPTER I.

### FOUND IN THE SNOW.

It was Christmas Eve. Two men and a woman sat, snow-surrounded, in the parlour of a small cottage in the valley of Deepdale, Yorkshire. One man was old, and the woman was his grey, world-worn wife; the other man was young, hale, and hearty.

"Here's Jack's health," said the old man, Jasper Heywood.

"And here's Jack's wife," said Joan.

"Nay, let us toast them together," interposed the young man; "for sure man and wife are one flesh—so here's to 'em both, and God send 'em safely home from these cruel wars."

"Thou mayst well say cruel, Jabez," replied Joan. "Ah, if I had my way, there'd be no fighting men abroad, nor weeping wenches at home!"

"Stop there, woman," said Jasper. "An there

B

was no fightin' men abroad, what'd become o' the weepin' wenches at home?—what'd become o' *us,* and our tight little island, I'd like to know—eh, Jabez?"

"Well, father, when the world grows older and wiser, perhaps folk will find something better to do than cut other folk's throats; but I fear that won't be in your time, or mine."

"Likely not," was the reply. "Meanwhile, since Christmas comes but once a year, let's be jolly. Load thy pipe, lad—here's a bit o' rare bird's-eye; and, good wife, mull us another mug o' elder, and come round t' fire, for sure it's a bitter neet."

The old man was right. It was a bitter night indeed. The wind, however, had dropped, and the snow, which had been falling almost incessantly for the past twenty-four hours, had almost ceased.

All was calm now, and still.

When Jabez Pryke came down from Deepdale Mills the night before, to pass Christmas with his adopted father, Jasper Heywood, and his wife Joan, the grey goose in the sky was only just beginning to shed her feathers; but now she had shed them till the heavens were bare.

The snowdrift had fallen in the valley breast high, and the roads were nigh impassable.

"Strikes me, Jabez," said Joan, "thou'lt have to stay here for t' next week; for sure, thou'lt never be able to get to t' mills wi'out a snow-sledge."

" Well, good mother," answered the young man, laughing, "I couldna wish for better company, nor a warmer welcome, though for certain I promised t' gaffer to dine up at t' Hall to-morrow; and he'll think I'm lost i' t' snow-drift if he doesna see me."

" Come i' t' ingle neuk; draw thysen up t' fire," replied Joan.

The yule log crackled on the hearth, and shed a ruddy glow on the cosy cottage and its occupants, as they gathered closer to the fire.

Old friends these—friends of many years' standing. Although Jabez Pryke had barely turned his five-and-twentieth year, while Jasper and his wife were approaching the meridian of life, Jabez remembered them as long as he could remember anything; for, when left an orphan, they had taken him home and brought him up, side by side with their own boy, the little fair-haired Jack; and from that time forth the two lads loved one another, even as David and Jonathan.

Once, and only once, an interruption occurred to their friendship. Of course it was a woman, and the old story. They both loved the same woman. But Jael Hoyle loved Jack; and no wonder, for he was a jovial, genial, good-looking, good-hearted lad, whom to look at was to love; while poor Jabez was gaunt, and gauche, and lantern-jawed, and looked twice his years. In truth, he had little or nothing about him to captivate a woman's eye, nothing but a heart of gold; but that was out of sight, and counted for little in the contest.

When he saw that the girl he loved loved his friend, he gulped down his sorrow and said nothing; nay, more, he was best man at the wedding, and, despite the hidden wolf gnawing at his heart, he kept a stiff upper lip and a smiling face till the hard day's work was done, and he reached his little chamber, and was alone with his God and his great grief.

Bride and bridegroom went on a visit to Jack's uncle, the dalesman in Cumberland, for their humble honeymoon. When they came back, a week later, Jabez had left his old home for good and all.

It was a wrench, but the thing had to be done, and so the sooner it was done the better.

The day after the wedding he went up to the master of the mills.

Jacob Dene was a shrewd, observant man; and when Jabez told him that he was bent on going to London to seek his fortune, Jacob soon learned the secret of his servant, and sympathized with him, remembering that he had once been young himself.

In the end, Jabez did not go to London; he stayed at Deepdale, took up his quarters at the mills, became a trusted servant and faithful friend. Henceforth his lines were cast in pleasant places —that is, if any place could be pleasant to him without the lass he loved.

All is not gold that glitters, and she had perhaps done better had she married him instead of her graceless Jack.

Twelve months after the marriage, Jacob Dene's only son came home with his beautiful young wife. This gay and gallant youth was a captain in the fighting Forty-First.

He and Jack and Jabez had been playmates. It is true he had never cared much for Jabez, but Jack and he had played truant together, stolen bird's nests, and robbed orchards together in their boyhood, and when they met after some years' absence they fraternized as of old. Jacob was a rich man's son, and Jack was poor; but they were made of the same stuff, and when the one was summoned to join his regiment, he had little difficulty in inducing the other to take the Queen's shilling, and accompany him over the sea.

They sailed the same day, and at the same hour, from Southampton for India, accompanied by their young wives.

That was two years past, and more.

Those were perilous times. The Oaks and Rowland Cottage heard regularly from the dear ones until the Mutiny broke out. Then tidings came fitfully, or came not at all.

At last came news which set every English heart on fire—news of the well of Cawnpore and the siege of Lucknow.

"It's strange," said Joan, "that we've no news of Jack or Jael."

" No news is good news, owd lass," cried her husband; " so let us hope that Jack and his wife have got clear with a whole skin from those Injun cut-throats."

"Amen!" replied Jabez.

Then, for a time, they subsided into silence as they communed with their own sad thoughts. The old dame's heart sank within her when she thought that her boy might have fallen into the hands of the bloody Nana; while Jabez conjured up in the fire a fair face and a pair of haunting, unforgotten eyes—a face which grew clearer and more distinct every moment.

At this very instant, when they heard, or thought they heard, nothing but the beating of their own hearts, the silence was broken by a low, soft wail from without.

" What's that ?" exclaimed Joan. "Hush ! "

Again the sound broke on the stillness, this time louder than before.

"The lantern—quick, the lantern!" cried Jabez.

Without pausing, he rushed out, followed by Jasper and his wife.

Struggling through the snow, they reached the garden gate.

In front of it, face downwards, lay a woman, clad in a large woollen shawl and a dark, travel-stained dress; a kerchief of vivid crimson from which her long dark hair had escaped streaming in abundance over her shoulders, was bound round her head.

Once more arose the soft, tender wail which had brought them forth. There was no mistake now from whence the sound came. There was something beneath the woman's shawl, something which breathed and stirred.

"A child!" exclaimed Joan.

"The lantern, Jasper—the lantern!" cried Jabez.

"Here, lad—here!"

Jabez climbed the gate, stooped, and, lifting the woman, turned her face to the light.

"My God! Jael!" he gasped.

"Jael—Jael!"

For a moment the two men stood as if they were frozen to ice; then the woman said, or, rather, shrieked, "What are you standing there for, you? Standin' like blocks of stone, while my boy's wife and her bairn are freezin' to death! Look alive—d'ye hear, d'ye hear? Gi' me t' lantern! Tear t' gate up by t' roots, gin ye canna push it back!"

Even as she spoke the two men tore the gate up, and plucked it forth from the snow, then laying the woman and the child upon it, they carried them to the cottage.

"Away wi' ye for five minutes," said Joan; "this is a woman's business, not yourn. Stay! Take t' mattress off t' bed, pillows, bolsters, and bring 'm here. Now t' sponge—t' panshion —mustard—hot water. That'll do; away ye go!"

When they returned from the kitchen, a quarter of an hour later, the child lay croodling on the hearth before the fire. The mother, pale and helpless, almost speechless, lay beside him.

"The doctor—send for the doctor, Jabez," cried Joan.

"Nay, mother," gasped Jael. "I'm past doctor's help. I've reached the end of my journey, and am grateful to God that He has brought me here to die."

"But you'll no die, hinny; we'll not let ye die—ye'll live, live for Jack's sake."

"I'm going to join him, mother."

"What! my Jack dead?—dead!"

"Yes, mother, I saw him struck down before my very eyes at Lucknow, while trying to save young Jacob Dene from one of the murdering savages. He had only time to say, 'Go home, take t' bairn to father and mother, and Jabez, and tell 'em to love him for poor Jack's sake.' And you see," she added faintly, "here I am with little Jack."

After a moment's pause, Jabez inquired tenderly, "And Lucy—Lucy Dene?"

"The well—the well of Cawnpore!" gasped the dying woman.

A thrill of horror passed through her listeners, and she herself fell back in an agony of past horror and present pain.

"The doctor, the doctor!" again cried Joan.

"Never mind t' doctor," moaned the dying

woman. "Kiss me, mother, father, kiss me. Jabez, won't you kiss me, too? My poor lad used to say out yonder, Jabez, that if aught happened to him thou'dst be a feyther to little Jack."

She looked for a moment into the face of her faithful friend and lover; then, smiling faintly as he bent and touched her forehead with his young lips, she sank back and died.

## CHAPTER II.

### BAD NEWS TRAVELS FAST.

As the distant bells of Deepdale rang in the Christmas Day, Jabez Pryke stood up on the snow-covered moorland, gazing down the valley towards the dark smoke-covered town and high buildings of the mills. He was quite alone, and remained for a long time like one in a dream. The winter morning was still and peaceful, the snow had ceased to fall, and the sky was quite light and clear. He had wandered thither before daybreak, to commune with his own sad thoughts.

So lonely and so pastoral was the scene, so devoid of all signs of life, that the solitary man might have been taken for a shepherd on some mountain far removed from men. On every side stretched the white moorland, rising up behind

him to hills of grass and heather, and strewn
everywhere with rocks and boulders glistening
moistly in the morning sun. To his left, half a
mile away, flowed the river, thinly sheeted with
glistening ice, and creeping silently down towards
the mills, and between him and Deepdale stood the
cottage which contained the dead form of the only
being he had ever loved.

Tall, gaunt, ungainly, with a thin, worn face,
and sad, weary eyes, he looked much older than
his years. His shoulders stooped habitually, as
if under some heavy burthen, and, shepherd-like,
he leaned upon a thick oaken staff; indeed, though
his life was spent in the busy whirl of manufacture,
he had the brooding, wistful air of men who dwell
constantly alone. He wore black to-day, an ill-
fitting suit of broadcloth, and a black slouch hat
was drawn down upon his brows.

When his hour of trial came, he had yielded
up Jael Heywood with scarcely a visible sign of
pain. It was not in the man's nature to parade
either his joy or his grief. But he had wandered
up to the moorland, as to-day, to the very spot
where he now stood, and had his dark hour alone.
How well he remembered it all! It was summer
then, and the moor was scented and alive; but his
heart was not less desolate and cold than on this
weary wintry day.

Even in his utter desolation there was a strange
sense of awe and rapture. She he loved was at
peace with God; she was God's only now, and all

bitterness was over; and, crowning grace of all, she had died with his name upon her lips, confiding to his care her little helpless child. Standing there alone, and gazing on the roof beneath which she lay in death, Jabez swore that he would fulfil that sacred trust, and be a father to the little Jack.

At last, slowly and sadly, he turned his steps towards Deepdale, toiling through the snow, and following the windings of the frozen river. Turning aside before he reached the outskirts of the little town, where Heywood's cottage stood, he followed the road eastward till he came in sight of the old church. He drew near the churchyard gate, and looked over upon God's acre, where his beloved Jael was soon to lie. As he paused thus a hand was laid upon his shoulder, and a cheery voice greeted him by name.

Turning, he saw the very man he was going to seek—John Lyster, the vicar of Deepdale.

"A merry Christmas, Jabez! Counting the tombstones, eh? A cheerless occupation, surely, for Christmas morning." Then, startled by the expression on the young man's face, the vicar added, "Is anything the matter?"

"I have bad news, sir," replied Jabez, gently. "Jael Heywood—our Jael, young Jack Heywood's wife—came back last night from India."

"Impossible! Came back, do you say?"

"Ay, sir; came back—to die. We found her fainting in t' snow, wi' her little bairn, and—and—

she's lying yonder in her father's cottage, waiting
till they carry her to her last home."

Despite his habitual self-control, the man's voice
was broken with sobs, and, leaning his head upon
the gate, he moaned as if in mortal pain.

"Bad news, indeed!" cried Mr. Lyster.  "Poor
Jael! she was a pretty lass!  And that bright
fellow, her husband—he——"

As he spoke, Jabez lifted his head and looked
full into his face, with a gaze so wild, so woebegone,
that he knew at once that there was more to come.
Then, in a few words, Jabez told him all the terrible
tale which Jael had told with her dying lips, of
the murderous work far away, of carnage, of horror,
and the hideous well of Cawnpore.

"My child!—my little Lucy!" cried the vicar,
hiding his face in his hands, and sobbing like a
child.

It was his turn now to suffer, and, after a few
more piteous words, he passed through the churchyard gate, and entered the church, to pass *his* dark
hour there.

Sick at heart, Jabez Pryke walked on.  His work
was not yet done.  He had to carry the sad news
onward, and, though his heart sank within him, he
would trust the task to no other man.

Following the road, he made the best of his way
to the house of his master and employer, Jacob
Dene, owner of the great Deepdale Mills.  The
Oaks, as it was called, was situated half a mile
from the church and Vicarage, on an eminence just

beyond the outskirts of the little town. It was a new mansion, and took its name from the young trees which had been planted in front of its spacious garden.

Reaching the iron gate, he passed up a winding carriage path, and stood on the broad stone steps of the house—a plain, but spacious building, of no pretensions to architectural beauty. With a deep sigh, he rang the bell. A plainly dressed serving woman opened the door.

"Is t' master in?" he asked.

"Yes, Mr. Pryke."

"And t' mistress?" he added, thinking with a tremor of the tale he had to tell.

"Nay; mistress has just stepped out to see a sick lass i' the town."

Jabez stepped into the hall, and stood there bareheaded.

"Tell t' master I wish to see him."

The woman disappeared, and returning almost immediately, ushered Jabez into a large, plainly furnished study at the rear of the mansion, where a tall man in the prime of life sat reading; a man with a square determined face and keen black eyes, but with lines of gentleness around his mouth. He looked up and nodded as the young man entered.

"Well, Jabez, what brings thee here on Christmas morning?"

"Bad news, sir," was the reply.

"Nothing wrong at the works, my lad?"

"Nay, sir; worse than that. It's bad news from far away—something that concerns your son."

Jacob Dene rose to his feet, and saw, as the vicar had done, the shadow of the coming sorrow on the man's grief-stricken face.

"Speak out, man! What is it? No harm has come to him? He is not—dead?"

Jacob did not reply in words, but the look in his eyes was enough, and Jacob Dene staggered as if before a blow. Then the story was told, as before. Silently, without tears, but pale as death, Jacob Dene listened; then, turning away his face, and gazing out through the window of the room, he motioned Jabez to leave him alone.

To understand the position of affairs, especially as it concerned the present head of the great Deepdale Mills, it will be necessary to go back a little.

The Denes had been settled at Deepdale since Jacob, first of that name, came back from America with William Penn, after having helped that astute man to found Pennsylvania.

Jacob Dene the first had been attracted to the beautiful Yorkshire valley by the bright eyes of Rachel Hunsden, a beautiful Yorkshire girl. When he married her, he settled down in the valley, and there the Denes had stayed from that day to this. Like the friend of the founder of the family, they had all been born and bred Quakers. Up to a hundred years ago they had all been farmers, but the Jacob (for the first-born lad was always a Jacob, as the first-born lass was always a Rachel) of that day became acquainted with Richard Arkwright, took up his famous invention, and went into the spinning business; and so from small beginnings were developed the great Deepdale Mills, and Dene, alpaca, subluna, and vecuna manufacturers, who traded all over the world. They employed several thousand hands, and the Deepdale Mills were the pride of all Yorkshire.

Every modern appliance and improvement had been brought to bear upon the manufactory for the good of employer and employed; while the little town itself, its church, its schools, its baths, its gardens, its college and park, were the envy and admiration of the country, and all broad England besides.

Jacob Dene, the present master of the mills, was an austere man; but he was a large-hearted and liberal, and, in many respects, a modern idea'd man—possibly a little too modern idea'd—for he loathed the profession of arms as much as he detested capital punishment. Except hanging a man, he maintained that the worst use to which a man could be put was the occupation of cutting throats for hire. He was not one of those men who confine their interest in a subject to a merely theoretical view of it; hence, upon a certain memorable occasion, he formed one of a deputation who travelled to St. Petersburg to wait upon the Tsar for the purpose of beseeching the Autocrat of the North to refer some impending war to arbitration. As everybody knows, the Quaker and his friends had their journey for nothing; still, they had done their best, and no one can do better than that.

These being Jacob's views, it may readily be conceived that he was distressed beyond measure when his only son and heir, young Jacob Dene, in direct defiance of the family traditions, became a soldier. Nor were matters much mended when he espoused Lucy Lyster, the vicar's pretty but penniless daughter.

True, poor Lucy was as good as she was beautiful; but the Denes had always married money and land, and when there was neither one nor the other, it widened the breach. And so, when they parted, and the last " good-bye " was said, although there was no bad blood 'twixt son and sire, there was some coldness between them, and more between Jacob Dene and the vicar of Deepdale.

The truth was, Jacob thought that the vicar had been too facile and compliant a father, and that, in point of fact, he had planted his penniless daughter upon the wealthy heir of the Deepdale Mills. Never was there a graver mistake, or a greater injustice. The young couple loved each other, and all the fathers and mothers in the world would have been powerless to have kept them apart.

As the reader already knows, when Captain Dene went out to India with his young wife, Jasper

Heywood's son Jack and his wife Jael sailed with them.

It was a heavy day at Deepdale when these young people left their native valley. Jacob Dene seemed hard and self-contained, and bade them a cold good-bye; but many days elapsed before he returned to himself. When the poor mother loses her only son, the blow falls as heavily in the palace as the cottage, and Susanna Dene bewailed her boy as much as Joan Heywood bewept hers.

Jabez Pryke, who suffered most of all, kept his sorrow to himself. He and the vicar accompanied the young people to Southampton to see the last of them; and from that time forth the lonely man and the lonely parson (for Mr. Lyster was a widower) were firm friends. The latter had instinctively divined Jabez's secret, and sympathized with his grief and self-abnegation.

Jabez Pryke left the master of the mills to brood over the terrible story which Jael Heywood had brought from Lucknow. The master of the mills remained for a long time silent, as a man transfixed to stone. Two hours later, however, he went down to the Vicarage. Extending his hand to his quondam enemy, he said—

"Friend, thou hast heard."

"The Lord giveth, and the Lord taketh away, blessed be the name of the Lord," replied the vicar.

"I have tried to school myself to say so," returned the millionaire, "but I cannot as yet;

c

my heart was ever rebellious. It runs in the blood of the Denes. Well, I am justly punished. We are two childless old men; those whom we loved have been taken from us, and have left no sign that they ever lived. It is hard to bear. Let us not make it harder still by enmity. Canst thou forgive me ? "

The vicar grasped his hand in silence, and no more was said; but from that time forth all was forgotten and forgiven.

When it was known at church time that little Jack and his mother had been found in the snow over night, outside Heywood's cottage, the whole valley was alive. Foremost among the visitors to the chamber of death were the vicar, Jacob Dene, and Susanna his wife. Over that scene of common suffering we will draw a veil.

Every one wondered how poor Jael had ever reached Deepdale. Subsequent inquiries served to show that the Government had provided for her passage to England, and that, on her arrival, although enfeebled by disease and privation, she persisted in pressing onwards to her native valley ; that when she arrived at Barford, unable to obtain a conveyance, she started forth to walk, was overtaken by the snowstorm, and fell death-stricken on the very threshold of her own old home.

As Jacob Dene gazed on the infant boy, who, all unmindful of his loss, lay crowing in his grandam's arms, he thought that he would have given all the wealth of Deepdale to have had a flower like that blossoming in his childless home.

# CHAPTER III.

TIME speedily confirmed the doleful tidings brought by Jael Heywood to Deepdale that memorable winter night. Full details arrived ere long, and there could no longer be any doubt that young Captain Dene had fallen at the moment of the relief of Lucknow, and Lucy his wife was among the victims at Cawnpore. As they read the horrible record, both Jacob Dene and John Lyster forgot their gentle creed; the one remembered no longer that he was a clergyman, the other that he was a Quaker. They felt only, in that supreme hour of sorrow, that they were fathers and Englishmen.

Their hands clenched, their eyes flashing fire, they stood together outside the churchyard, where poor Jael was now peacefully asleep.

The vicar exclaimed, "These things must not be thought of, but they make men mad!"

"Not thought of?" echoed the master of the mills. "Not thought of? I can think of naught but thy poor child, my boy's wife. Had *I* been there! had I been there!"

"Had we both been there!"

Then the clergyman said something very un-canonical, and parson and Quaker, after wringing each other's hands, strode off in opposite directions to walk their agony away. Women, however,

cannot relieve their pent-up sorrows in the manner
of strong men ; they can only suffer and endure.
In silence and alone, the poor bereaved mother,
Susanna Dene, mourned the loved ones whose loss
had made her home so desolate !

In that terrible hour of England's ghastly victory, when horror was piled on horror, and every
day brought fresh news of victory blended with
calamity, the cries of grief and agony were echoed
in a thousand English homes.  The nation, like
Christian in the fable, was passing through the
very Valley of the Shadow of Death.  Little wonder,
indeed, that men forget their magnanimity, and
women their faith in God, before the spectacle of
such tribulation.  Justice was shaken on her
throne; Mercy, like an avenging angel, changed
her nature and waved the bloody dagger of revenge, and wherever the English tongue was
spoken rose one common shriek demanding
retribution.

Nature, ever heedless of the fitful and unreasoning strife of man, continued her secret ministra-
tions, and drew over the graves of many dead her
coverlet of grass and flowers.  The winter had
passed away, and spring blew her windy clarion
on the hills.  Where snow had lain on the broad
upland moors, the thyme and heather waved, and
the air hummed with sounds of joyful life.

One Saturday afternoon in early summer, Jabez,
the overseer, left the mills, and, going along with
the stream of men and women homeward bound,

made his way to the churchyard, to gaze, as was his constant custom, on the grave of poor Jael. Work was over for the day, and the folk were swarming like bees out of a hive. Elderly men gathered in groups, lads went along arm in arm, lasses laughed and flirted with their sweethearts, and above the hum of stronger voices rose the clear cries of children. Jabez heard nothing, heeded no one; his thoughts were far away. Leaving the throng behind him, he strolled into the churchyard.

He knew the grave among all the rest. It lay in the sunny corner of the churchyard, and early spring flowers, crocus and anemone, had already been placed there by his hands. He stood for a long time looking down upon it, and thinking of the fragile form that slept below. At last, passing his hand across his dim eyes, he left the grave, and regained the open road.

Again he followed the road up towards the moor, and, after half an hour's walk, stood among the upland grass and heather and looked back at Deepdale. Sad and grief-worn as he was, his spirit was now quite at peace. Fresh from the stress of work and life, he enjoyed his own loneliness and that of the beautiful scene surrounding him.

Many a time, he remembered, he had wandered hither with Jael, he a tall, ungainly lad, she a bright, laughing girl. Both were too young to think of love, but he, the elder, felt something stirring in his heart which was to ripen in time to tender passion. He had followed his little play-mate like her shadow, he had obeyed like a slave the slightest waving of her hand; and then—and then, afterwards, had come the knowledge that it was all hopeless, and that the light in her young eyes, the love in her young heart, was not for *him!* Well, it was all over; and his love still lived, though Jael was dead. He would not have had it otherwise. He felt, that still spring morning, that were his life to be lived again, he would not change it. She had trusted him even unto death. She had left him her last blessing, and the care of her little child.

As he turned to stroll homeward he heard the sound of carriage wheels, and looking backward he saw an open waggonette coming slowly along the road which winds from distant Barford across the moor. In Deepdale every one knew his neighbour, and Jabez saw at a glance that the occupants of the vehicle were strangers. Behind the driver sat a lady of middle age, with a face worn but beautiful, and by her side, looking eagerly out at the prospect, stood a little dark-haired boy of three or four. Opposite to her sat a black woman, clad in the familiar costume of an Indian ayah, and holding in her arms an infant child.

As Jabez stood on the roadside, the carriage approached nearer. The sight of the Indian woman sent the thought at once to India, and called up the picture of wild scenes and terrible events.

"Who can they be?" thought Jabez; when, at a word from the lady, the waggonette drew up, and a clear, musical voice said—

"Do you belong to Deepdale?"

Jabez looked up, met the lady's gaze, and touched his hat respectfully.

"Yes, my lady. I work in 't mill. I'm overseer to Mr. Dene."

The lady stood up in the carriage, shading her eyes, and gazing towards the little town; then, glancing down again, she continued—

"I am going there—to the Vicarage. Can you direct me to it?"

"Nay, you can't miss it," replied Jabez. "Follow t' road, and keep straight on past t' church, and you'll see t' house before ye." He added quickly, before she could sign to the driver to go on, "Maybe you come from India?"

"Yes," replied the lady, with some surprise.

"I thought so," said the overseer, glancing at the Indian nurse. "Maybe, too, my lady, you knew t' young captain, Master Dene's son?"

"I knew him well," replied the lady. "He was an officer in my husband's regiment, and he fell at Lucknow during the siege. He died side by side with my husband, Colonel Hollis, of the Forty-First."

"And his wife, my lady—his poor wife—be it true, as we ha' heard, that she be dead too?"

Mrs. Hollis looked in surprise at the rough fellow in his working clothes, who, as he spoke, stretched

out his hands in agitation, and trembled with
sympathy.

"It is quite true," she answered sadly. "That
is why I have come here. I am bringing home her
child."

As she glanced at the infant in the ayah's arms,
Jabez climbed up on the step behind the vehicle,
and followed the direction of her eyes. The
child, a beautiful infant of only a few months
old, was sleeping peacefully in its nurse's lap.

"Did you know Captain Dene?" asked Mrs.
Hollis, gently.

"Ay, my lady, I knew him well; and his wife,
too, poor lass, poor lass! And this be their bairn?
Wonderful—wonderful! Brought home like t'
baby boy, the child o' our poor Jael."

The lady noticed with surprise that his eyes,
full of tears, looked with infinite regret and tenderness upon the infant, while his lips murmured
something that sounded like a blessing. The
next moment he leapt down, and stood bareheaded
in the road, watching the waggonette as it drove
on. The lady looked back and nodded. Jabez
waved his hand. The little boy, leaning over
the back of the carriage, watched him and
laughed.

"Wonderful! wonderful!" muttered the overseer to himself, as he followed them down the
road. "Two bairns come home out o' t' cruel
war—Captain's little daughter, and Jael's little
Jack. Minds me o' t' flowers new-blowing on t'

poor lass's grave i' the churchyard! Well, well, out o' death comes life, as parson says."

Before Jabez Pryke could carry his news home to the Heywoods, Mrs. Hollis had reached the Vicarage and had told her story to Mr. Lyster. She was the widow, as the reader has already heard, of Colonel Hollis, the commanding officer of the fighting Forty-First. The boy who accompanied her was her only son. The baby girl, already christened Rachel, was the child of Captain Jacob Dene, and Lucy Lyster his wife, brought back to England in accordance with a sacred pledge given to the poor mother before she died. That fragile snowdrop was all that remained to attest that the young soldier and his wife had ever been.

While the vicar, divided between joy and sorrow, held his little grandchild in his arms, Jabez Pryke, half a mile away, was bending over little Jack, and Jasper and Joan Heywood looked on in wonder and delight. Before the life that comes, the life that is buried becomes forgotten, and all they saw now was the light in the eyes of the boy poor Jael had left behind.

"Mother, look!" cried Jabez, holding out his forefinger to the crowing boy. "Isna t' bairn t' living image o' poor Jael? God bless him and gie him good luck for her sake!"

"Amen to that, Jabez," responded Joan. "And t' little one you saw up yonder—poor Miss Lucy's lass—does she favour her mother, too?"

"Nay, mother, I knew not. She were just like a white snowdrop blooming on t' black wench's heart. I had naut but a glimpse, but she seemed as pretty as God makes little childer."

There was a long pause; then Joan said, with a look of tender inspiration, "Little lass and little lad! Suppose t' Lord, by-and-by, should bring they two together!"

Jasper Heywood, seated in his armchair, and lighting his pipe, looked up and grinned.

"There thou art, mother! At it again, like all t' women! They'd ha' marrying and wedding among bairns i' the cradle, if they had their foolish way, wouldn't they, Jabez? Why, woman alive, little lass, yonder, will grow up a proud lady, while little Jack here will ha' to work wi' his hands like you and me."

Jabez answered, still looking gently at the child, 'Maybe, maybe!" But, God willing, and you two helping, t' little man shall ha' learning, and maybe he'll grow up a gentleman, after all."

Before many hours had passed the news had spread all over the place, and formed the only theme of that Saturday half-holiday. It was discussed at every fireside, and many another single woman, as if to illustrate Jasper Heywood's estimate of the sex, uttered some such prophesy, or forethought, as that expressed by Joan.

Meantime, in the natural course of things, word of Mrs. Hollis's arrival had been passed from the Vicarage up to the Oaks. First to hear it, in her

husband's absence, was Susannah Dene. Her
carriage was at the door, and away she drove at
once till she reached the Vicarage; then, leaving
her years behind her, she sprang out, and rushing
into the house, descended with tears and cries,
and inarticulate expressions of delight, upon her
grandchild.

She introduced herself, *sans cérémonie*, to Mrs.
Hollis—made love to little Ralph, and friends even
with the ayah.

Then nothing would do but the vicar, Mrs.
Hollis, the boy, the ayah, and the baby must come
at once to the Oaks, where Jacob Dene was now
to be found.

At sight of his son's child the stern man burst
into tears. When at length an eventful evening
came to an end, the vicar could not find it in his
heart to deprive Mrs. Dene of the child, who took
up her abode henceforth at the Oaks, to become
the heiress of the Denes.

Although the scion of a noble house, Mrs. Hollis
was a lonely woman, for her brother-in-law, the
Earl of Beauchamp, had been very much opposed
to her marriage with his brother Ralph. She,
therefore, wisely accepted an offer to keep house
thenceforth for the vicar, which was a sensible
arrangement for everybody concerned, inasmuch
as she contributed three hundred pounds a year
towards Mr. Lyster's slender income, and found a
home for herself and her fatherless boy.

The weft of life is ever woven with the warp of

sorrow; the one serves to accentuate the other with a keener pleasure, or a deeper pain. Thence there was joy in Deepdale that the poor siege-children lived, and sorrow that their parents had died; but the joy abided, and the sorrow in time was forgotten by all, save the one faithful heart which bewailed now, as it would bewail for ever, the lost love of his youth.

But, although he sorrowed, Jabez, the overseer, did not sorrow without hope. He had now something to live for—Jack's child henceforth the child of his adoption.

As for the Denes and the vicar, their dead children lived again in the little Rachel.

## CHAPTER IV.

### TWO LADS AND A LASS.

Do you know Deepdale? Do you know the splendid Yorkshire valley, surrounded on every side by green or heathery hills, watered by a rapid river, and bearing in its bosom the cleanest and happiest of little manufacturing towns? If you have ever passed that way, down the open moorland, into the clean, carefully-kept streets, past the great many-windowed, many-chimneyed mills, among the cottages and well-tended gardens, from the church to the Vicarage, from the Vicarage to

the fine home of the mills' master, you will understand how Rachel Dene, as she grew up, learned
to love the place and its people, and to think there
was no such pleasant home in all the world.

It was the boast of Jacob Dene that his connection with the place and people was quite
patriarchal. He had made it, and kept it, what
it was, a model for the world. The thriftless, the
idle, the vicious, and the depraved drifted away
from Deepdale like scum from the lips of a summer
sea; they were out of place there, and found no
congenial associations. Industry, cleanliness, and
sobriety were the order of the day. The old
Quaker saw to it all. He would have no vagabonds
among his people. He was kind and liberal to
those who set a good example, but stern to the
undeserving.

Through the centre of this Arcadian valley, up
through the waving moorland, Rachel Dene rode
one summer day, in company with Ralph Hollis—
she upon a high-mettled and slender little cob, he
upon an almost thoroughbred mare. They had
been cantering and trotting along for a couple of
hours, full of high spirits, health, and youth; for
Rachel was now nineteen, and Ralph only a few
years older.

They were following a bridle-path along the
river-side, and walking their horses, whilst they
kept up an animated conversation.

"How pretty it looks!" cried the girl, gazing
from her saddle on the sunny scene around her.

"I think there is no place in the world half so
beautiful."

"A pity, is it not," returned Ralph, "that it is
disfigured by the smoke and dirt of the dingy mills ?
I hate manufactures and manufacturing places."

"Nay, there thou art wrong," said Rachel, in
the quaint Quaker phraseology she had learnt from
her grandfather, and which so well became her
pretty lips. "I love the mills and the town best
of all. Think how many mouths the mills feed,
how many happy homes they make! They're like
a kind, hard-working mother to us all!"

The young man laughed somewhat con-
temptuously.

"I don't understand that kind of sentiment.
The place, as such places go, is well enough, no
doubt; but I confess I love more gaiety and more
life. Deepdale is so dismal and so dull. Even
on Sundays the people look begrimed as troglodytes
living in the bowels of the earth, and the women
work so hard it makes them ill-favoured."

Rachel laughed and shook her head.

"There we differ again," she answered. "I
often think—'tis foolish, but very true—that if I
hadn't been my father's daughter, I would have
loved to toil hard, and be one of the people."

"A worker in the mills! Fancy *you* dressed in
homespun like a mill-girl! Fancy *you* being
courted like a mill-girl by some fellow with coarse
hands and coarser speech!"

Rachel flushed, and cried, "I was not talking

of courtship, sir! But I would not care for a man's hands if his heart were clean!"

As she spoke she started, and flushed a deeper red. Approaching her along the river-side was a figure she knew well, that of a lad of about her own age, clad in a rough working suit, and carrying a fishing-rod and a small creel.

"'Tis Jack Heywood!" she exclaimed.

"So it is," answered Ralph, with the slightest shade of a frown. "Shirking his work, and angling—profitable occupation!"

Rachel beckoned, and Jack came up smiling. He was a fresh, hearty-looking lad, strong and erect, with a look of self-reliance. He lifted his hat to the riders, and stood looking eagerly at Rachel.

"I have got an afternoon's holiday," he said, "and am trying my luck with the fly; but the sun is too bright for angling."

"Are you all well at home?"

"Yes, Miss Rachel."

"I must come over soon, and see thy grandmother. Thou knowest, Jack, thou and I are almost like brother and sister—the two siegebairns, as the people call us, for the same trouble left us both in the world alone."

"Shall we get on?" said Ralph, impatiently. "My mare is restless."

Rachel nodded, and, with a light look and nod at Jack, rode on with her companion. Scarcely had they ridden out of earshot when Ralph, bending towards her, said, with a short laugh, "There's one of your hard-handed ones. Do you not thank your good fortune that you are so different?"

"Nay, indeed," answered Rachel, with a look of surprise. "My grandfather tells me that Jack is the cleverest boy in Deepdale!"

"Jack! That's familiar."

"And why not? I almost feel as if he were my brother. We are both motherless and fatherless, and our lots are so much alike."

"I hope they are very different."

"And we were friends when children. Thou, too, wast his friend. Thou hast a right to like him."

"So I do, in his way; but his way is not mine, Rachel. Look at the mare, how she pricks her ears; she thinks I am speaking of her. Come, shall we cross the moor, and gallop?"

Rachel nodded, and leaving the roadside, they came to a stretch of grass and heather, and hastened along side by side.

The years had come and gone, until some nineteen had passed away. Rachel had entwined herself round the hearts of the mill-owner and his wife until she had become the light and life of their desolate home. Nor was she less dear to the old vicar—for she reminded him of the wife and of the daughter he had lost. The same doves' eyes, the same sunny hair, the same fairy-like elastic figure, the same laugh, the very voice—came back again.

Ralph Hollis had grown into a strikingly handsome young man, of bright but unstable parts, and
petulant temper. He was an apt pupil when the
mood took him—but he was wayward and fractious
—and somewhat trying to his over-indulgent tutor
and his doting mother. This lad might be led, but
never driven. Of all his circle of acquaintances,
the one who could lead him the easiest was Rachel
Dene, who reigned over him, even as she reigned
at the Oaks, with autocratic, but benevolent sway.

As the years grew with her growth—the two
old men—her father's father and the father of her
mother—loved the girl more and more—while in
her young and innocent delight, the poor mother's
youth lived again. At first, indeed, they had
loved the child because she reminded them of the
loved and lost. As the years progressed, they
loved her for herself—not because she was by any
means a paragon, but simply because she was true,
and simple, and honest, and because she loved
them deeply in return.

She was not a young person of advanced culture
or remarkable beauty. Her accomplishments were
of quite an ordinary character; but, take her all
in all, she was adorable, as only a pretty Quakeress
can be. Her figure was slender, straight, and
well balanced, giving indications that at its
maturity it would leave little to be desired in the
way of symmetry. Her complexion was pale, but
transparent as alabaster; and when her heart
or emotions were touched, her cheeks flushed a

D

pearl-like pink, which quickened into loveliness. Her head was crowned with a wreath of hair which shimmered from lightest brown into ripest gold; square brow, dark eyebrows, and dark lashes; eyes grey; short, straight nose, with the slightest suspicion of a tip-tilt at the end; ripe rosy lips, and a firm set chin, which seemed to indicate that, should the emergency arise, she *might* have a will of her own.

The emergency had not arisen as yet.

She it was who wrote the paternal grandpa's letters—wrote them, too, in a good, round, readable hand, none of your feeble Italian scrawls. She it was who took grandma's tea up every morning, and relieved her of the cares of housekeeping; who visited the sick, and relieved the needy of the valley; assisted the maternal grandpa at Sunday school and Dorcas Society; and who, in point of fact, played Lady Bountiful Junior in Deepdale.

Not that her life was monopolized by these duties, for she had a notion that life was pleasant, and that the world was beautiful, and she enjoyed the spring-time of both. She it was who induced the old people to open their doors, and their hearts, to their friends; and it was astonishing how much pleasanter the Denes found it than shutting themselves up in their former insular exclusiveness.

As for Ralph Hollis, the master of the mills felt bound to do something for the lad, if only because his mother had brought, almost out of the jaws of

death, the angel who made Jacob's home happy.
Mrs. Hollis wanted to send the boy for a term or
two to Oxford, but considerations of expense intervened. Jacob had had enough of Oxford; he had
sent his own boy there, with the result already
described. No; he would put Ralph into the
counting-house.

"The rest," he said, "would depend on himself."

"The rest" is a vague phrase, which might
mean anything or nothing. It might, however,
mean a partnership in the firm. Perchance—who
knew?—a marriage with the heiress of Deepdale!

In the end, the mother concluded to let Ralph
go to the counting-house, not, it is feared, to that
young gentleman's delight, nor very much, in the
long run, to Jacob Dene's satisfaction.

Jack Heywood was a horse of another colour,
both figuratively and literally. Ralph was dark,
and somewhat saturnine; Jack was fair and frank,
with sunny hair and laughing eyes, eyes of English
blue. Ralph was slender, elegant, and tall; Jack
was equally tall, but he was stalwart, and, for his
age, was the best swimmer, oarsman, rider, leaper,
runner, cricket-player, boxer, and wrestler in the
valley of Deepdale or the West Riding. Ralph
was indolent; Jack was industrious. Ralph was a
great smoker, and fond, already too fond, of his
wine; Jack detested the smell of tobacco, and did
not care for wine. Ralph, like Rob Roy, despised
"weavers, and spinners, and a' sic mechanical
persons." Jack was a born inventor, and proud

of his craft. Ralph disliked books; Jack liked
them. He had learnt all that Jabez could teach
him of mechanics, and had now left his master
behind. Not that he was a book-worm—not the
least little bit.

Having enumerated their points of divergence,
it is satisfactory to note one or two points on
which these lads agreed. They both had a passion
for horses—all Yorkshiremen have. Ralph had a
horse of his own, or, rather, a mare, which he
called after Rachel; and a beauty she was, as
indeed she ought to be, considering the price she
cost Mrs. Hollis. Jack had picked up a rough-
looking cob at Wakefield horse fair for five or six
pounds, and had groomed him to such perfection,
that Jabez, as he called him, ran Rachel very hard
whenever he got the chance. Finally, both lads
were unanimous in their admiration for Rachel
Dene.

Mrs. Hollis had but one object in life—to see
her son happy, beloved, admired. To her, he was
everything. In him her dead husband, the lover
of her youth, lived again. A mother's love blinded
her to his faults, and, as we have hinted, they
were many.

To be just to the lad, he was devoted to her
beyond all things, but he was wrong-headed and
strong-headed. Moreover, he was a little impatient at his lot in life. He thought it hard that
he, the heir-apparent to an earldom—for his uncle
Algernon, though on the shady side of sixty, was

still a bachelor—should be condemned to a seat in
the counting-house, instead of one in the House of
Lords. The thought of Rachel, however, curbed
his impatience, and he did his best to fulfil his
duties, though it must be admitted that bad was
his best.

There was another mother who also kept watch
and ward over her boy. I have said "another
mother" advisedly, for as Jack approached man-
hood Joan saw in him the image of her dead son;
and as he grew day by day more like her first-born,
he found in her all a mother's care, she in him a
son's devotion.

He had his way in everything, however. He
was just as honest, tender, and true, and just as
petulant and as pugnacious as his father had been
before him. Jasper Heywood, too, was as proud
of the lad as he had been of his own son Jack. As
for Jabez, we have already referred to the pure,
unselfish devotion of this single-minded, simple
fellow for his dead sweetheart's son.

Meanwhile, while Ralph smoked, drank, and
idled, Jack worked and learnt. At fourteen he was
put on to assist his grandfather in looking after
the machinery at the mills; for Jasper was a
practical engineer, and foreman in his department.

Now, Jack had a positive genius for mechanics
of every description. In twelve months' time there
was not a bolt, a bar, a pin, a spring, a strap, that
he had not mastered the mystery of; while as for

steam-power, hydraulics, electricity, and chemistry, he had them at his fingers' ends.

From childhood he had been a visitor at the great house. He and Rachel and Ralph had played together as if they had been brothers and sister—that is to say, up to a certain period. At last "the pale spectrum of the salt " began to cast a shadow between them. Ralph was a born gentleman, the son of a distinguished officer ; Rachel was born a lady, daughter of a man of fortune; she was, moreover, an heiress. Jack was the son of a private soldier ; moreover, he was a mechanic, a man doomed to live by the sweat of his brow and the work of his hands. So, for that matter, he reflected sometimes, was Richard Arkwright, and so was Robert Stephenson.

Jabez was wont to say, "Dreams, my lad— idle dreams."

"Let me dream while I may, Jabez," the lad replied. "Perhaps I shall wake some day and find myself famous, and then you'll be proud of your pupil."

"I shall always be proud of him, Jack, and when you are a great man you'll still find a corner in your heart for the old folk and Jabez ?"

"Always, Jabez," cried the boy, with his mother's eyes.

Left alone on the roadside, young Heywood stood watching the form of Rachel until it disappeared. Then he threw down his fishing-rod and sat down in a brown study, looking at the stream. No more fishing for him that day. He was himself in too deep water.

Though only a lad of nineteen, he looked some years older, and he had all the manners and appearance of a man.

"They may come to favour each other some day," Joan had said when he was an infant, speaking of himself and little Rachel; and part, at least, of the prediction had come to pass. He was as hopelessly in love as ever boy could be with Rachel Dene.

"Brother and sister?" he muttered, echoing her words and shaking his curly head. Then he looked down at his coarse dress and hard, toil-worn hands, and felt quite hopeless and despairing. He might have been comforted a little had he known how eagerly Rachel, just before they met, had been discoursing to her companion, with "coarse hands" for a text.

## CHAPTER V.

### A GAME AT LAWN-TENNIS.

IT was a lovely summer afternoon, and there was a lawn-tennis party at the Oaks, to which some of the young people of the neighbourhood had been invited.

Of course, Ralph Hollis and his mother were

there, and the vicar and his curate; then there were Jack Vipont, the squire's son, fresh from Oxford, and his sister Julia; young Raggett, the civil engineer; and Wilkinson, the solicitor. Besides these, Ralph had got invitations for Captain Fitzherbert, and two or three of the officers of his father's old regiment, the fighting Forty-First, who happened to be quartered at Barford, hard by. The young man was great friends with these curly plungers—dined at mess with them, and afterwards adjourned to the rooms of some of the younger blood to play baccarat or poker.

They were having a pleasant time of it that afternoon, when Jack Heywood, accompanied by his grandfather and Jabez Pryke, called by appointment to show Jacob Dene a new invention which was to revolutionize the manufacture of alpaca.

The interview took place in the great man's study, and Jabez was the first spokesman.

"It be most all Jack's work. Jasper and I helped him a bit, but he worked the idea out for hissen mostly. The lad's a born talent for using cogs and wheels. Jack, show Mr. Dene how the machine works."

Jack blushed, and did as he was bid.

"Thou art a boy," said the Quaker. "'Tis but a boy's work, after all."

"We must all be boys sometime," replied Jabez, laughing. "Jack here's one in a thousand, master.

We're both born fools to him, Jasper, his grand-feyther, and me!"

Jacob inspected the model, and hummed and haa'd as Jack put it in motion.

"Very ingenious indeed! And what dost thou calculate will be the nett result of this pretty toy?"

"Only an economy of labour and material amounting to about cent. per cent.—that is all!" replied the lad, sturdily.

"Thou art reckoning thy chickens, lad, before they're hatched," replied the old Quaker.

"Perhaps so, sir; but I'm going to *try* to hatch 'em somewhere or other."

"Well, send the model to my office at the mills, and we'll see what we can do with it in the course of a few months."

"Beg pardon, sir," answered Jack, "but I can't do that. It has to go to town to-morrow to be registered at the Patent Office, and thence to the Manchester Exhibition."

"Thou art a self-reliant youth!" said Jacob Dene, astonished.

"I've no one but myself to rely on, sir; and I've been taught to believe that God helps those who help themselves."

"That's true. Well, since thou art here, thou hadst best come round to the lawn, and see thy old playfellow, Rachel. Thou knowest she's always glad to see thee."

Jack was not so sure of that. He knew that

there was a time when Rachel was really glad to see him, but that time was past and gone. Yet, after all, if the invention were to strike fire ? Ah, if it were ?

Jacob chatted pleasantly enough as he led the way to the lawn-tennis ground. Jack's face flushed, as ripples of laughter and pleasant sounds broke upon his ear ; above all, when he heard one voice, the voice he could tell out of a thousand.

The sight was pleasant enough to look at. Twenty or thirty young people of both sexes loafed about without formality, chatting or flirting as the case might be ; some playing at tennis on the lawn, others disporting themselves amongst the greenery and flowers in shrubbery or summer-houses. The girls, in their quaint Kate Green-away dresses and straw hats, lightened up here and there with a brilliant bunch of ribbons ; the young men in their flannels of vivid and varied colours, sashes, canvas shoes, and straw hats.

How bright, and simple, and natural, and unaffected it all seemed ; and yet, as Jack Heywood looked at it, what a gulf intervened between him and every one else there !

He stood alone on the edge of the lawn, look-ing at the play, while his grandsire and Jabez approached, with diffidence, to pay their respects to Mrs. Dene, who was in an arbour dispensing afternoon tea.

Within a stone's throw of Jack, with their backs turned to him, stood a young couple, talking

together. He had no need to see their faces to
tell him who they were.

"Rachel," said the youth, "you are coming to
dine at the Vicarage to-morrow?"

"I suppose so," she replied indifferently.

"Don't say 'suppose.' You will come."

"Grandpa has promised."

"I'm glad of that. You know that to-morrow
is my birthday?"

"Yes."

"I shall be one and twenty. May I speak to
Mr. Dene?"

"Of course thou mayst speak to him," she
replied simply.

"Don't say 'of course' in that cold-blooded way.
You know what I want to speak to him about."

"About going into the army, I suppose? But
you must not!"

"Confound the army! I want to speak to him
about you. You won't understand me! Surely,
you must feel—you must know, that I can't live
without you."

At this moment the ball came whizzing past
them, and as Ralph turned in the effort to stop it,
he came face to face with Jack Heywood.

"Hallo, Heywood!" he said, with the slightest
shade of pique in his voice. "What the deuce
brings you here?"

"My legs," replied Jack, laughing.

Rachel, too, laughed at the reply, as she shook
hands with the young workman.

At this moment the game finished.

"Wilt thou stand in with me for the next game?" inquired Rachel, with a smile.

"Nay," answered Jack; "I don't play tennis. If it were cricket, now——"

"Ah, if it were! I've seen thee hold the wicket against all comers."

"Rachel, may I bring you a cup of tea?" inquired Ralph, nervously.

"Nay, thanks; I'm going to take tea with Mr. Heywood. Come along" (Jack, she was going to say, but she thought better or worse of it),—"come along, Mr. Heywood," she continued, "and grandma will be glad to see thee. And how is the wonderful invention getting on?"

As they approached Mrs. Dene and her *al fresco* tea-table, Ralph turned angrily away towards his mother, who was dispensing tea, and more substantial refreshments, at the opposite end of the lawn.

Watching her opportunity, she whispered, "Well, have you made the most of your opportunities, Ralph?"

"I have; but she holds me on, and keeps me off, until I feel inclined to throw it up altogether."

"Foolish boy! Throw up ten thousand a-year, and the prettiest girl in Yorkshire!"

"It's of no use; I can't get her to come to the point. Just as we were coming to cues, up comes that lout of a Jack Heywood, and she declares on to him immediately, leaving me in the lurch."

" You can't suppose that she has any proclivities in that direction ? "

"I don't know. One would think not, for she is of gentle blood on both sides, while he belongs to the scum; but women are so confoundedly foxy."

"Methinks a gentleman might remember," said the widow, severely, "that his *mother* is a woman."

"Of course he does. You don't suppose that he thinks his mother is a man ? "

"No; but he sometimes forgets that his father was a gentleman, and that he owes something to his father's name."

Ralph laughed, and kissed her.

"Forgive me, you old darling; but I'm riled, and when I'm riled I'm forgetful even of what I owe to the best of mothers."

"Ah, Ralph, Ralph," she said, "you don't know how I love you ! "

"Yes, I do, mother ; but I suppose I inherit my father's temper as well as his name. So bear with me, for dad's sake."

While this conversation was going on at one end of the lawn, at the other, Jasper, Jabez, and Jack were being patronized by the world in general—that is to say, by everybody but the Denes.

The three men were in their Sunday go-to-meeting get-up, and in their dark rustic clothes and stove-pipe hats looked singularly out of place amongst these gay young people, in their airy and graceful costumes. To be sure, Mrs. Dene put them a bit at their ease. To her, Jack was still Jack, Jabez was Jabez, and Jasper, Jasper.

A muster of young men and women declared on to Rachel. She was obliged to be civil to everybody. So once more poor Jack found himself alone, chewing the cud of pleasant memories— memories which served to deepen the bitterness of his present loneliness. He recalled the time when, as children, they went out bird's-nesting; the time, too, when Burnside Beck was swollen, and the plank bridge broken down. Had he not carried her on his back, breast-high, through the water? Had they not rolled and romped in the new-mown hay when bairns? And once, while still children, and beyond the eyes of the prudish Jacob, had she not called him out at kiss-in-the-ring? That virgin kiss was still burning on his lips, while she had become a great lady, and he was only a poor operative.

Ralph, too, who used to be a bright, friendly boy, was changed. Yet how Jack envied him! Lost in a brown study, Jack found himself brought, by sheer accident, in contact with Mrs. Hollis.

Smiling sweetly upon him, she opened fire.

" Ah, Mr. Heywood, it is an age since I have seen you! What brings you here to-day?"

"I came to show my model to the master."

" You've seen my son, I suppose?"

"Yes."

"Do you know that to-morrow is his birth-day?"

"I've heard so."

"We have a dinner-party at the Vicarage in honour of the occasion—Mr. and Mrs. Dene, and Ralph's intended bride."

"His intended bride?" echoed Jack. "And who is that, pray?"

"Don't you know?"

"Nay, indeed."

"I thought everybody knew that my Ralph was going to marry Miss Dene."

The lad shrank as if from a blow.

"Yes, it is so," answered Mrs. Hollis. "I wish you'd come in to-morrow night after dinner to my room, and drink to Ralph's health."

Jack was silent; his lips felt dry as dust.

"Remember, too, if my son can help you in any way—if he can advance your prospects in life——"

She did not finish the sentence, for Jack was gone. He was seen no more that night.

At midnight it commenced to rain, and kept raining until daybreak. The sun was striving to emerge from the clouds when Jack turned up at the cottage, pale and wan as a ghost.

Joan Heywood had been up all night awaiting him.

"What's the matter, hinney?" she tenderly inquired.

"Nothing, grannie."

"Eh, lad, you may tell that to the men, who, although they know thou'st gotten a hard head, never guess thou'st gotten a soft heart. It's summat about *her*, for sure—I know it is. Rest thy head here, lad—here, where it has rested when thou wert nobbut but a bonnie wee bit bairnie. That's reet. Now, lad, what is it?"

"Oh, grannie, she's going to wed Ralph Hollis!"

"Who told thee so?"

"His mother."

"Dunna believe her. T' lass knows t' difference 'twixt a man and a mannikin."

"Oh, grannie, grannie," cried the lad, "you don't know how I love her!"

And he fell into a passion of tears.

"That's reet, lad—that's reet. It'll tak' t' soreness out of thy heart. Look—look yonder! Dost see t' rainbow stealing out o' t' clouds, while t' mists of t' neet are meltin' into mornin'? That's a good sign—a grand sign for thee, lad. And just listen to t' birds; they are singin' a weddin' march. Tak' heart, lad—tak' heart."

"I will, grannie—I will."

And he did take heart, as we shall see.

# CHAPTER VI.

## THE GREAT INVENTION.

JACK HEYWOOD might have spared his tears; his alarm was altogether premature. Jacob Dene held the opinion that all men are equal, that wars are detestable, and that money is the merest dross. This was all very well in theory; but, although our good Jacob called himself a Quaker, and "thee'd" and "thou'd" his friends, and was, for that matter, of amiable and peace-loving disposition, yet he was an aristocrat at heart, and one fully alive to the value of this world's goods. If he ever contemplated the marriage of his granddaughter, he looked much higher than Ralph Hollis for a suitable husband.

With the shrewdness of his class, moreover, he saw pretty deeply into the young man's character. He knew him to be a bad man of business, a light thinker, and the companion of other light thinkers; and though he tolerated him for his mother's sake, he entertained no very exalted hopes of his future. He was shrewd enough, of course, to perceive what the match-making mother had in contemplation; but he simply shrugged his shoulders and made no sign. He had perfect confidence in the good sense of Rachel, who was clearly not heart-struck yet.

The birthday party passed off without any sign

E

or omen.   The subject nearest to the heart of
Mrs. Hollis was never broached; she also perceived that the time was not yet ripe.   As may
naturally be supposed, she didn't for a moment
contemplate the possibility of her darling son ever
having a rival in Jack Heywood.   Jack was only
a common lad, an operative—a nobody, in fact.

A year passed rapidly away.   Ralph Hollis continued to dance attendance upon Rachel without
making any visible progress in his suit.   Jack
Heywood, relieved from his first great fear, toiled
late and early at mechanics, and especially at his
favourite invention.

From week's end to week's end old Joan kept
the lad's heart up.

"Coorage, lad," she would say.   "'Faint heart
ne'er won fine lady,' as the saying is, and I'll back
thee 'gin any lad i' t' county."

A little love goes a long way in the world, and
Jack had a great deal, for besides Joan, Jasper
doted on his grandson, while Jabez loved him with
"a love beyond the love of woman."   For the lone
man, this boy crystallized in one bright form the
lost love of his youth, the friend of his boyhood,
and the girl whom he had adored.   To his mind,
no woman was too good or good enough for Jack;
and it was a foregone conclusion with Jabez that
Rachel could never have the heart to say nay to
his boy when the good time came.

The great invention had been patented, and
exhibited at the Manchester Exhibition.   One

morning, to the delight, though not to the astonishment, of Jack and his friends, came the award of the Executive Committee, enclosing the prize of a silver medal. By the same post came a communication from the great firm of Briggs and Boodlum, of Bridge Vale, requesting to know Jack's terms for the application of his patent in their extensive factories.

He was beside himself with delight when he read the letter to grandfather and granny. Of course, Joan gushed, and hugged, and cooed over him.

"Let un alone, mother," said Jasper, the cynic. "I can't abear to see t' lad molly coddled i' that way."

"Thee never was a mother, Jasper."

"No, nor a grandmother, neither. Now what I say is this. Of course t' old gaffer has a reet to t' refusal of Jack's invention; but if he doan't come to time, why then close at once, my lad, wi' Briggs and Boodlum. What dost say, Jack?"

"Well, grandad," answered the lad, "I'd rather hear what Jabez has to say."

And away ran the lad as hard as he could go to the mills, and brought back Jabez with him, who delivered himself thus oracularly.

"Why, for sure, I'd rather the honour and the glory o' the thing should be wi' our own hoel Yorkshire than any other; so suppose we go and have a talk wi' Mr. Dene. But thou must muzzle thy mouth, Jasper, for the old man's apt to cut up rough if you scratch him the wrong way."

So it was resolved, there and then, that they should beard the Quaker lion in his den.

They got to the Oaks just after breakfast. When they were shown into the library, the "gaffer" was in the midst of the *Times* City article.

Jabez was right—Jacob Dene was a difficult person to deal with. He was a great man, in a small way—a kind of paternal despot—who liked to do kind and even generous things, but who objected to being driven into them—indeed, he could not bear his hand being forced. He not only liked his own way, but his own way of having it.

"What brings ye here?" he inquired curtly. "Anything wrong at the mills?"

"Nay, sir," responded Jabez, "but our Jack here has got the prize medal at the Exhibition, for t' new invention, and he just thought you'd like to have a look at it."

"Surely it doesn't want three big men to carry a bit jimcrack of a medal," returned the old man, curtly.

"It's no a bit jimcrack, sir; it weighs welly an ounce."

"Nonsense, nonsense!" cried the master. "Well, hand it over, and let's see it. Hem! I congratulate thee, Jack Heywood. Well, what's at back of medal?"

" The inscription," responded Jack.

"I've seen the inscription, lad, but there's something more than the inscription behind it. Three great fellows have not come from the mills, merely to show me a medal."

Jack looked at Jabez, who stepped forward and stammered, " Well, it be this, Mr. Dene," he said, placing Briggs and Boodlum's letter in his hand.

Jacob read it, and flushed with anger. Then he got up, and strode up and down the library in a most un-Quaker-like manner. Having relieved his mind by a little strong language, he cooled down a little.

" This is most unhandsome, lads, and unbusiness like ! The idea of Briggs and Boodlum coming between me and my people ! Well, if thou likest to go, Jack, go, and luck go with thee. Abandon thy old friends by all means—it's the way of the world."

" But it isn't my way, sir," said Jack. " The letter only came an hour ago. How am I to answer it ? "

" Answer it, lad ? " cried Jacob Dene. " Why say thou'lt see Briggs and Boodlum further first ! Say that Jacob Dene has secured the invention for Deepdale Mills, on thy own terms ; that is to say," continued the old man, warily drawing himself up, " always provided that the invention works to Jacob Dene's satisfaction. The first thing to be done is to go and show this pretty thing (and it is a pretty thing) to my wife Susanna, and her granddaughter ; the next, to order the machinery, and see how it works, and then we'll arrange about terms."

So saying, he led the way to the drawing-room, where Rachel and her grandmother gave them all a cordial welcome. Both ladies were delighted with the medal. Finally Jacob rang for a bottle of Madeira, and proposed success to Jack's invention.

When they were about to leave, Rachel shook hands with the lad, and said, smiling, " I hope, Mr. Heywood——"

"You used to call me Jack once," he said.

"Well, then, Jack, I hope thy invention will realize all thy desires."

"Do you really hope that ? " whispered Jack.

"Yes, truly."

"If it does, I shall be the happiest lad in the world."

As he looked her in the eyes, her face flushed rosy red, but she turned away without another word.

On their way back home Jasper and Jabez did all the talking. When they got to the mills, the two old fellows were in high spirits as they went from room to room showing the medal. Lads and lasses crowded round Jack, to congratulate him, but he walked about as if he were in a dream. At last he started off to the cottage, and ran every step of the way.

Joan was making a pudding for the dinner.

"Granny," said he, "the gaffer has arranged for the invention."

"Good news, lad—good news!"

"And, granny——"

"Well?"

"*She* called me *Jack!*"

Then Joan threw her arms, flour and all, round the lad's neck, and hugged him in an ecstasy of delight at the realization of her prophecy.

A month later, and one of the machines was fitted up in the mills for the purpose of ascertaining whether it would accomplish all that the young inventor had promised. Jacob Dene, the overseer of the spinning department, Mrs. Hollis, Mrs. Dene, Rachel, Ralph, and the vicar, were formed into an informal committee of inspection to see the result of the inaugural experiments.

Of course, the ladies knew as much of the matter as they knew of Euclid or Sanscrit, nor were Ralph or the vicar much wiser. The machine accomplished much, but the arrangements were still incomplete. However, the practised eyes of the overseer and Jacob Dene took in in a moment the enormous value which must ultimately accrue from the invention. At present, it required a cog here, a pin there, a strap round a certain barrel, and then—hey, presto! the entire trade would be revolutionized.

Jack was overwhelmed with congratulations, and a little dinner was improvised at the Oaks that night in compliment to the happy lad. A very pleasant gathering it was for everybody but Ralph and his mother, who were neither of them too well pleased. Jack was the hero of the hour. Could it have been his fancy that Rachel appeared a little more reserved than usual? Everybody else was full of the great event, but she had little to say about it, pleading ignorance as her excuse. This lack of appreciation was the only alloy to our inventor's triumph.

When he got home, while Jasper and Jabez foregathered over their pipes, he got Joan into a corner, and laid bare his heart.

"Granny," said he, "*she* was the only one who said nowt about the invention."

Joan laughed knowingly.

"Shows she *thought* all t' more. Of course, lad, thee doesn't understand. But, there, thou seest thee is na a woman, and dost na know the deceitful ways o' wenches. I know all about 'em; I was a wench once mysen. When thy grandfather used to come a-courtin' me, I allays looked as if I wished un at Kirby Lonsdale, though if he hadna come I should a' greeted my een out."

"Oh, granny, do you think that she really cares for me a bit—only a little bit?"

"Cares for thee? Why, of course she does! Only last Sunday, when she came into church, she smirked and nodded to Mrs. Hollis and Ralph quite sonsy like, then she looked over at our pew and turned pale as a lily. What did she turn

pale for, I should like to know? Why, because
thou was na theer; and when thou camest in by-
and-by, and she caught sight of thee, she flushed
up red as a rose in June. What was that for, I
should like to know? Thou'lt see, this invention
will win thee thy wife; if not to-day, to-morrow,
or next day. It'll come, lad—it's sure to come!"

Jack caught her in his arms and hugged her.

"And when thou art a great man, hinney," she
said, sobbing, "thou'lt no be ashamed o' thy old
granny—wilt thee, Jack?"

"Never—never!"


## CHAPTER VII.

### A BLACK MONDAY.

JUST as the new invention was in full swing, Jack
got a day off to have a run with the Brocklesby
hounds. When he reached the meet there was a
brave show of county people, and conspicuous
among the party were Ralph Hollis and Rachel
Dene. They belonged to the privileged class, and
were in the thick of the throng, while poor Jack,
being an intruder, merely hung upon the outskirts.

His blucher boots, bowler hat, and homely
jacket did not contrast to advantage with Ralph's
white hat, smart pink coat, boots, and breeches.
Evidently Master Ralph was well satisfied with
himself or with something else that morning, for

the fellow looked happy and handsome as he chatted away with Rachel. For that matter, so did she until she caught sight of Jack, to whom she bowed gravely. He returned the courtesy as coldly as it was given.

"Morning, Heywood—morning," said Ralph. "Got a day's holiday?"

"Yes," growled Jack, as he gave his cob the spur, and trotted off, half disposed to gallop back to Deepdale there and then.

But he was young. Besides, he was a Yorkshireman; so when he heard the yelping of the hounds, and the cry of the "view hallo,"—for they had found a fox almost immediately—he galloped back even more quickly than he had left the field.

There had been a heavy snowfall a few days before, a heavier thaw followed, a flood ensued, and all the rivers in Yorkshire overflowed their banks. The fox knew his ground, and led straight over hill and dale until they reached Blocklesby Ferry, where the Ouse was rushing down southward in a foaming torrent. Without hesitation, Reynard took the stream, the dogs followed, and, despite the strength of the current, made the other side a quarter of a mile lower down in safety.

Carried away by the example of the fox and the hounds, those who were foremost in the field boarded the ferry-boat, which, in a minute's time, was overcrowded with men and horses. Fortunately only one woman was aboard.

The boat had barely left the shore, when Jack

came up on his cob. Irritated at being left behind, he contemplated the departure of the boat with anything but equanimity. There was nothing for it, however, but to await its return.

As he looked on, impatiently, a terrified horse aboard the boat, which was now in mid river, began to rear, and kick, and plunge. The example was contagious; every horse aboard followed suit. Amidst the yells of the affrighted animals, and the wild cries of their riders, the boat capsized, and man and beast were flung headlong in one screaming, struggling mass into the rushing river. Jack never forgot that scene of horror; he never can forget it to his dying day. Man after man went down, wildly calling for help; they rose and sank, and rose and sank again, then drifted down to death. The noise, the struggle, and the commotion ceased. All was silent; nothing was to be heard to remind one of this sudden and awful tragedy but the roar of the river, and then—the wild face of a woman emerging from the waste of waters fifty paces lower down. There was but one face in all the world like that, and when Jack Heywood saw it rise, as it were, from death, for a moment his heart stood still !

Then he pulled himself together, and with the rapidity of lightning took stock of the situation. A hundred paces still lower down the river described an acute curve, shaped almost like the letter U. This curve somewhat broke and deadened the force of the torrent.

Keeping his eyes fixed on the fair, pale face, Jack spurred his horse till he reached the bend of the curve, and then, with set teeth and muscles of steel, he pulled up, ready to take the leap on which life or death depended.

As he looked, the face went down for the second time.

For the second time! There was still one chance left. At the edge of the curve, it rose for the third time. The eyes—the pleading eyes—met his!

All depended now upon when and how he should take the leap. A moment too soon, and he would be carried down the river, powerless to help, before her. A moment too late, and he would be behind her. There was a third and worse alternative, he might ride over her.

At the supreme moment he drew himself together, and the leap was made.

As she floated by in the last agony, he plucked her by her sunny hair, which fell in great dishevelled masses down her shoulders, flung her across his saddle-bow, and floated safely down the river, until he approached another curve, which enabled him to land in safety with his precious burden.

She was cold and inanimate as death. Save for the feeble beating of her heart, she might have been dead indeed. He held her in his strong arms—he pressed her to his heart—he laid her tenderly upon the ground—he chafed her hands—

he laid his cheeks to hers—he kissed her brow, her eyes, her lips—not with a lover's passion, but with a man's devotion, trying to breathe his own warmth and vitality into her expiring life, all the while beseeching Heaven with tears and prayers to spare her for the sake of those who loved her, and, perchance, a little for his own.

Surely his prayer was heard and answered; for —with a shudder which thrilled her from head to foot, quickening her blood into returning life—she opened her eyes, and looked at him.

"Jack!" she gasped. That was all.

But that was enough.

We have lost sight of Ralph, as, indeed, he had lost sight of Rachel half an hour before. The fact was, his mare had shied at Thorby Beck, which was swollen like a torrent, while Rachel, Squire Mordaunt, and a dozen others whose blood was up, had taken it flying, from the edge of the cliff.

Ralph was not alone—for two-thirds of the field shirked the leap, and concluded to make a detour. But Jack had made a way for himself; and while the others were crawling leisurely round to the left, he discovered a narrower arm of the dyke— leaped it—and hence it was that, guided by the hand of Heaven, he had arrived in time to save the life he loved.

Yes, she was safe—there was no doubt about that. But how to get her to some haven of refuge?

There was no sign of shed or shelter, far as the eye could reach.

While she lay shivering on the ground in her wet clothes—to make matters more agreeable, it began to snow. Then he pulled off his coat, and wrapped it round her. If he only had a flask now; but he carried nothing of the kind.

The snow thickened—he didn't feel it—for the fever in his heart had set him on fire.

Leaving his sturdy cob beside her, he ran two or three hundred yards towards one of those stone fences so common in Yorkshire. Leaping atop, he gave the view hallo! There was no response. Again, and yet again, he shouted—still no reply.

The snowflakes fell heavier and heavier—the grey clouds thickened, and became overcast—until a pall of darkness overshadowed the earth.

What was to be done?

He overleaped the intervening dyke, and ran over a ploughed field, sinking into the sludge, almost knee-deep at every step. Again he leaped the wall—again he shouted. This time, he was answered. He listened with his heart in his mouth. Presently he heard the murmur of distant voices, the galloping of horses.

At last, ten or a dozen horsemen, with Ralph Hollis at their head, emerged from the mist. When Jack told them what had happened, a thrill of horror passed through the group, and an awful silence befell as they thought of friends and comrades thus untimely called to their last account.

While they stood like men transformed to stone, Jack said to Tom Brixholme, the whipper-in, who bestrode a great sorrel mare, "Tom, give us a lift behind thee, lad. While these gentlemen stand gaping here, poor Miss Dene will be perished; so give the mare her head, and let her up."

Even as he spoke, off they went in a gallop, followed by the rest of the field, until they reached the spot where Rachel still lay shivering.

Dismounting rapidly he knelt beside her, and, raising her tenderly, placed his ear against her bosom. It still palpitated gently; so there was no immediate cause for alarm.

Up to this moment Ralph had not spoken.

At last he said, "How can I thank you?"

"I don't need *your* thanks," replied the other.

Ralph paused for a moment as he made answer.

"Of course I shall take her home at once."

"Excuse me," said Jack, "but I shall take care of her this turn. Happen one of you gentlemen may have such a thing as a drop of brandy about you?"

Half a dozen flasks were instantly placed at his disposal, and when he had succeeded in getting a few drops of the potent spirit down her throat she began to revive.

There was no conveyance—not even so much as a hurdle—so Jack did not hesitate as to his plan of action.

"Tom Brixholme," said he, "is there e'er a farmhouse nigh?"

"Yes, there's Farmer Sparrow's—at Barnolby-le-Beck, about a mile off."

Lifting Rachel from the ground, Jack continued, "As soon as I'm mounted, give her to me."

"Right you are, Jack," replied the whipper-in. "But first, lad, slip on this coat. It be t' Squire's. I brought it for un, sure. He'll never want it again, poor ge'l'man!"

Jack slipped on Squire Mordaunt's coat, sprang astride the cob, and rode leisurely to Barnolby-le-Beck, bearing his treasure in his arms—upon his heart. Poor Ralph felt that his nose was out of joint, and there was nothing for it but to follow and play second fiddle, which he did with a rueful face. There is no use, however, kicking against the pricks, and he had to accept the inevitable.

When they got to Farmer Sparrow's, the dame and her milking-maid took charge of Rachel. The honest soul stripped the girl of her wet clothing, chafed the frigid limbs, got her to bed, and administered a warm posset.

As soon as she came to, she inquired, "Where's Jack?"

"I don't know who Jack is," replied the dame, "but there be two young men downstairs. One carried you here in his arms on horseback; the other is in pink, and raal handsome he is."

"Prithee tell them to let Grandpapa and Grandma Dene know that I'm all right; only I'm so sleepy."

Five minutes later she was sleeping placidly as an infant.

While she slept, the two young men rode towards Deepdale together. Ralph smoked incessantly, and stopped at every halfway house to have a nip. It was in vain that he invited Jack to accompany him. The latter had already taken the precaution to fortify himself at Dame Sparrow's with hot coffee and a dish of ham and eggs. Both men were moody and taciturn, and spoke little to each other.

Upon arriving in the valley, Ralph went to the Vicarage. Jack paused for a moment at the cottage to hurriedly tell Joan and Jasper what had happened, and to ask the old woman to get some dry clothing ready for him; then he picked up Jabez at the mills, and they went to the Oaks together.

Mrs. Dene and Jacob were much alarmed at Rachel's absence, for it was now getting on for nine o'clock, and they had expected her back to dinner at six. When Jack told them what had happened, Jacob ordered the break out immediately. It was useless for Jack to assure him that there was no further danger. Jacob was impatient of opposition.

"Thy cob is worn out," he said. "Go to the stable, and take the best nag thou canst find. Take it, and keep it, lad, for this day's work. That'll do; spare thy speech. Gallop down to the Vicarage. Tell parson I'll call for him in half an hour; and, Jabez, do thou call on Doctor Whitaker, and ask him to make ready to go with us."

F

The poor cob was indeed done up; that struggle in the river, and the ride to Farmer Sparrow's double weighted, and the long ride to Deepdale, had taken the backbone out of him, so Jack was not sorry to give him a rest.   But in Jacob's stable there was a splendid young chestnut mare called Lucy, which Jack had long admired.

While the groom saddled her, Jack gave the cob a rub down; then he leaped upon the mare, and trotted down to the cottage, where he slipped on his dry clothing, which done, he galloped on to the Vicarage, which he found in a state of consternation.

Almost immediately upon Ralph's arrival he was taken suddenly ill.  Whether occasioned by fatigue, anxiety, vexation, or those repeated "nips" on the way, or all combined, no man may tell.

Doctor Whitaker had already been sent for.  He merely unloosed the young man's neck-cloth, smelt his breath, and shook his head.

"Is there any danger?" inquired Mrs. Hollis, anxiously.

"Nothing that a draught of bitter water in the morning will not obviate.  For the present, put him to bed, and let him sleep."

Ten minutes later the Denes, the vicar, the doctor, Jabez, and Rachel's maid were on their way to Barnolby-le-Beck, accompanied by Jack. To their inexpressible relief, they found their darling still sleeping soundly—so soundly that the doctor forbore to wake her,

Then came a difficulty. It was now too late to return to Deepdale. Dame Sparrow was, however, a woman of resources, and beds were improvised here, there, and everywhere, and soon after midnight the house was at rest.

Rachel did not awake until about nine o'clock. When she found her grandmother on one side of the bed, and the maid on the other, she said, " I've been dreaming, grandma, such a strange dream. I thought I was out with the hounds at Brocklesby Ferry; that the boat was capsized; that every one was drowned but me; that Jack came and saved me."

" And so he did, my darling! It was no dream. The brave lad did save thee, God bless him! But see, here's Jacob, and Grandpa Lyster, and Doctor Whitaker."

When the two old men saw their darling, radiant with youth and health, they kissed and caressed her; and at a signal from the vicar, all knelt beside the bed and offered up a silent thanksgiving that she had been delivered from the jaws of death.

By-and-by, when the doctor came and told Jack and Jabez that all the danger was past, the two men shook hands in silence, and while Jabez went to take his morning pipe in the farmyard, Jack went out for a stroll towards the Beck.

He walked along lazily, with his hands in his pockets, until he was out of sight of the house and its inhabitants.

Then Master Jack ran a little, he danced a little, he laughed a good deal, then he burst out crying, like a great baby; but finally he walked quietly back to the farm, softly whistling "The British Grenadiers." When he got to the kitchen, Jabez was sitting down to breakfast.

"Thou art happy, lad!" said he.

"Ay, and hungry, too, Jabez!"

Evidently he was, for he polished off his breakfast in fine style.

## CHAPTER VIII.

### RALPH HOLLIS.

WE have compared Ralph Hollis and Jack Heywood to the idle and industrious apprentices immortalized by Hogarth; but the comparison is, of course, an inadequate one, since the two lads of Deepdale, unlike their prototypes, didn't "start fair." Hollis had all the advantages of birth, blood, education, and refined surroundings; Heywood had all the disadvantages on the other side. And yet, as we have seen, the poorer lad was rapidly gaining on his social superior. He was recognized on every hand as a clever, industrious fellow, likely to rise to almost any position. He had already invented a mood of economizing labour which might bring him in a fortune; and, to crown all, he was a hero —he had saved Rachel Dene's life.

All this was gall and wormwood to the handsome son of Mrs. Hollis. To be surpassed in everything by a social inferior, and one his junior by several years, was a constant source of irritation. In his dilemma he turned for help to his mother, who, rendered preternaturally acute by maternal affection, kept her eyes fixed constantly on Rachel Dene, and saw, to her amazement, that Ralph was daily losing ground. True, Rachel liked the young man very well, for he was gay, dashing, and not ungenerous of disposition; but whenever there was a hint of love-making she shielded herself under the grey hood of Quakerdom, and couldn't or wouldn't understand. Attracted as much by her physical beauty as by her fortune, Ralph used all his powers of fascination, which were not very great, seeing that his experience lay chiefly among ladies of lighter disposition. He was quite at home with a handsome barmaid or a mirth-loving mill-girl, but he didn't understand the ways of pure and cultivated women.

The mother and son, like many who love each other much, wrangled a good deal over this and other subjects. Mrs. Hollis was proud and imperious; Ralph irritable and indolent; and sometimes they came to such high words that they hardly spoke afterwards for days together. Then Ralph would drive over to Barford to dine with the officers of the Forty-First, his father's old regiment; there would be cards, and dice, and billiards, and other amusements popular among such young gentlemen, and our idle apprentice would ride back to the counting-house with an aching head and an empty pocket, to go through the disagreeable drudgery of earning his daily bread. Over and over again, however, he had to appeal to his mother to help him out of his difficulties, and in doing so she got into difficulties herself. Still, it was for her darling's sake; and, as the young scapegrace constantly promised amendment, the poor, fond mother helped him, and prayed for better days.

There was one consolation—Ralph was the next-of-kin to an earldom. How fervently, amidst his pecuniary and other troubles, he prayed that his titled relative might remain a bachelor, and die at as early an opportunity as was convenient and possible.

More than once Jacob Dene lectured the young man on his conduct. One day, when Ralph returned from a night's orgy just in time to get to his desk in the morning, the old Quaker sent for him, and thus addressed him: "Thou art no flesh and blood of mine, Ralph Hollis, but I am sorry to see thy mother's son going so fast downhill to the place thou knowest. Thou wast at Barford last night, and rode over at daybreak?"

Ralph, who looked pale and wretched, and felt desperately ill and uncomfortable, forced a laugh.

"A friend was going away. We gave him a little dinner, and kept it up rather late."

"Who was thy friend?"

" Mr. Harkaway, of the Forty-First. His father and mine were intimately acquainted. I hope, Mr. Dene, you don't find me inattentive to my duties? I do my best, but the fact is, you know, I haven't much of a head for business."

" Nay," said Jacob Dene, dryly; "thou likest card-playing and folly better than honest work. Hast thou ever reflected, man, what it means to thee and thy mother?"

Ralph shrugged his shoulders.

"You see, I wasn't born for this sort of thing," he muttered, biting his lips, and scowling moodily.

"Born to be hung, maybe!" cried the Quaker, sharply. " What dost thou call thyself?"

" A gentleman, I suppose."

" I know a better word—a ne'er-do-well. Take warning and example! There's a lad in these mills who might teach thee, if thou art capable of learning a lesson."

" I suppose you mean young Heywood," returned Ralph. "I know, sir, he's your favourite, but allow me to say that a gentleman does not take example by his social inferiors."

"Thou art a jackanapes!" cried Jacob, angrily. " I have a mind to send thee packing! If it were not for thy mother's sake——"

" Pray don't mind her!" returned Ralph, hotly, for he was in the humour for a quarrel. " I can go, sir, whenever you like. I dare say I can pick up a living somehow and somewhere."

And he flounced out of his master's room, and

returned to his place in the counting-house. He was sick of the whole business, and did not care, for the moment, what might happen. In his irritation and anger, he forgot altogether about Rachel. When he recovered his temper, he regretted his hasty words on her account, and felt half-inclined to apologize. However, he was too proud for that.

But Jacob Dene made no further sign, beyond talking over matters with Mrs. Hollis, and begging her to use her influence towards the young man's reformation, which she tearfully promised to do. A few evenings later, when Ralph had finished his dinner, and sat by the fire in the vicar's sanctum reading a sporting newspaper, she came in and sat down opposite her son. The vicar was out on a sick call, and they were quite alone.

She did not speak for some time, but sat with her eyes fixed on the fire.

At last she said quietly, " Have you seen Rachel to-day ? "

" No," he replied, over his newspaper.

" She called this afternoon."

" Humph ! " muttered the young man, carelessly.

Another silence. It was clear that Ralph was prepared for a lecture, for without looking up he continued to read his newspaper with a scowl.

" Put down that paper and talk to me," said Mrs. Hollis. Ralph hesitated a moment, then threw the journal aside.

" What's the matter now ? " he exclaimed.

"I want to speak to you about yourself, and about Rachel."

"Well, mother?"

"You are behaving very foolishly and very badly. Mr. Dene is right."

"Oh, he has been sounding my praises!" cried Ralph. "Old humbug! I gave him a bit of my mind the other day when he began preaching to me down at the mill. He thinks me a fool, but he's mistaken."

"I'm afraid he's right," returned Mrs. Hollis.

"Thank you!"

"He complains, and justly, that you neglect your duties, and keep bad company."

"I keep company with gentlemen, which is more than he has ever done. Mother," he added hotly, "I'm sick of it all. I was never meant to be chained to a desk, or to pore over figures in a ledger. I'm determined to cut it as soon as possible."

"And Rachel?" asked Mrs. Hollis, coldly.

"Rachel is as bad as her grandfather. She never cared for me, and never will. Why should I keep on dangling at the heels of a methodistical flirt? Why should I humiliate myself by following a girl like that?"

"It is your own fault if you have not won her heart," said the lady. "You have had every chance, yet you let her go without an effort. You waste half your time with the men at Barford, and while you are playing cards and billiards, young

Heywood, who has not a tithe of your gifts, is
gaining every day in her esteem."

" Nice taste that ! " sneered Ralph. "A common
mechanic ! A fellow who can't speak decent
English ! "

" He's not so bad as that ; though, of course,
he is not a gentleman. Remember, however, that
Jacob Dene himself belongs to the people, and so,
for that matter, does Rachel herself."

Ralph rose impatiently, and stood with his back
to the fire, looking angrily at his mother.

" Let Rachel take the fellow, and welcome. I
am sick of humouring her human fancies ! "

" You know you love her, so don't talk so
absurdly," said Mrs. Hollis. " Oh, Ralph, do look
at the matter seriously. You are ruining your
own prospects and breaking my heart ! "

And the proud woman hung her head, while the
fast-streaming tears ran down her cheeks.

With all his faults, Ralph loved his mother.
She was the only living being, indeed, who inspired in him either deep respect or strong affection ; so her grief moved him, and, bending over
her, he asked her forgiveness.

" But you know, mother," he said, " I cannot
bear the life I am leading. I ought to have been
a soldier, like my father. After all, that's the only
life fit for a man ! "

In his secret heart Ralph was thinking more of
the amusements and dissipations of military life
than of its dangers and glories ; but the fond

mother looked at him in sudden pride, and thought, with a sigh, how closely he resembled his dead father.

"I wish it could have been," she said. "My boy, you must be patient; perhaps some day our fortunes may change, and then——"

She did not finish the sentence, but he understood her. Both were thinking of the one life which stood between Ralph Hollis and an earldom. Little did Mrs. Hollis know that, even in that faint expectation of the succession—faint because the present Earl was strong and hale, and might marry any day—the young man had already speculated largely. He was, in fact, far deeper in the mire of difficulties than any one suspected. That very morning a writ had been served upon him in the streets of Deepdale. He had got among a bad set, and in order to keep pace with its members he had used every device to raise money. His mother's resources were, as he knew, exhausted; his own were unsubstantial as thin air, for the small sum he received for his work at the mills would have scarcely sufficed to pay his tailor's bill.

## CHAPTER IX.

### A FOREWARNING.

THAT business at Brocklesby Ferry was a bad day's work for Ralph Hollis.

He was thankful, however, that it was no worse. Had he been beside Rachel at the critical moment, he might have been unable to restrain her from going on board the boat. Of course, he would have gone with her; then, in sporting phraseology, the odds were ten to one that he would have been drowned with the rest. On the other hand, had he come up with Jack, both would have certainly jumped into the river together in the endeavour to save her; and perhaps while the rivals were struggling for the honour of rescuing her, they would all three have perished. Of course, it was not Ralph's fault that his mare shied at Thorby Beck, but it was his misfortune. It left him out of the hunt, and gave Jack a chance which might never occur again in his lifetime.

Then there was that confounded brandy, of which he had taken enough, and to spare. Yes, he reflected; it was a bad day's work for him.

However that might be, that Black Monday could never be blotted out; and no one knew it better than Ralph himself—that is, when he *was* himself. At times he would be resolute, and never

touch alcohol for weeks together. Then a moment
of weakness or temptation occurred, and away
went his virtuous resolves like a handful of thistle-
down before the wind. So long as he was under
the influence of his mother he was right enough;
but he could not always be tied to her apron-
strings, and when once he got among his military
and racing friends, good-bye to prudence and
common sense.

His extravagance had involved Mrs. Hollis in
continual difficulties. So long as her father-
in-law lived she got a little help occasionally;
but he had been deceased for nearly a year,
and her brother - in - law, the new Earl, had
refused to give her a shilling. It was, however
almost a certainty that Ralph would inherit th.
earldom at some distant period, which was something to look forward to. If the lad would only
keep steady, and if that match could be brought
about with Rachel—— But, then, if it could
not?

He had set his heart upon her, and the thought
of losing her seemed beyond the bare pale of
possibility. Still, he could not help fancying that
she had never been the same to him since the day
at the ferry. He noted, too, with growing impatience and irritation, that Jack was a frequent
guest at the Oaks, that he had taken to dressing
in a more civilized manner, that he had even
taken to lawn-tennis, and that he was a deft and
dangerous opponent in that, or any other game

in which skill, or strength, or courage were necessary.

Now Ralph had so long taught himself to believe that Rachel was to be his wife, that the bare idea of any other man coming between them appeared an outrage. That a mere ordinary operative—a vulgar mechanic—should dare to aspire to Rachel —*his* bright and beautiful Rachel—was not to be thought of.

But Jack was not an "ordinary" operative—on the contrary, he was a very extraordinary one; and, though a mechanic, he was by no means a vulgarian. Moreover, he was now in a fair way to become a rich man.

They met daily at the mills, and though not particularly cordial, were always civil to each other. The proverb is as true as it is trite, that "lookers on see most of the game;" and Jabez saw with increasing anxiety, that distrust was ripening into dislike between these two young men.

As for the innocent cause of this contention, she scarcely knew her own heart, or, if she did, she did not care to scrutinize it too closely. She was really always glad to see Ralph—that is, when he was not too pressing in his attentions. On the other hand, she was grateful to Jack Heywood for having saved her life—and perhaps a little more than pleased to see evidences of some attempt at refinement in his manners and demeanour.

Time passed on, and the great invention, though

it scarcely justified its title, proved so far satisfactory, that it was adopted, with certain modifications, in the Deepdale Mills; and before Jack Heywood attained his majority, he found himself foreman of the department in which the machine was used, and in the receipt of a handsome income. This increased prosperity made no difference in his domestic habits. He continued to live at the cottage with the old people.

"Didna I allays say it!" Joan would constantly exclaim. "Thou wast born to be a gentleman, and some day, lad, thou'lt be master o' t' mill itself."

Jack would laugh, and blush, and look at himself in the glass, and think, very possibly, that the old woman was not far wrong. One thing, however, marred the completeness of his self-satisfaction. His new pride and happiness seemed to make no favourable impression on Jabez Pryke.

One day, therefore, he spoke out to Jabez. It was just after the dinner hour, and they were walking back to the mills together—he with a rose in the button-hole of his office-suit, Jabez in all the picturesque shabbiness of his working clothes.

"What ails you, Jabez?" he asked. "You seem changed a bit from old times. Sometimes I fancy you're sorry to know of my good luck."

The overseer stopped short, and looked at him quietly with his gentle, patient eyes—eyes so full of introspection, that they seemed to suffer from the tender light they shed upon him. Then he laid his hand upon the young man's shoulder.

"It's just this, lad," he replied. "I'm reet glad o' your good luck, and proud o't into the bargain; but I'm troubled whiles i' my own mind about what's to come o't. 'Taint allays the best or the cleverest colt as wins t' race, and 'twould be a bad look-out if t' luck were to turn thy head."

"What d'ye mean?" cried the lad, flushing angrily.

"I mean naut but what I say, Jack. T' luck, maybe, has come too quick to last. You're nobbut a boy, and you're reckoning the race o'er far ahead."

"How d'ye know that? I do my work and bide my time, and Master Dene has promised to help me along."

"That's reet enough," said the overseer. "But he'll ne'er help thee to Miss Rachel, if that's i' thy mind. T' master's proud, and he has the right to be proud; but he's a great man, lad, and try thy best, you're nobbut one of the people. Blood's thicker nor water, as t' saying is."

The lad looked angrily at the speaker, who continued quietly.

"But 'tis not that I were thinking o' altogether. You're gotten beyond us hardworking folk, and hankering after fine company. Up at Barford, holiday times, you spend your brass wi' swells. Last Leger, you went into t' ring, and lost money on t' favourite."

"Oh, that's it, is it?" said Jack, laughing, and looking a little relieved. "You think I'm going to the bad because I bet a bit, and like to enjoy myself once or twice a-year. Why, man, you love a horse as much as I do, and have staked thy brass many a time!"

"No doubt, lad; but I ha' done it sober. Last week a lad I know drove home fro' Barford i' Captain Fitzherbert's dog-cart, and when he got home he could scarce stand straight upon his legs."

"I wasn't drunk!" cried Jack, indignantly. "I was never drunk in my life. I'd only a glass or two with the Captain."

"You never used to touch it, lad," returned Jabez. "I wish I could persuade thee to take t' pledge."

"Not such a fool! You can't say that I ever neglect my work, or forget my duty. Now, can you?"

"Nay, lad, nay; but look at Mr. Ralph, and see what the liquor is doing for him. He's going downhill fast, and my heart turns cold when I think that a lad I love better may follow i' his footsteps."

"No fear of that," said Jack. "He's an idle beggar; and no man can ever call me that. Come, Jabez, be fair—do me justice, old man! You used to trust me and believe in me."

"And so I do now. I'd cut off my reet hand, lad, to keep you reet and square."

The two parted, each repairing to his particular part of the works. Jack was angry in his heart, and felt very much aggrieved. He felt that he had scarcely laid himself open to such a warning, for, beyond the taste for horseflesh of which we have spoken, he had few weaknesses and no vices. What irritated him most of all, however, was his old friend's insinuation, rather conveyed than spoken, that he was becoming too ambitious, and that his ambition was hopeless as well as dangerous. He had made up his mind to be a gentleman; and sometimes, if the truth must be spoken, he felt a little ashamed of his friends and belongings. Why were his birth and his position to be for ever used as silent arguments against him? His thoughts reverted, as of old, to Arkwright and to Stephenson, and to other men who had risen from the ranks to wealth and honour, and he felt indignant at his foster-father's want of faith.

Jabez was right, however. Guided by the instinct of unselfish affection, he perceived whither the lad was drifting. Success had intoxicated Jack Heywood. Though hardworking and stead-fast-hearted as ever, he thought more of pleasure and less of honest work.

# CHAPTER X.

THE great Yorkshire carnival came on again. Saint Leger was holding sovereign sway and masterdom on the Moor at Doncaster.

The mill hands had knocked off, and gone in thousands by a special train. Everybody in Deepdale had gone except Joan and Jasper Heywood, whose knee was as big as his head with a sudden and violent attack of rheumatism, so his wife stayed at home to nurse him. Though Jacob Done was a Quaker, a Quaker is still a man—especially a Yorkshire Quaker, when there is a horse in the way—and he accompanied his wife and granddaughter to Doncaster. Mr. Lyster, too, escorted Mrs. Hollis; Ralph Hollis went with his friends, Captain Fitzherbert and other plungers of the Forty-First from Barford; while Jack and Jabez drove over together to catch the train at Barnolby Junction. Jabez was for staying at home, but, seeing that Jack was bent on going, he determined to accompany him.

What a scene it was, to be sure, when they got to Doncaster! Train after train disgorged its thousands. The High Street was crowded—almost impassable. But the scene at the moor itself baffles description. Life, colour, gaiety, animation were everywhere ; and as for the crowd,

that could only be calculated by hundreds of
thousands.

A dozen different dialects of Yorkshire, contended for mastery with our own beloved Cockney
—with Scotch, with Irish, with French, with
German, and with shrill American.

The Denes, Rachel, Mr. Lyster, and Mrs.
Hollis were in the front of the Grand Stand, which
was thickly packed with human beings.  Save for
the fact that a Yorkshire horse was the first
favourite, our friends had no interest beyond
seeing the glorious strife for victory, and certainly
they had nothing in common with the gentry
below, amongst whom Ralph Hollis and his
friends were busy backing the favourite against
the field.

Hitherto, upon all former occasions, Jack and
Jabez had been content to gaze upon the race from
the outer fringe ; to-day they had sprung a point,
and paid their guinea apiece to enter the charmed
circle, where they encountered Ralph, Fitzherbert,
and his friends.

Jabez felt ill-at-ease in such fashionable
society; so he made his way alone to the Stand.
The plungers were civil to Jack, and Ralph gladly
took him under his wing, simply to keep him away
from Rachel.

It was a delightful day, and Jack enjoyed the
races.  It was pleasant to be in the thick of the
dazzling scene he had heretofore contemplated
at a distance—to be in the paddock, and to rub

shoulders with all the great people—especially to be introduced to the famous Jockey, with whom princes and dukes hobnobbed.

By-and-by there was a hastily improvised luncheon, washed down by champagne; and after that, a rough-and-ready race inaugurated the day's carnival. Jack didn't think much of that; but after it came more champagne with cigars, and soda and brandies to follow. Then another descent into the ring; then another raid upon the refreshment-room, more stimulants, and more cigars—a great deal more of them all than was good for Jack Heywood.

Ralph and his friends were seasoned vessels. Jack was unused to the process, and it began to take effect.

Back once more into the ring—back amongst a mob of howling ruffians, with books and pencils in their hands, and blasphemy in their mouths. To hear these fellows roar at each other, one would think Bedlam had broken loose amid a menagerie of wild beasts.

Bright and handsome, full of life and excitement, Jack pushed his way through the ring. Looking up towards the Grand Stand, he saw the eyes of Rachel fixed upon him, and smiling merrily, he lifted his hat. At that moment he felt a hand upon his shoulder, and turning quickly, saw his foster-father.

"Come away out o' this, lad," said Jabez; "'tis no fit place for a decent lad. Let's gang home."

" Gang home ! " echoed Jack, with a laugh, "and before the sport has half begun ?   Nay, not I ! Come along to the bar, and have a drink."

Jabez shook his head.

" Thou'st been tasting already, Jack.  Remember what I told you, and tak' no more.  If you won't gang home, at least, come and speak to Miss Rachel.  See, lad, she's beckoning fro' t' Grand Stand."

Jack looked up again.  Rachel was indeed beckoning, and, it seemed, to him.  He took his friend's arm and pushed his way out of the ring ; made the best of his way until he came close to the group from Deepdale.

" I hope thou art not wagering thy money, lad," said Jacob.  "Betting is a bad business, and unworthy of a decent man."

" I am only looking on, sir," answered Jack. "Isn't it splendid ?  They say the Yorkshire favourite is to win."

Then he leant over and talked to Rachel. Warmed with a glass or two of wine, he felt quite at his ease and familiar.  As he laughed and chatted, the girl looked at him in some surprise. Glancing from his flushed, excited face, she met the sad, wistful eyes of Jabez Pryke.

While this scene was taking place, two men stood watching it from the ring.  One was Ralph Hollis ; the other was his friend and boon companion, Captain Fitzherbert, a man nearly ten years his senior, seasoned in all kinds of dissipation, and a thorough "plunger" by habit as well as disposition. The Captain was thick-set and strongly built, with a high-coloured complexion, a black moustache, black hair, a little thin at the top, and a coarse, determined mouth. He was dressed in the height of fashion, sported a white hat, and was literally covered with jewellery.

"Look there, Fitz," said Ralph, in a voice thick with drink; "that infernal workman again talking to Miss Dene! They're whispering under the old Quaker's very nose. Ever since the fellow saved her life she has treated him as if he were a gentleman and an equal, though, at the best, he's only a confounded mechanic, working with his hands."

"Jealous, eh?" returned the Captain, with a laugh. "Gad, you've reason! Saved her life, did he? Ah, yes; I remember. You missed your best chance there, Ralph, my boy. Women like fellows of that sort, you know. Saved a woman's life myself out in India—widow woman—and, by George! she proposed to me on the spot. But Fitz didn't see it—oh, dear, no!"

Quite unconscious of Ralph's baleful gaze upon them, Jack and Rachel continued to converse in whispers. Never had the maiden seemed so gracious, never had the young inventor looked so happy.

"D——n them!" muttered Ralph Hollis.

"Certainly," said Fitzherbert. "But come along, and have a drink, and leave them alone;

—your rival's first favourite, and you're scratched!"

"Am I?" cried the young man, with a savage oath. "We'll see about that! Fitz, the old man hates me, and encourages this fellow! Only yesterday he took me aside and asked me to take example by young Heywood. Fancy that! Take example by a common mechanic!"

"Humph! An *uncommon* mechanic, I should say. I rather like the lad."

"And *I* hate him! There, they're shaking hands, and he's coming back to the ring. Listen to me, Fitz! It's a matter of life or death to me now to put things right with Rachel, and this clod is the only human being in my way."

They walked away together, eagerly conversing. Meantime, Jack Heywood, hurrying from Rachel's side, drifted away with the crowd. His excitement had increased tenfold by the reception he had met with from the Denes. His face was radiant; he could have leapt in the air. Laughing gaily, he pushed his way through the throng, again entered the ring, and at last came face to face with Ralph Hollis and Fitzherbert.

"Ah, Heywood," cried Ralph, smiling. "Better fun than the mills, eh? Come and liquor up."

"No, thank you," said the lad, hesitating. "I promised Miss Dene—— "

But Ralph Hollis took one arm, and Fitzherbert took the other. As they did so, they exchanged a significant glance.

" Just one glass ! " said the Captain. " Come,
we'll toast the great invention."

Bewildered and excited, Jack suffered himself
to be led away. His pride was flattered; he felt
himself a gentleman among gentlemen; and, to
speak the truth, he was pleased to be in such fine
company. He glanced round, and saw no sign of
Jabez, his self-appointed mentor; then, with a
laugh, he accompanied his friends to the refreshment-room.

Fitzherbert called for champagne. When the
bottle was opened, he and Ralph took care to
let Jack have the lion's share. Then, the lad, not
to be outdone, insisted on ordering and paying for
another bottle. Had he been a little sharper-
sighted and more suspicious, he might have
observed that his companions, always exchanging
looks of meaning, spilt the greater part of their
wine upon the grass.

Jack was no tippler; a little wine affected him;
and by this time he had drunk a large quantity.
He began to talk loudly, and to clap Fitzherbert
on the shoulder as he sallied back into the ring.

Above the Babel of sounds could be heard,
" Two to one, bar one ! " and " Fifty to one
against the favourite ! "

Jack believed in the Yorkshire horse—belief was
loyalty to his native county. He yielded to the
temptation, and, despite Mr. Dene's warning,
began to bet. Unluckily, he had five and twenty
pounds about him. He backed the favourite

against the field, with the result that he lost
his money.

Ralph Hollis, too, was betting furiously, and
losing—indeed, scarcely knew himself what he
had lost. He only knew one thing—that three
weeks ago he had borrowed two hundred pounds
from Fitzherbert, and that he had solemnly promised to pay him the day after the Leger; and,
amidst the riot, the confusion, and the pandemonium, he remembered that if this and other
moneys were not paid on settling-day, disgrace,
ruin, and all the rest of it might follow. But, in
the midst of all his excitement, he still kept his
eyes fixed on Jack Heywood. His plan had succeeded to admiration. The drink, and the excitement, and the loss had been too much for the
young workman. By this time he was quite drunk,
and very quarrelsome.

He had parted with his five and twenty pounds
like a man, but the bookmaker insisted that he
owed five and twenty pounds more, which, indeed,
he did, through some bungling in his betting.

At this moment Jabez came up.

When he saw the state of affairs he was ashamed,
and, indeed, a little angered, to see his boy in so
shameful a condition.

"Jabez, old man," cried Jack, clutching his arm,
"lend me five and twenty pounds."

In his intoxication he fell back into broad
Yorkshire.

"What for?" asked Jabez.

" Why, yon dog-faced reshil says I owe it him,
so shell out t' brass."

" My lad, I cannot. I havena got it."

" What ! " cried the lad ; " art *thou* gone back
on me ? Pretty chap thou art to stand by a friend
in a hoyle ! Hang such friends ! Get out for an
owd humbug ! "

The unhappy lad had indeed " put an enemy
into his mouth to steal away his brains," and he
let forth a flood of abuse upon his friend and more
than father. The plungers quite enjoyed the
scene, and added fuel to the fire by some not particularly elegant chaff. The bookmaker alleged
that he did not know Jack, and demanded that he
should immediately " pay up."

Jabez demurred ; the bookmaker swore that
both Jack and his friend were " nobbut, more or
less, nor a pair o' welshers "—words of direful
omen to a Yorkshireman. No sooner was it out of
his lips than the bookmaker was on his back, while
Jack strode over him, and requested him to get up
to be knocked down again.

The betting-man responded like a gamecock.
He was up in an instant, and going for Jack.
They rushed at each other like a pair of tigers,
amidst yells of encouragement from the by-
standers.

At the height of this scandalous scene, the
Denes, and Rachel, Mr. Lyster, and Mrs. Hollis,
appeared, passing from the Grand Stand above.
As Jack caught sight of them—above all, when

he caught sight of Rachel's eyes—her look of astonishment and disgust struck him with a sudden shock of pain. She scarcely paused a moment in passing; the next, she was gone; but she had seen it all.

As she passed forth, he said to the bookmaker, "Hold hard. There's my watch; it's worth nearly all thy brass. I'll send t' rest to-morrow."

"Nay, lad," replied the betting-man; "I'm sure thou art a pluck'd un, and we Sheffield grinders allays like a mon better after we've fowt un. My name's Tom Yondal; I'm to be found i' t' Pot Market, Sheffield, any time."

Jack was angered with Rachel, with Ralph, with the bookmaker, with everybody—above all, with Jabez. Had Jabez only lent him that twenty-five pounds, this calamity would not have occurred. With the unreasoning fury of an unaccustomed drunkard, he blamed every cause but the right one. As he reeled along, elbowing his way through the crowd to the railway-station, his demeanour was so strange and wild as to attract universal attention. He was so aggressive and pugnacious, that had it not been for Jabez he would have reached the police-station instead of the railway-station. When at last, however, he got there, he dragged Jabez into the refreshment-room, made a grab at a bottle of champagne, dropped it, and smashed it to pieces.

Then he snatched another, and knocked the neck off it, cutting his hand in the operation.

Some of the Deepdale lads were there, and he invited them to join him.

"Sup, lads, sup. Now, lass," he continued, "serve out some brandy and soda—lots of it. That's your sort!"

Finding it useless to attempt to restrain him, Jabez went to see if he could find the station-master to induce him to reserve a compartment, so as to get the wretched lad home without further mischief. While bent on this errand, he came in contact with Jacob Dene, the vicar, and the ladies.

There was no disguising from them the state of affairs; therefore, addressing his employer, Jabez said, "I've nowt to say for t' poor lad, save that he's had more than is good for un, and that it has been given to un by them as owt to know better. He's ne'er bin so afore, and please God'll ne'er be so agin. He's not only drunk, but mad—does na know what he's sayin' or doin'. Unless I can get him home, there'll be some mischief done. Please, Mr. Dene, gie us a good word wi' station-master to get t' lad in by hissen somewhere, if it be only in a horse-box."

Angered as Jacob was, his regard for Jabez was so great, that he assented to his wishes, and, at his request, the station-master was induced, with some difficulty, to reserve a second-class compartment for Jabez, Jack, and half a dozen Deepdale lads.

A very bad time they had of it until they got to

Barnolby Junction. Jack quarrelled with everybody in general, but with Jabez in particular.
Once, indeed, he threatened to throw him out
of the window. Drink had changed this genial,
gentle, lovable creature from a man into a wild
beast.

At last, his drunken fury wore itself out for the
time, and he fell into a stertorous sleep, which fortunately lasted until they got to Barnolby Junction.
Then Jabez drove him down to the mills, for he
could not bear that Joan should see the lad in so
sorry a condition.

Meantime, young Hollis was being driven home
from Barford by Fitzherbert in a high dog-cart
belonging to the Captain. Both were well warmed
with wine, and not a little excited, for Ralph had
lost large sums that day, and Fitzherbert was
clamorous for his money.

"Make your mind easy," Ralph said; "I can
get the money, and I'll pay you. After all, this is
a good day's work for *me*."

"How's that?" growled the officer.

"We doctored the favourite nicely! Rachel
and the old man saw it all. I don't think that
young cub will be backed for a place again."

Fitzherbert deposited his friend at the outskirts
of Deepdale, and then turned his horse's head
back towards Barford. It was now quite dark, and
not a sound broke the stillness of the night.

"About that money?" asked the Captain.

"You shall have it. I'll come over to-morrow."

The Captain nodded, and drove rapidly away.
Ralph Hollis walked on through the darkness in
the direction of the mill.

## CHAPTER XI.

### AFTER THE LEGER.

For some years past Jabez had resided per-
manently at the mills. He had a small living-
room in the front or main building, and immediately above the cashier's office. Here every
night he slept solitary and alone, ready for any
emergency which might occur. From his high
window could be seen, across a huge quadrangle,
the factories, the engine-rooms, and the great
warehouses in the rear. It was a lonely place by
night, and the overseer's life was lonely; but
Jabez Pryke, though he cared nothing for books,
had constant company in his own gentle thoughts.
His was an existence occupied with only two ideas
—devotion to his duty as his master's servant, and
love for the child of the woman sleeping in the
neighbouring churchyard. Among the treasures
in his barely furnished room was a picture of Jael,
a rude photograph taken one day at Barford. It
hung over his head, and night after night he raised
his eyes to it as to some pictured saint.

On that eventful night of the St. Leger, when
he arrived before the mills, supporting in his strong

arms the half-insensible form of his foster-son, he
found the great iron gate closed. He rang the
gate-bell, and the dull clanging echoed dismally
through the night, till at last a light appeared,
and Joe Styles, the watchman, came, lantern in
hand, to answer the summons. Behind him followed the great watch-dog Leo, a formidable
mastiff-bitch.

"Hullo, Jabez!" cried the watchman, unlock-
ing the gate, and swinging it open. "Back at
last?"

"Ay, mate," answered the overseer. "Here,
lend a hand, man; I want to take Master Jack up
to my room."

"What's the matter wi' un?" asked Joe, with
a grin. "I saw un up at Doncaster flinging t'
brass about like mad. Ower much lemonade, I
doubt?"

"The lad's ill, very ill. I canna tak un home
i' this state. He's got to sleep here i' t' mills."

"All reet, Jabez," replied the watchman.

It was no easy task to get Jack along. He
was comatose, and though he moved his legs
mechanically, his head and arms swung forward,
and without powerful assistance he would have
fallen. But the two strong men lifted him bodily,
and carried rather than led him up the steep stone
stairs till they reached the topmost landing, and
drew him into the overseer's little room. Then,
while Joe lit a candle, Jabez placed the boy in a
chair. He sat there with ruffled hair, pallid face,

and eyes half-closed, feverishly muttering to himself. One hand hung by his side like lead, the
other was thrust into his breast. The old watch-
dog, who knew him well, kept close, and licked the
hanging hand.

The watchman, a grim, grizzled veteran, stood
looking on, and, holding up the lantern, flashed
the light into his face.

"Poor lad, he's had his bellyful!" he said,
half amused and half shocked. "Say, Jabez,
Jem Wright t' stoker's sitting out wi' me i' the
engine-house, and we ha' a bottle o' good stuff
yonder. Will ye come and take a sup?"

"No!" cried Jabez, fiercely. "Curse t' drink!
Curse them that make it, and them that sell it!
See what it's done this neet!"

"Sure enough; but lad'll be reet i' the morning."

"He'll ne'er be reet again!" answered Jabez,
with a groan, like a deep sob. "Lea' us together;
I'll stop wi' him, and put him to bed."

The watchman nodded, and left the room, followed by the mastiff. The moment he had gone,
Jabez turned and locked the door; then, uttering
a low cry, knelt by the lad's side, and burst into
tears.

"Jack, Jack, my lad!" he cried. "Won't 'ee
speak to me? 'Tis me—Jabez! Look up, lad,
look up!"

But Jack made no sign; he still sat in a state
of collapse, murmuring vacantly to himself. Then

H

tenderly, like a woman, Jabez took off his coat and waistcoat, relieved him of his necktie and collar, and, raising him bodily, placed him upon the bed. He fell there like a log, with a low, suffocating moan.

Jabez bent over him, and looked into his face.

"'Tis strange," he said to himself; "I ha' seen many a mon o'erta'en wi' the cursed drink, but ne'er a one like this! He's more like a mon death-struck wi' poison! Poor lad! Poor lad!"

"Water!" moaned Jack, as if gasping for breath.

Jabez moistened his parched lips, and laid his head gently back upon the pillow. As he did so, he saw the picture of Jael hanging over the head of the bed.

"I promised to be a feyther to un," he cried, stretching out his arms to the picture, while the great tears rolled down his cheeks, "and I'll keep my word. I ha' been a lonely man for thy sake, Jael, but now thou hast gien me a son—thy living image, wi' the same blue een and bonny golden hair. Oh, my lass—my lass! just as your face looked when we found thee dying i' t' snow is t' lad's this neet!"

Then, mastered by his emotion, he sank on his knees by the bedside, and prayed aloud. Prayer more unselfish, more solemn and touching, never rose from the lips of man. And as he prayed, he took the boy's clammy hand, which hung loose on the coverlet, and kissed it again and

again. In his own name, in the name of his own
love and sorrow, he asked God to pardon the lad
for his folly that day; to watch over and preserve
him from future temptation ; to keep from his lips
the poison of drink; to strengthen him against
all evil; to make him a happy man, and to crown
him with honour and prosperous days. Lastly,
with an infinite tenderness, he interceded for a
happy sequel to the lad's love for Rachel Dene.

"Lord, Lord, turn not the lass's heart against
un, but be kinder to my lad than Thou hast been
to me! Keep him fro' lonesomeness like mine,
and answer his prayer wi' life and love ! "

Strong feeling makes even rough men eloquent,
and Jabez uttered his thoughts as if inspired.
Then rising to his feet, he looked down on Jack
with unutterable affection, for all the time it was
still Jael's face that he saw before him now, as he
had seen it the night she came home to die.

It was now getting late, and Jabez had still to
get down to the cottage, and break the news to the
old people. So, with one last look at the heavily-
sleeping lad, he left the room, closing the door
stiffly behind him.

"He'll be reet enough till I come back," he
muttered, "and I'll watch by his side all t' neet,
poor lad, poor lad! 'Twill be a bitter wakening
for him to-morrow morn."

Descending the dark stairs, he passed the offices
below, and came out upon the courtyard, and
reaching the gate, opened it with his master key,

which he had taken down from a nail in the room above. He was soon out in the open street, facing wind and rain, for it was a stormy night. Looking up at the mill building as he passed, he saw the windows all dark and desolate, and wafted another blessing to the lad lying asleep within.

His way lay through the town, and close past the churchyard. As he passed the shadow of the church, he ran up against a man.

"Confound you!" cried a voice; "where the deuce are you rushing? Who are you, eh?"

"Jabez Pryke," answered the overseer. "Is it thee, Master Ralph?"

"Yes. Where are you bound?"

"Down to Gaffer Heywood's cottage, sir."

"I thought you slept at the mill," said Ralph. "By the way, how's young Hopeful? Have you taken him home?"

"Nay, sir; he be lying asleep i' my room at t' mill. I'm going to tell the gaffer where he is, and then come back and look after un till morning."

"I see," returned Ralph, with a laugh. "I say, wasn't he awfully screwed? Never saw a man so gone in my life! How did it happen?"

"Maybe *you* can tell that better than me," said Jabez, significantly. "Though t' poor lad was o'erta'en, he's sober and hard-working, and never came to this pass before."

"Well, good night," cried Ralph, moving away.

"Good neet," replied Jabez, coldly. "You'll say nowt o' this to t' master?"

"I'm afraid he knows all about it, for everybody saw the lad in his mad fit. However, if I can put in a good word for him, I will!"

Leaving Jabez Pryke to make the best of his way down to the cottage, Ralph Hollis hurried on eagerly in the direction of the mill. Once or twice he paused and listened, but everything was still, and not a soul was in the street. In a few minutes he reached the street where the mill buildings were situated, and stood looking up, as Jabez had done, to the dark, dismal windows. The light of the lamp suspended over the gate fell upon his face, which was wild and pale as death. He was still excited with the drink he had taken during the day, and he shook like a leaf.

Drawing a flask from the breast-pocket of his great-coat, he took a long draught. Then, approaching the gate, and touching it with his outstretched hands, he peered in. All was dark and silent. Suddenly, as he leaned against the gate, it opened.

"The gate is unlocked!" he muttered, with a low cry of surprise. "That's unfortunate, but it shows the old fool will hasten back. If the thing is to be done, there is not a moment to lose!"

But his knees knocked together, and he trembled from head to foot. Another draught at the flask steadied him a little. For a minute yet he stood hesitating.

"It's sink or swim! If I don't pay up to-morrow everything will come out; and even if I

am discovered, Jacob Dene will never send me to
gaol. Curse the money! but I must have it, and
I know it's *there!* By God, I'll do it!"

He crept into the yard, and approached the
stairs leading to the cashier's office. He paused
and listened again; there was not a sound, save
the moaning of the wind, and the pattering of the
rain. Groping his way up the stairs, he reached
the first floor. As he paused there, a low moaning
sound broke upon the ear, coming from the rooms
above.

"Heywood! I forgot *him!*" thought Ralph.
"I must see if he is awake; if he is, and recog-
nizes me, I can soon frame an excuse for being
here."

He went on from stair to stair till he reached
the top floor, and paused outside the room where
Jack was lying. He knocked softly; there was
no answer. Then he quietly opened the door, and
peeped in. Jack lay tossing on the bed with his
eyes closed, muttering incoherently, seeing and
hearing nothing.

Ralph drew the door to, and slipt again down
the stairs.

# CHAPTER XII.

## JABEZ PRYKE'S VIGIL.

IT was getting late when Jabez Pryke reached the cottage, but there was a light in the window, and, entering without ceremony, he found the old couple sitting up by the parlour fire. Jasper lay back in his armchair, nursing his gouty knee, while Joan, spectacles on nose, sat at the table leaning on her elbows, and reading out of a newspaper some days old. She looked up as Jabez entered, and greeted him by name.

"Is it thee, Jabez? Welcome back, lad. But where's Jack?"

"Jack's not coming home t' neet," answered the overseer, quietly. "I left him yonder at t' mill."

"At t' mill!" echoed the old woman. Then, startled by the strange expression on Jabez's face, she added, "Summat's wrong. Speak out, Jabez Pryke!"

"It's nowt, grannie!" he replied, forcing a smile. "Come, let me sit down, and I'll tell thee all about it."

"Ay, sit down," said Jasper, hospitably. "Sit down, lad, and tell us about t' Leger."

But as Jabez took a seat by the fire, Joan rose angrily to her feet.

"T' Leger!" she cried. "Hark to t' owd fool—

he thinks o' nowt but racing and siccan folly. But I want to hear about Jack. Summat's wrong, I say. No humbugging, Jabez!"

"Nay, grannie."

"Thou mayst humbug Jasper theer, but 't won't do wi' me. Look me in t' face, Jabez. What's come to our lad? Where hast left him?"

"As I told thee," answered Jabez. "At t' mill, sound asleep in my bed."

"And why hast left him *theer*?"

Jabez answered again, not lifting his eyes.

"Well, then, he were a bit lively—he took a glass o'er much; and—and—I thought it best he should bide at t' mill till he came to hissen."

Jasper emitted a low whistle, Joan an indignant exclamation.

"*Drunk*, d'ye mean?" she cried.

"Well, a bit excited like," said the overseer. "He was put out about t' favourite, and got tasting with his friends, and—and—well, lads will be lads, and 'tis nobbut once in t' year."

Though he forced a smile, and tried to speak lightly, his face belied his words. His heart felt cold and dead within him, and he was miserable and ashamed. The old woman, watching him keenly, saw that the affair was serious.

"He must ha' been bad indeed," she cried, "if he couldna come home."

Jabez made no reply, but Jasper here took up the thread of talk.

"Jabez is reet. If t' lad did get merry, 'tis

nobbut once a year. Lord, I ha' been that way mysen, many a time ! "

"Jack's not like *thee*," snapped his wife— "an idle, foolish owd man, thinking o' nowt but idling and drinking, and smoking t' pipe in a corner."

"Thankee, wife," returned Jasper, with a grin.

"Nay, Jack comes o' better stuff; and if he were overta'en, there's been some foul play, I wager. Come, Jabez Pryke, I'll ha' the truth. Tell it out like a man ! "

Thus urged, the overseer gave a somewhat rose-coloured but fairly truthful account of what had occurred; described the scene in the betting-ring, the meeting with Rachel and the Denes, the encounter with Fitzherbert and Ralph Hollis, and the other occurrences of that eventful day.

The moment he mentioned Ralph's name, Joan interrupted him with a cry.

"Drinking wi' Ralph Hollis? Then 'tis young maister's doing! I was sure there was foul play in't. And Miss Rachel? Did she see him when the poor lad was o'erta'en like that ? "

"Ay, grannie," answered Jabez; "that's the worst on't. Miss Rachel seed him, and so did all our folk. I tried my best to quiet un, but 'twas a useless job."

"When t' drink's in, t' wit's out," observed Jasper, sententiously.

"Hold *thy* tongue !" cried Joan. "Ay, I see it all. 'Twas Ralph Hollis that made our lad drink, and maybe put some stuff i' the glass to steal away his brains."

"Nay, nay, grannie," said Jabez; "he'd ne'er do that!"

"I tell 'ee I know un. He'd gie his reet hand to shame Jack in Miss Rachel's een. Ay, he's a bad un, is Ralph Hollis, and comes o' a bad stock. My poor lad! who ne'er takes a sip o' liquor from one week's end to 'nother! I'd ne'er believe 't, Jabez, if thee hadna said it wi' thy own lips."

Poor Jabez heard the reproach, and for the first time in his life felt as if he had acted disloyal to the boy he loved so much. Yet what could he do? He was incapable of a lie, and he knew, moreover, that Jack was sure of gentle judgment, of tender sympathy in that house. And after all, as he had said, it was but a single slip. One rainy day does not make a flood; and one escapade, however wild, would not convert the boy into a drunkard. The fault could not be hidden now from any one; it would be redeemed by the future, and perhaps be a fruitful warning.

Yet there was a load upon his heart which he could not shake away. The shock had shaken him more strangely than he could have thought possible; the boy's downfall seemed his own death-blow.

"Cheer up," chirped Jasper. "The lad 'll be all reet i' t' morning. Joan, gie Jabez a cup o' our ale; he's soaken wi' t' rain."

" Nay, Jasper," returned the overseer ; " no ale
for me. I shall taste nobbut water fro' this day,
and if t' lad's wise he'll do t' same."

"Amen to that!" said Joan. "Drink's the
scaith o' t' world, and has killed more brave lads
than e'er fell i' bloody wars."

Jasper was dying to know about the St. Leger,
but in the presence of his wife he didn't dare to
speak. Fond of a glass himself, he thought that
a precious bit of trouble was being made out of a
very small affair. With Joan it was altogether
different. Through a grave woman's intuitive per-
ception she knew that Jack's conduct was at once
alarming and mysterious. He was not like other
lads; his whole life had been one steady progress
upwards, and though on one or two occasions of
late he had been a little merry, he had never made
his folly a public exhibition, or quite taken leave
of his sober senses. She saw, too, that Jabez
Pryke was deeply agitated and concerned, and she
suspected, as was the case, that he made the best
of a picture necessity compelled him to draw of
the lad's escapade.

The worst of the whole business was that the
Denes were aware of what had taken place.
Eager to see the fulfilment of her prophesies
concerning her grandson and Rachel Dene, poor
Joan had began to dread a castle in the air. For
the first time in her life, Rachel had seen the
young workman to serious disadvantage, excited
by drink, quarrelsome, reckless, transported out

of his usual gentle self. It was a bad day's business.

Jabez rose to go.

"I'll get back," he said. "I only came down to let thee know the lad was safe wi' me."

"I ha' a mind to gang wi' thee," returned Joan, sadly.

"Nay, bide here, granny; he's all reet in my bed, and I'll come down when he wakes i' the morning."

Eager to prevent even Joan from seeing her grandson in his physical and moral degradation, Jabez succeeded in persuading her to remain where she was. Besides, it was an ugly night, and it was a goodish stretch to the mill. He shook hands with Jasper, and then, bending over Joan, kissed her on the forehead.

"It's nowt, grannie, it's nowt," he said. "I'll go bail for our lad, he'll ne'er forget hissen again; and after all, lads will be lads."

He left her sitting in a brown study, tears in her kindly old eyes, which were fixed on the fire. Was it, she thought, a castle in the air, after all? Was Jack no hero, and she no prophetess, and would there never be the wedding of which she had long dreamed? Hopeful by nature, and full of faith in human nature, she soon began to brighten. Jasper was right. Jasper had been no saint, and yet he had been the best of husbands. As for Jack, he had his wild oats to sow, and it was just because he was so good that she had been shocked by the account of his backsliding. By-and-by, encouraged by her change of manner, Jasper put in another word, and this time his wife thought he spoke like a sensible man. When they rose to go to bed, they were both of a mind. Jack was a hero still, and that little affair of the wedding was bound to come right.

Meantime Jabez Pryke walked back to the town through the darkness and the rain. He did not hasten, though it was getting very late, and, full of his own disappointment, he was indifferent to the weather. Argue with himself as he might, he could not shake away the gloom which oppressed him. He had felt more passionately stirred on more than one occasion, but never so cheerless and depressed. His heart was like lead. Could it be that the shadow of some dreadful calamity was already upon him? If psychology be true, that was possible.

He passed the churchyard, and, instead of turning into the town, walked on towards The Oaks, and, full of some irresistible impulse, looked up at the house of the Denes. The house was dark, but a light burned in one of the upper windows. A shadow crossed the blind, and he recognized it was the shadow of Rachel Dene.

With the rain streaming upon his world-worn face, he watched the shadow come and go, and prayed that God might be pitiful, and not turn the maiden's heart against his boy. He would have liked to enter and stand before her, and plead

poor Jack's cause, explaining his faults away.
His instinct told him that she would be a partial
listener.  He had more dread of the stern old
Quaker, Jacob Dene.  Proud to the backbone, and
severe on human error, Jacob would be certain to
take the worst view of the case.

Sighing heavily, he turned back into the darkness, and walked slowly to the mill.

Alone in her chamber, daintily furnished with
every luxury that love and wealth can give, Rachel
sat before her mirror, thinking.  Her hair flowed
down in a shower of gold over her loose dressing-
gown, and her bare feet were thrust into satin
slippers.  She had dismissed her maid for the
night, and was quite alone.

All the evening she had been distraught and
sad, for her thoughts had been constantly with the
lad who had once saved her life.  Up till that day
she had thought of him with kindness, had been
tender and grateful to him, eager for his success,
hopeful of his future, but she had been unconscious
of any stronger feeling towards him than one of
womanly sympathy.  Now it was quite different.
The very shock she had received on witnessing his
degradation had opened her eyes, and she knew,
for the first time, how deep a place he had in her
young heart.

Jacob Dene had loudly expressed his indignation
—on the way home, at the dinner-table, in the
drawing-room after dinner—and she had been

unable to say a word in Jack's defence, for she,
too, in spite of her newly-discovered affection, was
indignant. She could not shut away the sight she
had seen—the wild, flushed face, the struggling
form, the laughing crowd, the whole horrible scene
in the ring at Doncaster. Even in his madness,
however, Jack Heywood had looked a splendid
fellow, and he had never seemed so handsome
in her eyes. Hitherto he had appeared a little
commonplace, somewhat too uniformly good and
virtuous, with all the rough worth and steadiness
of the dull mechanic; and Rachel, Quakeress as
she was, and innocent to the finger-tips, had been
inclined to patronize him. Now, he seemed another
being—wickeder and wilder, of course, and more
dangerous. The best of women love a man who
can be reckless upon occasion, and Rachel was no
exception to the rule. She was shocked, she was
offended, she was amazed, she was intensely
indignant. But she was in love !

She sat before the glass, looking wistfully at
herself, and thinking it all over. Her thoughts
went back to the time when she and Jack were the
poor siege-children, transplanted from India to
grow in Deepdale. She remembered Jack as a
boy, and afterwards as a bright, handsome lad,
whom she had almost looked upon as a brother.
All along she had been conscious of his timid
worship; but never until to-day had she realized
the sentiment which had been slowly growing in
her own heart. The dawning of love in a young

maid's heart is like the rosy flush of sunrise on
a summer dawn, when the leaves stir, the birds
begin to sing, and the air is full of a dewy sense
of joy. Full of her own loveliness, the warmth
of her own life, she felt her indignation die away
in a new sense of luxury, of yearning. She would
have liked to have gone to Jack that very minute,
and comforted him, and made him promise never
to go wrong again. He was so bright, so clever;
the world was beginning so well for him; and yet
he was in trouble. Love and pity struggled within
her, and for the time being, in spite of moral
indignation, in spite of surprise and sorrow, the
lad's cause was won.

"How foolish I am!" she thought. "I ought
to be very angry, for he looked dreadful, and 'tis
a shame indeed to see a man so degrade himself
before the world. I thought him so gentle and
quiet, too! No wonder grandpapa was shocked!
When I see Jack he shall know that I am very
angry!"

But, in a little while, she smiled at herself in
the glass, and murmured, softly, "Poor fellow!"

# CHAPTER XIII.

## UP AT THE MILL.

THE rain was falling fast, and Joe Styles, the watchman, after taking his accustomed rounds, which he did every two hours, was sitting in the engine-room, smoking his pipe, and playing a hand at cribbage with Jem Wright, the stoker, who was, of course, off duty. The watch-dog, Leo, lay fast asleep at his master's feet.

Both Styles and Wright had been to pay their respects at the shrine of St. Leger, and were full of the events of the day.

Both had lost in the mill sweepstakes, and both were considerably vexed at the defeat of the favourite. They kept a pretty sharp look-out on the game, though, and it was only during the intervals of dealing that they compared notes.

"Well, well," observed Styles; "hasn't Jack Heywood got his cargo aboard!"

"I never heerd o' un i' that way afore," replied Wright.

"Nor I either. He'll ha' an awful head on him i' t' mornin'. It's nowt to say he was screwed; he was clean daft. Well, t' lad will be sore 'shamed o' hissen to-morrow—that is, if he remembers owt about it. First game to me, Jem. It's thy deal, lad. Gie us a bit o' baccy while I mek cards for thee."

At this moment the clock struck twelve.

I

Just upon the last stroke Jabez reached the mill. As he got outside the quadrangle, looking up, he saw a light in the counting-house.

Now, a light there after business hours was unusual, but a light there at midnight was extraordinary.

"It canna be Styles," muttered Jabez; "he has no means o' gettin' in. Except t' gaffer, no one has the pass-key—nobbut mysen."

Quick as lightning it flashed through his mind that many heavy remittances had arrived by that morning's post, and that, in consequence of everybody hurrying off to Barnolby to catch the train, they might not have been paid into the bank.

"Anyhow," he continued, "the safe's all reet, for I've got t' key here i' my pocket."

To his horror, he found that he had lost his bunch of keys.

Then it occurred to him that, in his haste to get away—for Jack was dreadfully afraid they would miss the train—he had left the keys behind him.

For a moment the thought paralyzed him. It seemed as if he had been guilty of a criminal negligence, amounting almost to a breach of trust. Suppose a robber, a burglar, should have found his way to the counting-house?

He grasped his stick firmly, and disappeared rapidly down the passage which led to the congeries of offices amongst which the counting-house was situated. Without thinking of alarming the watchman, he passed alone up the stairs.

Meanwhile, fortune had been favourable to Jem Wright in the contest at cribbage, which was still going on at the engine-house.

"Fifteen two, fifteen four, fifteen six, a pair's eight, a pair's ten, and one for his nob's eleven. Game, Joe."

"Well, that's game and game; now for the conqueror, and I'll gang home. Tak' three while I deal."

As Styles proceeded to deal the cards, a loud cry, loud like a human cry, startled the players to their feet. It startled the dog, too, who leaped up, emitting a fierce growl.

"Jem," said Styles, dropping the cards, "there's murder goin' on somewhere, lad ! "

"It's a man a-callin'," responded the other. "If it had been a woman, now, I'd ha' thowt nought about it. Happen some chap might ha' been purrin' her a bit to keep her in order, and they wenches are apt to cry out afore theer hurt ! "

Again came the cry, this time shriller than before ; again Leo growled ominously.

"It's in t' mill, lad ! Bear a hand, and stir thy stumps," said Styles ; "and bring wi' thee yon crowbar—it may be useful."

So saying, they started for the front side of the mill—the side from whence the sounds arose. They reached the quadrangle. Once more came the voice, getting feebler and feebler still.

"Sure as death," said Styles, "that's Jabez

Pryke's voice, if ever Jabez spoke. Let's put on steam, or we may be too late."

As they rapidly crossed the quadrangle, they heard above them the tramp of struggling feet, the noise of furniture being overturned, and of men engaged in a deadly strife.

Looking up, they saw, in a confused mass, the shadows of two struggling human figures cast upon the lighted window-blind of the counting-house. Evidently two men were intertwined together in a death-struggle.

The watchers stood paralyzed for a moment; but as the dog leaped up, barking furiously, the shadows melted away like a dissolving view. Then they took a new shape. One figure stood erect and alone, with arms thrust forth in defence or defiance, while the other, recoiling from the fierce impact, staggered backward, and vanished from view. Simultaneously arose a terrible sound—a shrill, piercing cry, like that of a dying horse in the last moments of its agony, when torn to pieces by shot or shell upon some bloody battle-field; then came the dull, heavy thud of a falling body, then silence, for even the dog trembled and crouched in terror at his master's heel.

The weird phantasmagoria we have endeavoured to describe barely occupied thirty seconds; but such seconds !

As the solitary figure above stood erect and motionless, with arms uplifted, a colossal silhouette of despair, or remorse, or both, the watchman and the stoker had arrived beneath the window.

The one took out his revolver and examined it carefully in the moonlight, and grasped Leo by the collar, while the other shouldered his crowbar, and both men and dog disappeared noiselessly up the dark, tortuous passage before them.

It took them a minute or two to thread their way through the darkness before they could reach the corridor on the first floor, where they were brought to a halt by the sound of a voice exclaiming, in agonizing tones, "Oh, Jabez, Jabez, 'tis I who have killed thee!"

At the sound, the mastiff struggled to get free.

Releasing him, Styles said, "Good lad, go for un! Hi, lad, go!"

Growling fiercely, with eyes aflame, and bristling hair, the dog sprang into the counting-house.

The men without waited anxiously for what might come, for, when roused, Leo was a ferocious brute. To their astonishment his yells of defiance subsided into a howl so pathetic, that it reminded Joe (who had served in the constabulary in the sister isle) of the plaintive wailing of women at an Irish keening.

They stayed to hear no more, but burst into the room.

What a sight it was that met their eyes!

The safe, thrown wide open, appeared to have been rifled; the cash-box lay overturned on the floor, and its contents — coin, drafts, and bank-notes — were scattered in reckless confusion in every direction; the scanty furniture was over-turned and broken; while midst the *débris*, with white face, and glaring eyes, and gashed temples, lay Jabez Pryke, stone dead, in a pool of blood.

Over the body stood Jack Heywood.

He was half dressed, and seemed wholly demented.

His shirt and his hands were bedabbled with blood, his hair stood up erect, and his eyes were starting from his head. The dog lay whining and shivering at his feet; while, utterly regardless of the men's appearance, Jack continued to bewail the murdered man, with tears and cries, and sobs of half-stupefied remorse.

Finding it impossible to obtain any coherent or rational statement from him, Styles despatched the stoker to ring the alarm bell, while he, still gripping his revolver, continued to mount guard. A minute afterwards the bell rang out through the storm, startling hill and dale.

## CHAPTER XIV.

### THE DEAD MAN.

THE bell rang out in the night, high above the shrill crying of the wind, startling every dwelling in Deepdale, and sounding far away across the lonely rain-beaten moor. In an incredibly short

space of time the streets and lanes were thronged
with masses of people surging towards the mill in
a murmuring stream.

"What's t' matter?" "Hast t' reservoir bust
up at t' head, or is t' mill afire?" "Who's
ringing t' bell?" "Hark yonder!" "This way
—this way!" were some of the cries that rose
upon the night.

The throng swept in at the mill gate, and filled
the great quadrangle. Men, women, lads and
lasses, little children, confusedly mixed together.
They saw with wonder the lights in the upper
windows of the main building; they heard the bell
shrieking high above them; and while the rain
swept down upon them, and the wind moaned,
they were moving towards the passage leading
upward, when the bell suddenly ceased, and the
figure of the stoker appeared before them crying,
"Silence! keep back, lads!" And in answer to
their questioning cries, he added, "It's *murder*,
lads! T' overseer's lying up yonder, dead!"

Then, in spite of his warnings, they flocked up
the stair, and the foremost among them rushing
into the room, saw Jack Heywood standing over
the overseer's dead body moaning and wailing,
while the dog crouched at his feet, and the watchman looked on aghast. From those who crowded
into the room, to those who ranged outside, from
the counting-house to the quadrangle, from the
quadrangle to the street, and on through the little
town, the news spread like wild-fire. Murder had

been done! Jabez Pryke had been killed up at the mill, and young Jack Heywood had been taken almost red-handed in the act.

Had he been any other than Jack Heywood he would have been torn to pieces by the mob; but he was too well known and too beloved, and those who knew them could scarcely believe their eyes or ears. So, when the constables appeared pushing their way through the throng, and had their hands upon him, there was a murmur of wonder, almost of indignation. Rapidly and breathlessly the watchman panted out his story, and told all that he had heard or seen. Jack listened as if dazed, but when the constables seized him he uttered a shriek, and tried to tear himself free.

At this juncture Jacob Dene appeared, looking white and stern. Told the whole terrible truth, he gazed at the wretched lad, saying, "I warned thee, Jack Heywood. This comes of the drink that made thee mad at Doncaster. Thou hast slain thy best friend."

"Jabez, Jabez!" shrieked Jack, gazing in horror and despair on the dead man.

There was no doubt; he was dead indeed. A doctor, summoned in haste, pronounced life to be quite extinct. Horrified and awe-stricken, the crowd looked on, while the constables handcuffed their prisoner, in spite of his appealing cries.

Suddenly there came another sound, the shriek of a woman. Wild, ghastly, tottering, Joan Heywood pushed her way into the counting-house like one demented; but when she saw the man, who had parted from her full of lusty life only an hour before, lying dead upon the floor; when she beheld the other, whom she loved dearer than her own life, standing there with hair and hands bedabbled with blood, she fell wailing upon her knees, and with outstretched arms besought her grandson to prove his innocence of a crime so hideous. Dazed and stupefied, Jack ceased to struggle, and looked at her wildly; then, with a mad cry, he hid his face in his hands and sobbed aloud.

That night was one long remembered in Deepdale. Men and women thronged the streets till daybreak, discussing the terrible event. Hitherto, in that happy valley, crime of any serious kind had been almost unknown; and now, for the first time, the peaceful spell was broken by a deed so horrible, so infamous, as almost to transcend belief.

Meantime Ralph Hollis had let himself in with his latchkey, and gone to bed at once. When the news of the murder reached the Vicarage, as it did before many hours had passed, Mrs. Hollis tried her son's door and found it locked; then she knocked softly, but received no reply.

"Poor lad, he is tired out!" she said. "Let him rest till the morning—it will be time enough to tell him then."

But Ralph Hollis knew too well already. Crouching in his chamber, he had heard the tolling bell,

the tumult, the alarm; and peering from his
window he saw the lights moving about the town,
and the whole place awake. Towards daybreak
he fell into a troubled sleep, broken by bad dreams.
He was awakened by a knocking at his door, and
opening his eyes, saw the daylight streaming in at
the window.

"Ralph!" cried his mother's voice. "Are you
awake?"

"Yes, mother."

"There has been murder at the mill. Jabez
Pryke, the overseer, has been killed by young
Heywood. Get up at once!"

He heard her descend the stairs, and staggered
from his bed, his eyes wild, his face blanched and
terror-stricken. Instinctively he moved to the
glass, and shuddered at the reflection mirrored
there. His head went round, his brain was still
full of the fumes of drink, and he could hardly
realize what had occurred. When he did so, he
sank as if paralyzed on his knees by the bedside,
and hid his face in his hands. Nearly an hour
passed thus, when he was disturbed by a second
knocking at his door, and started up, trembling
like a leaf.

"Ralph, are you ready?" cried the voice.

"I am dressing, mother!"

His parched and bloodless lips could hardly
frame the words.

"Let me in! I *must* speak to you!"

He hesitated for a moment, then conquering

himself with an effort, he opened the door. To his surprise, his mother, scarcely looking into his face, threw her arms wildly around his neck.

"Mother, is it true," he gasped, "that the overseer——"

"Yes, he has been murdered, and the whole place is in alarm!" she replied. Then, looking into his face and seeing it so white and bloodless, she added, "No wonder you are horrified! It is terrible! Young Heywood did it, and has been arrested!"

"My God!" he murmured.

"But it is not that which has brought me back again. Oh, Ralph! I am sorry, very sorry, for Algy, but I cannot forget that he was always so unkind to you, my darling!"

"What do you mean?" cried Ralph.

"Read that!" she answered, putting a telegram into his hand. With eyes dim, and head swimming round, he read as follows:—

"To Ralph, Earl of Beauchamp, the Vicarage, Deepdale.

"MY LORD,

"Your uncle died this morning, at two o'clock. I await your lordship's commands.

"RICHARD BARKINS."

## CHAPTER XV.

### THE INQUEST.

ALTHOUGH Jack Heywood was a general favourite, opinion at the moment of his arrest was much divided against him. For the news had spread everywhere of the fight at Doncaster; of the violent altercation, and the yet more violent threats uttered against Jabez in Jack's drunken frenzy during the homeward journey; of the suspicious circumstances under which he was found with the murdered man; and, lastly, of his own self-upbraidings and self-accusations.

Despite all this, there were two or three women who believed in the lad's innocence, as truly as they believed in the justice of Heaven.

"Were they to lay down a pack o' Bibles, and swear he did it, I wouldn't believe 'em! My own heart knows my boy is innocent!" sturdily declared Joan Heywood. And Rachel? When Jacob Dene alleged that Jack was guilty, she said, quietly, "Grandpa, if that is thy opinion, we need not discuss the matter any further. I've known Mr. Heywood from childhood, and know that he is not capable of an act so wicked."

"I believe the child is right," chimed in Mrs. Dene.

"I hope it may prove so," rejoined Jacob; "but things look black against him."

Meanwhile the body of the murdered man had been left alone, while Jack was also put under lock and key at the Round House; nor was he alone either, for even the autocrat of Deepdale could not find it in his heart to say nay to Joan Heywood's request to be permitted to stay with her grandson.

The poor soul watched over his fevered sleep for the night, and administered such homely remedies as her own experience might suggest, or Doctor Whitaker's skill prescribe, but administered them in vain, for as yet the wretched lad lay void of sense and motion, almost of life.

When he returned to consciousness, and found himself in the Round House, he could not comprehend what had brought him there; or why his head was splitting, his throat parched and swollen, and his whole body a burning fire. As yet he could not form his thoughts into shape; indeed, he had no clear recollection of anything which had occurred after the affair in Doncaster. The drink which in the first instance had maddened him, in the second had stupefied his senses into oblivion.

After vainly trying to arrive at a conclusion whether he was awake or dreaming, he turned and caught sight of Joan Heywood.

Starting up, he tried to speak; but he was unable to articulate a syllable.

As he fell back, he pointed to his choking throat, and Joan quickly brought him some water.

When he had allayed his raging thirst he
gasped, "What's come, granny? and why am I
here?"

"They brought thee here last neet, lad," she
answered sadly.

"What for?"

"I canna tell thee."

"Canna tell, canna tell! Surely it's not for
punchin' that thief's head at Doncaster? Don't
cry, granny, don't cry, but send for grandad and
Jabez to get me out of this rat-trap."

"Jabez, lad, Jabez," moaned the old woman;
"woes me, poor Jabez!"

And she broke down utterly.

There was no help for it; he must know all.
Better that he should learn it from her than from
his gaoler.

When at length the truth was borne in upon
the wretched lad's mind, his amazement and
consternation were only equalled by his grief.
At first the thing appeared too monstrous, too
incredible for belief. Yet, even as she spoke, he
saw, or seemed to see, as if in some awful vision,
the white face of Jabez, the staring eyes, the pool
of blood, the open safe, the rifled cash-box, and the
dog crying at his feet.

Could it be possible that, in the delirium of
drink, he had dared to lift his parricidal hand
against his friend, his more than father? If he
knew himself, that could never be, for truly he
would gladly have laid down his own life for Jabez

Pryke. But, alas! he knew also that yesterday he was *not* himself!

Catching sight of his blood-stained linen, and his bloody hands, he flung himself on the ground in an agony of grief. His tears, his cries, his inarticulate expressions of anguish, pierced the poor grandam's heart. She tried to soothe him, but in vain; he was inconsolable. Under any circumstances, the loss of Jabez would have been one of the greatest calamities which could have befallen him; but to lose him under such circumstances was beyond horror. He tried to think, to recall what had happened; but some connecting link of memory was gone altogether, or, at any rate, refused to cohere. How came he at the mill at all? That was the very first question he asked himself; but he was unable to answer it. When Joan explained that Jabez had taken him there, he had not the faintest recollection of the occurrence. The pressure on his nerves was so great, the charge against him so awful, the crime itself so foul, strange, and unnatural, that the bare thought of it drove him to despair.

"Oh, grannie, grannie," he cried, "you know I *couldna* do it; my arm would have rotted from my body first! But could—oh, could I, while that infernal poison was working i' my brain—could I have been so mad, so wicked, as to lift my hand against him? Oh, that I were dead! God knows I would have died fifty times over for his sake. Oh, Jabez, Jabez, my dear old dad—my dear old dad!"

Joan tried by every means in her power to awaken his dormant memory and to supply the missing link, but in vain.

Meanwhile, the sad news had an unlooked-for effect on Jasper Heywood, for it cured his rheumatics like magic.

Jumping out of bed, he roared, "It's a lie—a lie of the devil's own making! An' Jabez, too—dear old Jabez! Why, t' lad wouldn't 'a harmed a hair o' his head! He loved un too well for that!"

With that he scrambled into his clothes, and, regardless of his rheumatism, ran up the valley to the Round House like a two-year-old.

Throwing his arms round Jack, he cried, "Cheer up, lad—cheer up! If all t' saints in t' calendar were to come back to life and swear they seed it, I'd tell 'em they were liars! And a thief, too! Why, dang un, theer never was a thief i' t' family, from curfew time upwards! As for brass, why, we've gotten enow, and to spare! Go thy ways, owd woman, to Barford, and see owd Grainger, t' lawyer, and tell un to come here and stand up for Jack at crowner's 'quest. Go at once, lass, and I'll stay here and blow a bit o' baccy wi' t' lad."

Without another word, Joan went off to Barford to retain the solicitor, while Jasper tried to cheer up his unfortunate grandson.

At the post-mortem examination it was discovered that Jabez's skull was badly fractured, and that the temporal artery of the right temple had been severed as clearly as if it had been cut in two with a lancet.

When the inquest took place the next day, the jury, after hearing the evidence of Stokes and Wright, at the coroner's direction, without a moment's hesitation, returned a verdict of " Wilful murder " against Jack, who was that night transferred to Barford. When brought before the stipendiary, Grainger, the solicitor, alleging that he had not yet had time to consult his client, requested a remand, which was granted to that day week.

Barford Gaol was not Deepdale Round House; and when, after a painful parting with his grandfather and grandmother, Jack was consigned to his solitary cell, he appeared quietly but utterly demented.

The mystery and the horror of the thing increased day by day, and no single ray of light appeared to illumine the darkness which enshrouded it. Up at the Oaks, and down at the cottage, and through the whole valley of Deepdale, men's minds, and women's, too, were occupied with nothing else. The men saw the case with their heads, and they were reluctantly compelled to arrive at the conclusion that, in a fit of mad drunkenness, Jack had done the deed. The women, who saw only with their hearts, refused to believe that it was possible for him, under any circumstances, to kill the man he loved so dearly. Both men and

K

women sympathized with the unhappy lad in his tribulation.

As for Rachel, angry, ashamed as she was at the disreputable scene in Doncaster, she never believed for an instant that his was the hand that struck the blow.

Jacob Dene and the vicar were both puzzled at the commission of such a crime in the absence of all motive. Their opinions, however, underwent a change in consequence of a piece of evidence which transpired at the next examination. The betting man from Sheffield, reading an account of " The Deepdale Mystery " in the *Yorkshire Post,* concluded to make tracks for Barford, to see if there was any chance of " copping " that five and twenty pounds which Jack had omitted to send him.

Now, it must be premised that, after repeated consultations with his client, Mr. Grainger could make neither head nor tail of his case. The evidence for the prosecution commenced with the statement of the Deepdale lads who had accompanied prisoner and deceased from Doncaster. They testified to prisoner's mad demeanour, his violence, his abuse, and his threats. Then came the watchman and the stoker; and, lastly, to the astonishment of everybody, Mr. Thomas Yondal.

That worthy had made some inquiries of the chief constable, with the result that, almost before he knew where he was, he found himself in the witness-box. He deposed as to the betting, and the fight at Doncaster; the debt of five and twenty pounds; prisoner's appeal to deceased to pay it; his refusal, and the subsequent quarrel.

As Grainger listened, he felt that every word of this evidence was a strand in the rope that was to hang his unfortunate client; and he merely shrugged his shoulders, stating that he reserved his defence.

"That being the case," said the stipendiary, "the prisoner is committed to take his trial at Leeds Assizes."

## CHAPTER XVI.

### THE EARL OF BEAUCHAMP.

WITHIN an hour after he had heard the news of his accession to the earldom, Ralph Hollis was on horseback, riding full-speed to Barford. Wild and pale, with blood-shot eyes, he had come from his chamber to receive the congratulations of his mother and the vicar; then, without breakfasting —for he declared he had no appetite—he had gone round to the stable, and ordered his horse to be saddled at once.

"Poor boy!" sighed his mother. "The surprise was a joyful one, but a shock notwithstanding. He can scarcely realize his good fortune."

Ralph returned to the front of the house, followed by the groom leading the horse. Mrs. Hollis came

out to the porch, and was again startled to see
how dazed and strange her son still appeared.

"Mother," he said nervously, "I am just going
over to Barford, and shall telegraph to London
from there."

"Won't you go first to the Oaks, and tell the
Denes ? "

"I leave that to you," answered the young man.
"I shall be back very soon.   What with one thing
and another, I feel rather upset.   I shall be all
right after a gallop in the fresh air."

Grasping the reins with hands that trembled
violently, he mounted his horse and rode rapidly
away, his mother watching him with proud and
loving eyes till he disappeared.   In her joy at the
good fortune, Mrs. Hollis had quite forgotten the
dark affair which had occurred the previous night.
All her heart was full of pride and happiness.

"I will go to Rachel," she said, "and tell her
the good news."

So, while Ralph was riding towards Barford,
she went and found Rachel Dene.   But when she
spoke of Ralph's good fortune, of his accession to
wealth and a great title, Rachel scarcely seemed
to hear or heed.   The young girl's whole heart
was occupied with two feelings — tenderness for
the poor lad just committed for a terrible crime,
and indignation against those who could possibly
believe him guilty.   All her soul was at last awake.
Sharp on her discovery of the true state of her
feelings towards Jack Heywood had come the

announcement that he was a criminal, arrested for murder. It was almost too horrible for belief.

"Are you not glad, Rachel," said Mrs. Hollis, "of my boy's good fortune?"

Rachel looked at her sadly, with eyes full of tears.

"Of course I am glad, for his sake," she answered; "but to-night I can think of one thing only—'tis so strange, so terrible! Mr. Heywood is accused of murdering his foster-father, and, although I am sure he is innocent, it looks so black against him."

Mrs. Hollis looked in her face, and saw there, with womanly instinct, the confession of the truth —that Rachel had given her heart to the man who had once saved her life. Well, after all, it did not matter much *now.* The new Earl of Beauchamp might look higher than the heiress of the Denes. The day before, such a match would have been social salvation for her son—for them all; but a few hours had changed the cards, and Ralph was master of the situation.

Meantime, Ralph rode towards Barford. Quitting Deepdale by the high road, he reached the open moor, and, drawing rein, looked back and saw, looming darkly against the morning sky, the black outline of the mills. A shudder ran through his frame as he thought of the dead man lying there, and of the living man already a prisoner in the Round House.

"My God!" he murmured. "If I had only known yesterday! Too late—too late!"

Full sunshine lay upon the moor and sparkled on the river, for the clouds of last night's rain had passed away, and fresh airs were winnowing the sky to purest azure. All the world looked bright and glad; but Ralph saw only darkness and desolation. Haggard and pale, he turned his horse's head again, and hurried on.

It was a good long ride to Barford, and more than once on the way thither he halted at roadside inns, and plied himself with ardent spirits. The liquor put some heart into him, and brought a little colour to his cheeks, so that by the time he reached the great town he was more master of himself. Riding up to the principal hotel in the High Street, he dismounted, handed his horse to an ostler, and strolled into the coffee-room. He had not yet breakfasted, but he felt no hunger whatever; so he ordered a glass of brandy, and had just drunk it when a hand was laid upon his shoulder. Starting, and growing deadly pale, he turned and encountered the familiar face of Captain Fitzherbert.

"Hullo, old fellow," said the Captain; "you've left your premises and come over early. Come to settle, eh? I'm glad of that, for some of our fellows were talking about you last night, and were rather rusty."

Ralph did not answer; his tongue clung to the roof of his mouth, and he trembled nervously.

"Anything the matter?" asked Fitzherbert, looking at him in some astonishment.

" Nothing, nothing ! " answered the young man.
" I'm a little upset after yesterday, that's all ! "

" Hot coppers, eh ? By-the-by, what's this
about a murder down at Deepdale ? The news
came over this morning by the carrier."

" It isn't exactly a murder," said Ralph, avert-
ing his eyes, and looking through the window into
the street. " A row of some sort between our old
overseer and that young fellow we had in tow
yesterday. The lad got blind drunk, there was a
quarrel, and something ugly happened. But it
isn't murder ! No, no ! not murder ! "

The Captain's face grew very grave.

" I'm confoundedly sorry," he said. " The old
man has been killed, at any rate, hasn't he ? "

Ralph nodded.

" Well, it's an ugly business for both of us ! "

" For us ! What business is it of ours ? "

" Well, we played the youngster a trick, didn't
we, and doctored his drink ? The cursed stuff
must have made a madman of him, and you
see—— "

" It was only a lark," cried Ralph, eagerly.
" How could we foresee what was going to
happen ? As for the lad, I'm sorry for him, and
I'll do my best to help him—yes, by the Lord, I
will ! "

" I hope you will," returned Fitzherbert. " But
now, about our fellows and that money ? Have
you got it ? "

" No," was the reply.

"Then I'm afraid there'll be a row. I warned you," said the Captain.

"I think they'll give me time," said Ralph, forcing a sickly smile. "*You* will, at any rate, won't you? The fact is, old fellow—but haven't you heard? I'm in clover at last! The old man died last night, and I got the telegram this morning."

Fitzherbert was at once astonished and delighted.

"I'll tell the boys," he cried. "Give you time? I should think they would *now.*" But he added as he wrung the young Earl's hand, "I'm sorry about that poor devil of a workman, though! I wish we hadn't met him yesterday."

While Fitzherbert went round to the barracks to tell the officers of his friend's change of fortune, Ralph ordered breakfast to be prepared in a private room. When the meal was ready he entered the chamber, and found a fire burning on the hearth, and everything very comfortable.

"I'll ring if I want anything more," he said to the waiter. "Stop, though; I want you to send me a telegram. Bring me a form at once."

When the man brought the form, Ralph wrote the telegram out as follows, and addressed it to Barkins, the confidential valet of the deceased Earl:—

"Yours received. I shall come on to London as soon as possible. Beauchamp, White Lion Hotel, Barford."

Directly the waiter left the room, Ralph rose up
and locked the door; crossing to the window,
which was on the first floor, he looked out
nervously into the street; then, secure from obser-
vation, he opened his coat, and took from the
breast pocket a roll of bank-notes and papers.
His hands shook like leaves, and his face was
as white as death, as he turned the papers
over.

Startled by the sound of footsteps along the
corridor, he thrust them back into his bosom, and
stood listening; but the steps passed by, and he
breathed again. Conquering his agitation with a
great effort, he knelt down before the fire, and
placing the papers one by one in the blaze,
watched them rapidly consuming; bank-notes,
bills of exchange, letters of credit, all shared the
same fate. In a few minutes, every one of them
had disappeared, save for a few charred fragments
and pieces of film that fluttered on the top of the
blazing coal. As if fearful that even these might
betray his secret, he seized the poker and dis-
persed the ashes into the surrounding flame. At
last, rising to his feet, he stood again listening.
All was quite silent. He went tip-toe to the door,
unlocked it stealthily, and then sat down to
breakfast.

He could not eat; he was too spirit-shaken and
terrified; but he hurriedly drank some cups of
tea, and swallowed a few morsels of dry toast. He
rose again, and looked in the mirror over the

mantelpiece; his face was like a dead man's, and his head was swimming round.

A sound of voices, mingled with merry laughter, came from below, and, ascending the stairs, approached nearer and nearer.

"Room twenty-five—all right!" cried the voice of Fitzherbert.

The next moment the Captain appeared, accompanied by several young officers of the fighting Forty-First.

"Here we are!" cried Fitzherbert. "Come to congratulate you, old boy!"

And Ralph, surrounded on every side by his friends, and felicitated on his good fortune, forcing a spasmodic gaiety, bade them welcome, and ringing the bell, ordered champagne and cigars. After a glass or two, he felt better, laughed and joked, and made as merry as possible. Not a word was said on either side of the paper with his signature which some of these young bloods held in their possession. Ralph was the hero of the hour.

He did not return to Deepdale that night, but, while Jack Heywood was languishing in prison, kept it up royally with the officers and Fitzherbert. Play ensued, of course, and the young Earl lost as usual; but he did not care, and distributed his paper merrily to the winners, who were well content to take it. It was long after midnight when he staggered to his bed in the hotel, and fell into a drunken sleep.

He woke next morning with a splitting head-

ache ; but in spite of that, his nerves were calmer,
and he had made up his mind to the situation.
The Barford newspapers were full of long accounts
of the Deepdale tragedy. Sitting at breakfast in
his private room, he read through all the horrible
details of the murder, the prisoner's arrest and
self-accusations, the overwhelming and damning
proofs against him.

"Poor devil !" thought Ralph the Earl. "One
comfort is, they can't make it anything worse than
manslaughter. If it was a hanging matter, I
think I should go mad ! "

He was now resolved not to return to Deepdale
until the affair had blown over. His nerves, he
felt, were quite unequal to the ordeal. So he
wrote a hasty letter to his mother, telling her
that it was necessary for him to go straight on
to London. There was an express train to the
metropolis at two p.m. ; he determined to take
it—a determination which he communicated to
Fitzherbert, who stepped in after breakfast.

The Captain, while expressing his approval of
the arrangement, returned again to the subject
of the murder.

"Seen the papers, of course?" he said.
"Well, I do hope the poor lad will get off clear,
or, at any rate, with a light punishment. I'd go
into the box myself to prove that he was blazing
drunk, and didn't know what he was doing."

"You'd better not do that," returned Ralph,
nervously.

" Well, perhaps not; but, by George, I won't
stand by quietly if they make out too black a case
against him ! I feel still as if it was all our doing
—don't you ? "

" No," said Ralph ; " and, for that matter,
there will be plenty of people to swear as to his
condition."

" It says in the papers that there was money
stolen and valuable papers, but the police can find
no trace of them. It's queer, now, seeing that he
was taken red-handed, that nothing of the sort
was found upon him. But what's the matter?
You look as white as a ghost ! "

" I've a confounded headache," stammered
Ralph. " Two nights of it, you know! Besides,
this business of the succession has come upon me
so suddenly that I don't know whether I'm standing
on my head or my heels."

" I suppose not," laughed the Captain. " By
George, though, I should like to be in your shoes !
You wanted the tin badly enough, old fellow, and
I suppose you don't object to the title thrown in ? "

" Not a bit of it," said Ralph, echoing the
laugh.

Presently Fitzherbert went away, promising to
meet his friend shortly in London; and Ralph
was again left alone to his self-reproaches and
nervous terrors. Determined to front the world
boldly, and put on the brightest face possible, he
strolled downstairs and stood at the inn door,
smoking his cigar and looking at the crowded

street. The news of his good fortune had spread
by this time; the landlord of the inn came forward to congratulate him, while the waiters and
chambermaids looked on obsequiously. Several
acquaintances came up, and after fresh congratulations, passed on. So the time wore away till
noon.

As twelve o'clock sounded from the neighbouring cathedral, a dog-cart drove up to the door,
and Ralph saw, seated beside the driver, the very
last person he could have wished to encounter at
the moment—Rachel Dene. She was quite alone,
and the moment she saw the young man she
uttered a joyful exclamation. He stepped forward,
and assisted her to alight.

"Why, what brings you to Barford?" he asked.
"And why are you without an escort?"

"Grandpapa could not come with me," she
cried quickly, "and as there was no time to be
lost, I hurried hither alone. I am going on to
Mr. Grainger about poor Jack Heywood. Oh,
Ralph, thou hast heard? Was ever such a
calamity? Yet he is innocent, I know!"

"I'm sure I hope so," answered Ralph, shrink-
ing from the gaze of the young girl's clear, truthful
eyes.

"I am so glad we have met, for thou wilt help
me, I am sure. Let me go on to Mr. Grainger
at once."

And she took his arm eagerly, as if to lead him
away.

"I am very sorry," he stammered nervously, "but it is absolutely imperative for me to go to London. The Earl is dead. My mother has told you, I suppose? and I must pay him the last respects, as his kinsman and heir."

"Thou canst not help the dead!" cried Rachel. "What we must all do now is clear. An innocent man is accused of murder, and perchance we can save him. Come with me, for God's sake, and come at once!"

Ralph would have done so gladly, but he dreaded the ordeal of the interview with the solicitor, and all his wish now was to get out of the way as quickly as possible. He was still full of a nervous terror.

"My dear Rachel, it is impossible!" he said. "Of course, I will do all I can; but they are waiting for me in London."

Again he felt her truthful eyes upon him, and shrank from meeting them. He felt for the moment as if he could have sunk through the earth in shame.

"Oh, Ralph, he saved my life!" sobbed the girl.

"Don't fret yourself unnecessarily," he replied. "Every one knows that the man was drunk, and if he did this thing it was in a drunken frenzy. That, of course, will plead in his favour."

But Rachel, drying her eyes suddenly, and setting her face to a look of clear resolve, cried, "He is innocent, I tell thee; nay, I could stake

my life upon it. Whoever killed poor Mr. Pryke,
it was not Jack Heywood! "

It was a hard task for Ralph Hollis to preserve
his self-command; he was tortured as if upon the
rack, and could scarcely refrain from uttering a
cry of pain. Trembling violently, he turned his
head away, when he felt the girl's hand clutching
his arm, and heard her saying, " The man who
did this thing was a thief, and had broken into
the counting-house. Jack Heywood was incapable
of such an act! Oh, Ralph, he was thy companion in childhood, and was ever so good and
true! Thou canst not think him guilty? Say
thou canst not? "

"Upon my life," answered Ralph, "I don't
know what to think or say! I'm only sure of one
thing—that I could cut off my right hand to set
the fellow free! "

A few more hurried words, and Rachel was gone.
The young man breathed again as soon as she
disappeared.

"Confound the girl!" he muttered. "Why
the deuce does *she* meddle in the matter? I was
right, then; it is clear enough that she loves
him! "

In his nervous alarm from other causes, he
scarcely felt at that moment even a qualm of
jealousy. All his wish now was to fly away from
the scene of his horror, and from the eyes which at
any moment might read his secret.

A little later, he was seated alone in a first-class

carriage, travelling by express to London, more like a fugitive from justice than the happy heir to fortune and an earldom.

## CHAPTER XVII.

### THE PRIMROSE PATH.

UPON arriving at Curzon Street, May Fair, Ralph found that his uncle's death had been occasioned by a fit of apoplexy upon returning from the Lord Mayor's banquet. A few days afterwards he attended the obsequies at Beauchamp Castle, as chief mourner, with little or no affectation of regret for a relative whom he had scarcely seen, and who had been systematically hostile to his mother and himself.

After the funeral, he returned to the Castle, looked through the stables, glanced at the coverts, conferred with the steward, the butler, and the housekeeper, the head groom, and the head game-keeper, confirmed them in their appointments, and returned to town by the next train, accompanied by Grimstone, the family solicitor.

They dined together that night in Curzon Street, where Ralph thenceforth took up his abode, having taken over the whole of his uncle's *ménage*, including Barkins, the valet, who had been in the Beauchamp family all his life, had known Ralph's father and mother, and who soon

succeeded, by the way, in attaching himself to
his new master.

That evening, Grimstone explained to his youth-
ful client that it would be requisite to go through
certain formalities for the administration of the
estate; but before the week was out, the new Earl
had taken his seat in the House of Lords, and
voted for the Government in an important
division.

The estate cut up better than was anticipated,
and Ralph found himself in the enjoyment of
something like thirty thousand a year—so, at
least, he wrote Jacob Dene, politely tendering his
resignation—expressing his regret for the overseer's untimely death, and volunteering the
opinion that Jack, he felt sure, was the last man
in the world capable of such a crime.

He wrote much to the same effect to Jasper
Heywood, telling him to draw upon him for all
moneys requisite for the defence. He touched
lightly upon the subject in his letter to Rachel, to
whom he sent some little presents just to remind
her of his existence. Nor did he forget his other
friends and relations. To his mother he sent an
open cheque, some valuable pieces of mourning,
gloves, etc., and to the vicar some books of reference. Then, having so far done his duty, he
invited Captain Fitzherbert to come and join him
in seeing life in London, to which occupation
these gentlemen devoted themselves assiduously.

It was astonishing what a number of friends

L

cropped up all at once at May Fair. Friends of
Ralph's father, friends of his mother—aristocratic
matrons with marriageable daughters, and friends
of his late lamented uncle. Besides these came a
*clientèle* of tradespeople who had fattened on the
Beauchamps for generations. Then there were
obliging gentlemen, olive-complexioned and large-
nosed, who inquired in the most delicate and
friendly manner if the new lord needed ready
money. There were other gentlemen with cropped
heads, low foreheads, bull necks, who called to
inquire if "my lord" required any lessons in the
noble arts of racing and self-defence.

The Honourable Augustus Torvin, the Government whip, put the new Earl up at the Junior
Carlton, and Tom Tressider nominated him for the
Jockey Club, in place of his noble uncle, deceased;
while Fitzherbert introduced him to the Ostriches,
where one night they encountered the famous
Major O'Gallagher, whose escapade with the Begum
of Upper Oude led to his quitting the service with
a certain *éclaircissement* a quarter of a century ago.

The Major, of course, was a native of the Sister
Isle, with just that flavour of the brogue on his
tongue, and those cordial and ingratiating manners,
which impart such a charm to the manners of the
well-bred Irishman.

Although on the shady side of sixty, he was a
fine, stalwart fellow, and in excellent preservation.
"Mick," as his friends called him, had a head as
white and as well polished as a billiard ball; a

celestially Irish nose; bright, twinkling blue eyes;
rosy, clean-shaven cheeks, which expanded into
dewlaps as they fell in glistening folds over the
white neck-scarf which he always affected.

He had met the late Colonel Hollis in India
during those bad times of the Mutiny, and he
received Ralph with effusion.

"I knew your father," he cried, "before ye were
born. The best player at poker and pyramids in
the Punjaub. And how is that gorgeous creature,
your mother? By my honour, I used to adore
her; that is, before I took to adoring my dinner.
Which reminds me you must come and dine with
me to-night, and your friend, too."

It was in vain that Ralph pleaded a prior engagement; the Major would not take no for an answer.

"Come, my boy, and take us without ceremony,"
said he. "Julia will be delighted to see you.
Sure, she played with you when you were a little
fellow the size of my thumb out there at Lucknow,
when the Nana, bad cess to him, gave poor Ralph
his quietus."

Both the young fellows were impressed by the
Major's frank and engaging manners, and the
little dinner at Montpellier Square was a break
in the run of bachelor banquets. To be sure, the
O'Gallagher apartments were not palatial, but
there was a cordial welcome from the Major and
the Major's daughter.

In appearance Julia O'Gallagher reminded Ralph
of some lost vision of his youth, or one of those

weird bizarre statues of some bronzed odalisque, partially clad in garments of white, from which the dusky limbs gleam forth bare and beautiful in the stately symmetry of their classic outlines. Had Cleopatra had the faintest tinge of Egyptian blood in her Greek veins, so might the serpent of Old Nile have looked in her golden prime. The tinge of olive which blended with the Milesian strain of the O'Gallaghers came from her mother, the Begum aforesaid. Thence also came the white teeth; the luscious, scarlet lips—lips like twin rosebuds; the dark, flashing eyes; the straight, black brows; the night of raven hair, which was wont upon provocation to tumble to the ground, covering her lithe and elastic figure as with an iridescent mantle of sable. The voice, too, had the soft, crooning music of the far East. To these Oriental attributes were added the accomplishments of Europe—a taste for music, painting, and the fine arts generally.

She came forward and welcomed the young men as if she had known them all her life; indeed, she professed to remember Ralph as her little play-fellow at Lucknow and Cawnpore.

Neither he nor Fitzherbert noted her garb, but saw vaguely that it was some soft flowing white stuff; nor did they even note the pearls which rose and sank upon her neck; in fact, they paled their ineffectual fires before the light of her splendid eyes. The men were captivated at the first look.

The repast was not particularly sumptuous, but

it was agreeable, well cooked, and well served, and
Miss O'Gallagher did the honours like a princess.
After dinner she left the gentlemen to their wine.
They didn't stay long, however, and when they
joined her she gave them some delicious tea in
dainty little cups of some quaint Indian ware,
arabesqued and inlaid with gold. Then she sang
and played to them, and did both divinely.

By-and-by, three or four men about town dropped
in to beg a cup of tea. Presently some one suggested
cards, whereupon Julia glided from the room without a word.

After an hour or two at half-crown points, the
guests began to drop away, and Ralph and Fitzherbert rose to follow suit.

"Make my adieux, Major, to Miss O'Gallagher,"
said Ralph. "Thanks for a delightful evening."

"Come again, my boys," replied the Major,
"without ceremony; there's always a knife and
fork, and a welcome."

"Capital fellow, the Major," said Ralph, as they
drove home.

"First rate," responded Fitzherbert. "But
isn't the girl splendid?"

"She's a beauty," returned Ralph, with a yawn,
"for a fellow whose taste lies in that direction.
I suppose, being nearly a nigger myself, I adore
fair women. Besides, there's only one woman in
the world for me, and she's down at Deepdale."

"By Jove!" cried the captain, "I begin to
think there's only one woman in the world for

me, and she's at Montpellier Square. Not that
I suppose she'd ever descend on a poor plunger
like myself. I expect she's looking out for higher
game—a prince or a lord, at least."

" They seem pretty well tiled in. I suppose the
Begum left her something worth having ? "

" Don't know," said Fitzherbert. " When we
were in the Punjaub our fellows used to look upon
all the natives as niggers. There's nothing of the
nigger about *her*."

" Not a bit."

" I say, Ralph, look here; the Major's worth
cultivating. I've won a fiver to-night. The first
lucky deal I've had since I've been in town."

" And I believe I'm a sovereign or two to the
good," laughed Ralph, full of his new independence
of such trifles.

That was the first of many pleasant nights
at Montpellier Square. Strange to say, Julia
O'Gallagher had no lady friends. She reigned,
therefore, with undivided sway, and distributed
her smiles or courtesies with perfect impartiality,
and an apparent absence of personal predilection ;
and yet how dangerously seductive she could be
when she played the artillery of her charms upon
any given object ! To-night one man thought
himself the especial favourite ; the next, another
man was made happy with a smile or a gracious
word. Tom Tressider was the first favourite one
night ; Fitzherbert took the premier *pas* upon
another occasion. Every man had his turn—turn

and turn about; perhaps Ralph came in for more than the rest. He said that was because Julia remembered him as an old playfellow. Fitzherbert thought, however, it was because she remembered he was an Earl.

Whenever the men took to cards, which they did every evening, she took herself to her own apartments.

"Boys will be boys," said the Major. "For myself, I object to going beyond a crown point. But never mind—go ahead; you can only be young once!"

Night after night the play became heavier and heavier, despite the Major's warnings. Other men sometimes dropped in. There was the Hon. Algy Fitz Urse, the Chevalier Vicoff, Major Deuceace, and a few other choice bloods of the Ostriches. That five pounds of Fitzherbert's had gone long ago, with many a note to boot.

Julia invariably suggested that both Ralph and Fitz should take their departure at the same time with herself, but they decided to remain. When she left the room, the men formed an avenue down which she passed with a smile and a kind good night for all.

Then came the real work of the night—baccarat, poker, and the rest of it. The Major smoked his cigarette and looked on while the youngsters went for each other.

What with the excitement of the game and copious libations, Ralph and Fitzherbert began to

plunge heavily, and to lose heavily, too. Some
nights they did not know what they had lost.
I.O.U.'s were circulated freely. They never remained long in doubt about these, for one or other
of their friends usually turned up the next day at
May Fair, requesting payment.

Sometimes, too, the Major himself put in an
appearance with a promissory note and a paternal
remonstrance.

This business of settling up didn't give Fitzherbert much trouble so long as Ralph paid the
piper; in the end, however, it upset him both in
health and in credit. Nights at Montpellier Square
were varied by nights at the Merozable and at the
Ostriches; but wherever these young gentlemen
went, the result was invariably the same. They
were by no means of the verdant-green fraternity;
and as their own object was plunder, they could
scarcely object when the tables were turned upon
them.

When Barkins found that his master and his
friend had the devil's books in their hands at all
hours; that they turned night into day; that they
went to bed late; that when they got up their
first demand was for soda-water; that they merely
trifled with a cup of tea and a devilled anchovy
toast before they returned to soda, copiously
diluted with brandy; when he observed that repeated doses of this potent beverage were accompanied by huge full-flavoured havannahs, he
ventured to remonstrate. He might, however,

have spared himself the trouble, for all the thanks he got.

Presently two or three race meetings came off. Ralph went to each of them, and plunged in every direction, losing right and left. He now became fretful, peevish, and angry upon the slightest provocation, and could not bear to be alone, especially since the receipt of a cold and repellent letter from Rachel, more than hinting that he had been the means of leading Jack Heywood astray at Doncaster. His mother urged him to come down to Deepdale at once, to settle his debts, and to conclude his engagement with Rachel; but from the tenor of that young lady's last communication, he thought it would not be desirable to put his fortune to the test for the present, and so he postponed his visit from day to day, from week to week. A giant's strength might well succumb to the life he was now leading, and Ralph was no giant.

It is the pace that kills, and the pace was beginning to tell upon him already. His cheeks became flushed and hectic, his hands trembled, and he was tortured with a hollow, racking cough, which never ceased, morning, noon, or night.

Obviously he needed rest and recuperation. Happy thought! He would take the Major, and a few sporting friends, down to the Castle for the shooting. He did do so, and returned worse than ever.

He now began to recall the old days in the

quiet Yorkshire valley with regret. Old days, indeed! Why, only a few months had elapsed since he quitted Deepdale, and yet it seemed ages ago. It was not yet too late to pull up; he would return to the Vicarage. Just as he had arrived at this sensible conclusion, the Major, the Captain, and Tom Tressider called one day to "give him a straight tip," as they expressed it, about a great bruising match which had just been arranged between two notorious gladiators.

The affair, which was known only to the initiated, was to come off in France. It was in the highest degree *chic*, and it would not do to be out of so good a thing, so next day off went my lord, accompanied by his noble friends. Being by no means a good sailor, Ralph had an awful passage to Dieppe, and landed very ill; but, despite Fitzherbert's remonstrances, he persisted in accompanying the Major and the rest to Rouen, in the neighbourhood of which city the famous pugilistic encounter was to take place.

By the time he got there Ralph was worse, and Fitzherbert begged him to stay in bed for a day or two. It was in the depth of a most inclement winter, and he was shivering from head to foot when, early next morning, he got aboard the small packet and steamed down the river, in company with the Brummagem Bulldog, the New York Hercules, their seconds, and upwards of a hundred and fifty shining lights of the *jeunesse dorée.*

After steaming about for some hours, at about two o'clock in the afternoon the boat was moored to an islet in the middle of the river; the motley crowd of peers, plungers, and pugilists landed, and the champions of the two hemispheres proceeded to batter each other's faces to pulp, until night spitefully put an end to the sport. The stakes were then drawn, and the twin bulldogs, having beaten each other out of all semblance to humanity, embraced and vowed eternal friendship.

It was late when our gallant sportsmen got back to Rouen. Ralph was shivering worse than ever, and coughing even more than usual. Fitzherbert urged him to stay, and get a day or two's rest; but the Major, Deuceace, Tressider, and the champions were for pushing on to Calais by the express, and Ralph resolved to push on with them.

With the aid of copious and repeated doses of *eau de vie* he succeeded in reaching Calais in time for the boat. When they embarked he could scarcely keep his feet, and he asked Fitzherbert to go below to secure a cabin, a pint of champagne, and a captain's biscuit.

It took some five minutes or more before Fitzherbert could see the steward. During this time the boat had left the pier, and was rapidly making way; and when Fitzherbert came on deck he couldn't find Ralph anywhere. The Major had seen him five minutes before; Tressider had seen him even later, and had given him a pull at his flask.

It now began to blow hard. Fitzherbert was a worse sailor even than Ralph, and he collapsed immediately. More than an hour elapsed after his arrival at Dover before he could struggle upon deck. When, at last, he turned out there was no sign of either Ralph or the Major, or, indeed, of any of his friends.

Doubtless, they had gone on to town by the tidal train. Obviously, there was nothing for it but for him to follow.

## CHAPTER XVIII.

### 'TWIXT DOVER AND CALAIS.

UPON Fitzherbert's arrival at May Fair, to his astonishment he found no sign of Ralph the Earl. When the following day came, and Ralph did not appear, Fitzherbert became anxious; anxiety gave place to alarm when a second day elapsed without any communication from his missing friend.

It now occurred to the Captain to look up the Major, and he drove down to Montpellier Square in Ralph's brougham.

The Major was out. He had gone down to Fleet Street to arrange about the drawing of the stakes and the division of the spoil among the noble sportsmen. But Julia was visible, and greeted him with her brightest smile.

"How are you to-day?" she inquired.

" Very seedy. I've not seen you for an age."

" And the young Earl ? "

" I don't know. I've not seen him since we left Calais."

" Indeed ! "

" No. The fact is, I was unfortunately compelled to succumb to the chops of the Channel, and as Ralph was seedy when we went aboard, I thought possibly the Major might have taken charge of him."

" I don't think so. Papa has never mentioned the subject to me."

" When did the Major get back ? "

" The night before last."

" I think I'd better look him up at once."

When Fitzherbert reached the Ostrich club the Major was at lunch.

" Well, dear boy, how's our Pylades—how's the golden youth ? "

" Don't know," cried the Captain. " I thought you could tell me."

" The deuce you did ! How's that ? "

" I've not seen him since we left Calais."

" You don't mane that ? " said the Major.

" I do, though."

" Perhaps you'll be after explaining ? "

" First, do you mean to say, Major, *you've* not seen him ? "

" Divil a bit ! Now, then, go ahead, dear boy, with the particulars."

" Well, then, I lost sight of him when we got

aboard, and I had such a devil of a time of it in crossing that I couldn't pull myself together to come on deck till long after you fellows had got ashore. I came on by the next train to Curzon Street, expecting to find him there. He has not been there, nor have I seen or even heard of him since."

"The dear boy seemed very queer. Perhaps he may be staying at Dover to recuperate."

"Not a bad idea. I'll telegraph the Lord Warden at once."

Having despatched his telegram, Fitzherbert joined the Major at lunch. By the time they had finished, there came a reply from Dover, stating that Lord Beauchamp was not at the Lord Warden, nor had he been there.

"I have it!" said the Major. "Boys will be boys; he's met with an adventure. I'll go bail, now, a pair of bright eyes have detained him on the other side of the streak."

"But I tell you I saw him aboard."

"So did I; but sure he'd plenty of time to get ashore. Ah, with youth the season is for joy; and I was young once myself."

"What time is it?" inquired Fitzherbert, looking at his watch. "Four o'clock! Just time to catch the tidal train. I'm off!"

"More power to ye. Let me know as soon as you have traced the truant."

Fortunately for Fitzherbert, this time the Channel was as smooth as a mill-pond.

Immediately on his arrival at Calais he went to the police-station. The Commissary was communicative and obliging. He stated that at the very moment the packet cast her moorings a man was seen rapidly running down the pier; that he tried to leap aboard; that he missed his footing, and fell headlong into the sea; that a couple of fishermen, who were fortunately cruising about in a small coble, fished him out more dead than alive; that he was now lying at the Hotel Montjoy, and that in all probability he was the missing English milord.

Half an hour later Fitzherbert was by Ralph's bedside at the hospital. He had been unconscious since the moment of his deliverance, and was still quite delirious.

The physician in attendance stated that a violent cold had supervened upon congestion of the lungs, and an aggravated attack of delirium tremens. It was perhaps as well that this gentleman did not understand a word of English, as Ralph's ravings would doubtless have astonished him.

'Twas in vain that Fitzherbert tried to restrain the wretched youth. At one moment he was at Brocklesby Ferry, at another in the ring at Doncaster. Anon, with a shriek of terror, he started bolt upright, screaming, "Don't—don't—don't glare at me with your pale face—don't, don't!"

Then he fell back, panting and exhausted.

Thus the days passed on, and the patient's

condition still gave great cause for alarm. The
bodily ailment seemed subsiding, but the mental
and spiritual condition seemed to border on some
serious form of brain disturbance or chronic
hallucination.

"Our young friend has something on his mind,"
said the doctor to Fitzherbert after one of these
violent outbursts. "I suppose he has been a
*bon vivant*—what you call in your English a free
liver?"

"Of course, he's gone the pace," returned the
Captain. You see, he has only just come into his
property, and he's been trying to see as much life
as possible."

"Well, you must keep him very quiet, or he
will never recover. Do you know of any serious
mental trouble?"

"No," replied Fitzherbert. "He has everything
a man can want, and, so far as I know, no trouble
at all. But he's been going it, you know, ever
since his change of fortune."

The constancy and devotion of Fitzherbert knew
no bounds. Night after night he sat up with his
friend, till he himself looked almost as sick and
haggard as the invalid. He liked Ralph, and had
stood by him in many a nasty affair. There was
something yet in store for him, however, which
was to test his friendship to the full.

One night Ralph Hollis had dozed off quietly,
and Fitzherbert, who sat by the bedside watching,
thought that he was going to have a long, sound

rest. Suddenly, however, the invalid awakened—not with the wild start of fever and delirium—and looked at his friend; then, reaching out a thin, trembling hand, he said quite gently, "Fitz, old fellow, is there any news?"

"News! Of whom?" asked the Captain, a little surprised.

"Of young Heywood?"

"None; only he has been committed for trial. Don't worry yourself about *him*. Close your eyes, and go to sleep."

But Ralph's hand closed tightly in his as the faint voice said, "I can't sleep! Sometimes, old fellow, I think there is no sleep for me this side the grave; and, to tell you the truth, I don't think I shall ever rise from my bed again. Well, so much the better. But I can't die with a lie upon my soul. You're a good fellow, and I can trust you, can't I?"

"Stake your soul on that," replied the Captain.

"Well, then, I'm going to make a clean breast of it, and, if I die, you'll try to put things right. Fitz, I've never been myself since that night at Doncaster. It was a dirty trick we played on that youngster, but there's worse than that to tell. If they hang him, and if there's a hell, as I believe, the devil will have me, for, as sure as there's a God above, *I*, and not Jack Heywood, killed Jabez Pryke!"

With a cry of horror, Fitzherbert started back, and almost sprang to his feet. At first, he thought

M

that Ralph was raving, but a look into his eyes
convinced him to the contrary.   White and calm,
with the firm resolve upon him to tell his secret
once and for ever, Ralph lay back upon the pillows,
watching the effect of his strange confession.

"*You* killed him ? " gasped Fitzherbert.   " No,
no ; you're raving ! "

"I'm telling you the gospel truth," said Ralph ;
" and, what's more, if you like to call in witnesses
and hear me swear it, I'll stand to what I say.
It's *that* which has made me mad, and driven me
headlong to the devil.   Listen, and I'll tell you
how it happened.   You know how badly I wanted
money—you know how the fellows were down on
me from every side ?   Well, that night when you
drove me over from Barford the devil tempted me
to enter the counting-house and take what I wanted,
to save me from exposure and ruin.   I was half-
drunk still, and I hardly know now how I got into
the place, but almost before I could realize what I
was doing I had opened the safe, and was collaring
the coin and the paper.   I had seized a handful of
gold and notes, and had thrust them into my
breast, when I heard a sound behind me, and,
turning round, I saw the overseer standing on the
threshold of the room, and looking on."

There was silence in the sick-room, save for the
low, faint voice of the speaker.   Fitzherbert sat
spell-bound.

"Well, then, I knew that it was all up, but
before I could think what to do, the old man had

seized me, and we were struggling together. As God is my Judge, Fitz, I never meant to harm him, but I tried to tear myself free. In the struggle he was hurled backward, and struck his head against the marble mantelpiece. My God, I think I see him now! I hear his dying cry! He gave one wild scream, and fell dead before me!"

As he proceeded, Ralph grew more and more excited, and he sat up in the bed wildly gesticulating.

"Then I heard another sound—some one behind me descending the stairs. Young Heywood, still drunk and half asleep, with his eyes closed, and his hands feeling before him, appeared in the passage. I stepped back behind the door as he entered, then out on the landing and into one of the recesses of the stair. A moment after, I heard a shriek from the room; it was the lad's voice, and then some men came running up the street, and with them the watch-dog Leo. They did not see me, and the dog, instead of taking my scent, rushed on into the room, where the lad was now wailing like a madman. There wasn't a minute to lose. I slipt down the stair, through the gate into the street, and ran like a madman till I reached the Vicarage door. I had my latch-key, and got in unheard and unseen. All the rest you know. Next morning my mother brought me the news of my uncle's death. Think of my feelings *then.* But, as God is my Judge, it was an accident, not murder! I never meant to kill the old man—no, no!"

He hid his face in his hands, and sobbed. Fitzherbert still sat silent, riveted with the horror of the tale.

"Now you can do what you think best," moaned the wretched man. "Denounce me if you like; I don't care!"

Yet he looked pleadingly at his friend, as if beseeching his sympathy and protection.

"It's an awful business," said the Captain at last. "I never suspected it was so bad as this. But that money and those papers; what became of them?"

"I threw the gold away on the moor, and destroyed the notes and papers next day at Barford. Fitz, old man, what am I to do? Now it's all up with me I don't mind making a confession; but if I should live—— "

"Leave me to think it over," returned Fitzherbert. "Go to rest now. Here, I'll give you your draught; it may send you off to sleep."

So saying, he measured out the potion which the doctor had left for the patient. Ralph drank it gratefully; and presently, as if relieved to some extent by the confession he had made, dozed off into a fitful sleep. The Captain sat pondering darkly. It was an ugly business, as he had said; yet, on reflection, he did not see as yet why he should interfere. Ralph was his friend, his pal, and in the Captain's dark code of morality, fidelity to a comrade was the cardinal virtue. Besides, Ralph was rich and powerful, and the downfall and exposure of one would mean certain ruin to the other. Of course, if the accused man were actually convicted and condemned to death, it might be a different matter. Fitzherbert determined to wait and see.

At daybreak Ralph opened his eyes, and saw the Captain still sitting by the bedside.

"Well, what is to be done?" he asked eagerly. "Unless I'm dreaming, I told you everything last night?"

"You did," replied Fitzherbert; "but make your mind easy. I never rounded on a pal yet, and I'm going to hold my tongue."

## CHAPTER XIX.

### GUILTY OR NOT GUILTY.

ON the very day—the very hour—that Ralph and his friends were "assisting" at that memorable contest on the river, Jack Heywood was on trial for his life at Leeds Assizes.

During repeated interviews Grainger had made persistent efforts to induce his client to confide in him, so as to prepare some theory for the defence; but he always obtained the same answer, the formula of which was simple and conclusive, and was contained in five words—

"I know nothing about it."

Then the lawyer endeavoured to persuade Jack to admit that a quarrel had occurred while he was intoxicated; that Jabez had struck him, and that in self-defence he had struck him against the mantelpiece (for Grainger had carefully examined the counting-house and everything in it); hence the catastrophe. Jack, however, declined to endorse this theory of the matter, and reiterated—

"I know nothing about it."

Grainger then tried another tack. He got a pair of medical experts to examine his client, with a view to propounding the defence of insanity. This line was more untenable than the other, and there was nothing for it but to obtain an eloquent advocate to plead extenuating circumstances to the jury. This gentleman did his duty to the best of his ability; but his eloquence was powerless against the damning weight of evidence. The case for the defence having closed, and the counsel for the prosecution having replied, the judge proceeded to sum up; and having put the case for and against the accused with judicial impartiality, he came to the theory of the defence—viz. that the crime had occurred during a drunken scuffle.

"It is almost trivial for me," said his lordship, "to observe that a man is not excused from his crime by reason of intoxication by alcohol. If that were to be accepted as a valid defence, the criminal courts might as well be closed at once, because there is no doubt drunkenness is the cause of a large proportion of the crime committed. The learned counsel for the defence has contended that the occurrence was accidental, or, rather, that it was one of those cases coming within the term of manslaughter. He has also enlarged upon the evidence as to character given by the witnesses for the defence, and the universal concurrence of testimony as to the known affection which for so many years had existed between prisoner and deceased, and the absence of motive for the commission of the crime. On the other hand, gentlemen, you have the statement of the witness Yondal as to the occurrence at Doncaster; the refusal of deceased to lend prisoner money; the quarrel on the homeward journey; the threats of violence; the burglarious entry into the counting-house; the breaking open of the safe; the rifling of the cash-box; the abstraction of certain bank-notes, drafts, and other moneys, and the subsequent death of Jabez Pryke.

"It is true, none of these notes, drafts, or moneys have been found upon the accused, and that point is clearly in favour of the prisoner.

"It is for you to decide upon the matter without fear or favour. If you believe that the accused committed this crime, it is your duty to find him guilty. If, on the other hand, you have any reasonable doubt on the subject, it is your duty to give the prisoner the benefit of the doubt."

At four o'clock the jury retired to consider their

verdict, taking with them the plan of the counting-house.

Then came an awful and unbroken silence.

Half Deepdale was in court—men and women who had known the prisoner from childhood. Jasper and Joan Heywood sat at the solicitors' table beside Grainger. A lady, closely veiled, was seated 'twixt Jacob Dene and the vicar, in the gallery to the left of the dock. Jack looked round, and took in the picture as if in a dream.

After what appeared an age, the jury returned to the court, and the judge to the bench.

The foreman was pale and agitated.

"How say you, gentlemen of the jury?" inquired the clerk. "Is the prisoner at the bar guilty, or not guilty?"

"Guilty."

The court surged and throbbed as if with one huge pulse.

"Guilty," repeated the foreman; "but the jury desire to recommend the prisoner to mercy on account of his youth, and also on account of the condition he was in when the crime was committed."

Then came the words, "Prisoner at the bar, have you anything to say why sentence of death should not be passed upon you?"

"Yes!" exclaimed Jack.

In this supreme moment he recalled, as if by miracle, all that had occurred on the night of the murder.

"My lord, and gentlemen of the jury," he continued, in a clear and sonorous voice, "I have nothing to say against t' verdict—it couldna be otherwise; but for the sake o' those I leave behind, I wish to clear my memory from this foul crime. I was ne'er drunk i' my life until that night at Doncaster, and t' poison went to my brain and made me mad. After we left Doncaster, I remember nowt until I was wakened from my sleep by a voice crying 'Murder!' Had I been dead, surely that voice would have brought me back to life. I leaped up, and ran as fast as my feet could carry me to the counting-house. As God is my Judge, Jabez lay there dead before me, bathed i' his own blood. From that moment until this, when it has pleased t' Lord to lift the cloud fro' my brain, all has been a blank; but now—now that I see and know all, now that I realize the dreadful truth, no punishment you can inflict can equal what I suffer already in the knowledge that had I been by his side, as was my duty—had I been a man, and not a drunken, besotted beast, this trouble would ne'er have befallen my best friend! As for his murderer, he is in the hands o' God, in whose name I declare that I am innocent! *He* knows it; Jabez Pryke knows it, too; and I can meet him wi' a clear conscience. That is all I have to say."

The judge was apparently more unmanned than the prisoner. With trembling hands he put on the black cap. As he proceeded to pass sentence, his voice was choked with emotion. Tears streamed down his aged cheeks; nor his alone, for there was scarcely a dry eye in the place.

When, at length, the last awful words were uttered, the condemned turned, and rapidly left the dock. As he did so, a piercing scream rang through the stillness. The veiled lady between Jacob Dene and the vicar fell swooning to the floor, and the court broke up in a tumult of excitement and confusion.

## CHAPTER XX.

### UNDER SENTENCE OF DEATH.

WHEN overhauling the *débris* of Jabez Pryke's rifled cash-box, Jacob Dene came upon a rough memorandum of the remittances received by the morning's post on the day of the murder. There were Bank of England notes to the value of two hundred pounds, drafts payable at sight for upwards of five or six hundred more, besides acceptances for various amounts. Payment of the notes was immediately stopped, although no notification to this effect was published. This precaution was adopted in the hope that the thief —always assuming the notes to be stolen—might be taken off his guard, and therefore induced to present them for payment.

Their disappearance was the one missing link of evidence against Jack Heywood. His statement

before the judge coincided entirely with the theory
that these notes and drafts might have been stolen
by a third person.

Assuming, for the sake of argument, that in
some aberration of intellect, caused by his mad
drunkenness, Jack had broken into the counting-
house for the purpose of robbery, that he had
been discovered in the act by Jabez, that a
deathly struggle had then ensued, there could be
no possibility of doubt of the fact that Jack had
been actually taken prisoner the next moment;
hence, had he stolen the notes they must have
been found upon his person, or about him. They
were not found upon his person, nor could any
trace of them be found anywhere.

That he might have had a drunken quarrel with
Jabez, that a struggle might have occurred which
culminated in the awful catastrophe which had
befallen, was possible, and even probable; but
that the lad could be a thief—his whole life and
character gave the lie to so improbable a sup-
position. The more Jacob Dene thought of the
matter, the more he gravitated towards the conclusion that Jack was innocent. But what of that
if a judge and jury had found him guilty? He
was condemned to death, and every day, every
hour, brought him nearer to his doom.

Had Jacob needed any incentive to exertion, he
would have found it on all hands, both at home
and abroad. At home, from morning to night,
his wife and his granddaughter dinned into his

ears, "Jack Heywood is innocent, and must be saved."

It was easy enough to emit that imperative "must," but 'twas difficult to give effect to it.

On Saturday, as the foreman of the mills gave utterance to the same opinion, when the hands knocked off for the half-holiday at noon they mobbed him. The result was that a mass meeting was held, a memorial was prepared then and there, and signed by every soul capable of signing a name or making a mark ; and on Monday morning Jacob himself, accompanied by Grainger, the solicitor, and Rachel, set off to town, taking the memorial with them.

Immediately on their arrival they went down to the House of Commons, where they obtained an interview with the member for Barford, who took them to the Home Secretary's private room. This important functionary promised to communicate with the judge who tried the case, and if the circumstances required investigation, to give the matter consideration.

"If they require investigation!" burst out Rachel. "They do demand it, sir. An innocent man is about to be put to death, and thou canst save him !"

"My dear young lady," replied the Secretary, "I can do nothing of the kind ; I cannot over-rule the law. People arrive at the conclusion that I am all-powerful, but I am as much the servant of the law as the humblest police officer."

"But he is innocent, sir!"

"I have been told that of many murderers. The other day I was assailed with a general howl of execration because I declined to interfere with the sentence passed on a cold-blooded assassin, who, within an hour of his execution, confessed that he had murdered his victim under circumstances of unutterable atrocity."

"But this man is no assassin. He is the best and bravest of men. He loved the murdered man from childhood. The murderer is a thief, who stole the money, and Jack Heywood never stole a farthing in his life."

"Well, well," said the Home Secretary, "I promise you the first hour I can spare from more pressing duties."

"More pressing!" interrupted Rachel. "None can be so pressing as this. His life is in danger."

"The prisoner has an eloquent advocate."

"Nay, not an eloquent, but an earnest one, sir," sobbed Rachel. "He saved my life, snatched me from the jaws of death, and I should take shame to myself were I to pause at any means to save him. Oh, do, sir, do, pray, see to it at once —now, this instant! For God's sake, save him!"

"Have you the papers about you?" inquired the Secretary of Grainger.

"They are here, sir," said he, presenting them.

"Very well; I will look over them to-night when I get home; and if I see any cause for interference I will communicate with the judge at once."

"May we see thee again, sir?" inquired Rachel.

"Hem, I'm not quite clear about that; the debate on the Address will last for a week or a fortnight. Indeed, I ought to be in my place now. You will excuse me."

"But surely, sir, we may see thee again?"

"On the whole, I think you had better not; but, on my honour, the matter shall have immediate attention, and my secretary shall acquaint you with the result."

With this cold comfort, he left them.

It was now Monday night, and the execution was fixed for the following Monday.

Six days from doom and death!

It was well for the Home Secretary that he had resolved to grant no further interview, for this intractable young lady haunted the Home Office, morning, noon, and night for the next two days.

Though the great man himself was unapproachable, his secretary was daily visible. He alleged that the chief had looked through the papers, but could not decide upon the matter till he had heard from the judge, to whom he had already written.

His lordship was on circuit.

"Where is his lordship?"

"At York."

"We'll go there at once, grandfather."

"It will be useless; the judge will not see us."

"He shall see us, and hear us, too!" cried Rachel.

It was idle to remonstrate with her, and to York they went by the mail train—Grainger and all.

It was two o'clock on Thursday morning when they reached the Anstruther Hotel.

By daybreak they were at the judge's lodgings. They might as well have stayed in town, for the judge was obdurate, and declined to see them. That day Rachel wrote quires of letters and scores of telegrams to his lordship, which all reached the same destination—the waste-paper basket.

Hour after hour passed while she waited impatiently for answers which never came. She could not eat, or drink, or sleep.

Burning with a fever of unrest, at sunrise she hurried out for a walk. Save for the casual labourer limping towards his daily toil, or the railway porter lazily coming towards the station, or the worn-out night policeman crawling home from his last beat, the city was still at rest. Crossing the railway-station, she walked down towards the Minster. Contemplating its rare quaint beauty with but languid interest, she hurried back and ascended the city walls, and strolled towards the Barbican.

It was now Friday morning. Only three days more, and then——

What was Jack doing now? Was he thinking of her? Did he know that she was devoting every energy of blood, and bone, and brain to his rescue? Of course he knew that she believed him innocent; she had written to say so; she had told the old people; she had told everybody so a thousand times.

Three days—only three days!

By this time she had crossed the Barbican, and had reached the walls which overhang the Convent. The nuns had turned forth for their constitutional after matins. As she leant down to look at them, they melted into air, and she saw, or thought she saw, a prison—a condemned cell —a face—his face, piteously, but speechlessly, appealing to her. While she still gazed, the mirage melted into the morning mist, and the mist itself faded away before the sun, which rose red as blood from behind the Convent.

With a gesture of despair she threw her arms aloft, crying, "Oh, God! must he die? Is there no help?—no hope?" As she spoke the words, she came face to face with a little gentleman, clad in a shabby, old-fashioned coat and vest, with a baggy pair of Oxford-grey continuations somewhat too short for his stumpy little legs, and disclosing half an inch of white stocking between their extremities and his loose-tied clumsy shoes. His body was too small for his head, which was broad and massive, and covered with a thatch of snowy whiteness. A pair of shaggy eyebrows, black as a blacking-brush, surmounted the eye of a lynx, the beak of an eagle, and the mouth of a badger. A huge white neckcloth was twisted in convoluted folds round his neck—the white cambric frill of his shirt was stained with snuff, with which he ever and anon furnished his nose in great pinches from his vestcoat pocket.

To complete his incongruous appearance, he wore a shabby felt parson's hat, pulled down over his brows after the fashion of the Plantagenet period.

This gentleman's face was cast in no ordinary mould—once seen, it was not easily forgotten. She had seen it once before. Then it was surrounded with a horse-hair wig, and he was in the act of placing a little black cap upon it; the scene —the voice—the face—came back to her as if by inspiration.

Throwing herself before him, she cried, "God hath not brought thee here for nothing. I am Rachel Dene! The man condemned to death at Leeds a little while ago is innocent! Save him, or at least grant time for his innocence to be proved."

The old gentleman gave a long, low whistle, and muttered to himself, "Here's a pretty kettle of fish! D——d hard a man can't take a constitutional or look at a pretty girl without being let in for an arrangement of this kind."

Although she heard him mumbling, she could not distinguish a word of what he said.

"Thou dost not speak," she continued. "For God's sake give me some hope."

N

"I'm not clear," he replied sturdily, "that I ought not to commit you for contempt of court for sending me those indiscreet letters, and those audacious telegrams; or, at least, to give you in charge to the nearest police magistrate. But I never could say no to a pair of bright eyes in my life; so get up, pray, lady, and dry your eyes, and don't snivel—zounds, don't snivel, but listen!"

"Yes, yes," sobbed Rachel.

"I shall be in town to-morrow night, and will see the Home Secretary. Beyond that, I can say nothing. Though the heavens should fall, justice shall be done—that, and nothing more or less."

Then, with a kind of grim, cynical humour, he continued, "Now get you gone, you handsome hussy! If you are wise—though I suppose it's idle to expect a woman that's pretty to be prudent —forget that you have seen me. That'll do. There, you needn't kiss my hand."

The next minute, with an activity beyond his years, the old gentleman had disappeared down the Barbican.

When she returned to the hotel, Rachel made an attempt at breakfast—a poor one; still, it was an attempt.

While she was hesitating how to break the ice for the journey, Grainger came from the Castle with news to the effect that the assizes would terminate on the morrow, and that the judge would return to town that night by the express.

"We had better get back at once, grandpa'," said Rachel.

So to town they went, having previously telegraphed Joan and Jasper to meet them at Wakefield, when they paused for five minutes to tell the old couple that every effort was being made for the reversal of the sentence.

Both Jacob Dene and Grainger urged upon the Heywoods not to buoy up Jack with false hopes. Rachel, however, sent her assurance of his innocence, and off they sped to town.

That night she slept a little, but woke at daybreak to go over her interview with the judge, to recall his words, his tones, his looks. He would be in town to-night; and then—then, only twenty-four hours more.

Were she a man she could go forth amongst the multitude which seethed up and down the Strand beneath the windows of the hotel. Being a girl, she could only sit still and suffer—no, not sit still, for she paced wildly to and fro. They tried to console her; but she had no thought for any one save the man who lay under sentence of death down yonder.

At length night came, and with it came a cruel, crawling fog, which wrapped the busy thoroughfare in darkness, through which only a gleam of some funereal torch could be seen, while a roar of hoarse voices arose from the pandemonium beneath. Presently the fog penetrated into the very room in which they sat, peopling it with phantoms. It

was in vain that Jacob Dene piled the huge grate
with fuel; the fog remained triumphant, and they
could scarcely see to the other end of the room.

By-and-by, Grainger glided in, grim, and grey,
and ghastly.

"The train has been two hours late," he gasped
hoarsely; "but the judge has arrived, and has
driven home to Berkeley Square."

"Will he not see the Home Secretary to-night?"

"It is now eleven; and to venture out again in
such a fog as this would be to tamper with his life."

"His life!—*his!*" At that moment she thought
of only one life in the world.

Dawn broke cold and wet, and the hours sped
faster and faster still, till the sun gave place to
shade.

Night was falling on Kirkdale Gaol.

With beating hearts, Jasper and Joan Heywood
were taking their last leave of the lad they loved
so well, when Rachel Dene burst into the prison,
bearing the news that his punishment was com-
muted to penal servitude for life!

## CHAPTER XXI.

### PRISON WALLS.

WHEN the news reached Calais that Heywood's
life had been spared, it exercised a salutary effect
on the young Earl's health.

Ralph got better daily, and in about a month's

time he was well enough to return to England. While he was travelling to town by the tidal train, Jack Heywood was travelling in the same direction from another point of departure. The Earl was fashionably attired, and a first-class saloon car was reserved for him and his friends. Jack was clad in a hideous suit of home-spun, marked with the broad arrow, and he and his friends—upwards of four and twenty of the greatest ruffians in England—were securely handcuffed to each other, and packed like cattle into a fourth-class compartment.

Our hero's journey was uneventful enough, save for one incident. To be sure, his new acquaintances beguiled the time with conversation full of obscenity and blasphemy; but, as far as he was concerned, they might have been talking in an unknown tongue. He sat near the window, and looked listlessly at the ever-changing panorama as the train whirled by; but neither sight nor sound made the least impression on his darkened brain.

At last, however, he heard the cry of "Doncaster!" and at the same sound he awoke with a shudder of horror. In an instant it all came back to him. That fatal Leger—the Grand Stand —the drink—the fight—her pale face, with its disdainful and reproachful look. Jabez, too! There was the refreshment-room opposite—where he had smashed the champagne bottles. Strange, too, the very girl who waited behind the bar then was now drawing tea from an urn.

As he looked forth, she caught sight of him. He shrank back, and hid himself in the corner—but it was too late; she had seen him.

The first bell rang. The passengers streamed out of the room and into the train. The girl came running out with a cup of tea in one hand and a jug of milk in the other.

Approaching the carriage, she said to Jack, "Sup, lad! It'll not scald thee; see, this is new milk."

His heart came to his mouth with a jump, and if it hadn't been for the ruffianly eyes upon him, he could have cried like a child.

As it was, he gulped down his emotion, and said, "Nay, thank ye; I cannot drink!"

"But you must!" replied the girl; "you will, to please me."

He took the tea, and drank it.

"God bless thee, lass!" he gasped.

"God bless thee, too, lad!" she responded, "and bring thee safe through."

The ruffians around were subdued to silence, and tears came from more than one case-hardened heart as the train glided away towards Peterborough.

When they got to King's Cross the van awaited them, and they were driven rapidly to Brixton. On their arrival at the prison, they were shunted into an open space for examination by the officials.

Their irons were now taken off, and they were checked and counted like so many beasts of

burthen. A receipt was given for them, and a
soldierly man, in an undress military uniform,
read the prison rules in a harsh voice, especially
impressing upon the new arrivals that they must
observe perpetual silence towards each other, and
that any breach of discipline would entail so many
days upon the crank, accompanied by bread and
water.

The intelligence was received with a growl that
was peremptorily suppressed,

Then the warder selected Jack and a fellow-
prisoner about the same height, and beckoned
them to follow into a large shed, inside which they
found a bath-room. Here they were ordered to
strip, and get into the bath. Jack's companion
evidently understood the process. At any rate,
he stripped from head to foot, plunged in and out
again on the other side, and slipped into a new
suit of prison clothes, marked with a number, and
certain hieroglyphics known to the initiated.

At first, Jack was disposed to kick at this
revolting business, but, finding the water clean,
and that he was surrounded by half a dozen
stalwart six-footers, he concluded not to resist.
When he had finished his ablutions, he was conducted to his cell, an apartment four feet wide, by
seven feet long, and seven feet high. A small
pane of glass from the inside, and a somewhat
larger from the outside, lighted up the place,
discovering a hammock, mattress, a blanket,
and a pair of sheets, some straps and hooks, a

stool, a pannikin, a copper washing-basin, and a Bible.

The warder under whose charge he was placed, said, "You seem a decent chap, and are not up to this game; take a straight tip—if you want to do your time easy, and shorten your stretch, keep your crib clean as a new pin; don't talk, don't grumble, do what you're told, and, above all, don't ask any questions. Baggin will be round in half an hour, and you can turn in to roost for the night."

The door closed with a bang, was locked, barred, and bolted, and Jack was alone, or rather he thought he was; but just as he had arrived at the conclusion that, at any rate, he was rid of his loathsome companions, he heard a scratching noise from the other side of the partition to his cell. Presently the sound was repeated—there came a scratch from the other side, and another. He didn't know what to make of it.

At last a voice whispered, "Mate, are you one of the new chums?"

Before he could reply, from the other side came the inquiry, "Mate, do you come from the smoke or the steel?"

"I don't understand," he replied.

"Don't you? Then where the blazes do you come from?"

"Yorkshire," he replied.

"Yorkshire?" continued his interlocutor. "The Yorkshire tykes are the downiest coves in the gang.

In course, you've got some stuff? Sling us a wing!"

"A wing?"

"A pinch of stuff!"

"What stuff?"

"What stuff? Why, baccy, to be sure!"

"I haven't got any!"

"You Yorkshire? Why, you're a regular wing!"

This interesting colloquy was interrupted by a loud, strident voice.

"What's this? What's this? Prisoners talking against regulations! No. 91, I shall report you to-morrow! Here's your baggin!"

With that, the door was unbolted, and an attendant threw a lump of bread and a can of hot cocoa into Jack's hands. By this time Jack was hungry, so he devoured it eagerly. Half an hour afterwards he got out his hammock, and slung it. Five minutes later he fell fast asleep; body and soul were wearied out. When, at last, he awoke, he could scarcely realize where he was; but the next minute it was all clear enough. He was a prisoner for life. For life!—for life! How could he ever live through it?

It was now broad day, and the warder opened the door.

"Attention, No. 91!" he said, in a whisper. "I'm not a-going to report you for last night, but mind it don't happen again! If you behave yourself, I'll get you put on a good gang among some decent fellows."

At this moment the bell struck four.

"Now pack up your traps! It only requires a little knack; I'll show you how to do it. That's your sort! In half an hour baggin will be served out; then you've an hour to do what you like with before chapel."

As yet, Jack retained his appetite, and he did ample justice to his bread and cocoa. When chapel time came, he was ordered to fall in amongst a hundred or more men, of all sorts, shapes, and sizes, all clad in the same hideous uniform of crime—all with cropped heads and clipped beards; some with foreheads villainously low, and the furtive, restless eye of the habitual criminal; some with features and demeanours which spoke of refinement, but few of remorse.

All regarded him with eager, anxious eyes.

He looked, endeavouring vainly to descry some of the companions of yesterday's journey; but evidently they were locked in another part of the prison.

As the word "Fall in—quick march!" was given, they went sharply down the corridor towards the chapel.

The service was somewhat inarticulately set forth by a sandy-haired youth, evidently not yet out of his first sleep. At a signal the pious congregation fell upon their knees and began to murmur the responses; then on either side of the new-comer, under cover of their prayer-books, the thieves whisper in half a dozen dissonant voices.

"Are you a new chum?" "How long have you got?" "Are you a lifer? or is it only a few years' stretch?" "What are you in for?"

These were something like the words, denuded of the blasphemy by which they were preceded and followed.

Being a man of the people, Jack had been accustomed to hear his friends garnish their daily talk with strong adjectives and other ornaments of speech, but the filth and obscenity which now assailed his ears made every drop of decent blood in his body boil with a loathing he could not conceal. Truly the House of God seemed changed to a Gehenna.

After chapel he was taken before the doctor, who examined him as to his bodily health; then before the curate, who examined him as to his health spiritual; after that he was conducted to the prison-barber, who cropped his head close to his poll, but spared his virgin beard, which, in truth, was only just beginning to sprout; then he was taken before the Governor, who was fortunately a soldier and a gentleman.

He took stock of the new prisoner, gave him permission to write home, which he did at once, and handed the letter to the warder for governmental inspection. The warder, in his turn, took stock of Jasper's address, with results to be hereafter chronicled.

When the letter was despatched Jack was ordered out for exercise. He prowled round and round the yard, following a shambling lot of gaol birds, who, despite the presence of the officer on guard, tried to incite him to conversation. He had no heed for them; he had only one thought— escape. But as he looked at the huge walls, surrounded with their impregnable buttresses; the iron-barred windows; the massive, iron-bound, oaken doors, trebly barred and bolted, hope died away in his heart.

It was still early in the day, and he was now taken to join the new company to which by the Governor's order he was allotted. In a large central hall, on stools apart from each other, sat forty or fifty men, variously employed; some were mending clothes; some, very old men, were knitting stockings; other men, apparently of a superior class, were colouring maps at a bench set apart for the purpose. To the last detachment he was conducted, and as this was a sort of thing to which he was accustomed, he soon polished off his work, and paused to take stock of his companions.

Despite the regulation as to silence, and the repeated interference of the warders, these men were as communicative as they were inquisitive. One vouchsafed the information that he was a barrister, who, in a moment of aberration of intellect, confounded a friend's signature with his own; another alleged that he had been a banker, who had made indiscreet speculations; a third was an author who had a misfortune; a fourth a sea-captain who was a victim to a conspiracy on the part of some unknown seamen; some alleged they were innocent; others, on the contrary, boasted of their guilt.

Presently they were all ordered to return to their cells for the midday meal, which consisted of meat, bread, and potatoes. A couple of hours' rest followed, for those who were so disposed; but for Jack there was no rest. Was there no means of escape? he asked himself again and again. He would find a way, or make one.

Were they thinking of him at home? he wondered. Of course they were; there could be no doubt about that. There could be no doubt, moreover, that they believed in his innocence. But she—did she believe him innocent? He thought she did; indeed, he knew in his heart of hearts she did. He thought, too, that she might have loved him if he only had had the chance to woo and win her; but no, it was all over!

Another bell, afternoon work, the evening meal, then locked up for the night.

Presently a warder came round with orders.

" Put your brooms under the door for candles."

Looking down, he saw a gap of some four inches between the door and the floor. Instinctively he shoved forth his broom, and a lighted candle was shoved into his cell by a convict who accompanied the warder. The door was slammed and locked, and they passed on.

The schoolmaster had given him " Sir John Mandeville's Travels " to read. He tried to in-

terest himself in the quaint old mariner's story,
but the letters danced up and down before him,
for his heart was far away.

The candle fell upon the floor. Even the light
had been a companion, and now that it was out he
was alone with his sad thoughts and his despair.

Amidst the silence came the crafty scratch of
the night before on the iron partition which sepa-
rated him from his neighbour. This time he
scratched in reply. Quick as thought came the
thieves' whisper he was beginning to understand.

" Mate ? "

" Well ? "

" What have you doused the glim for ? "

" It fell down and went out."

" Then sling it under the door, here to the
right."

" What for ? "

" What for! Why, you don't suppose I want
to curl my hair with it, do you ? "

" But you have a light burning? "

" In course I have. But I don't want your'n for
burning; I want it for eating. I am that 'ungry,
I could eat a bullock ! "

Jack couldn't withstand this appeal, and he
slung out his candle to his voracious neighbour,
who scraped it into his cell with his broom, whispering, " Jolly good luck to you, Yorkshire ; if
ever you're up a tree, and I can give you a lift,
count on Ginger ! "

Presently came the last bell, and the prison was

at rest. Fortunately, tired nature took compassion upon poor Jack, who for a time forgot his troubles in the blest nepenthe of sleep.

Thus passed a week or more in the dreary routine of prison life, until a letter came from Deepdale, so soft, so tender, and so sacred, that it inspired him with hope. Were all the world in arms against him, he was sure of the love of those two fond and faithful hearts. *She*, too, had been to inquire after him; she still believed him innocent. Ah, there was some comfort left; and after all, he was young, and life was strong within him; but, indeed, it was his ever-abounding vitality which, apart from the degradation, made prison life so hateful to him.

Jones, the friendly warder, took an early opportunity of informing him that *he*, too, had heard from Jasper Heywood, who had sent him money. This was news indeed! If Jack liked he could have "stuff" (tobacco). He didn't care for "stuff;" but Jones thought a little might be desirable to conciliate his neighbours, this being the luxury most prayed by these unhappy wretches. Tobacco was accordingly got, and Jack doled it out liberally amongst his immediate chums, with the result that "Yorkshire" became amazingly popular, more especially with a certain sandy-haired gent, with a twist in his eye, who confidentially informed him that he was "Ginger," his next door neighbour.

Thanks to the underground communication thus

established, through Jones, Jack was ˙enabled to
write home once a week, and got an answer the
next.

He was glad to hear that the invention was a
great and pronounced success, and that Jacob
Dene had behaved most handsomely in the matter.
Every week a considerable sum was placed in the
bank to Jasper Heywood's account, who held it in
trust for Jack.

By this time he had grown tired of colouring
maps, so he asked and obtained permission for
active work, and was put at the head of the building gang.

One day the Governor called him.

"No. 91," said he, "you have a clean slate and
a good record, without a single black mark. Every
good mark goes towards the remission of your
sentence; and, if you mind what you are about,
it will be remitted to five and twenty years, perhaps
even less. Think of that."

He did think of it; he thought of nothing else
by day or night. Five and twenty years! It might
as well be five and twenty thousand! Long before
five years had passed, Rachel Dene would be
married to Ralph Hollis, perhaps the mother of
Ralph's children. There was madness in the very
thought.

If he could get out—if he could only see her—
speak to her !

Time was getting on, days had lengthened into
weeks, weeks into months, months were crawling

up until the end of the year was at hand—the end of the period when Jack Heywood would have passed his probation at Brixton, and be transferred to Portland, Portsmouth, or Dartmoor. From those penal settlements escape was impossible!

## CHAPTER XXII.

### ANOTHER CHANGE.

At last one day the Black Maria drove up to the door of Brixton Gaol, and a tall, gaunt man, clad in convict's garb, and heavily ironed on either hand to two armed warders, slipped out of the prison into the van, followed by a third officer.

No one, not even Joan Heywood, would have recognized the prisoner, but the convict in question was No. 91—in other words, Jack Heywood.

Upon arriving at the railway-station, he and his guards were rapidly conducted to a compartment especially reserved for them; the third officer returned to the booking-office, took four tickets, despatched a telegram, rejoined his friends laden with newspapers and refreshments, solid and liquid.

Tickets were duly examined, the bell rang, and off went the train.

"Now, No. 91," said the officer in charge, playfully, "we don't want to make matters more disagreeable than is necessary. Them revolvers are

o

loaded; we shan't use the things unless we're
obleeged, but we've got to hand you over alive or
dead at Dartmoor.   Which is to be?"

"I don't care which," replied Jack, listlessly.

"Oh, that's all nonsense!  You're only a lad
yourself, and while there's life there's hope; you
don't know what may turn up.   Anyhow, what I've
got to say is this : If you'll give us your word not
to try no tricks with us, we'll take them bracelets
off your wrists, and you can smoke your pipe, and
read the papers, and enjoy yourself; and if you
like to make one at a game of 'nap,' why I sha'n't
say no."

"Take these cursed things off," replied Jack,
"and I pledge you my word I'll ne'er trouble
you!"

As much to the relief of Jack's captors as himself, the handcuffs were taken off.

"Have a smoke?" inquired the affable officer.

"No, thanks."

"Have the paper, then?"

"Thanks!"

He took the paper, and glanced over it listlessly.
There was nothing in it to interest him, so he
looked through the window.

As he took in the ever-changing beauty of hill
and dale, of wood and water, his thoughts reverted
to the peaceful Yorkshire valley, the village
churchyard where his mother lay sleeping, and
the old house at home, and those who loved him
there.

"What is the reason I have not heard from my grandfather?" he inquired abruptly.

"I don't know," replied one of the men.

"Look here, lads!" said Jack, eagerly; "I've got twenty pounds!"

"The devil you have! Why, you've been searched over and over again! How did you manage to hide it?"

"Never mind; that's my business! I'll give you ten pounds of it if you'll post me a letter!"

"Hand it over, then!" said the officer, smiling at his comrades.

Extracting a twenty-pound Bank of England note from the lining of his jacket, Jack handed it over to the officer, who said quietly, "I'll get change at the next station."

When he got to the station he jumped out, changed the note at the booking-office for ten sovereigns and ten-pound note, and bought at the bookstall a couple of sheets of note-paper, an envelope, an automatic pencil; then he bought a bottle of whisky in the refreshment-room, and, thus armed, returned to the carriage.

"There you are, No. 91; there's your tenner! Now, Tom, there's three pound for you; three for you, Dick; three for this child; and another for the party who negotiated the transaction! Now just a taste to wet the bargain!"

Then he opened the bottle of whisky, and sent it round, returned to his pipe and his game of nap, while Jack wrote his letter. It occupied

him some time, and took him a little out of his
trouble.

When he had finished and sealed it, he gave
it to the officer, who faithfully undertook to
post it.

The journey was long and fatiguing to the
officers, but Jack could have wished it twice as
long, for it was still a glimpse of freedom, the last
he would have for many a day. The warders grew
very jolly over their pipes and whisky, and, at last,
they prepared their dinner, and invited Jack to
join them, which he did.

Even a warder is a man—that is, when he's not
on duty; and as these fellows began to talk about
house and home, and wife and bairns, Jack's heart
softened to them. Their jollity was contagious.
He thought he would like a pipe; they gave him
one, and as he saw the blue fumes ascending, and
the blue waves toying with the bosom of the white
shore, or coyly kissing the bases of the crimson
tors, he remembered that, after all, he was only
three and twenty; that there are many years
betwixt that and three score and ten; that while
there's life there's hope; and finally, that time and
he were a match against any other two.

Night was falling when they reached Portland,
manacled together, as they were at the beginning
of the journey.

His last words before they entered the prison
were, " You won't forget the letter ? "

The officer nodded. Some writing took place,

and some official documents were exchanged. While this was being done, one of the officials said to the officer in charge, " I scarcely know where to put him, for there's been the devil to pay within the past few days ! There's been a mutiny—had to call in the sojers—and some of the ringleaders are going to catch toko to-morrow. I expect they'll get it hot, for our old man won't stand any nonsense ! Let me see, Jackson," he continued ; "you must put the prisoner into cell No. 171. We can arrange about his billet to-morrow; it's too late to-night."

Jack shook hands with his friendly escort, whispered once more " The letter ! " and was led to his cell, where he soon fell fast asleep.

He awoke refreshed. To his astonishment, he was not called up as early as usual. Habit had, however, become second nature, and up he jumped. As soon as he was stirring came the usual scratching on either side, and the usual inquiries from unknown companions.

From these interlocutors he gathered corroboration of the officer's story about the mutiny. One or two of the ringleaders had been shot down; others were to be stripped up to the triangles that morning.

Presently breakfast was served; the men, however, in this part of the prison, were all confined to their cells—an unusual occurrence, which was explained, however, later on, when the cracks of the cat, and the shrieks of the wretches under the lash, rang through the corridors. At the sound of a punishment, a chorus of sympathy arose from every cell, and filled the place.

"Silence there!" roared a strident voice.

Every man was silent, for he knew not whose turn might be next. The door of Jack's cell was suddenly unlocked; the same voice called out "No. 91, step out. Right about face—quick march!"

Following his guide past the quadrangle, he saw a sight which he never forgot, which he never will forget to his dying day.

In the centre of the square three half-naked men, tied up to the triangles, were writhing and shrieking beneath the cat, which was being vigorously applied to their bare backs. A company of soldiers, armed with guns and bayonets, formed round the square. Ten or twelve men were being led half-flayed alive to their cells, or, presumably, to the infirmary.

These, then, were the mutineers; and an awful set of ruffians they looked. As they staggered along, their yells of agony and their revolting blasphemies filled the air. At this moment Jack almost canoned against a convict with a black face and a bag of soot thrown over his shoulder.

"You here, Yorkshire?" said a familiar voice. "I thought you'd taken your hook."

"Ginger!" exclaimed Jack.

"Yes, Ginger. Brixton was purgatory; but this is hell!"

"Silence!" roared the officer, and the man passed on.

When Jack found himself in the presence of a stern military-looking man of three score and upwards, he brought himself to attention, and executed the requisite salute.

"Name and register?" demanded the Governor's clerk.

"Name, Heywood; I have no register yet," replied Jack.

"Officer, see that this man has a register. Prisoner, we have a good record in your favour from Brixton, so we'll give you a chance. Only mind, no nonsense; you've seen how we deal with mutiny here. Take him away."

The next moment he was led out of the office, and conducted towards the bath-room. The water looked cleaner; besides, as he had it all to himself, he rather enjoyed it than otherwise. Ten minutes later he found himself in a room filled with photographs of prisoners. Here he encountered Ginger disguised in a clean face. He had had his photograph taken twice, once in his prison dress, and once in a kind of nondescript civilian costume, which comprised in one and the same garment, coat, vest, shirt, neck-cloth.

"Ha, Yorkshire!" said the voice of Ginger; "come to have your pictur' taken? Mine's first rate. I'm goin' to ax the cove to let me have one to send home to the old ooman."

"Silence!—clear out!" said a warder.

Ginger disappeared, and another convict emerged from the inner room.

"This way," said the warder, as he led Jack to the studio.

The photographer, who was himself a convict, was busily arranging the camera.

"Sit down yonder," said he brusquely, "and put your head in the rest."

"To be handed down as a thief, in a thief's dress! I decline!"

"Now, my man," said the warder, "do listen to reason, or you'll get into trouble."

"You may spare your speech. I won't be taken in this infamous garb!"

"Then we shall have to tie you down."

"You'd better not."

Again the warder sounded his whistle, again came two of his myrmidons, and another conflict occurred, during which the camera was smashed to pieces, and Jack was overpowered and ironed, and taken before the Governor.

"Six days dry bread and cold water, and a hundred marks. Lock him up!" was all the autocrat vouchsafed to utter.

That night Jack was famished with hunger.

Directly after the lights were out, he heard a scratching at the wall. As soon as he scratched in reply, there came the thieves' whisper, to which he was now becoming accustomed.

"Hi, Yorkshire!"

"Here!"

"I'm Ginger!"

"Where are you?"

"Here to the right! Hist! I sweep the chimbleys, and have the run of the shop. I've got some grub for you—some toke and a piece of cold beef. I'm a-going to sling it under the door; put your broom out! Got it?"

"Yes!"

"That's right! Old Jenkins won't starve you while Ginger can nobble a bit!"

"Who's Jenkins?"

"Your warder!"

Thanks to Ginger, "Old Jenkins" did not quite starve his prisoner.

At the end of his six days, Jenkins came and marched Jack once more towards the photographer's studio. This time he positively refused to enter the room.

"All right, my lad," said Jenkins. "Now will you walk to the Governor's office, or must we carry you?"

"I'll walk," replied Jack.

The autocrat was more irate than ever.

"Nine days' confinement—bread and water—two hundred marks—put him into second probation—and send him with No. 16 to the West Quarry!"

"Please, sir—— " said Jack.

"Out with him!"

"One moment! I expect a letter—— "

"Obdurate refractories forfeit all right to letters. See Regulation No. 19."

"But I——"

"Take him away!"

Jack went back to his cell without a word. That night Ginger came to the rescue, with a hunch of bread, and a slice of boiled mutton.

"What's second probation?" inquired Jack, through a chink in his cell.

"You'll be moved to the punishment cells—a couple o' screws will be told off to look arter you, so that nobody can come a-nigh you; but, never you mind, Yorkshire; you can allays depend on Ginger!"

Jack did his nine days, and, thanks to the faithful Ginger, came out stronger than he went in. Next day, came two warders to escort him to the West Quarries. They were the two fellows with whom he had the conflict at the bath.

"It's our turn, mate, now," said one of these gentlemen; "and see if we don't cry quits!"

Jack had made up his mind to control his tongue. His escort handed him over to the officer in charge of the gang, who gave him a pickaxe, and set him at some utterly useless work, after giving certain directions. This done, he was set apart at a distance of ten or twelve paces from the rest of the gang, who worked in couples, tickling the ground with their pickaxes, while, despite the regulations, they laughed and talked to each other.

When they knocked off at meal-times, his two friends came and took charge of him, and marched him back to his cell for dinner. No reproaches of these fellows could move him to utter a word.

Back again to work after dinner—back to his cell for the evening, still guarded in the same manner. But the seclusion to which he was condemned was rather agreeable than otherwise, for he was left alone in chapel even, where he had now a pew to himself.

This daily routine was broken by the weekly bath—the weekly medical examination—a talk with the schoolmaster, who never failed to bring him some interesting book—a theological argument with the chaplain, and Sunday parade before the Governor, and a nightly banquet smuggled into his cell by his friend Ginger. Day after day he asked for letters, but with the stereotyped answer, "None!"

Then came upon him once more the ferocious desire for freedom. Morning, noon, and night, he thought of nothing else. In his mad eagerness he never paused to calculate the almost absolute impossibility of escape, or that his prison garb would inevitably lead to his immediate recapture. He remembered, too, that the warders were armed, and that, their orders being imperative, they would not hesitate to shoot him down if they caught him attempting to escape.

After all, he could but die once, and anything was better than this cruel life. If the chance came, he would take it. It came sooner than he had anticipated.

# CHAPTER XXIII.

### CAPTAIN FITZHERBERT.

MEANWHILE, while Heywood, the convict, was suffering a living death, Ralph, the Earl, had come back from death to life. But coincident with the recovery of his health was the deadening of his moral sense. Satisfied that his secret was safe with Fitzherbert, he no longer thought of personal martyrdom, and his thoughts again set to the old centre—Rachel Dene.

He returned to London, young, handsome, rich, courted and admired. What could the heart of man desire more? Unfortunately, however, there was a skeleton in his lordship's cupboard which gave him no rest by day, no sleep by night, which set his fevered blood afire, and drove him forth to seek forgetfulness in what men call pleasure. Go where he might by day or night, by bed and board, he was dogged by two ghostly phantoms—the ghost of a dead crime, and the present apparition of a living trouble.

There were times, indeed, when Ralph felt induced to end his misery. He would atone for the past—would speak the truth—would accept disgrace, infamy, punishment, and set his rival free. These movements of remorse, however, were of brief duration; he kept a smiling face to the world while his heart was tortured by ever present agonies

—agonies which were rendered doubly painful to bear from the knowledge that his guilty secret was known to another.

But although Fitzherbert now knew all, his attachment to his friend was great, his devotion sincere. What he knew he knew, but he kept the knowledge to himself, and all reference to the subject was tabooed between them.

To speak the truth, the Captain was just then deeply occupied with one object, destined to become the main object of his life. The Oriental charms of Julia O'Gallagher, with whom he was brought into almost daily contact through his intimacy with her father, had been too much for his peace of mind; but, with a reticence not too characteristic of his class, he kept his feelings to himself, and only proved them by a hundred acts of simple devotion. He was neither unselfish nor highminded; he lived to a great extent by professional gambling; he was familiar with every form of dissipation; but he was capable, when his affections were strongly awakened, of great tenacity and faithfulness. Every day strengthened the links of the chain which the beautiful girl had woven around him. Every day also drew him into closer connection with the gay old heathen, her father.

The Major was floating on thin ice; when once the thaw came, down they must go into the deep waters of wrecked reputations. At present the fifty or sixty per cent. people were accommodating enough, but the end was near at hand.

Meanwhile, there were cosy dinners and card parties at Montpellier Square and elsewhere, picnic parties to Lewes and Goodwood, and all the rest of it.

The gallant Major had called upon Mrs. Hollis upon his arrival in town, and Julia had accompanied him. The Colonel's widow had been struck with the girl's beauty and accomplishments, but had instinctively felt that she was a dangerous person to be near the Earl; indeed, she was still convinced that there was but one possible bride for her darling, and that was the heiress of Deepdale.

But Julia O'Gallagher was innocent of any designs on the young Earl's heart. She was, considering her education and her surroundings, singularly pure and unworldly. Had she possessed more subtlety and less sincerity, more head and less heart; had she been a little less honourable, and a little more unscrupulous; in fact, had she been the least bit wicked, she might have been the queen of the *demi-mondaine* world.

Consciously or unconsciously, she accepted the single devotion of one man. Fitzherbert was not a very brilliant person, or a very handsome man, but he had pleasant ways, was loyal and devoted, modest and manly. Of course, he was not clever; but then, as he remarked to Ralph, "She was clever enough for both." In fact, Julia regarded him more as a great mastiff to run her errands, to guard her here and there to the theatre or the pictures while papa was playing poker at the club.

The girl was lonely, she had no companions of her own sex, while the men of her father's set were ostentatious in their admiration of her beauty. One fellow of high lineage actually dared to insult her. Fitzherbert saw it and said nothing, but he thought the more. Next night he picked a quarrel with my lord at the club, ostensibly about cards, and thrashed the offender within an inch of his life.

The Major was present. If there was one thing more than another the O'Gallagher delighted in it was a fight, and the next morning at breakfast he entertained Julia with a full, true, and particular account of the combat.

"How did it begin, papa?" inquired Julia, unsuspiciously.

"It was something about a murder. My lord said something rude to Fitz, and then somehow the fight began. But you'll see all about it in the evening papers."

Julia listened with heaving breast and flashing eyes, but said nothing.

The Major had to break a horse, and he disappeared soon after breakfast. The Captain usually looked in either before or after luncheon, but to-day he did not come at all. Julia missed him as she had never missed him before. The day was long and dreary; with a woman's instinct, Julia had guessed the truth from the first. *She* was the cause of the encounter, and poor Fitzherbert was her champion. She began to love him from that moment.

At last came the evening papers, with a sensational account of the fracas of the night before.

She waited up till her father came home. She looked down from the landing on to the hall below. When she found the Major was alone she hurried away with a sigh of disappointment, and crept up to bed. But not to sleep; there was little sleep for her that night.

Another day passed in the same manner. The Major did not dine at home, and she was alone all the evening. She went to the piano, and began to play some of Mendelssohn's "Songs without Words." By-and-by she took down a volume of Tennyson, and sought "Mariana in the Moated Grange." All the loneliness of her life, all the misery of her position, came upon her as she read, and she cried like a child. Fitzherbert's cause was now as good as won.

The Earl and the Captain were due at dinner next day. About one o'clock Ralph called, but he was alone.

"I've called," said he, "to ask you to excuse Ned and myself to-night. The Denes are up in London. They are only here for a day or two, and they are strangers in town. They've asked me to dine with them."

"Does Captain Fitzherbert accompany you?" asked Julia.

"No, not exactly," answered Ralph, with a laugh.

"We have not seen him these three days,"

continued the girl. "There is nothing the matter, I hope?"

"Nothing particular," laughed Ralph. "Only he is not quite presentable."

"I do not understand you."

"Well, you see he has a pair of black eyes, and he doesn't care to be seen."

"Tell him to come here; never mind his eyes," said Julia, eagerly.

"At once?"

"Immediately! I must see him on particular business."

When Ralph gave the message, Fitzherbert jumped into the first passing hansom, and drove to Montpellier Square. When he entered the drawing-room Julia was at the piano playing the "Bridal March" from Mendelssohn. At the sound of his footstep she sprang up; and, falling on his neck, she kissed him. Then she burst out crying, and he consoled her.

When the Major came in to dinner she took the Captain by the hand and led him to her father.

"Your blessing, papa," she said; "we are going to be married!"

The Major started as if shot.

"Do you mean it?" he cried. "Sure you're joking! What are you going to live upon?"

"On love, papa," answered Julia, smiling.

"Well, that's poor sustenance; but there! I know you'll have your own way—so take her, Fitz.

my boy, and take my blessing along with her.
But mind, there's to be no hurry about the marriage! You'll have to wait a bit."

"As long as you like," returned the Captain;
"that is, any time in reason."

So it was settled, and from that day forth Fitzherbert, in spite of debts and duns, was the
happiest fellow in the world. His whole nature
seemed to change. He cared no more for billiards
or for cards, and was never happy away from
Montpellier Square. Again and again he said to
himself that he would turn over a new leaf when
Julia became his wife. He dreamed of a cottage
in a wood, of rural felicity, of a bright fireside, of
loving little children. Many were the delicious
*tête-à-têtes* he had with Julia in those happy days
of their first engagement.

"My darling," he would say, "you've made a
new man of me. I wish—I wish I had known you
earlier; it might have saved me from a deal of
misery. I know I'm not worthy of you—no one
could be worthy of you—but, God willing, I'll do
my best."

He meant what he said, and had Fortune been
kinder to him, he might have effected a complete
reformation. Nature had intended him for an
honest man; Fortune, which so often mars the
handiwork of Nature, had done her best to blacken
his character, but could not altogether change his
disposition. He had shown that he could be
faithful, even culpably devoted, to an unworthy

friend. Time was to show to what heights of self-sacrifice even this poor fellow could attain, when stimulated and strengthened by the one ennobling passion of his otherwise wasted life.

## CHAPTER XXIV.

### RACHEL ON THE WATCH.

THE lines of our life drama, which are destined to unite in the sequel, have been wandering far away from Rachel Dene, who has been standing, as it were, apart, a spectator of certain acts in which she scarcely took a part. She had not been idle, however, but had been working with all her might for the deliverance of the man she loved. When she found that all her efforts were in vain, that beyond securing his reprieve from the capital punishment she could do nothing, she felt as if her heart was broken. A long and serious illness followed; and when she emerged again from her chamber she looked several years older, and full of weariness of the world. To deepen her trouble, she found that the stern heart of Jacob Dene was firmly set against her lover. The proof of his guilt had, indeed, been overwhelming, and the old Quaker, as we know, had little or no mercy on wrong-doers.

"Thou must forget him," he said. "He has

sinned against God and man, and must take his punishment. From this day forth, think no more of him or his."

"But he is innocent," she pleaded. "I *know* he is innocent. I have known it from the first. Let me go to him? Let me write to him? Let me show him that one soul, at least, believes in him, and prays for his deliverance?"

This, however, was forbidden, and all the poor girl could do was to share her grief with the old couple at the cottage. From there she heard of Jack from time to time, though there came loving messages, to which, in spite of her grandfather's warning, she returned tender answers. But as time went on, and no hope came, Rachel drooped more and more under the weight of her heavy sorrow.

Since the night of the murder, Ralph Hollis had not returned to Deepdale; but he had heard at intervals from the Denes, and knew all that was going on, so that when Rachel appeared in London he was not astonished to find her so greatly changed. The sight of her face, which seemed the more beautiful for its sorrow, revived in the young man's heart all the fire of his old passion. He was wise enough, however, to hide the true nature of his feelings, and to offer her only the most respectful sympathy. She found, to her surprise, that he was quite prepared to become her confidant, to talk to her for hours together on the theme nearest to her heart, and

in her simplicity she trusted him, and was very
grateful.

Coming straight from Montpellier Square after
the interview described in our last chapter, he
drove to the hotel in South Kensington, where the
Denes were staying, and found Rachel alone in
the drawing-room. His heart leapt joyfully as
she came to him with outstretched hands.

"I'm so glad thou hast come early," she cried.
"Grandpapa is away in the City, and I am very
lonely."

The young man took her hands and pressed
them tenderly. They sat down side by side, and
there was a long silence. Glancing at Rachel's
face, he saw that her eyes were full of tears.

"You are fretting yourself to death," he said
gently. "Try to forget what has passed. Try to
be comforted."

"Nay, I do my best," she answered; "but I
feel now as if I could never be happy again—and
indeed I cannot till the truth is known, and *he* is
cleared. Oh, Ralph! it is so good of you to be
gentle with me in my affliction. I shall never
forget that you have proved so true a friend."

"You know my heart, Rachel," he said, with a
sigh. "It is the same as ever; but a man must
accept the fortune of war, and I see now that I
had never any chance. You always preferred him
to *me!* Well, I don't blame you for that, though
it's hard, very hard! All I ask you is—for my
sake, for all our sakes—to keep up a good heart."

She rose from his side, and paced up and down the room.

"Can nothing be done?" she cried. "Oh, Ralph! I am sure thou wilt help him if thou canst!"

"Certainly," was the reply. "But, there! it is quite hopeless. He'll have to 'dree his weird,' as they say in Scotland; and after all, you know, prison life isn't so dreadful—the suffering is more in the imagination than in the reality. Then, again, what they call a 'lifer' doesn't mean exactly imprisonment for life. If he keeps a good record, a man often gets out at the end of fifteen years."

"Fifteen years! But when he is innocent——"

"I believe he is," said the young Earl, emphatically.

"God bless thee for saying so!" cried Rachel, looking at him with grateful eyes. "All are against him save thyself and those who know him and love him best."

Never in all his days had Ralph Hollis felt so miserably mean, so full of remorse. At that moment, indeed, he would have liked to perform an act of heroism, and make a clean breast of everything. But, no! life was too sweet, and the world too full of charm. He thought, too, of his mother—the one being in the world for whom he had any unselfish affection—and said to himself, with characteristic self-deception, "For myself I should not care so much, but for her sake I must keep silence to the end."

They dined together that day—Jacob and Susannah Dene, Rachel and the young Earl. It was a dismal enough affair; but, thanks to Rachel's society and sweet looks, Ralph enjoyed himself immensely. Quitting the house at an early hour, he went off to the club, where he met some choice spirits, and played at cards for heavy stakes. Flushed and feverish, he went at last to his room to spend a sleepless night.

"I'm a miserable cad," he said to himself; "but, after all, is it my fault? Had my uncle died a few hours earlier I should have been spared this life-long misery. God knows I never intended to be a murderer—it was all an accident, as I told Fitzherbert; and though an innocent man is suffering on my account, I *can't* face a prison, and give myself up."

Then, with the innate selfishness of his nature, he thought rapturously of Rachel—her beauty, her tenderness, her confidence in him. There was hope yet, if he played his cards carefully, that she might forget the other, and begin to care for *him.*

"I've loved her all my life!" he cried. "If that fellow had not come in the way, all would have been different. And *now——* Why should I waste time in self-reproaches? Why should I mar my good fortune by making myself miserable? It's the fortune of war! Life's a lottery; prizes to some, blanks to others; and the prize I want is Rachel Dene."

Selfish and vacillating himself, he entirely miscalculated the strength of the young girl's nature. Once awake to the fact that she loved Jack Heywood, Rachel never faltered for a moment in her first faith; and though with her own eyes she had seen him brutalized with drink, and though she knew the world thought him guilty of a hideous crime, she held tenaciously to the belief in his innocence. The old Quaker stubbornness asserted itself in this gentle being. She thought of the poor prisoner all day, and her prayers were wafted to him every night. Fifteen years! She would wait fifty rather than turn her simple thoughts to any other living man.

A few days later the young Earl had a long talk with Jacob Dene. They met at Ralph's rooms by appointment, unknown to Rachel, but the conversation was chiefly of her. The old Quaker deplored what he called her infatuation for a man who had, by his own act, placed himself beyond the pale of human sympathy.

"Let it be a lesson to *thee*," he added. "I thought once that young Heywood was the steady horse, and Ralph Hollis the unbroken colt; but see to what a pass drink and the love of money can bring a man. I hope, lad, thy new-found fortune has not turned thy head, and that it has brought thee better manners and better company."

"I hope so," returned Ralph, with an obedient smile. "You see, sir, I was a little spoiled by my bringing up. It is bad for a young fellow to be waiting for an old one's shoes."

"Right! As for worldly titles, they are all vanity; but once thou art a peer, set a good example to thy kind."

"I'll try, sir," answered Ralph. "But Rachel —do you think she will ever get over this great sorrow?"

"She is a girl, a child, and *must* get over it; it is sin, I hold, to have set her heart upon a criminal."

"And, indeed, he was ever far beneath her!"

The eyes of the two men met, and each knew what was passing in the other's mind. Ralph saw his opportunity, and availed himself of it— nervously, awkwardly, but with a certain show of manly candour.

"Oh, sir, I need not play the hypocrite!" he cried. "I have loved Rachel all my life, and till this man came between us, I thought that she cared a little for me in return. Not for the world, however, would I seem to her selfish and unfeeling. All I wish you to know is that my heart is still unchanged."

Jacob Dene nodded approvingly. He liked the young man's modesty and gentleness of demeanour, and, above all, he knew that he was a suitable match.

"I have thy word," he said, "that thou hast changed thy ways. What was this I heard of a great prize-fight in France—a disgraceful affair? They tell me thou wast present?"

"By the merest accident," stammered Ralph.

"More shame for thee! Dost thou gamble still on the turf?"

"No, sir; I have given that up long ago. Remember, I was only a boy."

"Thou art a boy still," said Jacob. "What's thy present life?"

"A very dull one. I have cut most of my old friends—I confess they were a bad set—and found few new acquaintances. I live very quietly, as you see."

"Well, good fortune has not spoiled thee—that is in thy favour," returned the old Quaker. "I will not deny that I once mistrusted thee; but now, things are changed, and perchance—nay, I promise nothing—perchance, I say, Rachel and thee may come together. But not a word of this to Rachel herself. She is of stubborn disposition, and if she thought I approved of thee for her husband, poor would be thy chance of gaining her affection."

Thus it came to pass that Ralph became, with her grandfather's secret approval, the close companion of the young Quakeress. He had played his cards very cleverly, and, posing as a sympathetic friend, daily gained a firmer place in her affection; indeed, he was now almost the only person in the world to whom she could open her heart unreservedly, and with the certainty of finding due sympathy. Under these favourable circumstances, all his fears, all his scruples, were forgotten. He thought of nothing now but the hope of winning Rachel's love, and to secure this he humoured, with diabolic cunning, that other love which had become the mainspring of her maiden life.

So long as the Denes remained in town, he was very careful in his social conduct. His only intimate companion was Fitzherbert, whom he instructed to keep as much as possible out of the old Quaker's way. He avoided the gambling clubs, went to no race-meetings, and was zealous in his attendance at the House of Lords, even going the length of making a short maiden speech on a manufacturing question, which speech occupied just two lines in the newspaper next day. Those who knew him better looked on and wondered.

"Beauchamp has sown his wild oats," they said, laughing, "and is going in for respectability. Who knows? some day he may become Prime Minister!"

By the time that Rachel left for Deepdale, the young Earl had succeeded in fully establishing himself in her esteem. The season was just over; everybody else of any importance was leaving London, and Ralph began to think of going somewhere for a holiday.

"I'd like to go down to Deepdale," he said to his mother; "but the place is too full of sad associations. Fitzurse tells me of some capital salmon-fishing in a river close to the mouth of the St. Lawrence. I think I shall try Canada."

## CHAPTER XXV.

### FITZHERBERT GETS INTO TROUBLE.

ONE winter's day, when confined to the house by his asthma, which was becoming chronic, O'Gallagher said to Fitzherbert, "'*Dum vivimus*,' my boy, is my motto. Sufficient for the day is the evil thereof. As for the future, bad luck to the blackguard, I haven't the honour of his acquaintance, so let him look out for himself, as I had to do before him. It's the present is the botheration. Julia has taken charge of the cheque-book, and bowled me out and at the bank. Where she gets this niggardliness from God knows, for I don't; not from her mother or me. I never could keep my expenses within bounds, because of the insufficiency of my income. What can a man do when he's born a gentleman? Sure he must spend whether he has it or no. The girl is good enough to see that I have my wine, my meat, my tailor, my stable-keeper, my butcher, and my baker; but where is the use of those without my horse in the stable, my box at the play, a quiet rubber, or a monkey or two on the last race? By Jove!" he added; "there she comes."

As Julia made her appearance, followed by Ralph Hollis, the O'Gallagher continued.

"Ah, Ralph, my boy, here you are. And how's that superb creature, your mother? And the young Quakeress, too—how's she? By my honour, she's an angel; she's better than an angel, for she has no wings to fly away with! Ah! when I see a face like that, my heart always goes out to it, and I'm a boy again."

"Papa will still be talking, Lord Beauchamp," said Julia. "But you must excuse him, for he is still the youngest member of the family."

"Faith," laughed the Major, "you may say that, darling. Sure, as long as I'm a man, I hope to be a boy."

"I've come to say good-bye," said the Earl. "I'm going to take a run over to Canada and do some salmon-fishing."

"When do you start?" asked the Major.

"To-morrow."

"To-morrow is it? Then good-bye and good luck to you!" cried the Major,

"Thanks! Good-bye, Miss O'Gallagher!"

"Good-bye and *bon voyage,* Lord Beauchamp. I hope you will have a pleasant time," said Julia; then she gave her hand to Ralph.

"Thanks!" returned his lordship. "Fitz, are you coming my way?"

"In one moment," replied Fitz. Then he whispered to the Major, "I say, Major, about that five-hundred-pound bill that's due on Wednesday?"

The Major made a wry face.

"Try if you can't get Beauchamp to spring something towards it, and come round to-morrow," he whispered.

"All right. Coming, Ralph!" And off went the two young fellows together.

"Papa," said Julia, who had been regarding this whispered conference with observant and anxious eyes, "I wish you would not be always leading Captain Fitzherbert into these monetary difficulties."

"He has told you of them?" cried O'Gallagher, sharply.

"He has told me nothing, papa; but I'm neither blind nor deaf."

"No, by Jove, nor dumb either!" the Major cried. "Ah! how can you, while rolling in wealth, leave your poor old father to the mercy of those rascally bill-discounters?"

"It is because I do not wish to leave my father to their mercy that I seek to restrain his extravagance. Ah, papa! you have already squandered your own fortune in dissipation, and why should you seek to squander mine?"

The Major looked indignant.

"Squander yours!" he cried. "Let me tell you, Julia, that what you call dissipation a gentleman calls doing his duty in that state of life in which it has pleased Providence to place him. A gentleman is a circulating medium, or nothing. For Her Majesty herself is neither more nor less than a circulating medium, and an O'Gallagher can't go wrong in following so illustrious an example!"

"I think, papa," returned Julia, sadly, "were

I to follow my natural instincts I should be even more thoughtless than you are, but my love for you has taught me to learn prudence. But what is the present difficulty, papa?"

"Well, it's just that bit of a bill for five hundred pounds that I got poor Fitz to accept for me, and if *I* don't take it up, *he* must."

"Oh, papa, how could you?" cried the girl.

"Well, my darling, needs must when the Derby drives, and I came to grief over the favourite."

"When is the bill due?" asked Julia.

"The day after to-morrow."

Without another word she hurried from the room. As she went, the old Pagan smiled, and murmured, complacently, "She'll do it, the darling, she'll do it. I never met a woman yet who could say no to an O'Gallagher."

Then he lit a cheroot, and before he had half finished smoking it Julia returned with a cheque for five hundred pounds.

"There, papa," she said lightly; "now promise to be very good, and never do this any more."

"Never, by the honour of an O'Gallagher," returned the Major. "But I think, my darling, we ought to get out of this land of fogs, and go to the south, the sunny south. What do you say to the Riviera?"

"Yes, papa, that will do. Anywhere but Monte Carlo."

"Certainly not Monte Carlo, my lovey; that would be too much for me," said the Major. "It would recall my lost youth, and that angel, your mother. It was there we spent our honeymoon; and, faith! that was not all we spent there."

"Make your own arrangement for the future, papa; but for to-night let me make mine. We will dine *tête-à-tête*, and dine early."

"By all means. By the way, Julia, tell James to put a bottle of Chateau Margaux down to the fire."

"Very well, papa, and—oh, Fitz has a box for the theatre, and if you will promise not to play more than one rubber, you may go to the club."

It was impossible to be long angry with the Major, and Julia beamed upon him and kissed him that evening as she and Fitzherbert deposited him at the club, and they started on their way to the Frivolity Theatre. It was a bad night's work, however, for her and for her lover, too, when she left the hardened old gambler at the club with the five hundred pounds in his pocket. By the time he had taken a dozen whiskies he went for baccarat, with the result that he lost Julia's five hundred pounds, and having disposed of all the loose coins he had about him, he was compelled to borrow half a crown from the porter for a cab home. The morning brought a headache, repentance, and remorse. Meanwhile that bill would be due the next day.

Previous to his departure for America, Ralph had given his friend a hundred pounds, which

Fitzherbert had that morning handed over to the Major.

"One hundred, however, is not five hundred," said the Major. "I'm very seedy to-day, Fitz, my boy," he continued. "Never mix your drinks. It's not the quantity, but the mixture, that does it. Now, suppose you run down to Lazarus, and give him a pony to stave him off for a week till my dividends are due."

Fitzherbert, who knew as much about dividends as he did of discounts, called at Sackville Street, and put off Lazarus for a week.

In the mean time, Julia made preparations for the journey, greatly to Fitzherbert's discomfiture, since it would be quite impossible for him to accompany her. The Major got out as frequently as his cough and the east wind would permit him, but, as the week came to an end, his cough grew worse, and he was confined to the house. Then he wrote a note to Fitzherbert, begging him to see Lazarus again, and to get time. The Captain saw the Jew, who refused point blank. When Fitzherbert called to consult the Major on the subject, he found him in bed.

"It's about that infernal bill, I suppose," said the Major. "Well, I presume it's all right?"

"No; it's all wrong," answered the poor Captain, gloomily.

"You don't say that?"

"But I do, though. Lazarus is furious—vows he'll make us both bankrupt. Then some one has

Q

told him you're going abroad next week, and he swears he'll issue a judge's warrant, and lay you by the heels and throw you into prison. I'm afraid he'll come here and make a fuss, and frighten Julia."

"He mustn't do that, Fitz!" cried the Major, in alarm. "My daughter knows nothing of all this?"

"Not from me," returned Fitzherbert. "And now what's to be done? For myself I don't care, but I'm thinking of you and of *her*."

"I know you are, my boy. Well, then, just run back and tell him to hold hard for twenty-four hours, when I pledge you my honour I'll find either money or paper. Look me up at twelve to-morrow; and remember, Fitz, my boy, not a word of this to Julia!"

"All right!"

And off went the Captain once more to face the obdurate bill-discounter.

When Fitzherbert returned the next day, the Major was still confined to his bed, and his cough was worse than ever.

"Hand over my writing-case, my boy," he gasped. "In here's a bill at three months for seven hundred pounds. It's accepted by Lord Dunsinane. You needn't look surprised; his lordship has owed it me for months past. I put the screw on him last night, and instead of sending a cheque he sent this. I can't get out with this infernal north-easter, so I must just trouble you to see Lazarus once more. There's to be five hundred to take up the present bill; a hundred for interest, and the other hundred you can keep for yourself!"

"I can do without it," said Fitzherbert.

"No, dear boy. Well, if you put it that way, it's all in the family, so suppose we split it between us; you keep one half and I'll take the other!"

When, an hour later, Fitzherbert explained his business to Lazarus, the astute Israelite hummed and hawed.

"I suppose it'll be all right?" he muttered. "The old Marquis is shaky, and when he dies, young Dunsinane will inherit. However, three names are better than two, and as a mere matter of form, you'd better back the bill."

Without hesitation, Fitzherbert endorsed the new bill, retained the old one, and came out triumphant with a cheque for a hundred pounds, which he cashed on his way to Montpellier Square. When the old Major heard the crackle of five new crisp Bank of England notes for ten pounds each, the effect was magical.

"Thank God that's paid!" said he, as he jumped out of bed. "Fitz, I feel ever so much better. Go to Julia; say I'll come down to dinner. Stay and dine with us, and we'll have a pleasant evening!"

That was the last pleasant evening poor Fitzherbert had for a long time, for two days later the lady of his lifelong devotion and the great

O'Gallagher left town for San Remo, and the dis-
consolate Captain was left alone in London.

Quite alone, for Ralph had already sailed.
Before the separation the two friends had several
long talks together, and touching once more on the
subject of the Deepdale murder, Fitzherbert assured
the real culprit of his intention to hold his tongue.
He would have liked to borrow a few hundreds
more, but he knew that Ralph himself had been
spending a great deal lately, and to press him just
then looked like levying blackmail.

"Never mind," he thought; "if I get into a
very bad fix I can write to him, and he'll never
leave me out in the cold."

So the two parted, and the Captain remained
in the great city. A few weeks passed before
he began clearly to realize his situation. On
investigating his affairs he found they were worse
than even he himself had suspected. He was in
debt here, there, and everywhere, and saw no way
out of it. He could not dig, and to beg he was
ashamed. He was not ashamed, though, of running into debt with tradesfolk.

"A younger son is, as he observed, born to that
line of business; in fact, it is the only line of
business he is born to. He has to learn billiards,
that is, if he wishes to earn a living by that
pleasant pastime; while, as to cards, well, card-
playing is an exact science, unless you can carry
the ace up your sleeve, and that a fellow is debarred
from in reference to vulgar prejudice. If I'd only

the goodwill of a fashionable crossing now, like the fellow in the story, I might turn an honest penny ! "

Meanwhile the Major and his daughter had reached the Riviera, which was not a pleasant place that winter. Wherever the two went the winter still followed and preceded them. Hail, rain, sleet, snow, ice before or behind them in every direction. The Major's cough got worse and worse, and he began to think he'd better have stayed at home. As he sat one day muffled up to the chin and shivering over the stove, or the miserable handful of damp wood which did duty for fire at the Hotel Splendide at Cannes, he growled, " Curse the weather ! Sure it's the marrow in my bones that's congealed into ice; and, as for this infernal cough, it's my heart it's bringing up ! "

" I'm so sorry, papa," said Julia; " but you would come, you know."

" That's right—that's right; reproach your old father who's sacrificed his life for you ! Confound this cough ! Ring the bell, and call for the stoker ; see if that old cat can make this conglomeration of chips into a fire, and let me have a hot whiskey, blazing hot."

When he had swallowed the beverage as hot as he could put it down without scalding, he said, " Ah, darling, you're the best of daughters, and I'm an ungrateful old vagabond ! "

" No, no, papa; I won't hear you talk like that," said Julia.

"But I must and I will!" returned the Major. "I ruined your mother, I've ruined myself, and I was near ruining you; but thank God you had the common sense to save yourself from me, and now I can die easy, knowing that you are provided for."

"Don't talk about dying, papa," cried Julia.

"And why shouldn't I?" returned the Major, sadly. "Death is the one debt that must be paid; we can't escape it, try as we will. You may renew a bill, or stave off a tradesman, but when the Dun of Death lays his hand upon our heads there is no escape. It reminds me, Julia darling, that my little bill is nearly due, and that at any hour of the day or night I may expect to see that cold, relentless face. I shouldn't mind the thought of death, Julia, but that I can't bear to know that I must leave you alone. Ah, it's a bad lot we are —the O'Gallaghers; a set of godless heathens wandering about the face of the earth, instead of being settled down as good Christians among our own kith and kin, and doing good to the poor devils born on our land. Help me into bed, darling. Perhaps I shall be better to-morrow."

On the morrow, however, he was worse, and the following day he was worse still. Poor Julia loved him—for he had been to her father and mother— in fact, everything in the world. In his way he loved *her;* he had petted and spoiled her, and he would have ruined her with equal facility. Her origin and her dubious position and past always kept her in doubtful society, and even then she was alone. Women avoided her, and men regarded her as an anomalous compound of the Eastern odalisque and the European money spinner; she who, despite the hot blood of her Indian mother, was chaste as snow.

It was the quiet, unostentatious, yet respectful admiration of Fitzherbert which had made the heart of this poor girl go out to him. She had learned to love him just as she loved the old gambler and *roué* who lay dying before her.

Yes, there could be no doubt about one thing. The Major was near the end of his journey, but he managed to struggle to San Remo.

" Send for Fitz, darling," he said one afternoon; " I'd like to see you man and wife. He's not a brilliant match for you, but he loves the very ground you walk on. Send for him at once—send for him, for the love of God, Julia; I must see him before I die ! "

Suddenly he was seized with a wild paroxysm of coughing. When he withdrew the handkerchief from his mouth it was drenched with blood.

" It's all over, Julia," he gasped, " and I've no time to make my peace with Heaven. Kiss me, darling. I'm a bad lot, but I've always loved you. Sure, I've had a fine time of it, and if I could but see you settled I should die happy; but what must be must be. Kiss your wicked old father, and say you forgive him."

As Julia knelt sobbing by the bedside, he continued.

"And there's a bill—a bill for seven hundred pounds; it's due to-day, or to-morrow, or next week. Bad luck to the bills! I always get into a muddle about them. But mind, my life's insured. Give Fitz seven hundred pounds directly —directly, mind, for the bill—the bill—— "

"Yes, papa," sobbed Julia; "I understand."

"And settle the rest on the eldest boy, if you have one; and call him Gerald, after his wicked old grandfather. It's getting dark, Julia, or it is the end that's coming. Hold on to me, dear; hold on to me," he whispered, faintly; and then he fell asleep, holding her hand in his.

She sat there till the hand grew cold, the breathing short; then she knew that the stupor was that of death.

The next morning Captain Fitzherbert went down to his club, and found a foreign telegram to this effect :—

"My poor father died last night. Come at once. Julia. Hotel d'Italie, San Remo."

Poor Fitzherbert was overwhelmed at this intelligence. Making the best of his way to the smoking-room, he dropped into a chair, and endeavoured to collect his thoughts. His first impulse was to start for San Remo at once; a little reflection showed him this would be impossible. Without money, how was he to get a suit of mourning, and how was he to get to San Remo? Well, he still had his watch and chain and a diamond ring, and a shirt stud worth a hundred guineas. He would dispose of these.

Just as he had arrived at this conclusion, two of his boon companions, Algernon Fitzurse and Major Deuceace, lounged in.

" What's up, Fitz ? " asked Algy.

" The Major—poor old Major O'Gallagher—has just died."

" You don't say so ! "

" Yes ; he died at San Remo last night."

" Poor old chap ! " muttered Algy; " he was a good cribbage-player."

" Well, he's pegged his last hole, anyhow," interposed the Major. " Hawkins, brandy and soda. Have a cigar, Algy ? "

At this moment Lord Dunsinane burst into the room, followed by Lazarus, the bill-discounter. Both were pale with excitement.

" Oh, there you are ! " cried Lazarus, accosting Fitzherbert.

" Of course, I am here," returned Fitzherbert, coldly. " But may I ask what brings *you* here ? "

" What brings me here ?—my money ! " shrieked Lazarus. " I want my money, and, what's more, I'll have it—do you hear, Mr. Fitzherbert ?—I'll have it, if not out of your pocket, out of your life ! "

Fitzherbert sprang to his feet.

"This is neither the time nor the place for a bill-discounting blackguard——" he began, when the Jew interrupted him.

"A bill-discounter is better than a thief!"

"Not much," retorted Fitzherbert; "it's a distinction without a difference. Anyhow, if you have any claim against me, send it in, and we will discuss it at the proper time and in the proper place."

"This is the proper time and place," said the Jew.

"No, it is not. This club is for gentlemen, not for people of your stamp. Davison, show this person the door!"

"Davison, do nothing of the kind!" cried Lord Dunsinane. "Mr. Lazarus is here as my guest."

"Very good, my lord, very good," cried Fitzherbert. "I know whom to make responsible for this outrage."

By this time an eager and excited crowd had gathered around. Dunsinane drew himself up indignantly.

"A gentleman does not fight with a forger and a thief!" he said.

As the last word left his lips, Fitzherbert knocked him down.

"Police, police!" shrieked Lazarus.

In answer to the cry, two detectives in plain clothes made their appearance.

"There's your man," continued Lazarus, pointing to Fitzherbert; "take him away, and lock him up."

"Hands off!" cried Fitzherbert, fiercely. "I'll knock the head off any man who dares to touch me!"

An ominous growl arose of "You shan't take him!"

"Come, gentlemen, it's a serious thing to interrupt an officer in the discharge of his duty!" said one of the men.

"Duty be hanged!" cried Major Deuceace. "You've no right to come here on your dirty work. This club is as sacred as the House of Commons."

"Don't know anything about that, sir," was the reply; "we were brought here by Lord Dunsinane."

"Cowardly hound!" said Algy; "that's because of the thrashing Fitz once gave him."

"Nothing of the kind," retorted Dunsinane, now livid with rage; "it is because he has forged my name!"

"And he has robbed me of seven hundred pounds!" continued Lazarus. "He brought me a bill for seven hundred pounds, which he pretended was O'Gallagher's. Here it is with his own endorsement, and it bears the forged signature of Lord Dunsinane!"

A murmur went round the room, for the thing looked very serious. Even Fitzurse and Deuceace, who were hand in glove with Fitzherbert, looked anxiously at one another.

"A forgery, did you say?" cried Fitzurse.

"Yes, a forgery!" screamed the Jew. "Here's his lordship to say so!"

"Say so? To swear it!" cried Lord Dunsinane. " I'll do so in any court in Christendom!"

Fitzherbert was stunned; but when his senses cleared, he understood everything. The Major, always reckless and unscrupulous, had got him into this dreadful trouble, hoping, no doubt, before the bill came mature, to take it up or square it in some way. Death had intervened, and Fitzherbert had to pay the penalty. Even in the moment of his dire extremity, he had only one thought—to shield the woman he loved. The O'Gallagher had paid his last account, and he was her father.

By this time the sleek and swarthy and respectable members of the club had strolled away, leaving Fitzherbert to my lord, to Lazarus, and the detectives.

Fitzurse and Deuceace were both notorious black sheep; their hands were against every man, and every man's hand was against them; but the Captain was their comrade, and they elected to stand by him.

"Algy," growled Deuceace, in a fierce whisper, "this is a plant between the Jew and Dunsinane. I don't believe Fitz is in it; let's see him through."

"If we can only do it!" muttered Fitzurse.

"Well, I can spring half; will you spring the other half?"

"Yes; if I have to pawn my last shirt!"

"Then let us try if we can square Lazarus!"

"All right! Go ahead!"

"Here, Lazarus," said Algy; "come and have a drink."

So while Fitzherbert sat perfectly stupefied, under guard of the detectives, and Lord Dunsinane strode to and fro in a fever of fury, Algy and Fitzurse took Lazarus away, and talked to him quietly. They then agreed to raise the seven hundred pounds and costs, and the Jew seemed disposed to meet their views. After the matter had been argued for some time, he said, "Well, gentlemen, I must consult my principal; if he is willing, I am, but I must tell you it is quite in his lordship's hands. Half a minute, and I'll tell you what he says." With that he approached Lord Dunsinane, and repeated the proposal.

"Never! never!" growled the peer; "would you have me compound a felony? No, not for the Bank of England!—a thousand times no!"

"It's no use, gentlemen," said Lazarus, returning to Algy and Fitzurse; "we can't compound a felony; it's an indictable offence."

"Take him away, do you hear?—take him away!" growled my lord.

Fitzurse and Algy went up to Fitzherbert.

"We are coming with you, old man. Don't believe a bit of it," said Fitzurse.

"Not a word!" chimed in Deuceace. "Davison, call a four-wheeler!"

"I'm ready!" said the Captain, pulling himself together. "I'll go quietly—only hands off, that's all!"

"Right you are, sir!" returned the detective, while one opened the door, and both followed the Captain down the stairs.

"Lazarus," said Algy, "stay a moment while you hear me speak to this fellow."

With that, he went up to Dunsinane.

"My lord," he said, "you're a liar and a cad! In your heart of hearts you know that Fitzherbert didn't do this; you know it was old O'Gallagher; and you are putting this upon my friend because he once gave you a thrashing. But if Fitz comes to grief over this business, I'll thrash you within an inch of your life, as sure as my name's Algernon Fitzurse!"

"And when Algy has done with you, you'll have to settle with me!" said Deuceace; and the two men left the room together.

"I think, my lord," said Lazarus, "you'd better have accepted their offer. What I do, I do in the way of business, but you do it for pleasure. Every man to his taste, but I'd rather not be in your shoes."

"Pshaw! The law will protect me!" cried the peer.

" Yes, as far as forty shillings goes, but that's not much to pay for a luxury. But there ! we had better be off to Bow Street."

So to Bow Street they went, where the charge was duly entered.

Upon being brought before the magistrate the next day, Fitzherbert was committed to take his trial on a charge of forgery and obtaining money under false pretences. He was removed at once to the Old Bailey.

Fitzurse and Deuceace stood manfully by him to the last, procured the best legal advice, and paid for it. Yet, despite all that could be said or done on his behalf, the evidence was so conclusive, and he himself bore such a shady character, that he was convicted.

He was found guilty, and sentenced to fifteen years' penal servitude.

He might have saved himself by accusing the O'Gallagher, but he refused point blank to give any explanation of how the dead man's name came upon the bill.

When sentence was passed his head swam ; it seemed as if the roof of the court was tumbling down upon his head. When the warders carried him out of the dock he had a semi-consciousness of two pair of hands grasping him, of two choking voices, those of Deuceace and Fitzurse, saying, " It's a cowardly shame ! God bless you, old man ! We won't forget you ! "

## CHAPTER XXVI.

### THE TWO PRISONERS.

FITZHERBERT had been set to pick oakum. He might as well have been set to construe the Prometheus Vinctus. He was not allowed to write till he had accomplished his allotted task. He never could accomplish it—he never did.

His poor soft, delicate fingers were torn to pieces. The experienced gaol-birds around could do in three hours what it took him three days to attempt. He struck work in despair. He was pulled up for insubordination, and got five days on the crank and a remission of forty days.

When he had gone through this ordeal, he demanded an interview with the Governor, from whom he requested permission to write again to Earl Beauchamp and Julia O'Gallagher. The great man inquired if they were relatives, and on being informed that they were merely friends, he refused permission point blank. It was in vain that poor Fitzherbert pleaded; remonstrance and reproach were alike wasted. Had he possessed money, means of communication with the outer world would have been easy enough; but he had no money, nor had he any means of obtaining it. The knowledge of his innocence did not make his punishment the lighter to bear; on the contrary, it fell all the heavier.

At length, in the efflux of time, came the period when the other prisoners were to be removed to Portland. While they were being transferred from the prison van to the railway carriage at Waterloo, the crowd stared at them as if they were packs of wild beasts. Up to this moment Fitzherbert had retained some hope of seeing or hearing from Julia, for the sake of whose good name he had suffered himself to be branded as a felon.

His fellow-prisoners for the most part beguiled the journey with song and jest, while he sat apart in silence, till at length the prison peninsula rose before him. Immediately on his arrival he had to undergo the degrading routine of prison discipline. He was stripped from head to foot, examined as though he were some animal whose points were to be approved before being put to action. Unfortunately, he commenced by kicking against this revolting business. A quarrel ensued, which ended in his being dragged before the Governor of Portland on the very first day of his arrival. Poor fellow, he had not brought a clean slate from Brixton; so the interview was short, and the result, " Ten days on the crank ; bread and water ; four marks. Take him away ! "

This was not a good beginning. At the end of his punishment Fitzherbert thought he would try another trick, and became obedient. Surely Julia and Ralph would hear of his unhappy condition through the papers ; failing the papers, they might come in contact with Fitzurse or Deuceace, in

R

which case help would surely arrive sooner or later to enable him to effect his escape.

When he had done his ten days, he was sent to work in the West Quarry at stone-dressing. He was enfeebled by his bread and water diet, and he couldn't do much work.

"Look alive, No. 79," said the warder, peremptorily.

"I can't do much to-day, sir," replied the convict; "I've been on bread and water for the past ten days. Only let me get a little stronger, and I'll do my best, I'll promise you."

"All right, my lad," replied the warder, good-naturedly; then he added, in a whisper, "Keep your weather eye open, and in a day or two you'll be able to slip into it like one o'clock. You can bring yourself to anchor. Sit down a bit."

Fitzherbert availed himself of this permission, and looked round to take stock of his fellow workmen. One gang was engaged in removing stone in huge masses; another, in levelling a mound of earth; a third, in building it up again; a fourth, in dressing the famous Portland stone in lumps about the size of a cocoa-nut; a fifth, in loading carts with these lumps; a sixth, like beasts of burthen, were hauling cartloads of stone up the mountain side.

The prisoners appeared to be of every station, and almost of every nationality. Cheek by jowl with criminals, such as burglars, coiners, pickpockets, and area-sneaks, were dynamitards and

Fenians, mixed up with an occasional gentleman, a fraudulent banker, a forger, a barrister, or even a parson.

Misery makes strange bedfellows. Though some of these men seemed conscious of their degradation, the bulk of them laughed and talked, whistled and sang, despite the rule that such amusements are strictly prohibited. The warders, who were all fully armed, kept a sharp look-out on their flocks, prepared to shoot any one of them down upon the slightest provocation; but beyond an occasional "Hold your tongues!" "Silence!" or "I'll report you!" they made no effort to control.

One tall, slender-looking fellow, with fair hair, aquiline nose, and clean-cut features, attracted Fitzherbert's attention by the way in which he toyed with his pickaxe; indeed, he handled it as gingerly as if it had been a croquet-mallet. For fully five minutes he leant upon it in a position of languid elegance; then, transferring it to his left hand, with his right he twisted the ends of an imaginary moustache. This occupied another four minutes or more; then he laboriously lifted the pick, examined both points, dropped it to earth, and twisted the airy moustache again. At length he appeared to be roused to activity by the sound of approaching footsteps, inasmuch as he spat upon his hands, uplifted the pick, and worked with a will as the warder came in view. The moment, however, that he passed out of sight, the gentleman with the aquiline nose returned to his ruminations, and his companions to the process of tickling the earth with their pickaxes.

"Jem's thinking," said one of the convicts, lifting his left thumb over his shoulder towards the man with the aquiline nose.

"No, he isn't," responded another, in an educated but cynical voice. "He'd scorn the action; he thinks he's thinking, which is quite a different thing."

"I'll bet two to one," continued the first convict, "he's guessing what's on for lunch at the Carlton this minute."

"Done with you!" laughingly drawled the man with the aquiline nose. "I was actually thinking how I could get a quid of tobacco, so hand it over!"

"I will, as soon as I get it," laughed the convict; "but there's not been a bit of stuff in the place this while past. Ginger has promised to get in some to-morrow."

"I wish to-morrow'd hurry up, then, for I'm dying for a quid; it's the only thing worth living for in this infernal place!"

"Try the Johnny Raw there," said convict number one; "perhaps he's got a bit of stuff about him."

Lounging lazily up to Fitzherbert, the man with the aquiline nose said, "I say, you fellow—— Fitz, by Jove!" he cried, dropping his voice.

"Pelham!" exclaimed Fitzherbert.

"Hush! Stow that; I'm only Jim Swindon here," whispered the other.

"I thought you were dead," continued Fitz-herbert.

"No such luck, old man," was the reply. "I wish I were."

"Your brother told me you were drowned."

"The man that is born to be hanged 'll never be drowned!" chimed in the cynic.

This brilliant sally was greeted with a roar of laughter, which, however, subsided into silence as the warders were seen returning. Up went the pickaxes, and at it went the elegant gentleman with the rest.

Fitzherbert by this time had recognized in the loquacious convicts two or three other old chums. Besides the wretched Pelham (born a lord and brother of a duke), there was the son of an Irish judge, a nobleman who was said to have been killed in the American war, a barrister, and the vicar of an English parish.

"Well," thought Fitzherbert, "I am not alone unfortunate. Poor Pelham!"

This unexpected advent of old acquaintances did something to make the hateful place less endurable. The weather was genial and bracing, and in a few days he began to get better. Fortunately he was dropped into Pelham's gang, nicknamed "the Devil's Own" by the other convicts.

Some of the Devil's Own kept up by occult means communication with the outer world. They could command money; money meant smuggling letters in and out and obtaining tobacco, without which some of those lost wretches would have gone mad. In this respect Fitzherbert found himself as bad as any of them. He would encounter any danger for a few puffs of a good cigar.

Pelham told him he had got into trouble through mistaking another man's signature for his own, and had been convicted and sentenced by the name of Swindon, under which he had concealed his shame. His poor mother bewailed him as dead.

"Better so," said he, to Fitzherbert, "than that she should dream of this!"

One of the most trusty agents of the Devil's Own for communicating with the outer world was "Ginger." This worthy, whom our readers will remember, appeared privileged to come and go exactly when he pleased, and many a coin he brought in, and many a letter he took out.

While Fitzherbert was endeavouring to accommodate himself to circumstances as best he could, Jack Heywood had become rebellious, desperate, and even ferocious. He had refused point blank to be stripped and searched, had thrashed one brutal warder within an inch of his life, and disabled another, for which offences he had various periods of punishment in the cells set apart for the purpose—bread and water, plank beds, and sometimes no bed at all. It was of no avail—they might break this man, but they could never bend him. He was still as determined to effect his escape as ever. Every one of these offences against discipline entailed special punishment for

" Sulky Jack." His cruelest punishment, though, was that he was refused permission to write home or to receive a letter from home. At length Ginger smuggled in writing materials—paper, envelopes, and pen and ink—into Jack's cell—a perilous proceeding for both, if found out.

"Here ye are, Yorkshire," said Ginger; "I'll get it posted somehow, if I get fourteen days' bread and water for it!"

But Jack was a marked man, and no warder would risk his place without the certainty of a heavy reward. Thus in vain Ginger represented that there was money behind the job.

"'Tain't behind it, Ginger," was the reply, "that I want it; it's before, laddie. If Sulky Jack can spring a flimsy, I'll chance it!"

When Ginger reported progress that night, Jack had recourse to that ten-pound note which he had managed still to retain.

"Ginger," said he, "you might get this fellow to give you five back!"

That gentleman took the ten-pound note and stuck to it, refusing to return any change. He forwarded that letter, though, and in a few days' time Jack got an answer, dated from the town of Portland itself.

The letter was full of sweet and sacred words, recitations of belief of his innocence. Jasper and Joan Heywood were outside the prison walls; money was plentiful, escape was possible; now it was a mere question of time.

Despite everything, he now kept a good heart. He was sure of money to bribe his gaolers—above all, he was sure of the two faithful hearts who from without kept watch and ward by day and night upon his prison gates.

One day, as the Devil's Own were marching to the West Quarry, they came full butt upon a tall, stalwart fellow in charge of two warders. Apart from the man's appearance, which was striking enough, he was attired in a costume which fixed, and, indeed, riveted attention, for he was clad in a parti-coloured dress, after the fashion of a mediæval jester, one-half of it being a bright canary colour, the other half black. The man wore irons, too, which clanked as he walked briskly along.

In passing each other he and Fitzherbert encountered each other face to face, and eye to eye. Each gave an imperceptible start.

" Who's that ? " inquired Fitzherbert, of Pelham.

" Sulky Jack, the Deepdale murderer ! " replied Pelham, in a whisper.

" My God ! " exclaimed Fitzherbert.

Could it be retributive justice which had brought him there face to face with this innocent, long-suffering man ?

# CHAPTER XXVII.

## A ROMANTIC EPISODE.

RETURNING to England shortly after her father's death, Julia O'Gallagher scarcely rested by day or night in her inquiries for Fitzherbert, from whom, to her astonishment, she had received no communication whatever. She went first, however, on personal business to the family solicitor, an old-fashioned and highly respectable person, who represented an eminent conveyancing firm, which had flourished in Lincoln's Inn Fields for nearly a century. This old gentleman, the soul of honour, was a hundred years behind the age. He saw immediately to the business about the insurance on the Major's life, and invested the money to the best advantage, but he did not display any remarkable alacrity in making the requisite inquiries about Fitzherbert. Of course, Julia could not explain the motives which influenced her so strongly in the matter, nor did she permit herself to display the anxiety she felt. She had no one but her maid to confide in, and that young lady was not a person to inspire confidence. It was Julia's misfortune, therefore, to be still alone in the world.

The discovery of the truth came upon her like a thunderclap.

The man she loved, the man who had filled her with such simple devotion, was in a convict prison; and further inquiry elicited the truth, known only to herself, that he had been condemned on account of a crime really committed by her own father. Not a sign had he made, not a complaint had he uttered, but had accepted his fate like a hero, to spare her pain.

If she had loved him before, she adored him now; on her knees, night after night, she wept and prayed for her lover.

Then she took a firm resolve.

"With God's help," she said, "I will save him and justify him."

Dassiter, the lawyer, had been unable to obtain any information about Fitzherbert's place of confinement beyond the fact that he had been removed to some distant convict prison; but fortunately at or about this time Julia encountered a gentleman she had formerly known—Algernon Fitzurse, recently translated to the peerage by the death of his elder brother.

He was delighted to see her, and she was glad to see him.

Fitzurse had sown his wild oats, and had become impressed with the duties of his new position; but he requested permission to call next day, and when he had done so some spontaneous expression of his regard for Fitzherbert caused the girl to open her heart to him. He sympathized with her loyalty to his friend, and with her lonely situation, so greatly, that upon leaving her he went direct to his mother, the Dowager Countess, a charming old lady. He

was the Dowager's only son, and even in his wildest
days he had been her darling, so had little difficulty
in persuading her to accompany him in his next
visit to Miss O'Gallagher. The two ladies took a
fancy to each other, and Julia found in the Countess
a valuable ally and friend.

Meantime Fitzurse, or Lord Delamere as we
must now call him, took the matter of Fitzherbert
in hand, and engaged a famous criminal lawyer to
make the requisite inquiries. After a few weeks
the lawyer reported that there was every reason to
believe that Fitzherbert was confined at Portland ;
so to Portland Delamere and Julia went the next
day.

It was the custom, whether in romance or reality,
to depict the Governor of a penal establishment as
a stereotyped monster in human shape; but as a
matter of fact many of these persons are gentlemen of the most humane feelings, whom inexorable
necessity has condemned to become professional
gaolers. In this case, however, public sentiment
was right. The Governor of Portland was a
jaundiced, ill-conditioned individual, who was pre-
judiced in his likes and dislikes.

For all that, he dearly loved a lord, and more
than that a handsome lady.

So having been duly advised over-night of Lord
Delamere's intended visit, he laid himself out to
receive his lordship with all honours due to his
lordship's station. Orders were given for everything to be brightened up and made clean as a

new pin. The "Devil's Own" occupied the model cells, which were to be thrown open for inspection. Every cell was holystoned, every tin can or copper utensil was brightened up like silver, or like burnished gold, and the men, instead of being sent out to the quarry, were ordered to stay in their cells, an order received with universal dissatisfaction, for not one amongst them cared about being pruned up for inspection; possibly more than one had good reason to desire to escape recognition from the outer world.

Upon their arrival, Lord Delamere and Julia were received by the Governor, who escorted them in the first instance to the infirmary, where the large dreary dormitory and spotless linen excited their admiration, while the poor careworn prisoners claimed their sympathy. Julia looked in vain from side to side for her lover, whom she feared to find dead or dying with shame and grief. From the infirmary they were led to the kitchen and the bakehouse, where piles and piles of newly-baked bread emitted a fresh and wholesome odour; thence they proceeded to the great kitchen, where they found spread out on the table samples of the prisoners' food for dinner. Here was a magnificent leg of mutton, there a fine joint of beef, and there a steaming hot copper full of potatoes like huge balls of flour.

This was one side of the picture. If they had only seen the other!

Delamere and his companion tasted the mutton

and the bread, and found them both delicious; but the girl's heart was too full to admit of her paying the requisite attention to each detail.

At last they were conducted to the model cells occupied by the Devil's Own; the doors were unlocked by the warders in attendance, and at the word of command the men stepped out, faced in a line, and saluted the Governor.

Julia looked into one or two of the cells; then the Governor led the way down the hall, inspecting the prisoners as they passed.

As they got about half-way down, a choking voice gasped "Julia!" The word had scarcely left his lips when, with a wild cry of joy, she leaped into the arms of her lost lover.

A scene of the wildest amazement followed. "God bless my soul! This is monstrous!" exclaimed the Governor. "Monstrous! Scandalous! A breach of discipline! Take the gang to the quarry, and remove No. 79 to his cell!"

"Silence, there!" roared a gigantic warder. "Fall in! Right about face! Quick march!" As the men rapidly defiled down the central avenue, two warders advanced to Fitzherbert on the one side and to Julia on the other, and despite their prayers and entreaties that they might speak to each other, if only for a few minutes, pulled them asunder.

"Oh, my darling!—my darling! Thank God, I've seen you!" cried Fitzherbert as they dragged

him to his cell. "Don't fear for me; I'm all
right *now!*"

Fortunately Julia had fainted, and was utterly
unconscious. It was in vain that Lord Delamere
appealed to the Governor, who was furious with
rage. Had his lordship approached him in a
different manner—had he requested an interview
for Julia with the prisoner, the chances are that
the Governor might have been induced to yield
assent; but he was under the impression that
advantage had been taken of him, and he would
listen to nothing. Indeed, he cut short the interview by exclaiming, as he left the hall, "Show
this lady and gentleman out!"

Two warders bore Julia to the carriage, which was
waiting at the prison gates; but Delamere, not to
be daunted, went on to the door of his friend's cell.

"Fitz!" said he; "Julia's all right! She's
only fainted! I'll take care of her."

"God bless her!" gasped Fitzherbert.

"And, Fitz, I've kept my word, and given that
rascal Dunsinane a thrashing!"

Here a hand was laid upon his arm. "I must
trouble your lordship to follow the lady," said the
principal warder.

"One moment, my good fellow; I want just a
word with my friend."

The warder glanced round, and saw that the
Governor had disappeared.

"Prisoners are forbidden to talk; it's against
the regulations."

"Hang the regulations!  Fitz!"

"Here!" answered Fitzherbert from his cell.

"Keep up your heart, old man; we know where you are, and will soon have you out."

"God bless you, Algy!"

As Delamere walked down the corridor, he looked round to see if he was unobserved, and took the opportunity to slip a ten-pound note into the warder's hand.

"I shall be staying at the Red Lion for the next week," he whispered; "try to see me there."

"It's as much as my place is worth!"

"I'll make it worth much more.  Mind, I shall expect to see you."

"All right, my lord."

By the time Delamere returned to the carriage, Julia had recovered.  She took his hand, and grasped it cordially.

"Now that I know where he is, my mind is easy.  I will not rest night or day till he is free."

The news of the scene of the morning spread like wildfire through the prison, and added to the growing dissatisfaction amongst the prisoners.  It is true it was a trifle compared with what had gone before, but it was a romantic and sensational trifle, and it was in a thousand mouths that night.  The Governor was universally detested, and no wonder.  Even to his own officers he was insolent and overbearing.  Many of the important officials were superior men, who, although they were compelled to yield obedience to his orders, did so most unwillingly.

In one word, the prisoners were in a state of semi-mutiny, which was only kept down by the most vigorous means. The separate cells were crowded; indeed, scores of men were reported and brutally punished by the director at the instigation of the Governor.

This same director was a gentleman who went in for flogging as a panacea for insubordination. Men were frequently strapped up to the triangles, and some were maimed for life. One man, it is a matter of history, actually died from the infliction.

How Jack Heywood had escaped this punishment is to this day a mystery; but now, after he was assured that the means of escape were at hand, he became less refractory; he did whatever work was allotted him with assiduity, and without grumbling. Consolation had come to his bruised heart in various ways. First he had caught in the quarry a beautiful little white mouse, and had trained it to come and go at his call, and to sleep in his bosom. Secondly, he had learnt that Rachel had sent him loving messages, and that she still remained Rachel Dene! Thirdly, Joan Heywood had written, begging him that every morning at seven (for the winter had now set in), and every night at the same time, he would say the Lord's Prayer, and at the same hour day and night she would say the same prayer, with a little one thrown in for his deliverance. This simple

act of piety soothed, softened, and consoled him,
and gave him courage and strength to look forward
to the hour of his vindication.

Christmas was now approaching. There would
be some merriment going on even amongst the
stern officials; and if so, that was the golden
opportunity to be utilized.

The warder who carried his letters to and fro
entered into negotiations with the Heywoods; the
chief warder followed suit with Lord Delamere.
These two worthies put their heads together,
squared the porter at the portcullis, and agreed,
in consideration of a large sum of money, to
release the two prisoners. Finally, it was arranged
that on Christmas Day a boat should be ready on
the shore, which would take them to a sailing
vessel which lay in the offing. Once aboard, they
would be safe. This last was Delamere's plan.
The vessel was chartered by him, and he was
quite willing to act in concert with the other
prisoner.

As Christmas came nearer, the excitement and
anxiety of the prisoners increased. The faithful
Ginger was the go-between, who kept them both
posted up as to the progress of affairs.

Christmas Day dawned ominously, for the sky
was overcast, and it seemed as if it would turn to
snow. Providentially this passed away, and the
sun broke forth bright and glorious. There was
no work that day, but church in the morning, and
some attempt at a choral service. With husky

s

throats the assembled congregation sang, "For
unto us a Child is born, for unto us a Son is given,
and the punishment shall be upon his shoulders!"

After church there was an hour's exercise in the
open at the West Quarry before dinner. The men
took open order, and wandered to and fro at their
own sweet wills. Clouds of thick mist floated
everywhere, now veiling and again disclosing the
dreary prospect of land and sea. A wind,
gradually rising, came from the north-west. The
air was bitterly cold, and the prisoners had much
ado to keep themselves warm. They laughed and
shouted, whistled and sang, and romped boisterously
together, while the armed warders looked on phleg-
matically, their hearts a little softened, perhaps,
because it was Christmas Day.

While this merriment was going on, Fitzherbert
leaped to the summit of the crags, and took a look
round. In his youth he had been on garrison
duty at Gibraltar. How the scene recalled his
old station! He thought, for the moment, he was
at Gibraltar again; and he saw that the chances
of escape would have been ten to one in favour of
the fortress in the Mediterranean.

The prison itself stood upon the summit of a
lofty hill. The rocky peninsula, wrongly called an
island, was surrounded in part, to the right and
the left, by the sea, in the rear by the military
district of the Verne, beyond which lay a bare and
thickly misted district of swamp and marshes. To
the right and left the prison fortress was guarded

by the naval harbour forts. Except by strategy or
treachery, escape was impossible. But in the
offing towards the south lay a sailing vessel, with
bunting flying at the fore. The word had been
passed, and Fitzherbert knew the word was Lord
Delamere's, and that once aboard, he would be
free.

At this moment the signal was given to fall in.
With empty stomachs and aching hearts—for even
the most lost wretch there thought of other Christ-
mases, of home and friends, of father and mother,
sisters and brothers, sweetheart, or wife and child
—they marched slowly back to the prison. On
their return they stopped in the square for inspection before being dismissed for dinner.

The Governor was about to give them their
*congé*, when, as ill luck would have it, he caught
sight of Ginger, disguised in a clean face, attempting to smuggle a letter into the hands of Fitzherbert; a letter, in fact, containing the formal
plan of action for the escape.

"Halt, there! Fall in, No. 79 company!"
roared the martinet.

The word of command was obeyed; but before
the men could form in file, the letter had disappeared as if by magic. In point of fact, Ginger
had rolled it up, and swallowed it like a pill.

"Hand over the letter!" shouted the Governor.

"I have no letter, sir!" replied Fitzherbert.

"Then *you*, sir!" he roared to Ginger.

"Me, sir?" said Ginger, innocently.

"Yes, you, sir!"

"Never had no letter in my life—can't read, sir!" returned Ginger, smiling.

"Don't humbug me! Some one has it in his possession, for I saw it—I saw it with my own eyes! Hand it over!"

A dead, ominous silence was his only answer.

"Very well! Deputy-director, march gang No. 79 round to the bath-room; strip, and let every man be searched from head to foot; then bring me the letter!" And so saying, he retired.

When the men heard the deputy-director give the command, "Right about face! Quick march!" they instantly obeyed; but when they reached the bath-room, and were ordered to strip, they paused.

"Strip, do you hear? Strip!" cried the chief warder.

They looked at each other; then they looked at him with a stony glare; but no man moved hand or foot—no man spoke. There was a dead silence.

Then the deputy held a whispered colloquy with one of his men, with the result that the latter hastily quitted the bath-room.

The men still remained at "attention," and might have been so many statues.

Four minutes later the Governor returned in person.

"What's this I hear? Refuse obedience to my orders! Strip!—do you hear?—strip! Very well —very well! I shall know what to do to-morrow.

Deputy-director, march these men back to their cells."

Again the word of command was given. Again the men obeyed, and were marched back to their ward and locked up.

Their implacable tyrant followed, growled some order to one of the warders, and paced up and down outside the cells.

Presently the dinner-bell was heard. Tramp, tramp, came the warders, passing by, carrying steaming rations of roast beef and plum-pudding to the prisoners in the other wards.

When the last footfall had died away, and the delicious odours had permeated every cell of the Devil's Own, the Governor said in a hard voice, " Now, men, will you produce that letter ? "

Silence was still his only answer.

"Very well, then ! Officer, serve out to these men rations of bread and water for their Christmas dinner. Perhaps that may bring them to their senses."

This barbarous order broke the silence, and, as the Governor passed down the avenue, a howl burst on either side as if it had risen from opposite cages of wild beasts. The warders in charge vainly tried to obtain silence ; they were overpowered by a torrent of execrations.

At last they locked the cells, and returned to their Christmas dinners. Then Ginger appeared upon the scene. How it was he was not locked up no one could understand, but there was collusion somewhere. He had obtained—stolen, most likely —from the kitchen one or two grills of beef and pudding, which he conveyed to Jack and Fitzherbert, and one or two other favourite persons. He had also got a quantity of tobacco and methylated spirit; one or the other, sometimes both, were thrust under the door of every cell. At first the men were soothed by the unwonted stimulant, and, in nearly every case, they sank into a stupid torpor of sleep.

Night fell soon. When the gas was lighted in the corridor, empty and hungry stomachs began to assert themselves. By-and-by came strains of distant music, and sounds of laughter from the Governor's quarters, from the officers' quarters, from the warders' quarters. Evidently these gentlemen are keeping Christmas.

Pleasant this for hungry and empty men !

It wanted some four hours for the time fixed for the escape. Jack Heywood and Fitzherbert were in a fever. Still more music—more laughter from within and without. The prisoners became angry, then they became furious.

Presently a merry ballad is heard from the Governor's quarters. In reply, a ruffian, with a stentorian voice, roars out a ribald song, and every man from every cell roars forth the chorus. The sound is taken up in the next ward, and the next, and the next, till it arises to one infernal roar, which rings through every ward.

The man on guard summoned the principal

night warder, who in his turn summoned his men.
Cell after cell was opened; innocent or guilty were
dragged out and flung, neck and crop, into the
punishment cells. Instead of allaying the blood-
fever, this brutality made it worse. Half-drunken
officers were summoned from the song and dance,
from the wassail bowl and the yule log. Cells
were unlocked, refractory men — not without
desperate hand struggles—were beaten into sense-
lessness, and flung, head foremost, into punishment cells, while the torrent of groans, and
shrieks, and shouts of "Murder!" made night
hideous. Amidst this foretaste of Pandemonium,
the Governor made his appearance in evening
dress.

In vain he tried to make himself heard above
the din.

At last, during a momentary pause, he roared
out, "A mutiny!"

Then he wheeled round, and telephoned to the
town for soldiers.

Meanwhile, the rebels remained rebellious. More
cells were thrown open, more men were dragged
out and punished. It was difficult to say which
was the maddest, the prisoners or the gaolers.

Suddenly a stentorian voice shouted out from
the main corridor, "Burn the d—d place down—
burn it! We can die but once, any how!"

A thousand voices responded in a hoarse chorus,
"Tear down the gas—burn the prison!"

The frantic prisoners were in the act of carrying

out this threat, the confusion was worse confounded, the tumult was at its height, when the
tramp of soldiers were heard in the distance. It
came nearer and nearer. A cry of " Halt ! " was
heard ; the tramp ceased. Then, locks, bolts, and
bars were heard to fly asunder, and again the word
of command was given.

" Quick march !  This way ! "

Tramp, tramp again, the soldiers filed in the hall
at the double ; and side by side with the Captain,
walked the Governor.

" Halt !  Attention !  Fix bayonets ! "

At this instant, and at the same moment, the
cells of Jack Heywood and Fitzherbert were thrown
rapidly open. They were in the rear of the soldiers and unnoticed.

A friendly voice whispered, " Coast clear !  Now's
your time. Cut away ! "

No further incentive is needed to speed their
fleeting feet. They now carry their lives in their
hands, and are liable to be shot down like dogs.
As they reach the outer gate, the porter, who has
been squared, occupies himself in leisurely lower-
ing the portcullis ; but an assistant, called in at
the last moment, catches sight of the convicts,
rings the alarm bell, and shrieks out, " Prisoners
escaping through the portcullis ! "

The signal is responded to, and a non-com-
missioned officer and half a dozen soldiers come
dashing up. The portcullis had just dropped to
the ground, but although it interposed for the

moment a barrier between the pursued and the pursuers, unfortunately it interposed no barrier to the pursuers' rifles. The moon, too, was at its full, and lighted up every movement of the fugitives, who were half-way down the zig-zag path, below which the boat was concealed.

"Present! Fire!"

The order is instantly obeyed, and Fitzherbert fell wounded to the ground. But, strong as Hercules, Jack Heywood stooped for a moment, lifted his lifeless comrade upon his shoulder, and again took to his heels down the precipitous side of the cliff.

By this time the soldiers came rushing down the path. They gain the brink of the precipice just as Jack has reached the boat, in which four men are lying to their oars. Jack threw the body of Fitz aboard, leapt in himself, and as he did so a volley of musketry came from the precipice. The bullets whisked harmlessly over his head.

The next moment a thick black cloud obscured the moon, darkness fell upon the scene, and under its cover they were pulling safely down the Channel towards the open sea.

# CHAPTER XXVIII.

## IN BRITTANY.

THE prime mover in this desperate attempt to interfere with legal justice was Algernon, Lord Delamere, and he was aided and abetted by that amiable blackleg, Major Deuceace. Algernon, we may mention, was second cousin to the famous Ned Barnaby, of the Guards, whose escapades in and out of the battlefield were the talk of Europe; and he, like his relation, carried into modern affairs the adventurous spirit of the Middle Ages. Apart from his affection for Fitzherbert, he looked upon the whole affair as a "lark;" but when the Captain, bleeding and unconscious, was brought on board the little cruiser, Delamere, who was waiting on the deck, saw that it was no laughing matter.

No sooner were the men on board than the vessel stood out to sea. Fitzherbert was carried below, and his wounds dressed by Deuceace, who was a bit of a surgeon. When the poor fellow opened his eyes he saw a dear and familiar face bending over him.

"Julia, is it you?" he murmured, gratefully. "Where am I? What has happened? Ah! I remember!" and he again became unconscious.

Julia turned to Deuceace, who stood quietly looking on.

"Will he recover, sir? Are his wounds dangerous?"

"They've peppered him," returned the Major; "but I've stopped the bleeding, and I think there's a chance yet. The cowards! To shoot him in the back, like a dog!"

Sobbing wildly, the girl knelt by her lover, and passionately kissed his hand.

"You'd better not disturb him," said Deuceace, gently. "I think he's sleeping. Poor Fitz! I wish there was a proper sawbones on board, but I've done my best."

"Let me stay with him," pleaded Julia. "I will be very quiet—only do not drive me away!"

Deuceace could do no more; so he left her to her sorrow, and went on deck, where he found Lord Delamere conversing with the other convict, Jack Heywood. The vessel was by this time right out at sea, and heading westward through cloud and rain.

"What's to be done now?" said Delamere, as his friend came up. "A pretty mess we appear to have made of it! By this time the escape will be telegraphed to every station, and we shall have her Majesty's cruisers running the seas in pursuit."

"Penal servitude for every one of us, I suppose!" cried the Major, lighting a cheroot, and looking Jack from head to foot. "I'm afraid, too, poor Fitz is booked!"

"I hope not," returned Delamere. Then, leading Deuceace aside, he whispered, "That fellow is named Heywood, who was convicted for a murder done in Yorkshire. I've told him that his friends were in the job with us, and planked down their money to help us; but, upon my life, it's an ugly business for all concerned!"

Here the captain of the vessel, a squat, thickset man of the Dirk Hatteraick type, came up and joined them.

"Bad look-out, this!" he said. "Which way are we to steer? As sure as Davy Jones, the cruisers will be after us!"

"You knew that before you undertook the job," cried Delamere. "We're all in the same boat; now, old man, what's to be done?"

"We might run along there, and put these lubbers out somewhere in Devon. I know every creek and anchorage there," said the sailor.

"No good," returned his lordship. "The coast-guards will be watching everywhere. No, turn about, and steer for the coast of Brittany. The wind's veering round, and we can run."

The order was obeyed, sullenly enough, for though the men were to receive for the affair enough money to make them independent of the sea for life, they had only just begun to realize the danger of the whole proceeding. Delamere and Deuceace stood smoking and talking together, when Jack Heywood again approached and saluted them.

"You said, gentlemen, that friends of mine helped you. Where are they now?"

"In the town of Weymouth," returned Delamere. "An old man and woman. They did not
tell me, by the way, who you were."

"My name is Heywood," said Jack, drawing
himself up, "and I was unjustly convicted of
murder!"

"So I've just heard," answered my lord, dryly.

"I see you don't believe me," continued Jack;
"but, as God is my Judge, I'm an innocent man.
'Twas the knowledge o' that made me mad sometimes yonder i' prison. But I thank you with all
my heart for what you've done, though what's to
become of me now I don't know."

And he turned aside, to hide the tears that
were streaming down his face.

"Poor devil!" muttered Delamere. "Don't look
like a murderer, either! But, for that matter,"
he added, with a grin, "we're all convicts now. I
say, Deuceace, suppose we hoist the black flag,
and take to piracy. We shall never be able to
return to civilized life again!"

The night passed, and Fitzherbert still sur-
vived, though more or less unconscious of his condition. Fortunately, though there was a strong
north-westerly wind, the sea was comparatively
smooth, and the little vessel sailed gallantly on to
the coast of France. The sailors kept a sharp
look-out, but saw only a few sailing ships and
fishing-boats. Early the next morning, however,
they sighted a large English vessel, which they
recognized as a man-of-war. She passed within

a couple of miles of them, with the English colours
flying, and, for the moment, every man's heart
was in his mouth, but she disappeared presently,
to their infinite relief.

Not until the second morning did they sight the
Breton coast. Creeping close in the morning grey,
they found themselves in the neighbourhood of a
small fishing village at the mouth of a river. The
shallows thereabouts were very dangerous, and
they had constantly to take soundings.

"Know where you are?" asked Delamere of
the captain.

"All right, my lord," was the reply. "Been
here before with a cargo."

"We must get the wounded man ashore as soon
as possible," continued Delamere. "I think we're
safe here."

It was decided, however, that both Fitzherbert
and Heywood should exchange their prison dresses
for a couple of rough suits purchased of the sailors.
As the vessel ran in towards the mouth of the
river, the change was effected—not without some
inconvenience and pain to poor Fitzherbert. Then
the anchor was run down, and a boat was lowered.
While they were bringing Fitzherbert on deck,
Delamere took the sailors aside, and paid them
their money out of a heavy bag of gold.

"What shall you do now?" he asked the
captain.

The sea-dog grinned, and jingled the money in
his pockets.

"Run down to Brest, and go on the spree," he replied.

"I needn't ask you fellows to keep quiet," said his lordship. "No one knows of this business but ourselves, and we're all equally culpable. So mum's the word!"

A couple of hours later Fitzherbert was lying in bed, in a small village inn, half-farm, half-cabaret. His friends had brought a French surgeon to him, who, after carefully examining his wounds, pronounced that with care he might possibly recover. It was a very bad case, however; and by this time the patient was tossing about deliriously, in a state of violent fever. Julia O'Gallagher sat by the bedside, eager to nurse him back to life.

"If you knew—if you knew!" she sobbed. "Oh, gentlemen, it was all my father's doing! Your friend was too noble to say a word in his own defence. He was silent that he might spare me pain!"

"Poor Fitz!" muttered Delamere, dashing away a tear. "He was always staunch, wasn't he, Deuceace?"

"Rather!" said the Major. "Well, he's got a good nurse, at any rate."

They left Julia alone with the patient, and walked down to the window. Here they found Jack Heywood, dressed in his sailor's suit, and looking sadly out to sea.

"How is he, gentlemen?" asked Jack.

"Much the same. Sawbones thinks he may pull round."

"It's very strange that we should be here together," continued Jack. "I saw him once or twice in prison, and recognized him directly. He was a great friend of Ralph Hollis, of Deepdale."

"Now Earl Beauchamp," said Delamere. "Yes, that's right enough. Beauchamp and he have always been close pals."

"I met them together at Doncaster t' very night before t' murder," continued Jack; and as he proceeded, he fell from excitement into the old familiar Yorkshire dialect. "I had gotten more drink than was good for me, and I ha' sometimes thought they two played me a scurvy trick. Anyhow, after I had drank wi' Hollis and t' Captain, I lost my senses. When I got them again, I was a prisoner in t' gaol, accused o' killing t' best man that ever lived—t' man I loved best of all men in t' world—my poor foster-father, Jabez Pryke."

The two gentlemen looked at him in wonder, for his voice was choked with tears, and he was sobbing like a child.

"Jabez is yonder up i' heaven," he cried, lifting his hands, "and he knows—God bless him!—that I loved him dear. I couldna have done 't! I couldna have raised a hand to harm Jabez! But 'tis all a blank still 'tween the time when I drank wi' those chaps and the time I were a prisoner in gaol!"

"You were drunk, you see," suggested Delamere. "At any rate, I'm sure poor Fitz would never play you a scurvy trick, as you call it."

And he turned on his heel, and walked towards the shore with Deuceace. Though capable of doing so much for a comrade of his own set, he had little or no sympathy with the criminal classes, and in his eyes Jack was a commonplace convict.

"Queer, ain't it?" he muttered. "Well, it's a queer world!"

"Doocid queer!" chimed in Deuceace, who was no more eloquent than his friend.

Jack watched them, and his heart swelled indignantly, for he felt that they did not believe a word of his story. He was a free man, but the taint of the prison was still upon him, the shadow of a hideous crime. What was he to do? He had escaped, but he was still an outcast. He thought of his faithful old friends, of Rachel Dene. How was he to communicate with them? Would he ever see them again? Better, far better, he thought, if the bullets had struck him instead of the other, and he had died at the moment of his escape.

While he stood in despair, the two gentlemen returned.

"We've been talking it over," said Delamere. "We think you'd better not stay here. Your best plan, if you don't want to get caught again, is to make tracks for America."

"I have no money," answered Jack.

T

"I'll get that all right. I'll lend you fifty pounds."

"Why do you want me to go, my lord ? Can't I stay here a while, and see if that poor chap gets better ? "

"It isn't safe," replied Delamere. "There is certain to be a bother, and I rather fancy the extradition treaty would be put in operation as soon as our hiding-place is discovered. Now we can manage to cook up some story about the sick man ; but if you hang about, it might get us into trouble."

"Very well, my lord," said Jack, sturdily. "I see what it is : you want to get rid of me, because in the eyes of t' law I'm a murderer and a scoundrel! But I'll go—I'll go ! "

"The best thing you can do. Here's the money ! " He placed some notes and gold in Jack's hand ; then, turning to Deuceace with a laugh, he added, "I say, old man, I'm nearly cleared out ! I never told you how they stared at Coutts's when I handed in my cheque and asked for a thousand pounds in fivers. I shall consider it a cheap investment if we pull poor Fitz round."

It was now growing late in the afternoon. On inquiry, Jack ascertained that a diligence would leave the village at midnight, with Brest for its destination ; and by that diligence he arranged to depart. He would doubtless find a vessel at Brest to take him on to the Far West. As soon as the arrangements were made, he again sought out

Delamere and Deuceace, who were sitting in the little *café* attached to the inn.

"Only one favour before I go, gentlemen," he said. "I want to have one last look at t' poor chap upstairs."

"Very well," replied his lordship. "Only you must not speak to him; he is to be kept quiet."

They went upstairs together and knocked at the bedroom door. Julia O'Gallagher, pale and calm as any sister of mercy, let them in.

"He is very restless," she whispered. "I have given him the doctor's draught, but it does not seem to do him good."

They approached the bedside. Fitzherbert lay on his back, his eyes wide open, breathing heavily as if in pain.

"Poor chap!—poor chap!" murmured Jack, looking down upon him.

At that moment the wounded man gave a start, and turned his head. His eyes looked straight into Julia's face.

"Who's that?" he cried.

"It's me—Jack Heywood," answered Jack, with a sob, "who was with you in t' prison. Don't you know me, Captain? I met you long ago wi' Ralph Hollis, at Doncaster."

"Come away, man," said Delamere, taking Jack by the arm.

But before they could leave the room Fitzherbert called them back.

"Stop! Don't go!" he cried. "I remember

now. Come here, I say. It's all coming back
upon me before I die. Give me some brandy—
quick!"

Julia glanced at Deuceace, who nodded assent,
and bending gently over him, she wet his lips with
spirits and water. He was quite conscious now,
and sensible. Haggard and wild, panting for
breath, he waved to Jack and the others, beckoning them to the bedside.

"Ah, Algy, old man! God bless you for what
you've done; but it's no use—no use! I'm going!"

"No, no!" sobbed Julia. "Calm yourself,
dear; you'll soon be well."

"I shall never be well again," he answered,
reaching out for her hand. "My poor Julia!
God will look after you when I am gone. Algy,
old man, I loved her—remember that!"

"I'll remember," replied Delamere, almost
breaking down.

"But I can't die till I've told you the God's
truth. You see that man? Look at him! God
brought us together, and punished me. Listen,
all of you. You *shall* listen! We met him at
Doncaster, Ralph Hollis and I, and doctored his
drink. Next day we heard he had been taken up
for murder. I thought him guilty, for he was
taken red-handed with the murdered man. It was
a lie! He didn't do it! He was as innocent as I
was, poor devil! I wouldn't have let him hang,
but I let him go to a fate worse than hanging.
God forgive me!—God forgive me!"

In his wild frenzy of truth-telling, Fitzherbert sat up in the bed, his eyes fixed on Jack, his mouth twitching as if with palsy.

"Come away," said Delamere; "it's killing him! Lie down, old fellow, and go to sleep."

"*No!*" said Fitzherbert. "Don't leave me, Algy! Hear all I've got to say! He's innocent, I tell you! I know it, because I had the truth from the other man's own lips. And it wasn't murder, after all! He *swore* it wasn't murder, but an accident!"

"*Who—who* swore it?" exclaimed Jack. "Tell me, for God's sake!"

"Ralph Hollis!" replied Fitzherbert; and he fell, fainting, back upon the bed.

## CHAPTER XXIX.

### A SUNBEAM IN DEEPDALE.

RACHEL DENE sat alone in the drawing-room of the great house at Deepdale.

Her grandfather and grandmother were both away in London, and she was left in solitude, to entertain her own sad thoughts.

The monotony of her life had been broken, only a few days before, by a letter from Joan Heywood, announcing the escape of Jack from Portland, following close upon which had come the sensational accounts in the newspapers of the mutiny in the prison, and the escape of the two prisoners. With a wildly-beating heart, she had read the reports, which culminated in the description of the flight down the shore by night, the wounding of one of the convicts, and the disappearance of both on board an unknown sailing vessel. One of the two had been dangerously hurt. But which of them? The reports didn't tell—the reports did not know. Was it her lover?—or was it his companion? Sick with sympathy and terror, she read the wild record over and over again, but could come to no conclusion.

Later details proved that all the machinery of police had been set to work to trace the fugitives, in vain. The coasts were everywhere patrolled and watched, armed ships were scouring the sea, the hue and cry was out on every side, but the missing vessel had cunningly evaded pursuit. Jack, then, had escaped? But how?—and was he dead or living? Rachel Dene would have given the world to know.

Ralph Hollis was still in the Far West. After some months of salmon-fishing in Canada, he had gone on to Manitoba, and thence across country to Denver and San Francisco. He had written frequently—long letters, to which her grandfather had replied, and in one of which, received only a few weeks past, he had boldly expressed the hope that Rachel might some day become Lady Beauchamp.

Jacob Dene had read her the words, and they seemed so kindly, so respectful, and so loyal, that she was deeply touched; but she had only said, with a sad smile, "Nay, grandpapa, thou knowest I shall never marry."

She had long seen, nevertheless, that the old people were working zealously on Ralph's behalf— a knowledge which would have made her very angry if she had not been completely possessed with the sentiment of the young Earl's kindness in her time of trouble.

In point of fact, Ralph had been on the point of returning to England; had actually taken his passage home by the North German Lloyd line from New York, when he read in the English newspapers an account of Fitzherbert's arrest and conviction. A nameless terror filled him, and he dared not return, lest the only man who knew his secret should involve him in his downfall. No; he would let the thing blow over, and, before sailing, discover if there was any danger. Meeting an old comrade in New York, he went on with him to New Orleans, where he fell back into some of his old habits, and relapsed into gambling and dissipation.

As Rachel sat looking out at the wintry prospect, thinking of Jack, and wondering if he were alive or dead, a knock came to the door, and the waiting-maid brought in a card, saying that a gentleman wished to see her on particular business. She looked at the card and read, "Lord

Delamere," a name quite unfamiliar to her; but she asked the maid to show the visitor into the drawing-room, and as he entered, rose to meet him with characteristic self-possession.

" Good afternoon, Miss Dene," said his lordship, beaming upon her with his good-humoured boyish face. " You must let me apologize for intruding upon you without an introduction. I have come a long way to see you, and am glad to find you at home." Then, seeing her look of surprise, he added, " I've often heard of you, Miss Dene, from one whom you know very well."

" Indeed ! " said Rachel, wondering still more. " Prithee, sit down."

Delamere took a chair, and became a little confused and nervous—a very unusual circumstance with one generally so cool. He fidgeted with his hat, dropped his umbrella, and all the time kept his eyes fixed nervously on the young girl's face.

" Can you keep a secret ? " he said, at last.

" I hope so," she answered, smiling.

" Because," he continued, smiling also, " I'm going to place myself in your power. If the police knew what I am going to tell *you*, I should very likely wear a sample of steel bracelets before to-morrow morning. I've broken the laws, my dear Miss Dene, in an awful way. I'm a regular criminal, egad ! "

She gazed at him with fresh wonder, and began

to think that he was, at least, very eccentric. He
certainly did not look like a criminal, though, for
his face was the picture of indolent good humour.
His next words startled her, and her colour came
and went wildly as he spoke them.

"Have you read in the papers of that affair at
Portland?"

"The escape from prison?" she cried. "Yes,
yes!"

"Well, you'll hardly believe it, but *I* was in it,
and that is what has brought me here."

Rachel rose to her feet with a cry.

"Thou hast news of Jack—of Mr. Heywood?
Tell me quickly, is he alive or dead?"

"Make your mind easy. He is very much
alive."

"But one was wounded. I have been in terror
ever since lest——"

"It was not *your* friend whom the rascals shot
down," said Lord Delamere; "it was poor Fitz,
my chum—the best fellow in the world! We
planned their escape. It was well managed; but
poor Fitz got his quietus. He's—he's dead!"

And the speaker drew his hand across his eyes,
while his hearty face grew sad and clouded.

"But I gave him a promise before he died,"
continued Delamere to Rachel, who scarcely heard
him, for she was weeping joyfully, and gazing
silently. "I gave him a promise, and I'm going to
keep it. With his dying breath, Miss Dene, he
cleared an innocent man; more than that, he had

everything set down, and legally witnessed, and
signed it with his own hand."

"What dost thou mean?" cried Rachel.   He
said—he said—— "

" That young Heywood was no murderer.   That
the murder—it wasn't murder, though—was done
by some one else."

" I knew it—I knew it !   Oh, thank God—thank
God ! "

At the joyful news, all her love sprang up like a
fountain, and she wept like a child.   As she tried
to dry her eyes, she glanced towards the door, and
uttered a wild cry.   On the threshold of the room,
framed in the doorway, stood a pale, bearded man,
looking at her.   He wore a rough sailor's suit, and
was otherwise much changed ; but she knew him
in a moment.

" Jack ! " she cried ; and he sprang forward and
caught her in his arms as she fainted away.

When she recovered she was lying on the sofa,
and Jack—the same kind, gentle Jack of old—was
bending over her.

"Forgive me, Rachel ! " he said.   "I thought
you would be glad to see me again, and I think
you were ; but I'd no right to take thee by surprise like that, my lass.   I've come all the way to
Deepdale to see thee, and tell thee some good news."

She blushed and shrank away, for in a moment
of joyful impulse she had revealed her whole heart
to the man who had scarcely ever dared to speak
to her of love.

"Thou canst prove thy innocence," she said.
" Oh, I am so glad, so glad ! "

The man's face saddened.

" Maybe, lass ; when 'tis all proved, you'll be a
bit sorry too ; and I'm in trouble still. The
hue and cry is out after me, and if the police
knew I was here, they would take me back to
gaol."

She looked round. The room was empty, for
Lord Delamere had discreetly retired. She sprang
up, and closed the door.

" Take thee ? But thou art innocent ! Ah, I
knew it ! "

" I'll have to *prove* it, my lass," said Jack, " and
that'll cause more sore hearts than one. But
there, let me look at thee ! Let me see the sweet
face I ha' dreamed of so many nights i' my
trouble ! I ha' had a bad time, my lass, since last
we met, but I'd go through it all again right gladly
to be sure o' one thing, and that one thing's thy
love ! "

He held her in his arms, and she didn't offer
any resistance. Their lips met for one moment
of supreme happiness. Then she looked up, and
whispered, " I *knew* thou wouldst come back to
me, Jack ! "

" Call me that again," he said.

" Jack—dear Jack ! "

" I was right, after all. You do love me,
then ? "

" I have loved thee always, I think ! "

"Always?"

"At least, as long as I can remember. Most of all, Jack, in thy great trouble."

There was a gentle tap at the door. Lord Delamere walked in, smiling.

"Sorry to intrude, my lad, but we must get back to London. My dear Miss Dene, make your mind easy. Heywood here is going to walk right back into the lion's mouth, but he won't stay there. We'll prove he's innocent, right up to the hilt, egad!"

And he took Jack's hand.

"This is our best friend," Jack cried. "We mustn't get him into trouble. No man must know how it all came about."

Jack Heywood proceeded straight to London and surrendered himself to the authorities, while Lord Delamere went off to his friend the great criminal lawyer, and put the whole matter in his hands. A white lie was necessary to free Delamere and Deuceace from complicity in the escape from Portland, so it was suggested that the two gentlemen, when rambling in Brittany, had found Fitzherbert at the point of death, and by the merest accident received his last confession. Suspicion pointed to them as agents in the escape, but proof was difficult, not to say impossible. But money and influence in plenty were brought to bear on the authorities. In a very short time Jack's innocence was proved, and a warrant issued for the arrest of Ralph Hollis, Lord Beauchamp.

That warrant, however, was never executed. On the very day of its issue, information was received by cable that an English peer, Earl Beauchamp, had been shot dead in a gambling affray at New Orleans. The shock of the news killed his mother. She was thus spared the knowledge of her son's great crime. Further details confirmed the cable report, and added shocking particulars, with which we decline to trouble the reader.

Jack Heywood walked forth into the sunshine, a free man. His first impulse was to go to Lord Delamere, and thank that kindly peer for all his goodness. He found his lordship in the smoking-room of the club, in company with Major Deuceace. They were looking sorrowfully at a letter, which ran as follows :—

" DEAR LORD DELAMERE,

" I am leaving England for India. Before I go I wish to send you my last adieux, for we shall never meet again. God will reward you for your loyalty to your friend, the man I loved, and shall love until I die. I do not mourn him; I am too proud, too glad. He died like an English gentleman, and was happier in such a death than in his life.

" Yours always truly,
" JULIA O'GALLAGHER.'

"Poor Fitz!" said Delamere, folding up the letter.

" Poor Fitz!" echoed Deuceace.

Then they shook hands with Jack, and asked him to join them in a brandy and soda. He declined, saying he had sworn off strong drink for ever, but took some lemonade.

"I say, you're wanted in Yorkshire," said Lord Delamere, smiling.

Jack laughed, and wrung the gentlemen's hands. He would have hugged them both. Then he rushed from the room, almost crying.

"Queer world!" soliloquized Delamere.

" D—d queer!" echoed the gallant Major.

" Poor Fitz!"

" Poor Fitz!"

Then both gentlemen looked at each other dolefully.

" Can't stand this," said Algernon, Lord Delamere. "Ring the bell! Here, waiter, bring me some more brandy and soda."

Our tale is told. If the reader demands any further sequel, let him betake himself some day to the happy and prosperous valley of Deepdale. There he will learn, what he already guesses, that John Heywood, once tried and convicted for murder, reigns where Jacob Dene reigned, and is now, thanks partly to the great invention, the richest manufacturer in Yorkshire; and that his wife Rachel, once Rachel Dene, is his fit helpmate, his companion in all things noble, and the gentle mother of his many children. So the dark cloud turned, and the silver lining shone out upon the night at last.

THE END.

PRINTED BY WILLIAM CLOWES AND SONS, LIMITED,
LONDON AND BECCLES.

# ALPHABETICAL CATALOGUE OF BOOKS
### IN
# GENERAL LITERATURE AND FICTION
#### PUBLISHED BY

[JAN.]   CHATTO & WINDUS   [1915]

### 111 ST. MARTIN'S LANE, CHARING CROSS

*Telegrams*
*Bookstore, London*      LONDON, W.C.      *Telephone No.*
1624 *Gerrard*

---

**ADAMS (W. DAVENPORT).—**
**A Dictionary of the Drama:** A Guide to the Plays, Playwrights, Players, and Playhouses of the United Kingdom and America, from the Earliest Times to the Present. Vol. I. (A to G). Demy 8vo, cloth, 10s. 6d. net.

**ALMAZ (E. F.).—Copper under the Gold.** Crown 8vo, cloth, 3s. 6d.

**ALLEN (GRANT), Books by.**
Crown 8vo, cloth, 3s. 6d. each ; post 8vo, illustrated boards, 2s. each.
**Babylon.** With 12 Illustrations.
**Strange Stories.**
**The Beckoning Hand.**
**For Maimie's Sake.**
**Philistia.**   |   **In all Shades.**
**The Devil's Die.** | **Tents of Shem.**
**This Mortal Coil.**
**Dumaresq's Daughter.**
**Under Sealed Orders.**
**The Duchess of Powysland.**
**Blood Royal.** | **The Great Taboo.**
**Ivan Greet's Masterpiece.**
**The Scallywag.** With 24 Illustrations.
**At Market Value.**

**Dumaresq's Daughter.** Crown 8vo, cloth, 1s. net.
**The Tents of Shem.** POPULAR EDITION, medium 8vo, 6d.

**ALEXANDER (Mrs.), Novels by.**
Crown 8vo, cloth, 3s. 6d. each ; post 8vo, picture boards, 2s. each.
**Valerie's Fate.** | **Mona's Choice.**
**A Life Interest.** | **Woman's Wit.**
**Blind Fate.**

Crown 8vo, cloth, 3s. 6d. each.
**The Cost of her Pride.**
**A Golden Autumn.**
**Barbara, Lady's Maid & Peeress.**
**Mrs. Crichton's Creditor.**
**A Missing Hero.**
**A Fight with Fate.**
**The Step-mother.**

**ANDERSON (MARY).—Othello's Occupation.** Crown 8vo, cloth, 2s. 6d.

**ANTROBUS (C. L.), Novels by.**
Crown 8vo, cloth, 3s. 6d. each.
**Quality Corner.** | **Wildersmoor**
**The Wine of Finvarra.**

**The Stone Ezel.** Crown 8vo, cloth, 6s.

---

**ART : A Critical Essay.** By CLIVE BELL. With 6 Illustrations. Crown 8vo, buckram, 5s. net.

**APPLETON (G. W.).—Rash Conclusions.** Crown 8vo, cloth, 3s. 6d.

**ARNOLD (E. L.), Stories by.**
**The Wonderful Adventures of Phra the Phœnician.** Crown 8vo, cloth, with 12 Illusts, by H. M. PAGET, 3s. 6d. : post 8vo, illustrated boards, 2s.
**The Constable of St. Nicholas.** With a Frontispiece. Crown 8vo, cloth, 3s. 6d. ; picture cloth, flat back, 2s.

**ART and LETTERS LIBRARY**
(The) Large crown 8vo. Each volume with 8 Coloured Plates, and 24 in Half-tone. Bound in cloth, 5s. net per vol. EDITION DE LUXE, small 4to, printed on pure rag paper, with additional Plates, parchment, 10s. 6d. net per vol.
**Stories of the Italian Artists from Vasari.** Collected and arranged by E. L. SEELEY.
**Artists of the Italian Renaissance:** their Stories as set forth by Vasari, Ridolfi, Lanzi, and the Chroniclers. Collected and arranged by E. L. SEELEY.
**Stories of the Flemish and Dutch Artists,** from the Time of the Van Eycks to the End of the Seventeenth Century, drawn from Contemporary Records. Collected and arranged by VICTOR REYNOLDS.
**Stories of the English Artists,** from Van Dyck to Turner (1600-1851). Collected and arranged by RANDALL DAVIES and CECIL HUNT.
**Stories of the French Artists,** from Clouet to Delacroix. Collected and arranged by P. M. TURNER and C. H. COLLINS BAKER.
**Stories of the Spanish Artists** until GOYA. By Sir WILLIAM STIRLING-MAXWELL. Selected and arranged by LUIS CARREÑO. With Introduction by EDWARD HUTTON.
**Stories of the German Artists.** By Prof. Dr. HANS W. SINGER.
**The Little Flowers of S. Francis of Assisi.** Translated by Prof. T. W. ARNOLD. With 8 Illustrations in Colour and 24 in Half-tone.

1

**ART & LETTERS LIBRARY**—*contd.*
**Of the Imitation of Christ.** By
THOMAS À KEMPIS. Translated by
RICHARD WHYTFORD. With Historical
Introduction by WILFRID RAYNAL,
O.S.B., and 8 Reproductions in Colour
and other decorations by W. RUSSELL
FLINT. The EDITION DE LUXE has four
additional Plates in Colour and may be
had bound in pigskin with clasps. 25s. net.
**The Confessions of Saint Augustine.** Translated by Dr. E. B. PUSEY.
Edited by TEMPLE SCOTT. With an Introduction by Mrs. MEYNELL, and 12
Plates in Colour by MAXWELL ARMFIELD.
The EDITION DE LUXE may be had bound
in pigskin with clasps. 25s. net.
**The Master of Game:** The Oldest
English book on Hunting. By EDWARD,
Second Duke of York. Edited by W. A.
and F. BAILLIE-GROHMAN. Introduction
by THEODORE ROOSEVELT, Photogravure
Frontispiece and 23 full-page Illustrations.
Large crown 8vo, cloth, 7s. 6d. net ;
parchment, 10s. 6d. net.

**ARTEMUS WARD'S Works.**
Crown 8vo, cloth, with Portrait, 3s. 6d. ;
post 8vo, illustrated boards, 2s.

**ARTIST (The Mind of the).**
Edited by Mrs. LAURENCE BINYON. With
8 Plates. Small cr. 8vo, cloth, 3s. 6d. net.

**ASHTON (JOHN).—Social Life
in the Reign of Queen Anne.** With
85 Illustrations. Crown 8vo cloth, 3s. 6d.

**AUSTEN (JANE), The Works of,**
in Ten Volumes, each containing Ten
Illustrations in Colour by A. WALLIS
MILLS. With Notes by R. BRIMLEY
JOHNSON. Post 8vo, cloth, 3s. 6d. net per
vol. The Novels are as follows : I. and
II., PRIDE AND PREJUDICE ; III.
and IV., SENSE AND SENSIBILITY ;
V., NORTHANGER ABBEY ; VI., PERSUASION : VII. and VIII., EMMA ;
IX. and X., MANSFIELD PARK.

**AUTHORS for the POCKET.**
Choice Passages, mostly selected by
A. H. HYATT. 16mo, cloth, 2s. net each ;
leather, 3s. net each.
**The Pocket R. L. S.**
**The Pocket George Borrow.**
**The Pocket Thackeray.**
**The Pocket Charles Dickens.**
**The Pocket Richard Jefferies.**
**The Pocket George MacDonald.**
**The Pocket Emerson.**
**The Pocket Thomas Hardy.**
**The Pocket George Eliot.**
**The Pocket Charles Kingsley.**
**The Pocket Ruskin.**
**The Pocket Lord Beaconsfield.**
**The Flower of the Mind.**

**AUZIAS - TURENNE (RAYMOND).—The Last of the Mammoths:** A Romance. Cr. 8vo, cl., 3s. 6d.

**AYESHA (MARION).—The
Truth about a Nunnery.:** Five Years
in a Convent School. Cr. 8vo, cloth, 6s.

**AYSCOUGH (JOHN), Novels by.**
Crown 8vo, cloth, 6s. each.
**Prodigals and Sons.**
**Outsiders—and In.**
**Mezzogiorno.** | **Hurdcott.**
**Monksbridge.** | **Faustula.**
**Marotz.** Crown 8vo, cloth, 2s. net.

**BACTERIA, Yeast Fungi, and
Allied Species, A Synopsis of.** By
W. B. GROVE, B.A. With 87 Illustrations.
Crown 8vo, cloth, 3s. 6d.

**BAILDON (H. B.). — Robert
Louis Stevenson:** A Study. With 2
Portraits. Crown 8vo, buckram, 6s.

**BALLADS and LYRICS of LOVE,**
selected from PERCY'S 'Reliques.' Edited
with an Introduction by F. SIDGWICK.
With 10 Plates in Colour after BYAM
SHAW, R.I. Large fcap. 4to, cloth, 6s. net.
**Legendary Ballads,** selected from
PERCY'S 'Reliques.' Edited with an
Introduction by F. SIDGWICK. With 10
Plates in Colour after BYAM SHAW, R.I.
Large fcap. 4to, cloth, 6s. net.
\*\*\* The above 2 volumes may also be had in
the ST. MARTIN'S LIBRARY, pott 8vo, cloth, gilt
top, 2s. net each; leather, gilt edges, 3s. net each.

**BARDSLEY (Rev. C. W.).—
English Surnames:** Their Sources
and Significations. Cr. 8vo, cloth, 7s. 6d.

**BARGAIN BOOK (The).** By C. E.
JERNINGHAM and LEWIS BETTANY. With
9 Illustrations and 9 Tabular Charts.
Demy 8vo, cloth, 7s. 6d. net.

**BARING-GOULD (S.), Novels by.**
Crown 8vo, cloth, 3s. 6d. each ; post 8vo,
illustrated boards, 2s. each ; POPULAR
EDITIONS, medium 8vo, 6d. each.
**Red Spider.** | **Eve.**

**BARKER (E. HARRISON).—A
British Dog in France:** his Adventures in Divers places, and conversations
with French Dogs. 43 Illustrations
by L. R. BRIGHTWELL. Large crown
8vo, cloth, 6s. net.

**BARKER (ELSA).—The Son of
Mary Bethel.** Crown 8vo, cloth, 6s.

**BARR (AMELIA E.).—Love will
Venture in.** Crown 8vo, cloth, 3s. 6d. ;
CHEAP EDITION, cloth, 1s. net.

**BARR (ROBERT), Stories by.**
Crown 8vo, cloth, 3s. 6d. each.
**In a Steamer Chair.** With 2 Illusts.
**From Whose Bourne,** &c. With 47
Illustrations by HAL HURST and others.
**Revenge!** With 12 Illustrations by
LANCELOT SPEED and others.
**A Woman Intervenes.**
**A Prince of Good Fellows.** With
15 Illustrations by E. J. SULLIVAN.
**The Unchanging East.**
**The Speculations of John Steele.**
Crown 8vo, cloth, 3s. 6d. ; POPULAR
EDITION, medium 8vo, 6d.

2

**BARRETT (FRANK), Novels by.**
Post 8vo, illust. bds., 2s. ea.; cl., 2s. 6d. ea.
The Sin of Olga Zassoulich.
Little Lady Linton.
John Ford; and His Helpmate.
A Recoiling Vengeance.
Honest Davie. | Lieut. Barnabas.
Cr. 8vo, cloth, 3s. 6d. each; post 8vo, illust.
boards, 2s. each; cloth limp, 2s. 6d. each.
Found Guilty. | Folly Morrison.
For Love and Honour.
Between Life and Death.
Fettered for Life.
A Missing Witness. With 8 Illusts.
The Woman of the Iron Bracelets.
The Harding Scandal.
A Prodigal's Progress.
Crown 8vo, cloth, 3s. 6d. each.
Under a Strange Mask. 19 Illusts.
Was She Justified? | Lady Judas.
The Obliging Husband.
Perfidious Lydia. With Frontispiece.
POPULAR EDITIONS. Medium 8vo, 6d. each.
Fettered for Life. | Found Guilty.
The Error of Her Ways. Crown 8vo,
cloth. 3s. 6d.; CHEAP EDITION. cl. 1s. net

**BARRINGTON (MICHAEL),**
Novels by.
The Knight of the Golden Sword.
Crown 8vo, cloth. 6s.
The Lady of Tripoli. With Illustrations. Crown 8vo: buckram gilt, 5s.

**BASKERVILLE (JOHN).** By
RALPH STRAUS and R. K. DENT. With
13 Plates. Quarto, buckram. 21s. net.

**BATH (The) in Skin Diseases.**
By I. I. MILTON. Post 8vo. 1s.: cl., 1s. 6d.

**BAYEUX TAPESTRY, The Book**
of the. By HILAIRE BELLOC. With 76
facsimile Coloured Illustrations. Royal
8vo, cloth, 10s. 6d. net.

**BEACONSFIELD, LORD.** By T.
P. O'CONNOR, M.P. Crown 8vo, cloth, 5s.
The Pocket Beaconsfield. 16mo,
cloth gilt, 2s. net.; leather gilt, 3s. net.

**BEARD (JOHN, D.Sc.).— The**
Enzyme Treatment of Cancer.
With Illusts. Demy 8vo, cl. 7s. 6d. net.

**BENNETT (ARNOLD), Novels**
by. Crown 8vo, cloth. 3s. 6d. each.
Leonora. | A Great Man.
Teresa of Watling Street.
Tales of the Five Towns. | Hugo.
Sacred and Profane Love.
The Gates of Wrath.
The Ghost. | The City of Pleasure.
The Grand Babylon Hotel.
Leonora. POPULAR EDITION, 2s. net.
POPULAR EDITIONS. medium 8vo, 6d. each.
The Grand Babylon Hotel.
The City of Pleasure. | Hugo.
Sacred and Profane Love.
A Great Man. | Leonora.
CHEAPER EDITIONS, cr. 8vo 1s net each.
Sacred and Profane Love.
The Ghost.

**BELL (CLIVE). Art: a Critical**
Essay. With 6 Illustrations. Cr. 8vo,
buckram, 5s. net.

**BELLOC (HILAIRE). The Book**
of the Bayeux Tapestry. With 76
facsimile Coloured Illustrations. Royal
8vo, cloth, 10s. 6d. net.

**BENNETT (W. C.).—Songs for**
Sailors. Post 8vo, cloth, 2s.

**BESANT and RICE, Novels by.**
Cr. 8vo, cloth, 3s. 6d. each; post 8vo,
illust. bds. 2s. each; cl. limp, 2s. 6d. each.
Ready-Money Mortiboy.
The Golden Butterfly.
My Little Girl.
With Harp and Crown.
This Son of Vulcan.
The Monks of Thelema.
By Celia's Arbour.
The Chaplain of the Fleet
The Seamy Side.
The Case of Mr. Lucraft.
'Twas in Trafalgar's Bay.
The Ten Years' Tenant.

**BESANT (Sir WALTER),**
Novels by. Crown 8vo, cloth, 3s. 6d.
each; post 8vo, illustrated boards, 2s.
each; cloth limp, 2s. 6d. each.
All Sorts and Conditions of Men.
With 12 Illustrations by FRED. BARNARD.
The Captains' Room, &c.
All in a Garden Fair. With 6 Illustrations by HARRY FURNISS.
Dorothy Forster. With Frontispiece.
Uncle Jack, and other Stories.
Children of Gibeon.
The World Went Very Well Then.
With 12 Illustrations by A. FORESTIER.
Herr Paulus.
The Bell of St. Paul's.
For Faith and Freedom. With
Illusts. by A. FORESTIER and F. WADDY.
To Call Her Mine, &c. With 9 Illusts.
The Holy Rose, &c. With Frontispiece.
Armorel of Lyonesse. With 12 Illusts.
St. Katherine's by the Tower.
With 12 Illustrations by C. GREEN.
Verbena Camellia Stephanotis.
The Ivory Gate.
The Rebel Queen.
Beyond the Dreams of Avarice.
With 12 Illustrations by W. H. HYDE.
In Deacon's Orders, &c. With Frontis.
The Revolt of Man.
The Master Craftsman.
The City of Refuge.
Crown 8vo, cloth, 3s. 6d. each.
A Fountain Sealed.
The Changeling.
The Fourth Generation.
The Orange Girl. With 8 Illustrations
by F. PEGRAM.
The Alabaster Box.
The Lady of Lynn. With 12 Illustrations by G. DEMAIN-HAMMOND.
No Other Way. With 12 Illustrations.

3

BESANT (Sir Walter)—*continued.*
Crown 8vo. picture cloth, flat back, 2s. each
**St. Katherine's by the Tower.**
**The Rebel Queen.**

FINE PAPER EDITIONS, pott 8vo, cloth gilt,
2s. net each : leather gilt, 3s. net each.
**London. | Westminster.**
**Jerusalem.** (In collaboration with Prof.
E. H. PALMER.)
**Sir Richard Whittington.**
**Gaspard de Coligny.**
**All Sorts and Conditions of Men.**

CHEAP EDITIONS, cr. 8vo, cloth, 1s. net each.
**The Alabaster Box.**
**Verbena Camellia Stephanotis.**
**The Rebel Queen.**
**St. Katherine's by the Tower.**

POPULAR EDITIONS, medium 8vo, 6d. each.
**All Sorts and Conditions of Men.**
**The Golden Butterfly.**
**Ready-Money Mortiboy.**
**By Celia's Arbour.**
**The Chaplain of the Fleet.**
**The Monks of Thelema.**
**The Orange Girl.**
**For Faith and Freedom.**
**Children of Gibeon.**
**Dorothy Forster. | No Other Way.**
**Armorel of Lyonesse.**
**The Lady of Lynn.**
**My Little Girl.**

Demy 8vo, cloth, 5s. net each.
**London.** With 125 Illustrations.
**Westminster.** With Etching by F. S.
WALKER, and 130 Illustrations.
**South London.** With Etching by F. S.
WALKER, and 118 Illustrations.
**East London.** With Etching by F. S.
WALKER, and 56 Illustrations by PHIL
MAY, L. RAVEN HILL, and J. PENNELL.

Crown 8vo, cloth, 3s. 6d. each.
**Fifty Years Ago: 1837-1887.** With
144 Illustrations.
**The Charm,** and other Drawing-room
Plays. 50 Illus. by CHRIS HAMMOND, &c.

**St. Katherine's by the Tower.**
CHEAP EDITION picture cover, 1s. net.
**The Eulogy of Richard Jefferies.**
With Portrait. Crown 8vo, buckram, 6s.
**Art of Fiction.** Fcap. 8vo, cloth, 1s. net.

**BIERCE (AMBROSE).—In the**
Midst of Life. Crown 8vo, cloth, 3s. 6d. :
p. 8vo. bds., 2s. : cr. 8vo, pic. cov. 1s. net

**BINDLOSS (HAROLD),** Novels by.
Crown 8vo, cloth. 3s. 6d. each.
**The Mistress of Bonaventure.**
**Daventry's Daughter.**
**A Sower of Wheat.**
**The Concession-hunters.**

**Ainslie's Ju-ju.** Crown 8vo, cloth,
3s. 6d. ; picture cloth, flat back, 2s.

POPULAR EDITIONS, medium 8vo, 6d. each.
**The Concession-hunters.**
**The Mistress of Bonaventure.**

**BLAKE (WILLIAM): A Critical**
Study by A. C. SWINBURNE. With a
Portrait. Crown 8vo, buckram, 6s. net.
**The Marriage of Heaven and**
Hell, and A Song of Liberty. With
Introduction by F. G. STOKES. A FLOR-
ENCE PRESS BOOK. Cr. 8vo, hand-made
paper, bds., 3s. 6d. net ; parchmt., 5s. net.

**BOCCACCIO.—The Decameron.**
With a Portrait. Pott 8vo, cloth, gilt
top. 2s. net : leather, gilt edges. 3s. net.

**BODKIN (McD., K.C.). — Shil-**
lelagh and Shamrock. Crown
8vo, cloth. 3s. 6d.

**BORDEAUX (HENRI). — The**
Parting of the Ways. Translated by
LOUISE S. HOUGHTON. Cr. 8vo. cl., 6s.

**BORENIUS (TANCRED).—The**
Painters of Vicenza. With 15 full-
page Plates. Demy 8vo., cloth, 7s. 6d. net.

**BORROW (GEORGE), The**
Pocket. Arranged by EDW. THOMAS.
16mo, cloth, 2s. net ; leather, 3s. net.

**BOSSES AND CORBELS OF**
EXETER CATHEDRAL. By E. K.
PRIDEAUX and G. R. HOLT SHAFTO.
With Illusts. Dy. 8vo. cl., 7s. 6d. net.

**BOURGET (PAUL).—A Living**
Lie. Translated by JOHN DE VILLIERS.
Crown 8vo, cloth, 3s. 6d. ; CHEAP
EDITION, picture cover. 1s. net.

**BOYLE (F.).—Chronicles of No-**
Man's Land. Post 8vo, pict. bds., 2s.

**BRAND (JOHN).—Observations**
on Popular Antiquities. With the
Additions of Sir HENRY ELLIS. Crown
8vo, cloth, 3s. 6d.

**BREWER'S (Rev. Dr.) Diction-**
ary.
The Reader's Handbook of Famous
Names in Fiction. Allusions,
References, Proverbs, Plots,
Stories, and Poems. Crown 8vo,
cloth, 3s. 6d. net

**BREWSTER (Sir DAVID),**
Works by. Post 8vo, cloth, 4s. 6d. each.
**More Worlds than One:** Creed of
Philosopher, Hope of Christian. Plates.
**The Martyrs of Science:** GALILEO,
TYCHO BRAHE, and KEPLER.
**Letters on Natural Magic.** With
numerous Illustrations.

**BRIDGE CATECHISM: QUES-**
TIONS AND ANSWERS: Including
the PORTLAND CLUB CODE. By ROBERT
HAMMOND. Fcap. 8vo, cloth, 2s. 6d. net.

**BRIDGE (J. S. C.).—From Island**
to Empire: A History of the Expansion of
England by Force of Arms. With Maps
and Plans. Large crown 8vo, cl., 6s. net ;
also crown 8vo, cloth, 2s. net.

4

## BROWNING'S (ROBT.) POEMS.

Large fcap. 4to, cl., 6s. net ea.; LARGE PAPER EDITION, parchment, 12s. 6d. net each.— Also in the ST. MARTIN'S LIBRARY, pott 8vo, cloth, 2s. net each; leather, 3s. net each.

**Pippa Passes;** and **Men and Women.** With 10 Plates in Colour after E. FORTESCUE BRICKDALE.

**Dramatis Personæ;** and **Dramatic Romances and Lyrics.** With 10 Plates in Colour after E. F. BRICKDALE.

**Browning's Heroines.** By ETHEL COLBURN MAYNE. With Front. & Title in Colour and other Decorations by MAXWELL ARMFIELD. Cr. 8vo, cloth, 6s. net.

## BRYDEN (H. A.).—An Exiled Scot.

With Frontispiece by J. S. CROMPTON, R.I. Crown 8vo, cloth, 3s. 6d.

## BUCHANAN (ROBERT), Poems and Novels by.

**The Complete Poetical Works of Robert Buchanan.** 2 Vols., crown 8vo, buckram. with Portrait Frontispiece to each volume. 12s.

Crown 8vo, cloth, 3s. 6d. each ; post 8vo, illustrated boards, 2s. each.

**The Shadow of the Sword.**
**A Child of Nature.**
**God and the Man.** With 11 Illustrations by F. BARNARD.
**Lady Kilpatrick.**
**The Martyrdom of Madeline.**
**Love Me for Ever.**
**Annan Water.** | **Foxglove Manor.**
**The New Abelard.** | **Rachel Dene.**
**Matt:** A Story of a Caravan.
**The Master of the Mine.**
**The Heir of Linne.**
**Woman and the Man.**

Crown 8vo, cloth, 3s. 6d. each.
**Red and White Heather.**
**Andromeda.**

POPULAR EDITIONS, medium 8vo, 6d. each.
**The Shadow of the Sword.**
**God and the Man.**
**Foxglove Manor.**
**The Martyrdom of Madeline.**

**The Shadow of the Sword.** FINE PAPER EDITION. Pott 8vo, cloth, gilt top, 2s. net ; leather, gilt edges, 3s. net.

**The New Abelard.** Cr. 8vo, cl., 1s. net.

**The Charlatan.** By ROBERT BUCHANAN and HENRY MURRAY. Crown 8vo, cloth, with Frontispiece by T. H. ROBINSON, 3s. 6d. ; post 8vo, illustrated boards, 2s.

## BYZANTINE ENAMELS IN MR. PIERPONT MORGAN'S COLLECTION.

By O. M. DALTON. With Note by ROGER FRY, and Illustrations in Colour. Royal 4to, boards, 7s. 6d. net.

## BRYDGES (HAROLD). — Uncle Sam at Home.

With 91 Illusts. Post 8vo, illust. boards 2s. ; cloth limp, 2s. 6d.

## BURTON (ROBERT). — The Anatomy of Melancholy.

With a Frontispiece. Demy 8vo, cloth. 7s. 6d.

## CAINE (HALL), Novels by.

Crown 8vo, cloth. 3s. 6d. each ; post 8vo, illust. bds. 2s. each ; cl. limp, 2s. 6d. each.

**The Shadow of a Crime.**
**A Son of Hagar.** | **The Deemster.**

Also LIBRARY EDITIONS, crown 8vo, cloth. 6s. each ; POPULAR EDITIONS, picture covers, 6d. each ; and the FINE PAPER EDITION of **The Deemster,** pott 8vo, cloth, 2s. net ; leather, 3s. net.

## CAMBRIDGE FROM WITHIN.

By CHARLES TENNYSON. With 12 Illustrations in Colour and 8 in Sepia by HARRY MORLEY. Demy 8vo, cloth, 7s. 6d. net.

## CAMERON (V. LOVETT).—The Cruise of the 'Black Prince' Privateer.

Cr. 8vo, cloth, with 2 Illusts., 3s. 6d. ; post 8vo. picture boards, 2s.

## CANCER, THE ENZYME TREATMENT OF.

By JOHN BEARD, D.Sc. Demy 8vo, cloth, 7s. 6d. net.

## CANZIANI (ESTELLA), Books by.

**Costumes, Traditions, and Songs of Savoy.** With 50 Illustrations in Colour and some in Line. Demy 4to, cl. gilt, 21s. net ; vellum gilt. 31s. 6d. net.

**Piedmont.** By ESTELLA CANZIANI and ELEANOUR ROHDE. With 52 Illustrations in Colour and many in Line. Demy 4to. cloth, 21s. net.

## CARLYLE (THOMAS).—On the Choice of Books.

Post 8vo, cloth, 1s. 6d.

## CARROLL (LEWIS), Books by.

**Alice in Wonderland.** With 12 Col. and many Line Illus. by MILLICENT SOWERBY. Large cr, 8vo, cl. gilt, 3s. 6d. net.

**Feeding the Mind.** With a Preface by W. H. DRAPER. Post 8vo, boards, 1s. net ; leather, 2s. net.

## CARRUTH (HAYDEN).—The Adventures of Jones.

With 17 Illusts. Fcap. 8vo. picture cover. 1s. ; cloth, 1s. 6d.

## CASTELLANE (MARQUIS DE). —Men and Things of My Time.

Translated by A. TEIXEIRA DE MATTOS. With 13 Portraits. Demy 8vo, cl., 6s. net.

## CHAMBERLAIN (With MR.) IN THE U.S. AND CANADA.

By Sir WILLOUGHBY MAYCOCK. K.C.M.G. With 30 Illusts. Demy 8vo, cloth, 12s. 6d. net.

## CHAPMAN'S (GEORGE) Works.

Vol. I., Plays Complete, Including the Doubtful Ones. — Vol. II., Poems and Minor Translations, with Essay by A. C. SWINBURNE.—Vol. III., Translations of the Iliad and Odyssey. Three Vols., crown 8vo, cloth, 3s. 6d. each.

**CHATFIELD-TAYLOR (H. C.).—**
Goldoni: a Biography. With 16 Illustrations. Demy 8vo, cloth, 16s. net.
**Fame's Pathway.** Cr. 8vo., 6s. cloth.

**CHAUCER for Children: A Golden Key.** By Mrs. H. R. HAWEIS. With 8 Coloured Plates and 30 Woodcuts. Crown 4to, cloth, 3s. 6d.
**Chaucer for Schools.** With the Story of his Times and his Work. By Mrs. H. R. HAWEIS. Demy 8vo, cloth, 2s. 6d.
*.* See also THE KING'S CLASSICS, p. 16.

**CHESNEY (WEATHERBY),** Novels by. Cr. 8vo, cloth, 3s. 6d. each.
**The Cable-man.** | **The Claimant.**
**The Romance of a Queen.**

**CHESS, The Laws and Practice** of; with an Analysis of the Openings. By HOWARD STAUNTON. Edited by R. B. WORMALD. Crown 8vo. cloth, 5s.
**The Minor Tactics of Chess: A** Treatise on the Deployment of the Forces in obedience to Strategic Principle. By F. K. YOUNG and E. C. HOWELL. Long fcap. 8vo, cloth, 2s. 6d.
**The Hastings Chess Tournament,** Aug.-Sept., 1895. With Annotations by PILLSBURY, LASKER, TARRASCH, STEINITZ, SCHIFFERS, TEICHMANN, BARDELEBEN, BLACKBURNE, GUNSBERG, TINSLEY, MASON and ALBIN; also Biographies and Portraits. Edited by H. F. CHESHIRE. Crown 8vo, cloth, 5s.

**CHILD-LOVER'S CALENDAR** (The) for 1915. Illustrated in Colours by AMELIA BOWERLEY. 16mo, picture cloth, 1s. net.

**CHRISTMAS CAROLS, AN-CIENT ENGLISH.** Collected and arranged by EDITH RICKERT. Post 8vo, cloth, 3s. 6d. net. Parchment, 5s. net. See also NEW MEDIEVAL LIBRARY. o. 20.

**CLARE (AUSTIN).—By the Rise** of the River. Crown 8vo, cloth, 3s. 6d

**CLAYTON (MARGARET), Books** for Children by.
**Camping in the Forest.** With 12 Coloured Illusts., and many in Line, by the Author. Fcap 4to, cloth, 3s. 6d. net.
**Amabel and Crispin.** With many Illustrations. Demy 8vo, cloth, 3s. 6d. net.

**CLODD (EDWARD). — Myths** and Dreams. Crown 8vo, cloth, 3s. 6d.

**COBBAN (J. MACLAREN),** Novels by.
**The Cure of Souls.** Post 8vo, illustrated boards, 2s.
**The Red Sultan.** Crown 8vo, cloth, 3s. 6d.; post 8vo, illustrated boards, 2s.
**The Burden of Isabel.** Crown 8vo, cloth, 3s. 6d.

**CLIVE (Mrs. ARCHER), Novels** by. Post 8vo. cl. 3s. 6d. ea; bds, 2s. ea.
**Paul Ferroll.**
**Why Paul Ferroll Killed his Wife.**

**COLLINS (J. CHURTON, M.A.). —Jonathan Swift.** Cr. 8vo, cl., 3s. 6d.

**COLLINS (MORTIMER and FRANCES),** Novels by. Cr. 8vo, cl., 3s. 6d. each; post 8vo, illustd. bds., 2s. each.
**From Midnight to Midnight.**
**You Play me False.**
**Blacksmith and Scholar.**
**The Village Comedy.** | **Frances.**

Post 8vo, illustrated boards, 2s. each.
**Transmigration.**
**A Fight with Fortune.**
**Sweet Anne Page.**
**Sweet and Twenty.**

**COLLINS (WILKIE), Novels by.** Cr. 8vo, cl., 3s. 6d. each; post 8vo, picture boards, 2s. each; cl. limp. 2s. 6d. each.
**Antonina.** | **Basil.** | **Hide and Seek**
**The Woman in White.**
**The Moonstone.** | **Man and Wife.**
**The Dead Secret.** | **After Dark.**
**The Queen of Hearts.**
**No Name** | **My Miscellanies.**
**Armadale.** | **Poor Miss Finch.**
**Miss or Mrs.?** | **The Black Robe.**
**The New Magdalen.**
**Frozen Deep.** | **A Rogue's Life.**
**The Law and the Lady.**
**The Two Destinies.**
**The Haunted Hotel.**
**The Fallen Leaves.**
**Jezebel's Daughter.**
**Heart and Science.** | **"I Say No."**
**The Evil Genius.** | **Little Novels.**
**The Legacy of Cain.** | **Blind Love.**

**The Legacy of Cain.** Crown 8vo, cloth, 1s. net.

POPULAR EDITIONS, medium 8vo, 6d. each.
**Antonina.** | **Poor Miss Finch.**
**The Woman in White.**
**The Law and the Lady.**
**Moonstone.** | **The New Magdalen.**
**The Dead Secret.** | **No Name.**
**Man and Wife** | **Armadale.**
**The Haunted Hotel.** | **Blind Love.**
**The Legacy of Cain.**

**The Woman in White.** LARGE TYPE, FINE PAPER EDITION. Pott 8vo, cloth, gilt top, 2s. net : leather, gilt edges, 3s. net.
**The Frozen Deep.** LARGE TYPE EDIT. Fcap. 8vo. cloth, 1s. net.

**COLQUHOUN (M. J.).—Every** inch a Soldier. Crown 8vo, cloth, 3s. 6d.; post 8vo, illustrated boards, 2s.

**COLT-BREAKING, Hints on. By** W. M. HUTCHISON. Cr. 8vo, cl., 3s. 6d.

**COLTON (ARTHUR). — The** Belted Seas. Crown 8vo. cloth, 3s. 6d.

**COLVILL (HELEN H.).—The** Incubus. Crown 8vo, cloth, 6s.

6

## COMPENSATION ACT (THE),
1906: **Who pays, to whom, to what, and when it is applicable.** By A. CLEMENT EDWARDS, M.P. Crown 8vo, 1s. net: cloth, 1s. 6d. net.

## COMPTON (HERBERT), Novels by.
**The Inimitable Mrs. Massingham.** Crown 8vo, cloth, 3s. 6d.; POPULAR EDITION, medium 8vo, 6d

Crown 8vo, cloth, 3s. 6d. each.
**The Wilful Way.**
**The Queen can do no Wrong.**
**To Defeat the Ends of Justice.**

## COOPER (E. H.), Novels by.
Crown 8vo, cloth, 3s. 6d. each.
**Geoffory Hamilton.**
**The Marquis and Pamela.**

## CORNWALL.— Popular
**Romances of the West of England:** Collected by ROBERT HUNT, F.R.S. With two Plates by GEORGE CRUIKSHANK. Cr. 8vo, cloth, 7s. 6d.

## CRADDOCK (C. EGBERT), by.
**The Prophet of the Great Smoky Mountains.** Crown 8vo, cloth, 3s. 6d.: post 8vo, illustrated boards, 2s.
**His Vanished Star.** Crown 8vo, cloth, 3s. 6d.
**The Windfall.** Crown 8vo, cloth, 3s. 6d.; CHEAP EDITION, cloth, 1s. net.

## CRESSWELL (C. M.) — The
**Making and Breaking of Almansur.** Crown 8vo, cloth, 6s.

## CRIM (MATT).—Adventures of
a **Fair Rebel.** Crown 8vo, cloth, 3s. 6d.; post 8vo, illustrated boards, 2s.

## CROCKETT (S. R.) and others.—
**Tales of our Coast.** By S. R. CROCKETT, GILBERT PARKER, HAROLD FREDERIC, 'Q.,' and W. CLARK RUSSELL. With 13 Illustrations by FRANK BRANGWYN. Crown 8vo, cloth, 3s. 6d.

## CROSS (MARGARET B.), Novels
by. Crown 8vo, cloth, 6s. each.
**A Question of Means.**
**Opportunity.**
**Up to Perrin's.**

**A Question of Means.** POPULAR EDITION, medium 8vo, 6d.

## CRUIKSHANK'S COMIC AL-
MANACK. Complete in TWO SERIES: the FIRST from 1835 to 1843; the SECOND, from 1844 to 1853. With many hundred Woodcuts and Steel Plates by GEORGE CRUIKSHANK and others. Two Vols., crown 8vo, cloth, 5s. net each.

## CUMMING (C. F. GORDON),
Works by. Demy 8vo, cloth, 6s. each.
**In the Hebrides.** With 24 Illustrations.
**In the Himalayas and on the Indian Plains.** With 42 Illustrations
**Two Happy Years in Ceylon.** With 28 Illustrations.
**Via Cornwall to Egypt.** Frontis.

## CROKER (Mrs. B. M.), Novels
by. Crown 8vo, cloth, 3s. 6d. each; post 8vo, illustrated boards, 2s. each; cloth limp, 2s. 6d. each.
**Pretty Miss Neville.**
**A Bird of Passage.** | **Mr. Jervis.**
Diana Barrington. | Interference.
Two Masters | A Family Likeness.
**A Third Person.** | **Proper Pride.**
**Village Tales & Jungle Tragedies.**
**The Real Lady Hilda.**
**Married or Single?** 'To Let.'

Crown 8vo, cloth, 3s. 6d. each.
**In the Kingdom of Kerry.**
**Miss Balmaine's Past.**
Jason. | **Beyond the Pale.**
Terence: With 6 Illusts. by S. PAGET.
**The Cat's-paw.** With 12 Illustrations.
**The Spanish Necklace.** With 8 Illusts. by F. PEGRAM.—Also a Cheap Ed., without Illusts., picture cover, 1s. net.
**A Rolling Stone.**

Crown 8vo, cloth, 3s. 6d. each ; post 8vo, cloth limp, 2s. 6d. each.
**Infatuation.** | **Some One Else.**

POPULAR EDITIONS, medium 8vo, 6d. each.
**Proper Pride.** | **The Cat's-paw.**
Diana Barrington.
Pretty Miss Neville.
A Bird of Passage.
Beyond the Pale.
A Family Likeness.
Miss Balmaine's Past. (Cr. 8vo.)
Married or Single?
The Real Lady Hilda.
The Spanish Necklace.
**A Rolling Stone.** | **Infatuation.**

## CUPID AND PSYCHE (from 'The
Golden Ass' of Apuleius in Adlington's translation). With 8 Illustrations in colour by DOROTHY MULLOCK. Fcap. 4to, decorated cover, 5s. net.

## CUSSANS (JOHN E.).—A Hand-
book of Heraldry. With 408 Woodcuts and 2 Colrd. Plates. Crown 8vo, cloth, 6s.

## DANBY (FRANK).—A Coquette
in Crape. Foolscap 8vo, picture cover, 6d.; cloth, 1s. net.

## DAUDET (ALPHONSE). — The
Evangelist; or, Port Salvation. Cr. 8vo, cloth, 3s. 6d.; post 8vo, bds., 2s.

## DAVENANT (FRANCIS).—Hints
for Parents on Choice of Profession for their Sons. Crown 8vo, 1s. 6d.

## DAVIDSON (H. C.).— Mr. Sad-
ler's Daughters. Cr. 8vo, cloth, 3s. 6d.; CHEAP EDITION, cloth, 1s. net.

## DAVIES (Dr. N. E YORKE-),
Works by. Cr. 8vo, 1s. ea.; cl., 1s. 6d. ea.
**One Thousand Medical Maxims and Surgical Hints.**
**Nursery Hints:** A Mother's Guide.
**The Dietetic Cure of Obesity** (Foods for the Fat).
**Aids to Long Life.** Cr. 8vo, 2s.; cl.2s.6d.
**Wine and Health:** How to enjoy both. Crown 8vo, cloth, 1s. 6d.

## DEAKIN (DOROTHEA), Stories
by. Crown 8vo, cloth, 3s. 6d. each.
**The Poet and the Pierrot.**
**The Princess & the Kitchen-maid.**

## DEFOE (DANIEL). — Robinson
**Crusoe.** With 37 Illusts. by GEORGE
CRUIKSHANK. Pott 8vo, cloth, gilt top,
2s. net ; leather, gilt edges, 3s. net.

## DE MILLE (JAMES).—A Strange
**Manuscript found in a Copper
Cylinder.** Crown 8vo, cloth, with 19
Illustrations by GILBERT GAUL, 3s. 6d. ;
post 8vo, illustrated boards, 2s.

## DEVONSHIRE SCENERY, The
**History of.** By ARTHUR W. CLAYDEN,
M.A. With Illus.Demy 8vo,cl.,10s.6d. net.
**Devon : Its Moorlands, Streams,
and Coasts.** By Lady ROSALIND
NORTHCOTE. Illustrated in Colours by
F. J. WIDGERY. Fcap. 4to, cl., 20s. net.
Also a CHEAPER EDITION, with 50 Illustra-
tions Fcap. 4to, cloth, 7s. 6d. net.
**Folk Rhymes of Devon.** By W.
CROSSING. Demy 8vo, cloth, 4s. 6d. net.

## DEWAR (GEORGE A.B.), Books
by. Crown 8vo, cloth, 6s. net each.
**The Airy Way.**
**This Realm, This England.** With
9 Illustrations. Also published at 2s. net.

## DEWAR (T. R.). — A Ramble
**Round the Globe.** With 220 Illustrations. Crown 8vo, cloth, 7s. 6d.

## DICKENS (CHARLES), The
**Speeches of.** With a Portrait. Pott
8vo, cloth, 2s. net ; leather, 3s. net.
**Charles Dickens.** By ALGERNON
CHARLES SWINBURNE. Crown 8vo,
cloth. 3s. 6d. net.
**Dickens's Children.** With 10 Draw-
ings in Colour by JESSIE WILLCOX
SMITH. Crown 4to. cloth, 3s. 6d. net.
**The Pocket Charles Dickens :** Pass-
ages chosen by ALFRED H. HYATT.
16mo, cloth, 2s. net ; leather, gilt, 3s. net.

## DICTIONARIES.
**A Dictionary of the Drama.** By
W. DAVENPORT ADAMS. Vol. I. (A to G)
Demy 8vo, cloth, 10s. 6d. net.
**The Reader's Handbook.** By Rev.
E. C. BREWER. LL.D. Crown 8vo,cloth,
3s. 6d. net.
**Familiar Allusions.** By W. A. and C.
G. WHEELER. Demy 8vo, cl., 7s.6d. net.
**Familiar Short Sayings of Great
Men.** With Explanatory Notes by
SAMUEL A. BENT, A.M. Cr. 8vo, cl., 7s. 6d.
**The Slang Dictionary :** Historical
and Anecdotal. Crown 8vo, cloth, 6s. 6d.
**Words, Facts, and Phrases:** A
Dictionary of Curious Matters. By E.
EDWARDS, Crown 8vo, cloth. 3s. 6d.

## DIMNET (ERNEST). — France
**Herself Again.** Demy 8vo, cloth,
16s. net.

## DIXON (W. WILLMOTT), Novels
by. Crown 8vo, cloth, 3s. 6d. each.
**The Rogue of Rye. | King Hal.**

## DOBSON (AUSTIN), Works by.
Crown 8vo, buckram, 6s. each.
**Four Frenchwomen.** With Portraits.
**Eighteenth Century Vignettes.**
In Three Series, each 6s. ; also FINE-
PAPER EDITIONS, pott 8vo, cloth, 2s. net
each ; leather, 3s. net each.
**A Paladin of Philanthropy, and
other Papers.** With 2 Illustrations.
**Side-walk Studies.** With 5 Illusts.
**Old Kensington Palace, &c.** With
6 Illustrations.
**At Prior Park,** &c. With 6 Illustrations.
**Rosalba's Journal.** 8vo, with 6 Illus.

## DONOVAN (DICK), Detective
**Stories by.** Post 8vo, illustrated
boards, 2s. each ; cloth, 2s, 6d. each.
**In the Grip of the Law.**
**Suspicion Aroused.**
Cr. 8vo, cl., 3s. 6d. each ; picture cl., 2s. ea. ;
post 8vo, boards, 2s. ea ; cloth, 2s. 6d. ea.
**The Man from Manchester.**
**The Mystery of Jamaica Terrace.**
**Wanted !**
Crown 8vo, cloth, 3s. 6d. each.
**Tales of Terror. | Deacon Brodie.**
**Tyler Tatlock, Private Detective.**
Crown 8vo, cloth, 3s. 6d. each ; post 8vo,
boards, 2s. each; cloth limp, 2s. 6d. each.
**Chronicles of Michael Danevitch.**
**Tracked to Doom.**
**Tracked and Taken.**
**A Detective's Triumphs.**
**Who Poisoned Hetty Duncan ?**
**Caught at Last.**
**Link by Link. | Riddles Read.**
**From Information Received.**
**The Man-Hunter.** Crown 8vo, picture
cloth, 2s. ; post 8vo, illust. bds,, 2s. ; cloth
limp, 2s. 6d.
**Dark Deeds.** Crown 8vo, cloth limp,
2s. 6d. ; picture cloth, flat back, 2s.
**The Records of Vincent Trill.**
Cr. 8vo, cl., 3s. 6d. ; pict. cl., flat bk., 2s.
**Suspicion Aroused.** Crown 8vo,
cloth, 1s. net.

## DOSTOEVSKY (FYODOR),
**Letters of.** Translated by ETHEL
COLBURN MAYNE. With 16 Illustrations.
Demy 8vo, buckram, 7s. 6d. net.

## DOWLING (RICHARD). — Old
Corcoran's Money. Cr. 8vo, cl., 3s. 6d.

## DOYLE (A. CONAN).—The Firm
of Girdlestone. Cr. 8vo, cloth, 3s. 6d. ;
POPULAR EDITION, medium 8vo, 6d.

## DRAPER (W. H.). — Poems of
the Love of England. Crown 8vo,
Decorated cover. 1s. net.

## DU MAURIER (GEORGE), The
**Satirist of the Victorians.** By T.
MARTIN WOOD. With 41 Illustrations.
Fcap. 4to, cloth, 7s. 6d. net.

8

**DRAMATISTS, THE OLD.**
Edited by Col. CUNNINGHAM. Cr. 8vo,
cloth, with Portraits, 3s. 6d. per Vol.
**Ben Jonson's Works.** With Notes
and a Biographical Memoir by WILLIAM
GIFFORD. Three Vols.
**Chapman's Works.** Three Vols.—Vol.
I. The Plays complete; Vol. II. Poems
· and Translations, with Essay by A. C.
SWINBURNE; Vol. III. The Iliad and
Odyssey.
**Marlowe's Works.** One Vol.
**Massinger's Plays.** One Vol.

**DUMPY BOOKS (The) for**
Children. Royal 32mo, cloth, 1s. net
each.
**1. The Flamp, The Ameliorator,
and The School-boy's Apprentice.** By E. V. LUCAS.
**4. The Story of Little Black
Sambo.** By HELEN BANNERMAN.
Illustrated in colours.
**7. A Flower Book.** Illustrated in
colours by NELLIE BENSON.
**8. The Pink Knight.** By J. R. MON-
SELL. Illustrated in colours.
**9. The Little Clown.** By T. COBB.
**10. A Horse Book.** By MARY TOURTEL.
Illustrated in colours.
**11. Little People:** an Alphabet. By
HENRY MAYER and T. W. H. CROSLAND.
Illustrated in colours.
**12. A Dog Book.** By ETHEL BICKNELL.
With Pictures in colours by CARTON
MOORE PARK.
**15. Dollies.** By RICHARD HUNTER.
Illustrated in colours by RUTH COBB.
**17 Peter Piper's Practical Prin-
ciples.** Illustrated in colours.
**18. Little White Barbara.** By
ELEANOR MARCH. Illustrated in colours.
**20. Towlocks and his Wooden
Horse.** By ALICE M. APPLETON.
Illus. in colours by HONOR C. APPLETON.
**21. Three Little Foxes.** By MARY
TOURTEL. Illustrated in colours.
**22. The Old Man's Bag.** By T. W.
H. CROSLAND. Illus. by J. R. MONSELL.
**23. Three Little Goblins.** By M.
G. TAGGART. Illustrated in colours.
**25. More Dollies.** By RICHARD HUN-
TER. Illus. in colours by RUTH COBB.
**26. Little Yellow Wang-lo.** By M.
C. BELL. Illustrated in colours.
**28. The Sooty Man.** By E. B.
MACKINNON and EDEN COYBEE. Illus.
**30. Rosalina.** Illustrated in colours by
JEAN C. ARCHER.
**31. Sammy and the Snarlywink.**
Illustrated in colours by LENA and NOR-
MAN AULT.
**33. Irene's Christmas Party.** By
RICHARD HUNTER. Illus. by RUTH COBB.
**34. The Little Soldier Book.** By
JESSIE POPE. Illustrated in colours by
HENRY MAYER.
**35. The Dutch Doll's Ditties.** By
C. AUBREY MOORE.

**DUMPY BOOKS**—*continued.*
Royal 32mo, cloth, 1s. net each.
**36. Ten Little Nigger Boys.** By
NORA CASE.
**37. Humpty Dumpty's Little Son.**
By HELEN R. CROSS.
**38. Simple Simon.** By HELEN R.
CROSS. Illustrated in colours.
**39. The Little Frenchman.** By
EDEN COYBEE. Illustrated in colours by
K. J. FRICERO.
**40. The Story of an Irish Potato.**
By LILY SCHOFIELD. Illust. in colours.

**DUNCAN (SARA JEANNETTE),**
Books by. Cr. 8vo, cloth, 7s. 6d. each.
**The Simple Adventures of a
Memsahib.** With 37 Illustrations.
**Vernon's Aunt.** With 47 Illustrations.
Crown 8vo, cloth, 3s. 6d.

**DUTT (ROMESH C.).—England
and India:** Progress during One
Hundred Years. Crown 8vo, cloth, 2s.

**EDWARDES (Mrs. ANNIE),**
Novels by.
**A Point of Honour.** Post 8vo,
illustrated boards, 2s.
**Archie Lovell.** Crown 8vo, cloth,
3s. 6d.; post 8vo. illustrated boards, 2s.
**A Plaster Saint.** Cr. 8vo, cloth, 3s. 6d.

**EDWARDS (ELIEZER).—
Words, Facts, and Phrases:** A Dic-
tionary of Curious, Quaint, and Out-of-the-
Way Matters. Crown 8vo, cloth, 3s. 6d.

**EGERTON (Rev. J. C.).—
Sussex Folk and Sussex Ways.**
With Four Illusts. Crown 8vo, cloth, 5s.

**EGGLESTON (EDWARD).—
Roxy.** Post 8vo, illustrated boards, 2s.

**ELIZABETHAN VERSE, The
Book of.** Edited, with Notes, by W. S.
BRAITHWAITE. Crown 8vo, cloth, 3s. 6d.
net : vellum gilt, 7s. 6d. net.

**ENGLISHMAN (An) in Paris:**
Recollections of Louis Philippe and the
Empire. Crown 8vo, buckram, 3s. 6d.

**EPISTOLÆ OBSCURORUM
Virorum (1515-1517).** Latin Text,
with Translation, Notes, &c., by F. G.
STOKES. Royal 8vo, buckram, 25s. net.

**EXETER SCHOOL, The Found-
ing of.** By H. LLOYD PARRY. Crown
4to, cloth, 5s. net.

**EYES, Our :** How to Preserve. By
JOHN BROWNING. Crown 8vo, cloth, 1s.

**FAIRY TALES FROM
TUSCANY.** By ISABELLA M. ANDER-
TON. Square 16mo, cloth, 1s. net.

**FAMILIAR ALLUSIONS:** Mis-
cellaneous Information. By W. A. and C.
G. WHEELER. Demy 8vo, cl., 7s. 6d. net,

**FAMILIAR SHORT SAYINGS** of Great Men. By S. A. BENT, A.M. Crown 8vo, cloth, 7s. 6d.

**FARADAY (MICHAEL), Works** by. Post 8vo, cloth, 4s. 6d. each.
**The Chemical History of a Candle:** Lectures delivered before a Juvenile Audience. Edited by WILLIAM CROOKES, F.C.S. With numerous Illusts.
**On the Various Forces of Nature, and their Relations to each other.** Edited by WILLIAM CROOKES, F.C.S. With Illustrations.

**FARMER (HENRY).—Slaves of** Chance: A Novel. Cr. 8vo. cloth, 6s.

**FARRAR (F.W., D.D.).—Ruskin** as a Religious Teacher. Square 16mo, cloth, with Frontispiece, 1s. net.

**FARRER (J. ANSON).—War:** Three Essays. Crown 8vo, cloth, 1s. 6d.

**FENN (G. MANVILLE), Novels** by. Crown 8vo, cloth, 3s. 6d. each; post 8vo, illustrated boards, 2s. each.
**The New Mistress.**
**Witness to the Deed.**
**The Tiger Lily.**
**The White Virgin.**

Crown 8vo, cloth, 2s. 6d. each.
**A Woman Worth Winning.**
**Cursed by a Fortune.**
**The Case of Ailsa Gray.**
**Commodore Junk.**
**Black Blood.** | **In Jeopardy.**
**Double Cunning.**
**A Fluttered Dovecote.**
**King of the Castle.**
**The Master of the Ceremonies.**
**The Story of Antony Grace.**
**The Man with a Shadow.**
**One Maid's Mischief.**
**The Bag of Diamonds, and Three Bits of Paste.**
**Running Amok.** | **Black Shadows.**
**The Cankerworm.**
**So Like a Woman.**

**A Crimson Crime.** Crown 8vo, cloth. 3s. 6d.; picture cloth, flat back, 2s.

POPULAR EDITIONS. medium 8vo, 6d. each.
**A Crimson Crime.**
**A Woman Worth Winning.**

**FILIPPI (ROSINA).—Inhaling:** A Romance. Crown 8vo, cloth, 6s.

**FIREWORK - MAKING, The** Complete Art of. By T. KENTISH. With 267 Illusts. Cr. 8vo, cloth, 3s. 6d.

**FITZGERALD (PERCY), by.**
**Fatal Zero.** Crown 8vo, cloth, 3s. 6d.; post 8vo, illustrated boards, 2s.

Post 8vo, illustrated boards, 2s. each.
**Bella Donna.** | **Polly.**
**The Lady of Brantome.**
**Never Forgotten.**
**The Second Mrs. Tillotson.**
**Seventy-five Brooke Street.**

**FISHER (ARTHUR O.).—The** Land of Silent Feet. With a Frontispiece by G. D. ARMOUR. Crown 8vo, cloth, 6s.

**FLAMMARION (CAMILLE).—** Popular Astronomy. Translated by J. ELLARD GORE, F.R.A.S. With Illustrations. Medium 8vo, cloth, 10s. 6d.

**FLORENCE PRESS BOOKS** (The). Set in the beautiful FLORENCE TYPE designed by Mr. HERBERT P. HORNE. Printed on hand-made paper.
**Virginibus Puerisque, &c.** By R. L. STEVENSON. With 12 Illustrations in Coloured Collotype after the Drawings of NORMAN WILKINSON. (235 numbered copies.) Crown 4to, bds., £2 12s. 6d net; vellum, £3 3s. net.
**The Fioretti or Little Flowers of S. Francis.** Translated by Prof. T. W. ARNOLD, M.A. With 29 Illustrations in Collotype from the MSS. in the Laurentian Library. (475 numbered Copies.) Printed in red and black. Demy 4to, boards, 30s. net; vellum, 42s. net.
**Songs before Sunrise.** By ALGERNON CHARLES SWINBURNE. (475 numbered copies.) Printed in red and black. Crown 4to, boards, 26s. net; limp vellum, 36s. net.
**The Marriage of Heaven and Hell;** and **A Song of Liberty.** By WILLIAM BLAKE. With Introduction by F. G. STOKES. Crown 8vo boards, 3s. 6d. net; parchment 5s. net.
**Sappho:** One Hundred Lyrics. By BLISS CARMAN. Small crown 8vo, boards, 5s. net; parchment gilt, 6s. net.
**Memorials di Molte Statue e Pitture, Sono Incyta Cipta di Florentie.** (Edition limited to 450 copies.) Demy 8vo, 5s. net; limp vellum, 12s. 6d. net.
**Olympia: The Latin Text of Boccaccio's Fourteenth Eclogue,** with an English rendering, and other supplementary matter, by ISRAEL GOLLANCZ, Litt.D., and a Photogravure facsimile of a part of the MS. Limited to 500 copies fcap. 4to, hand-made boards, 6s. net; vellum, 12s. 6d. net.
**Stevenson's Poems.** Complete Edition. Small fcap. 4to, cloth, 12s. 6d. net; velvet calf, 18s. net.
**The Poems of John Keats.** Newly arranged in chronological order, and Edited by Sir SIDNEY COLVIN. In 2 vols., small 4to, boards, 15s. net; buckram, 21s. net. LARGE PAPER EDITION, limited to 250 copies, fcap. 4to, hand-made paper, parchment, 31s. 6d. net; vellum 45s. net.
**Flanders, The Little Towns of.** 12 Woodcuts by ALBERT DELSTANCHE, with a Prefatory Letter from EMILE VERHAEREN. Edition limited to 500 numbered copies. Demy 4to, bds., 12s. 6d. net; vellum, £1 1s. net.

**FLOWER BOOK (The).** By CONSTANCE SMEDLEY ARMFIELD and MAXWELL ARMFIELD. Large fcap 4to, cl., 5s. net; parchment gilt, 7s. 6d. net.

**FORBES (Hon. Mrs. WALTER).** —Dumb. Crown 8vo cloth. 3s. 6d.

**FORTESCUE'S (MISS)** REMINISCENCES. With Portraits and other Illusts. Demy 8vo, cl., 16s. net.

**FRANCO - BRITISH EXHIBITION (The).** Folio, cloth, 10s. 6d. net.

**FRANKAU (GILBERT).—One of** Us: A Novel in Verse. Demy 8vo, 3s. 6d. net; crown 8vo, paper, 1s. net.
**"Tid'Apa":** A Poem. Demy 8vo, boards, 2s. 6d. net.

**FRANCILLON (R. E.), Novels by.** Crown 8vo, cloth, 3s. 6d. each ; post 8vo, illustrated boards, 2s. each.
**One by One.** | **A Real Queen.**
**A Dog and his Shadow.**
**Ropes of Sand.** With Illustrations.

Post 8vo, illustrated boards, 2s. each.
**Romances of the Law.**
**King or Knave?** | **Olympia.**
**JackDoyle's Daughter.** Cr.8vo,cl,3s.6d.

**FREDERIC (HAROLD), Novels by.** Post 8vo, cloth, 3s. 6d. each; illustrated boards, 2s. each.
**Seth's Brother's Wife.**
**The Lawton Girl.**

**FREEMAN (R. AUSTIN).—John Thorndyke's Cases.** Illustrated by H. M. BROCK, &c. Crown 8vo, cloth, 3s. 6d. POPULAR EDITION, medium 8vo, 6d.

**FRY'S (HERBERT) Royal Guide to the London Charities.** Edited by JOHN LANE. Published Annually. Crown 8vo, cloth, 1s. 6d.

**FURNITURE.** By ESTHER SINGLETON. With Illusts. Roy. 8vo,cl., 16s. net.

**GARDENING BOOKS.** Post 8vo, 1s. each : cloth, 1s. 6d. each.
**A Year's Work in Garden and Greenhouse.** By GEORGE GLENNY.
**Household Horticulture.** By TOM and JANE JERROLD. Illustrated.
**The Garden that Paid the Rent.** By TOM JERROLD.
**Our Kitchen Garden.** By TOM JERROLD. Post 8vo, cloth, 1s. net.
**Vine - Growing in England:** a Practical Guide. By H. M. TOD. With Illusts. Cr. 8vo, bds., 1s. net ; cl., 1s.6d. net.

**GARNETT (EDWARD). — The Three Great Russian Novelists (Tolstoy, Turgenev, Dostoevsky).** Crown 8vo, cloth, 6s. net.

**GIBBON (CHARLES), Novels by.** Crown 8vo, cloth, 3s. 6d. each; post 8vo, illustrated boards, 2s. each.
**Robin Gray.** | **The Golden Shaft.**
**The Flower of the Forest.**
**The Braes of Yarrow.**
**Of High Degree.**
**Queen of the Meadow.**

Crown 8vo, picture boards, 2s. each.
**For Lack of Gold.**
**What Will the World Say?**
**For the King.** | **A Hard Knot.**
**In Pastures Green.**
**In Love and War.**
**A Heart's Problem.**
**By Mead and Stream.**
**Fancy Free.** | **Loving a Dream.**
**In Honour Bound.**
**Heart's Delight.** | **Blood-Money.**
**The Dead Heart.** Post 8vo, illust. bds. 2s.; POPULAR EDITION, medium 8vo, 6d.

Crown 8vo, cloth, 1s. net.
**A Heart's Problem.**
**In Love and War.**

**GAULOT (PAUL). — The Red Shirts:** A Tale of 'The Terror.' Translated by JOHN DE VILLIERS. Crown 8vo, cloth, with Frontispiece by STANLEY WOOD, 3s. 6d.; picturecloth, flat back, 2s.

**GERARD(DOROTHEA).—A Queen of Curds and Cream.** Cr.8vo. cl., 3s.6d.

**GIBBS (A. HAMILTON).— Cheadle and Son.** Crown 8vo, cl., 6s.

**GIBNEY (SOMERVILLE). — Sentenced!** Crown 8vo. cloth, 1s. 6d.

**GIBSON (L. S.), Novels by.** Crown 8vo, cloth, 3s. 6d. each.
**The Freemasons.** | **Burnt Spices.**
**Ships of Desire.**
**The Freemasons.** Cheap Edition, picture cover, 1s. net ; medium 8vo, 6d.

**GILBERT'S (W. S.) Original Plays.** In 4 Series, FINE-PAPER EDITION, Pott 8vo, cloth, gilt top, 2s. net each ; leather, gilt edges, 3s. net each.
The FIRST SERIES contains : The Wicked World — Pygmalion and Galatea — Charity—The Princess—The Palace of Truth—Trial by Jury—Iolanthe.
The SECOND SERIES contains : Broken Hearts -- Engaged — Sweethearts — Gretchen — Dan'l Druce—Tom Cobb —H.M.S. 'Pinafore'—The Sorcerer— The Pirates of Penzance.
The THIRD SERIES contains : Comedy and Tragedy — Foggerty's Fairy — Rosencrantz and Guildenstern—Patience— Princess Ida—The Mikado—Ruddigore —The Yeomen of the Guard—The Gondoliers—The Mountebanks—Utopia.
The FOURTH SERIES contains : The Fairy's Dilemma—The Grand Duke—His Excellency—'Haste to the Wedding'—Fallen Fairies—The Gentleman in Black—Brantinghame Hall—Creatures of Impulse— Randall's Thumb—The Fortune-hunter —Thespis. With Portrait of the Author.

**Eight Original Comic Operas.** Two Series, demy 8vo, cl., 2s. 6d. net each.
The FIRST SERIES contains : The Sorcerer —H.M.S. 'Pinafore'—The Pirates of Penzance — Iolanthe — Patience — Princess Ida—The Mikado—Trial by Jury.
The SECOND SERIES contains : The Gondoliers—The Grand Duke—The Yeomen of the Guard—His Excellency—Utopia, Limited—Ruddigore—The Mountebanks —Haste to the Wedding.

**The Gilbert and Sullivan Birthday Book.** Compiled by A. WATSON. Royal 16mo, cloth, 2s. 6d. ; decorated cover, 1s. net.

**GISSING (ALGERNON), Novels by.** Cr. 8vo, cloth, 3s. 6d. each.
**Knitters in the Sun.**
**The Wealth of Mallerstang.**
**An Angel's Portion.** | **Baliol Garth.**
**The Dreams of Simon Usher.** Cr. 8vo, cloth, 3s. 6d.; CHEAP EDIT., 1s. net.

**GILBERT (WILLIAM).—James Duke, Costermonger.** Post 8vo. 2s.

**GLANVILLE (ERNEST), Novels by.** Crown 8vo, cloth, 3s. 6d. each; post 8vo, illustrated boards, 2s. each.
**The Lost Heiress.** With 2 Illusts.
**The Fossicker:** A Romance of Mashonaland. Two Illusts. by HUME NISBET.
**A Fair Colonist.** With Frontispiece.
Crown 8vo, cloth, 3s. 6d. each.
**The Golden Rock.** With Frontispiece.
**Tales from the Veld.** With 12 Illusts.
**Max Thornton.** With 8 Illustrations by J. S. CROMPTON, R.I.
**A Fair Colonist.** Cr. 8vo, cl., 1s. net.

**GLOVER (JAMES). — Jimmy Glover and His Friends.** With Illustrations. Demy 8vo, cloth, 7s. 6d. net.

**GODWIN (WILLIAM). — Lives of the Necromancers.** Post 8vo, cl., 2s.

**GOLDEN TREASURY of Thought, The.** By THEODORE TAYLOR. Cr. 8vo, cl., 3s. 6d.

**GOODMAN (E. J.)—The Fate of Herbert Wayne.** Cr. 8vo, cl.. 3s. 6d.

**GRACE (ALFRED A.).—Tales of a Dying Race.** Cr. 8vo, cl.. 3s. 6d.

**GRACE, Dr. E. M.: A Memoir.** By F. S. ASHLEY-COOPER. Crown 8vo, cloth, 5s. net.

**GREEKS AND ROMANS, The Life of the,** By ERNST GUHL and W. KONER. Edited by Dr. F. HUEFFER. With 545 Illusts. Demy 8vo, cl., 7s. 6d.

**GREEN (F. E.) — The Surrey Hills.** Illustrated by ELLIOTT SEABROOKE. Fcap. 4to, cloth, 7s. 6d. net.

**GREENWOOD (JAMES).—The Prisoner in the Dock.** Crown 8vo, cloth, 3s. 6d.

**GREY (Sir GEORGE). — The Romance of a Proconsul.** By JAMES MILNE. Crown 8vo, buckram, 6s.

**GRIFFITH (CECIL).—Corinthia Marazion.** Crown 8vo, cloth, 3s. 6d.

**GRIFFITHS (Major A.).—No. 99, and Blue Blood.** Crown 8vo, cloth, 2s.

**GRIMM.—German Popular Stories.** — Collected by the Brothers GRIMM and Translated by EDGAR TAYLOR. With an Intro. by JOHN RUSKIN. Illustrated by GEORGE CRUIKSHANK. Square 8vo, cloth, gilt top, 6s.

**GRONER (AUGUSTA). — The Man with the Black Cord.** Translated by GRACE I. COLBRON. With 2 Illustrations. Crown 8vo, cloth, 6s.

**GYP.—CLOCLO.** Translated by NORA M. STATHAM. Cr. 8vo, cl.. 3s. 6d

**HABBERTON (JOHN).—Helen's Babies,** With Coloured Frontis. and 60 Illusts. by EVA ROOS. Fcap. 4to, cl., 6s.

**HAIR, The: Its Treatment.** By Dr. J. PINCUS. Cr. 8vo. 1s.; cl., 1s. 6d.

**HAKE (Dr. T. GORDON), Poems by.** Crown 8vo, cloth. 6s. each.
**New Symbols. | The Serpent Play Legends of the Morrow.**
**Maiden Ecstasy.** Small 4to, cloth, 8s.

**HALL (Mrs. S. C.).—Sketches of Irish Character.** Illusts. by CRUIKSHANK and others. Demy 8vo. cl., 7s. 6d.

**HALL (OWEN), Novels by.**
**The Track of a Storm.** Crown 8vo, picture cloth, flat back, 2s.
**Jetsam.** Crown 8vo, cloth. 3s. 6d.

**HALLIDAY (ANDREW).— Every-day Papers.** Illust. bds., 2s.

**HAMILTON'S (COSMO) Stories Two Kings, &c.** Cr. 8vo., cl., 2s. net. Crown 8vo, 1s. net each.
**The Glamour of the Impossible. Through a Keyhole.**
Crown 8vo, cloth. 6s. each.
**Nature's Vagabond, &c.**
**Plain Brown.**
**The Door that has no Key.**
**Plain Brown.** POPULAR EDITION. medium 8vo. 6d.
**A Plea for the Younger Generation.** Crown 8vo, cloth, 2s. 6d. net.

**HANDWRITING, The Philosophy of.** By DON FELIX DE SALAMANCA. 100 Facsimiles. Post 8vo, cloth, 2s. 6d.

**HAPPY TESTAMENT, The.** By CHARLES LOUNDSBERRY. Illustrated in Colour by RACHEL MARSHALL. Post 8vo, decorated cover, 1s. net.

**HAPSBURGS, The Cradle of the.** By J. W. GILBART-SMITH, M.A. With numerous Illusts. Cr. 8vo, cloth, 5s. net.

**HARDY (IZA DUFFUS), Novels by.** Crown 8vo, cloth. 3s. 6d. each
**The Lesser Evil. | A Butterfly.**
**Man, Woman, and Fate.**

**HARDY (THOMAS). — Under the Greenwood Tree.** Post 8vo, cloth, 3s. 6d.; illustrated boards, 2s.; cloth limp, 2s. 6d.; FINE PAPER EDITION, pott 8vo, cloth gilt, 2s. net; leather gilt, 3s. net; CHEAP EDITION, medium 8vo, 6d. Also the LARGE TYPE EDITION DE LUXE, with 10 Illustrations in Colour by KEITH HENDERSON. Fcap. 4to., cloth, 6s. net; velvet calf or parchment, 12s. 6d. net.
**The Pocket Thomas Hardy.** 16mo, cloth gilt, 2s. net; leather gilt, 3s. net.

**HARRIS (JOEL CHANDLER):**
**Uncle Remus.** With 9 Coloured and 50 other Illustrations by J. A. SHEPHERD. Fcap. 4to cloth, gilt top, 6s.
**Nights with Uncle Remus.** With 8 Coloured and 50 other Illustrations by J. A. SHEPHERD. Fcap. 4to, cloth, 6s.

**HARTE'S (BRET) Collected Works.** LIBRARY EDITION. (Ten Volumes now ready). Crown 8vo, cloth, 3s. 6d. each.

Vol. I. POETICAL AND DRAMATIC WORKS. With Portrait.

" II. THE LUCK OF ROARING CAMP— BOHEMIAN PAPERS—AMERICAN LEGENDS.

" III. TALES OF THE ARGONAUTS— EASTERN SKETCHES.

" IV. GABRIEL CONROY.

" V. STORIES — CONDENSED NOVELS.

" VI. TALES OF THE PACIFIC SLOPE.

" VII. TALES OF THE PACIFIC SLOPE—II With Portrait by JOHN PETTIE.

" VIII. TALES OF PINE AND CYPRESS.

" IX. BUCKEYE AND CHAPPARRL.

" X. TALES OF TRAIL AND TOWN.

**Bret Harte's Choice Works** in Prose and Verse. With Portrait and 40 Illustrations. Crown 8vo, cloth, 3s. 6d.

**Bret Harte's Poetical Works**, including SOME LATER VERSES. Crown 8vo, buckram, 4s. 6d.

**In a Hollow of the Hills.** Crown 8vo, picture cloth, flat back, 2s.

**Maruja.** Crown 8vo, cloth, 3s. 6d.; post 8vo, picture boards, 2s.; cloth limp, 2s. 6d.

Post 8vo, cloth, 2s. net ea.; leather, 3s. net ea.
**Miss, Luck of Roaring Camp, &c.**
**Condensed Novels.** Both Series.
**Complete Poetical Works.**

Crown 8vo. cloth, 6s. each.
**On the Old Trail. | Trent's Trust.**
**Under the Redwoods.**
**From Sandhill to Pine.**
**Stories in Light and Shadow.**
**Mr. Jack Hamlin's Mediation.**

Crown 8vo. cloth. 3s. 6d. each ; post 8vo, illustrated boards, 2s. each.
**Gabriel Conroy.**
**A Waif of the Plains.** With 60 Illustrations by STANLEY L. WOOD.
**A Ward of the Golden Gate.** With 59 Illustrations by STANLEY L. WOOD.

Crown 8vo, cloth, 3s. 6d. each.
**The Bell-Ringer of Angel's**, &c. With 39 Illusts. by DUDLEY HARDY, &c.
**Clarence:** A Story of the American War. With 8 Illustrations by A. JULE GOODMAN.
**Barker's Luck**, &c. With 30 Illustrations by A. FORESTIER, PAUL HARDY, &c.
**Devil's Ford**, &c.
**The Crusade of the 'Excelsior.'** With Frontis. by J. BERNARD PARTRIDGE.
**Tales of Trail and Town.** With Frontispiece by G. P. JACOMB-HOOD.

Crown 8vo, cloth, 3s. 6d. each ; picture cloth flat back, 2s. each.
**A Sappho of Green Springs.**
**Colonel Starbottle's Client.**
**A Protégée of Jack Hamlin's.** With numerous Illustrations.
**Sally Dows**, &c. With 47 Illustrations by W. D. ALMOND and others.

Post 8vo, illus. bds., 2s. each; cloth, 2s. 6d. each.
**Flip.**
**A Phyllis of the Sierras.**

---

**HARTE (BRET)**—continued.

Post 8vo, illustrated boards, 2s. each.
**Luck of Roaring Camp**, and **Sensation Novels Condensed.** Also in picture cloth at same price.
**An Heiress of Red Dog.**
**Californian Stories.**

**A Ward of the Golden Gate.** Cr. 8vo, cloth, 1s. net.

**Three Partners.** Medium 8vo, 6d.
**New Condensed Novels.** Cr. 8vo, cloth, 3s. 6d. : Cheap Edition, 1s. net.

**The Life of Bret Harte.** By H. C. MERWIN. With 11 Illustrations. Demy 8vo, cloth, 10s. 6d. net.

---

**HASELDEN, W. K.—The Sad Experiences of Big and Little Willie.** Thirty-six Cartoons reprinted from *The Daily Mirror*. Demy 4to, cloth, 5s. net (limited to 500 copies signed by the author). Paper cover, 1s. net.

---

**HAWEIS (Mrs. H. R.), Books by.**
**The Art of Dress.** With 32 Illustrations. Post 8vo, 1s. ; cloth, 1s. 6d.
**Chaucer for Schools.** With Frontispiece. Demy 8vo, cloth, 2s. 6d.
**Chaucer for Children.** With 8 Coloured Plates and 30 Woodcuts. Crown 4to, cloth, 3s. 6d.

---

**HAWTHORNE (JULIAN), Novels by.** Crown 8vo, cloth, 3s. 6d. each; post 8vo, illustrated boards. 2s each.
**Garth. | Ellice Quentin.**
**Fortune's Fool. | Dust.** Four Illusts.
**Beatrix Randolph.** With Four Illusts.
**D. Poindexter's Disappearance.**
**The Spectre of the Camera.**

Crown 8vo, cloth, 3s. 6d. each.
**Sebastian Strome.**
**Love—or a Name.**
**Miss Cadogna.** Illustrated boards. 2s.

---

**HEAD (Mrs. HENRY).—A Simple Guide to Pictures.** With 34 Illustrations (24 in Colour). Fcap. 4to, cloth, 5s. net.

---

**HEALY (CHRIS), Books by.** Crown 8vo, cloth. 6s. each
**Confessions of a Journalist.**
**Heirs of Reuben. | Mara.**
**The Endless Heritage.** Cr. 8vo. 3s. 6d.

---

**HELPS (Sir ARTHUR). — Ivan de Biron.** Crown 8vo, cloth, 3s. 6d.; post 8vo, illustrated boards, 2s.

---

**HENDERSON (ISAAC).—Agatha Page.** Crown 8vo, cloth, 3s. 6d.

---

**HENTY (G. A.), Novels by.**
**Rujub, the Juggler.** Post 8vo, cloth, 3s. 6d.; illustrated boards, 2s.

Crown 8vo, cloth, 3s. 6d. each,
**The Queen's Cup.**
**Dorothy's Double.**
**Colonel Thorndyke's Secret.**

**HERBERTSON (JESSIE L.).—Junia.** Crown 8vo, cloth, 6s.

**HILL (HEADON).—Zambra the Detective.** Crown 8vo, cloth, 3s. 6d.; picture cloth, flat back, 2s.

**HILL (JOHN), Works by.**
Treason-Felony. Post 8vo, boards, 2s.
The Common Ancestor. Crown 8vo, cloth, 3s. 6d.

**HOEY (Mrs. CASHEL).—The Lover's Creed.** Cr. 8vo, cl., 3s. 6d.

**HOFFMANN (PROF.).—King Koko.** A Magic Story. Cr. 8vo, cl., 1s. net

**HOFFMANN, TALES OF. Retold from OFFENBACH'S Opera.** By CYRIL FALLS. Illustrated in Colour by A. BRANTINGHAM SIMPSON, R.O.I. Small 4to, cloth, 6s. net : velvet calf, 12s. 6d. net.

**HOLIDAY, Where to go for a.** By several well-known Authors. Crown 8vo, cloth, 1s. 6d.

**HOLMES (CHARLES J., M.A.), Books by.** Dy. 8vo, cl., 7s. 6d. net each.
Notes on the Science of Picture-making. With Photogravure Frontis.
Notes on the Art of Rembrandt. With Frontispiece and 44 Plates.

**HOLMES (OLIVER WENDELL). The Autocrat of the Breakfast-Table.** Illustrated by J. GORDON THOMSON. FINE PAPER EDITION, pott 8vo, cloth, 2s. net ; leather, 3s. net.

**HOOD'S (THOMAS) Choice Works in Prose and Verse.** With Life of the Author, Portrait, and 200 Illustrations. Crown 8vo, cloth, 3s. 6d.

**HOOK'S (THEODORE) Choice Humorous Works.** With Life and Frontispiece. Crown 8vo, cloth, 3s. 6d.

**HOPKINS (TIGHE), Novels by.** Crown 8vo, cloth, 3s. 6d. each.
'Twixt Love and Duty.
The Incomplete Adventurer.
The Nugents of Carriconna.
Nell Haffenden. With 8 Illustrations.
For Freedom.

**HORNE (R. HENGIST).—Orion.** With Portrait. Crown 8vo, cloth, 7s.

**HORNIMAN (ROY), Novels by.** Crown 8vo, cloth, 6s. each.
Bellamy the Magnificent.
Lord Cammarleigh's Secret.
Israel Rank. Crown 8vo, cloth, 3s. 6d.
POPULAR EDITIONS, crown 8vo, cloth, with pictorial outer covers, 2s. net each.
Bellamy the Magnificent.
Israel Rank.

**HORNUNG (E. W.), Novels by.** Crown 8vo, cloth, 3s. 6d. each.
Stingaree. | A Thief in the Night.
The Shadow of the Rope. Cr. 8vo, cloth, 3s. 6d. ; pictorial cloth, 2s. net.

**HOUGHTON (MARY). — In the Enemy's Country.** With a Foreword by EDWARD GARNETT. Crown 8vo, cloth, 5s. net.

**HUEFFER (FORD MADOX), Novels by.** Crown 8vo, cloth, 6s. each.
A Call: The Tale of Two Passions.
The Young Lovell.

**HUGO (VICTOR).—The Outlaw of Iceland.** Translated by Sir GILBERT CAMPBELL. Crown 8vo, cloth, 3s. 6d.

**HULL (ELEANOR), Selected and Annotated by.—The Poem-book of the Gael.** With Decorations from Irish MSS. Small crown 8vo, cloth, 6s. net.

**HUME (FERGUS), Novels by.**
The Lady From Nowhere. Cr. 8vo, cloth, 3s. 6d.; picture cloth, flat back, 2s.
The Millionaire Mystery. Crown 8vo, cloth, 3s. 6d.
The Wheeling Light. Crown 8vo, cloth, gilt top, 6s.

**HUNGERFORD (Mrs.), Novels by.** Cr. 8vo, cl., 3s. 6d. each ; post 8vo, boards, 2s. each ; cloth, 2s. 6d. each.
The Professor's Experiment.
Lady Verner's Flight.
Lady Patty. | Peter's Wife.
The Red-House Mystery.
An Unsatisfactory Lover.
A Maiden All Forlorn.
A Mental Struggle.
Marvel. | A Modern Circe.
In Durance Vile. | April's Lady.
The Three Graces. | Nora Creina.
Crown 8vo, cloth, 3s. 6d. each.
An Anxious Moment.
A Point of Conscience.
The Coming of Chloe. | Lovice.
POPULAR EDITIONS, medium 8vo, 6d. each.
The Red-House Mystery.
A Modern Circe.

**HUNT (Mrs. ALFRED), Novels by.** Crown 8vo, cloth, 3s. 6d. each ; post 8vo, illustrated boards, 2s. each.
The Leaden Casket.
Self-Condemned.
That Other Person.
Mrs. Juliet. Crown 8vo, cloth, 3s. 6d.
Thornicroft's Model. With a Prefatory Chapter by VIOLET HUNT. Crown 8vo, cloth, 2s. net.
The Governess. By Mrs. ALFRED HUNT and VIOLET HUNT ; with a Preface by FORD MADOX HUEFFER. Cr. 8vo, cl., 6s.

**HUNT (VIOLET).—The Desirable Alien at Home in Germany.** With additional Chapters by FORD MADOX HUEFFER. Crown 8vo, cloth, 6s.

**HUTCHINSON (W. M.).—Hints on Colt-Breaking.** With 25 Illustrations. Crown 8vo, cloth, 3s. 6d.

**HYAMSON (ALBERT).—A History of the Jews in England.** With 18 Illusts. Demy 8vo, cloth, 4s. 6d. net.

**HYATT (A. H.), Topographical Anthologies** compiled by. Crown 8vo, cloth, full gilt side, gilt top, 5s. net each; velvet calf, 7s. 6d. net each. Also, FINE-PAPER EDITIONS, without Illustrations, in the ST. MARTIN'S LIBRARY. Pott 8vo, cloth, gilt top, 2s. net each; leather, gilt edges, 3s. net each.
The Charm of Venice: an Anthology. With 12 Ill. in Colour by HARALD SUND.
**The Charm of London.** With 12 Illusts. in Colour by YOSHIO MARKINO.
**The Charm of Paris.** With 12 Illustrations in Colour by HARRY MORLEY.
**The Charm of Edinburgh.** With 12 Illusts. in Colour by HARRY MORLEY.

**INCE (MABEL), Novels by.**
Each with Frontispiece, cr. 8vo, cl., 6s. each.
**The Wisdom of Waiting.**
**The Commonplace & Clementine.**

**INCHBOLD (A. C.), Novels by.**
**The Road of No Return.** Cr. 8vo, cloth, 3s. 6d.
**Love in a Thirsty Land.** Cr. 8vo, cloth, 6s.

**INDOOR PAUPERS.** By ONE OF THEM. Crown 8vo, 1s.; cloth, 1s. 6d.

**IRVING (WASHINGTON).—Old Christmas.** Square 16mo. cl., 1s. net.

**JAMES (C. T. C.).—A Romance of the Queen's Hounds.** Cr. 8vo. cl. 1s.6d.

**JAMES (G. W.).—Scraggles:** The Story of a Sparrow. With 6 Illustrations. Crown 8vo, cloth, 2s. 6d.; decorated binding, 1s. net.

**JAPP (Dr. A. H.).—Dramatic Pictures.** Crown 8vo, cloth, 5s.

**JEFFERIES (RICHARD), by.**
**The Pageant of Summer.** Long fcap, decorated cover, 1s. net.
**The Life of the Fields.** Post 8vo, cloth, 2s.6d.; LARGE TYPE, FINE PAPER EDITION, pott 8vo, cloth, gilt top, 2s. net: leather, gilt edges, 3s. net. Also a NEW EDITION, with 12 Illustrations in Colours by M. U. CLARKE, cr. 8vo, cl., 5s. net.
**The Open Air.** Post 8vo, cloth, 2s. 6d. LARGE TYPE, FINE PAPER EDITION, pott 8vo, cloth, gilt top, 2s. net: leather, gilt edges, 3s. net. Also a NEW EDITION, with 12 Illustrations in Colours by RUTH DOLLMAN, crown 8vo, cloth 5s. net.
**Nature near London.** Crown 8vo, buckram, 6s.; post 8vo, cl., 2s. 6d.; LARGE TYPE, FINE PAPER EDITION, pott 8vo, cl., gilt top, 2s. net: leather, gilt edges, 3s.net. Also a NEW EDITION, with 12 Illustrations in Colours by RUTH DOLLMAN, crown 8vo, cloth, 5s. net.
**The Pocket Richard Jefferies:** Passages chosen by A. H. HYATT, 16mo, cloth gilt, 2s. net; leather gilt, 3s. net.

**JENKINS (HESTER D.).—Behind Turkish Lattices.** With 24 Illustrations. Crown 8vo, cloth, 6s. net.

**JEROME (JEROME K.).—Stageland.** With 64 Illustrations by J. BERNARD PARTRIDGE. Fcap. 4to, 1s.

**JERROLD (TOM), Books by.**
Post 8vo, 1s. each; cloth, 1s. 6d. each.
**The Garden that Paid the Rent.**
**Household Horticulture.**
**Our Kitchen Garden:** The Plants We Grow, and How We Cook Them. Post 8vo, cloth, 1s. net.

**JOFFRE (General).—My March to Timbuctoo.** With a Character Sketch by ERNEST DIMNET. Cr. 8vo, cloth, 2s. net.

**JOHNSTONE (Arthur).—Recollections of R. L. Stevenson in the Pacific.** With Portrait and Facsimile Letter. Crown 8vo, buckram, 6s. net.

**JONES (CECIL DUNCAN).—The Everlasting Search:** A Romance. Crown 8vo. cloth, 6s.

**JONSON'S (BEN) Works.** With Notes, etc., by WILLIAM GIFFORD. Edited by Colonel CUNNINGHAM. Three Vols., crown 8vo. cloth, 3s. 6d. each.

**JOSEPHUS, The Complete Works of.** Translated by WILLIAM WHISTON. Illustrated. Two Vols., demy 8vo, cloth, 5s. net each.

**KEATS (JOHN), The Poems of.** Arranged chronologically, and Edited by Sir SIDNEY COLVIN. Printed in the FLORENCE PRESS TYPE. 2 vols., small 4to, boards, 15s. net; buckram, 21s. net. LARGE PAPER EDITION, fcap, 4to, limited to 250 copies, parchment, 31s. 6d. net; vellum, 45s. net.

**KEMPLING (W.BAILEY-).—The Poets Royal of England and Scotland.** With 6 Portraits. Small 8vo, parchment, 6s. net; vellum, 7s. 6d. net. (See also KING'S CLASSICS, p. 16.)

**KERSHAW (MARK).—Colonial Facts and Fictions.** Post 8vo, illustrated boards, 2s.; cloth, 2s. 6d.

**KEYNES (HELEN MARY), Novels by.** Crown 8vo, cloth, 6s. each.
**The Spanish Marriage.**
**Honour the King.**
**Khaki Library, The.** A Series of Copyright Novels. Crown 8vo, cloth, 1s. net. Full list on application.

**KING (R. ASHE), Novels by.**
Post 8vo, illustrated boards, 2s. each.
**'The Wearing of the Green.'**
**Passion's Slave.** | **Bell Barry.**
**A Drawn Game.** Crown 8vo, cloth, 3s. 6d.; post 8vo, illustrated boards, 2s.

15

## KING (LEONARD W., M.A.).—

**A History of Babylonia and Assyria from Prehistoric Times to the Persian Conquest.** With Plans and Illustrations. 3 vols. royal 8vo, cloth. Each vol. separately, 18s. net; or the 3 vols. if ordered at one time, £2 10s. net.

Vol. I,—**A History of Sumer and Akkad:** An account of the Early Races of Babylonia from Prehistoric Times to the Foundation of the Babylonian Monarchy. [*Ready.*]

„ II.—**A History of Babylon** from the Foundation of the Monarchy, about B.C. 2000, until the Conquest of Babylon by Cyrus, B.C. 539. [*Shortly*]

„ III.—**A History of Assyria** from the Earliest Period until the Fall of Nineveh, B.C. 606. [*Preparing.*]

## KING'S CLASSICS (The).

Under the General Editorship of Prof. ISRAEL GOLLANCZ, D.Litt. Post 8vo, quarter-bound antique grey boards or red cloth, 1s. 6d. net; Double Vols., 3s. net. Quarter vellum, grey cloth sides, 2s. 6d. net; Double Vols., 5s. net. Three-quarter vellum, Oxford side-papers, gilt top, 5s. net; Double Vols., 7s. 6d. net. † signifies Double Volumes. * can be supplied for School use in wrappers at 1s. net each.

1. **The Love of Books: the Philobiblon of Richard de Bury.** Trans. by E.C.THOMAS.
†2. **Six Dramas of Calderon.** Trans. by EN FITZGERALD. Edited by H. OELSNER, M.A.
*3. **The Chronicle of Jocelin of Brakelond.** Trans. from the Latin, with Notes, by L. C. JANE, M.A. Introd. by ABBOT GASQUET.
4. **Life of Sir Thomas More.** By WILLIAM ROPER. With Letters to and from his Daughter.
5. **Eikon Basilike.** Ed. by ED. ALMACK, F.S.A.
6. **Kings' Letters.** Part I.: From Alfred to the Coming of the Tudors. Edited by ROBERT STEELE, F.S.A.
7. **Kings' Letters.** Part II.: From the Early Tudors; with Letters of Henry VIII. and Anne Boleyn.
*8. **Chaucer's Knight's Tale.** *In modern English* by Prof. SKEAT.
*9. **Chaucer's Man of Law's Tale, Squire's Tale, and Nun's Priest's Tale.** *In modern English* by Prof. SKEAT.
*10. **Chaucer's Prioress's Tale, Pardoner's Tale, Clerk's Tale, and Canon's Yeoman's Tale.** *In modern English* by Prof. SKEAT. (See also Nos. 8, 47, 48.)
11. **The Romance of Fulk Fitzwarine.** Translated by ALICE KEMP-WELCH; Introduction by Prof. BRANDIN.
12. **The Story of Cupid and Psyche.** From "The Golden Ass," APULEIUS'S Translation. Edited by W. H. D. ROUSE.
13. **Life of Margaret Godolphin.** By JOHN EVELYN.
14. **Early Lives of Dante.** Translated by Rev. P. H. WICKSTEED.
15. **The Falstaff Letters.** By JAMES WHITE.
16. **Polonius.** By EDWARD FITZGERALD.
17. **Mediæval Lore.** From BARTHOLOMÆUS ANGLICUS. Edited by ROBERT STEELE. With Preface by WILLIAM MORRIS.
18. **The Vision of Piers the Plowman.** By WILLIAM LANGLAND *In modern English* by Prof. SKEAT.
19. **The Gull's Hornbook.** By THOMAS DEKKER. Edited by R. B.MCKERROW,M.A.
†20 **The Nun's Rule, or Ancran Riwle,** in modern English. Edited by ABBOT GASQUET.
21 **Memoirs of Robert Cary, Earl of Monmouth.** Edited by G. H. POWELL.
22. **Early Lives of Charlemagne.** Translated by A. J. GRANT. (See also No. 45.)

## KING'S CLASSICS—*continued.*

23. **Cicero's "Friendship," "Old Age," and "Scipio's Dream."** Edited by W. H. D. ROUSE, Litt.D.
†24. **Wordsworth's Prelude.** With Notes by W. B. WORSFOLD, M.A.
25. **The Defence of Guenevere, and other Poems by William Morris.** With Introduction by ROBERT STEELE.
26, 27. **Browning's Men and Women.** Notes by W. B. WORSFOLD, M.A.[*In 2 Vols.*]
28. **Poe's Poems.** Notes by EDWARD HUTTON.
29. **Shakespeare's Sonnets.** Edited by C. C. STOPES.
30. **George Eliot's Silas Marner.** With Introduction by Dr. R. GARNETT.
31. **Goldsmith's Vicar of Wakefield.** With Introduction by Dr. R. GARNETT.
32. **Charles Reade's Peg Woffington.** With Introduction by Dr. R. GARNETT.
33. **The Household of Sir Thomas More.** By ANNE MANNING. With Preface by Dr. R. GARNETT. (See also Nos. 4, 49.)
34. **Sappho: One Hundred Lyrics.** By BLISS CARMAN.
35. **Wine, Women, and Song: Mediæval Latin Students' Songs.** Translated with Introd. by J. ADDINGTON SYMONDS.
36, 37. **George Pettie's Petite Palace of Pettie His Pleasure.** Edited by Prof. I. GOLLANCZ. [*In Two Volumes.*]
38. **Walpole's Castle of Otranto.** With Preface by Miss SPURGEON.
39. **The Poets Royal of England and Scotland.** Original Poems by Royal and Noble Persons. Edited by W. BAILEY KEMPLING.
40. **Sir Thomas More's Utopia.** Edited by ROBERT STEELE, F.S.A.
*41. **Chaucer's Legend of Good Women.** *In modern English* by Prof. SKEAT.
42. **Swift's Battle of the Books, &c.** Edited by A. GUTHKELCH.
43. **Sir William Temple upon the Gardens of Epicurus, with other XVIIth Century Essays.** Edited by A. FORBES SIEVEKING, F.S.A.
45. **The Song of Roland.** Translated by Mrs. CROSLAND. With Introduction by Prof. BRANDIN. (See also No. 22.)
46. **Dante's Vita Nuova.** The Italian text, with ROSSETTI'S translation, and Introd. by Dr. H. OELSNER. (See also No. 14.)
*47. **Chaucer's Prologue and Minor Poems.** *In modern English* by Prof. SKEAT.
*48. **Chaucer's Parliament of Birds and House of Fame.** *In modern English* by Prof. SKEAT.
49. **Mrs. Gaskell's Cranford.** With Introduction by R. BRIMLEY JOHNSON.
50. **Pearl.** An English Poem of the Fourteenth Century. Edited with Modern Rendering, by Prof. I. GOLLANCZ. [*Preparing.*]
51, 52. **Kings' Letters.** Parts III. and IV. Edited by ROBERT STEELE, F.S.A. [*In Two Volumes. Preparing.*]
53. **The English Correspondence of Saint Boniface.** Trans. by EDWARD KYLIE, M.A.
56. **The Cavalier to His Lady:** XVIIth Century Love Songs. Edited by FRANK SIDGWICK.
57. **Asser's Life of King Alfred.** Translated by L. C. JANE, M.A.
58. **Translations from the Icelandic.** Translated by Rev. W. C. GREEN, M.A.
59. **The Rule of St. Benedict.** Translated by ABBOT GASQUET.
60. **Daniel's "Delia" and Drayton's "Idea,"** Ed. by ARUNDELL ESDAILE, M.A.
61. **The Book of the Duke of True Lovers.** Translated from CHRISTINE DE PISAN by ALICE KEMP-WELCH.
62. **Of the Tumbler of Our Lady, and other Miracles.** Translated from GAUTIER DE COINCI, &c., by ALICE KEMP-WELCH.
63. **The Chatelaine of Vergi.** Translated by ALICE KEMP-WELCH. With Introduction by L. BRANDIN, Ph.D.

**KNIGHT (WILLIAM and EDWARD).** — The Patient's Vade Mecum: How to Get Most Benefit from Medical Advice. Crown 8vo, cloth, 1s. 6d.

**LAMB'S (CHARLES) Collected Works** in Prose and Verse, including 'Poetry for Children' and 'Prince Dorus.' Edited by R. H. SHEPHERD. Crown 8vo, cloth, 3s. 6d.

The Essays of Elia. (Both Series.) FINE PAPER EDITION, pott 8vo, cloth, gilt top, 2s. net: leather, gilt edges, 3s. net.

**LAMBERT (GEORGE).** — The President of Boravia. Cr. 8vo, cl. 3s. 6d.

**LANE (EDWARD WILLIAM).** —The Thousand and One Nights, commonly called in England The Arabian Nights' Entertainments. Illustrated by W. HARVEY. With Preface by STANLEY LANE-POOLE. 3 Vols., demy 8vo, cloth, 5s. net each.

**LASAR (CHARLES A.).—Practical Hints for Art Students.** Illustrated. Post 8vo cloth, 3s. 6d. net.

**LAURISTOUN (PETER).** — The Painted Mountain. Cr. 8vo, cloth, ns

**LEHMANN (R. C.).** — Harry Fludyer at Cambridge, and Conversational Hints for Young Shooters. Crown 8vo, 1s.; cloth, 1s. 6d.

**LEITH (MRS. DISNEY).—The Children of the Chapel.** Including a Morality Play, The Pilgrimage of Pleasure, by A. C. SWINBURNE. Crown 8vo, cloth, 6s. net.

**LELAND (C. G.).—A Manual of Mending and Repairing.** With Diagrams. Crown 8vo, cloth, 5s.

**LEPELLETIER (EDMOND).** — Madame Sans-Gêne. Translated by JOHN DE VILLIERS. Post 8vo, cloth, 3s. 6d.; illustrated boards, 2s.; POPULAR EDITION, medium 8vo, 6d.

**LEYS (JOHN K.).—The Lindsays.** Post 8vo, illust. bds., 2s.

**LILBURN (ADAM).—A Tragedy in Marble.** Crown 8vo, cloth, 3s. 6d.

**LINDSAY (HARRY), Novels by.** Crown 8vo, cloth, 3s. 6d. each.
Rhoda Roberts. | The Jacobite.

**LITTLE (MAUDE), Novels by.** Crown 8vo, cloth, 6s. each.
At the Sign of the Burning Bush.
A Woman on the Threshold.
The Children's Bread.

**LLOYD (Theodosia).—Innocence in the Wilderness.** Cr. 8vo, cloth, 6s.

**LINTON (E. LYNN), Works by.** Crown 8vo, cloth, 3s. 6d. each; post 8vo, illustrated boards, 2s. each.
Patricia Kemball. | Ione.
The Atonement of Leam Dundas.
The World Well Lost. 12 Illusts.
The One Too Many.
Under which Lord? With 12 Il'usts.
'My Love.' | Sowing the Wind.
Paston Carew. | Dulcie Everton.
With a Silken Thread.
The Rebel of the Family.
An Octave of Friends. Crown 8vo, cloth, 3s. 6d.
The Atonement of Leam Dundas. Crown 8vo, cloth, 1s. net.
Patricia Kemball. POPULAR EDITION, medium 8vo, 6d.

**LONDON CLUBS: Their History and Treasures.** By RALPH NEVILL. With Coloured Frontispiece and 8 Plates. Demy 8vo, cloth, 7s. 6d. net.
Clubs and Club Life in London. By JOHN TIMBS. With 41 Illustrations. Crown 8vo, cloth, 3s. 6d.

**LORIMER (NORMA).—The Pagan Woman.** Cr. 8vo, cloth, 3s. 6d.

**LUCAS (ALICE).** — Talmudic Legends, Hymns, and Paraphrases. Post 8vo, half-parchment, 2s. net.

**LUCAS (E. V.), Books by.**
Anne's Terrible Good Nature, and other Stories for Children. With 12 Illustrations by A. H. BUCKLAND, and Coloured End-Papers and Cover by F. D. BEDFORD. Crown 8vo, cloth, 6s.
A Book of Verses for Children. Crown 8vo, cloth, 6s.
Three Hundred Games and Pastimes. By E. V. LUCAS and ELIZABETH LUCAS. Pott 4to, cloth, 6s. net.
The Flamp, and other Stories. Royal 16mo, cloth, 1s. net.

**LUCY (HENRY W.).—Gideon Fleyce.** Crown 8vo, cloth, 3s. 6d.; post 8vo, illustrated boards, 2s.

**LYRE D'AMOUR (La).—An Anthology of French Love Poems.** Selected, with Introduction and Notes, by C. B. LEWIS. With Photogravure Frontispiece. Crown 8vo, cloth, 5s. net.

**McCARTHY (JUSTIN), Books by.**
A History of the Four Georges and of William the Fourth. Four Vols., demy 8vo, cloth, 12s each.
A History of Our Own Times from the Accession of Queen Victoria to the General Election of 1880. LIBRARY EDITION. Four Vols., demy 8vo, cloth, 12s. each.—Also the POPULAR EDITION, in Four Vols., crown 8vo, cloth, 6s. each.—And the JUBILEE EDITION, with an Appendix of Events to the end of 1886, in 2 Vols., large post 8vo, cloth, 1s.
A History of Our Own Times, Vol. V., from 1880 to the Diamond Jubilee. Demy 8vo, cloth, 12s.; crown 8vo, cloth 6s.

**McCARTHY (JUSTIN).**—*continued.*
**A History of Our Own Times,**
Vols. VI. and VII., from 1897 to Accession
of Edward VII. 2 Vols., demy 8vo, cloth,
24s.; crown 8vo, cloth, 6s. each.
**A Short History of Our Own
Times,** from the Accession of Queen
Victoria to the Accession of King
Edward VII. Crown 8vo, cloth, gilt
top, 6s.; also the POPULAR EDITION,
post 8vo, cl., 2s. 6d. net : and the CHEAP
EDITION (to the year 1880), med. 8vo, 6d.
**Our Book of Memories.** Letters
from JUSTIN MCCARTHY to Mrs. CAMP-
BELL PRAED. With Portraits and
Views. Demy 8vo, cloth, 12s. 6d. net.

FINE PAPER EDITIONS.
Pott 8vo, cloth, gilt top, 2s. net per vol. ;
leather, gilt edges, 3s. net per vol.
**The Reign of Queen Anne,** in 1 Vol.
**A History of the Four Georges
and of William IV.,** in 2 vols.
**A History of Our Own Times** from
Accession of Q. Victoria to 1901, in 4 Vols.

Crown 8vo, cloth, 3s. 6d. each ; post 8vo, pict.
boards, 2s. each ; cloth limp, 2s. 6d. each.
**The Waterdale Neighbours.**
**My Enemy's Daughter.**
**A Fair Saxon.** | **Linley Rochford.**
**DearLadyDisdain.** | **The Dictator.**
**Miss Misanthrope.** With 12 Illusts.
**Donna Quixote.** With 12 Illustrations.
**The Comet of a Season.**
**Maid of Athens.** With 12 Illustrations.
**Camiola.**
**Red Diamonds.** | **The Riddle Ring.**

Crown 8vo, cloth, 3s. 6d. each.
**The Three Disgraces.** | **Mononia.**
**Julian Revelstone.**

**'The Right Honourable.'** By JUSTIN
MCCARTHY and MRS. CAMPBELL PRAED.
Crown 8vo, cloth, 6s.

## McCARTHY (J. H.), Works by.
**The French Revolution.** (Consti-
tuent Assembly, 1789-91.) Four Vols.,
demy 8vo, cloth, 12s. each.
**An Outline of the History of
Ireland.** Crown 8vo, 1s. ; cloth, 1s. 6d.
**Hafiz in London.** Cr. 8vo, cloth, 3s. 6d.
**Our Sensation Novel.** Crown 8vo,
1s. ; cloth, 1s. 6d.
**Doom:** An Atlantic Episode. Crown 8vo, 1s.
**Lily Lass.** Crown 8vo, 1s. ; cloth, 1s. 6d.
**A London Legend.** Cr. 8vo, cloth, 3s. 6d.

## MACAULAY (LORD).—The His-
tory of England. LARGE TYPE. FINE
PAPER EDITION, in 5 vols. pott 8vo,
cloth, gilt top, 2s. net per vol.: leather,
gilt edges. 2s. net per vol.

## MACCOLL (HUGH).—Mr.
**Stranger's Sealed Packet.** Cr. 8vo,
cloth 3s. 6d. ; post 8vo, illus. boards, 2s.

## McCURDY (EDWARD).—
**Essays in Fresco.** With 6 Illustrations. Crown 8vo, buckram, 5s. net.

## MACDONELL (AGNES).—
**Quaker Cousins.** Post 8vo, boards, 2s.

## MACDONALD (Dr. GEORGE),
Books by.
**Works of Fancy and Imagination**
Ten Vols., 16mo, Grolier cloth, 2s. 6d. each.
Also in 16mo, cloth, gilt top, 2s. net per
Vol.; leather, gilt top, 3s. net per Vol.

Vol.   I. WITHIN AND WITHOUT — THE
HIDDEN LIFE.
 "    II. THE DISCIPLE — THE GOSPEL
WOMEN—BOOK OF SONNETS—
ORGAN SONGS,
 "   III. VIOLIN SONGS—SONGS OF THE
DAYS AND NIGHTS—A BOOK
OF DREAMS—ROADSIDE POEMS
—POEMS FOR CHILDREN.
 "    IV. PARABLES — BALLADS — SCOTCH
 "    V. & VI. PHANTASTES       [SONGS.
 "   VII. THE PORTENT.
 "  VIII. THE LIGHT PRINCESS — THE
GIANT'S HEART—SHADOWS.
 "    IX. CROSS PURPOSES—GOLDEN KEY
CARASOYN—LITTLEDAYLIGHT.
 "    X. THE CRUEL PAINTER—THE WOW
O'RIVVEN—THE CASTLE—THE
BROKEN SWORDS—THE GRAY
WOLF—UNCLE CORNELIUS.

**Poetical Works.** 2 Vols., cr. 8vo,
buckram, 12s. ; pott 8vo, cloth, gilt top,
2s. net per vol. ; leather, gilt edges, 3s.
net per vol.
**Heather and Snow.** Crown 8vo, cloth,
3s. 6d. ; post 8vo, illustrated boards, 2s.
**Lilith.** Crown 8vo, cloth, 6s.
**The Pocket George MacDonald :**
Passages Chosen by A. H. HYATT, 16mo
cloth gilt, 2s. net : leather gilt, 3s. net.

## MACHRAY (ROBERT), Novels
by. Crown 8vo, cloth, 3s. 6d. each.
**A Blow over the Heart.**
**The Private Detective.**
**Sentenced to Death.**
**The Mystery of Lincoln's Inn.**
Crown 8vo, cloth, 3s. 6d. ; CHEAP
EDITION, picture cover, 1s. net.
**Her Honour.** Crown 8vo, cloth, 3s. 6d. ;
CHEAP EDITION, cloth, 1s. net.
**The Woman Wins.** Cr. 8vo, cloth, 6s.

## MACKAY (Dr. CHAS.).—Inter-
ludes and Undertones. Cr. 8vo, cloth, 6s.

## MACKAY (HELEN).—Half
Loaves; A Novel. Cr. 8vo, cloth, 6s.

## MACKAY (WILLIAM). — A
Mender of Nets. Crown 8vo, cloth, 6s.

## MAGIC LANTERN, The, and its
Management. By T. C. HEPWORTH.
With 10 Illusts. Cr. 8vo, 1s. ; cloth, 1s. 6d.

## MAGNA CHARTA: A Facsimile of
the Original, 3 ft. by 2 ft. with Arms and
Seals emblazoned in Gold and Colours, 5s.

## MALLOCK (W. H.), Works by.
**The New Republic.** FINE PAPER
EDITION, pott 8vo, cloth, gilt top, 2s. net ;
leather, gilt edges, 3s. net ; also post 8vo,
illustrated boards, 2s.
**Poems.** Small 4to, parchment, 8s.
**Is Life Worth Living?** Cr. 8vo, 6s.

**MALLORY (Sir THOMAS).—**
**Mort d'Arthur,** Selections from, edited
by B. M. RANKING. Post 8vo. cloth, 2s.

**MARGUERITTE (PAUL and**
VICTOR), Novels by.
**The Disaster.** Translated by F. LEES.
Crown 8vo, cloth, 3s. 6d. WAR EDITION,
cloth, 2s. net.
**Vanity.** Translated by K. S. WEST. Crown
8vo, cloth, Portrait-Frontispiece, 1s. net.
**The Commune.** Translated by F. LEES
and R. B. DOUGLAS. Cr. 8vo. cloth. 6s.

**MARKINO (Yoshio), Books by.**
**A Japanese Artist in London.** By
YOSHIO MARKINO. With 8 Illusts. in
Three Colours and 4 in Monochrome by
the Author. Cr. 8vo, cloth. 6s. net.
**My Recollections and Reflec-**
**tions.** By YOSHIO MARKINO. With
9 Illusts. in Colour and 6 in Sepia by the
Author. Crown 8vo, cloth, 6s. net.
**The Charm of London.** Passages
selected by A. H. HYATT. With 12 Illusts.
in Colour by YOSHIO MARKINO. Cr. 8vo,
cloth gilt, 5s. net ; velvet calf, 7s. 6d. net.
**Oxford from Within.** By HUGH DE
SÉLINCOURT. With a Note and 12 Illus-
trations in Three Colours and 8 in Sepia
by YOSHIO MARKINO. Demy 8vo, cloth.
7s. 6d. net. : parchment, 15s. net.
Large fcap. 4to. cloth, 20s. net each ; LARGE
PAPER COPIES, parchment, 42s. net each.
Also a CHEAPER EDITION of each book,
fcap. 4to, cloth. 7s. 6d. net.
**The Colour of London.** By W. J.
LOFTIE, F.S.A. With Introduction by
M. H. SPIELMANN, Preface and 48 Illus-
trations in Colour and 12 in Sepia by
YOSHIO MARKINO.
**The Colour of Paris.** By MM. LES
ACADÉMICIENS GONCOURT. With Intro-
duction by L. BÉNÉDITE, Preface and 48
Illustrations in Colour and 12 in Sepia
by YOSHIO MARKINO.
**The Colour of Rome.** By OLAVE M.
POTTER. With Introduction by DOUG-
LAS SLADEN, Preface and 48 Illustra-
tions in Colour and 12 in Sepia by
YOSHIO MARKINO.
Crown 8vo, cloth 6s. net.
**The Story of Yone Noguchi.** By Him-
self. With 8 Illusts. by YOSHIO MARKINO.

**MARLOWE'S Works,** including
his Translations. Edited with Notes by
Col. CUNNINGHAM. Cr. 8vo, cloth, 3s. 6d.

**MARSH (RICHARD), Novels by.**
**A Spoiler of Men.** Crown 8vo, cloth,
3s. 6d.; POPULAR EDITION, med. 8vo, 6d.
Crown 8vo, cloth, 6s. each.
**Justice—Suspended.**
**Margot—and her Judges.**
**His Love or His Life.**

**MASSINGER'S Plays.** From the
Text of WILLIAM GIFFORD. Edited by
Col. CUNNINGHAM. Cr. 8vo, cloth, 3s. 6d.

**MASTERMAN (J.).—Half - a -**
**dozen Daughters.** Post 8vo, bds., 2s.

**MASTER OF GAME (THE):**
**The Oldest English Book** on
**Hunting.** By EDWARD, Second Duke
of York. Edited by W. A. and F.
BAILLIE-GROHMAN. With Introduction
by THEODORE ROOSEVELT. Photogravure
Frontis. and 23 Illustns. Large cr. 8vo.
cl., 7s. 6d. net ; parchment, 10s. 6d, net.

**MATTHEWS (BRANDER).—A**
**Secret of the Sea.** Post 8vo, illustrated boards, 2s.

**MAX O'RELL, Books by.**
Crown 8vo, cloth, 3s. 6d. each.
**Her Royal Highness Woman.**
**Between Ourselves.**
**Rambles in Womanland.**
H.R.H. **Woman,** POPULAR EDITION,
medium 8vo. 6d.

**MAYCOCK (Sir WILLOUGHBY,**
K.C.M.G.) With Mr. Chamberlain in
the United States and Canada. With 30
Illus. Demy 8vo, cloth, 12s. 6d. net.

**MAYNE (ETHEL COLBURN).—**
**Browning's Heroines.** With Frontis-
piece and Title in Colour. and other
Decorations by MAXWELL ARMFIELD.
Large crown 8vo, cloth, 6s. net.

**MEADE (L. T.), Novels by.**
**A Soldier of Fortune.** Crown 8vo,
cloth, 3s. 6d.; post 8vo, illust. boards, 2s.
Crown 8vo, cloth, 3s. 6d. each.
**The Voice of the Charmer.**
**In an Iron Grip.** | **The Siren.**
**Dr. Rumsey's Patient.**
**On the Brink of a Chasm.**
**The Way of a Woman.**
**A Son of Ishmael.**
**An Adventuress.** | **Rosebury.**
**The Blue Diamond.**
**A Stumble by the Way.**
**This Troublesome World.**

**MEDIEVAL LIBRARY** (The
New). Small crown 8vo, pure rag
paper, boards, 5s. net per vol. ; pigskin
with clasps, 7s. 6d. net per vol.
1. **The Book of the Duke of True**
**Lovers.** Translated from the Middle
French of CHRISTINE DE PISAN, with
Notes by ALICE KEMP-WELCH. Woodcut Title and 6 Photogravures.
2. **Of the Tumbler of our Lady,**
**and other Miracles.** Translated
from the Middle French of GAUTIER DE
COINCI, &c., with Notes by ALICE KEMP-
WELCH. Woodcut and 7 Photogravures.
3. **The Chatelaine of Vergi.** Translated from the Middle French by ALICE
KEMP-WELCH, with the original Text,
and an Introduction by Dr. L. BRANDIN.
Woodcut Title and 5 Photogravures.
4. **The Babees' Book.** Edited, with
Notes, by EDITH RICKERT. Woodcut
Title and 6 Photogravures.
5. **The Book of the Divine Con-**
**solation of Saint Angela da**
**Foligno.** Translated by MARY G.
STEEGMANN. Woodcut Title and Illusts.

**MEDIEVAL LIBRARY (The New)**—*cont.* Small crown 8vo, pure rag paper, boards, 5s. net per vol.; pigskin with clasps, 7s. 6d. net per vol.

6. **The Legend of the Holy Fina, Virgin of Santo Geminiano.** Translated by M. MANSFIELD. Woodcut Title and 6 Photogravures.

7. **Early English Romances of Love.** Edited in Modern English by EDITH RICKERT. 5 Photogravures.

8. **Early English Romances of Friendship.** Edited, with Notes, by EDITH RICKERT. 6 Photogravures.

9. **The Cell of Self-Knowledge.** Seven Early Mystical Treatises printed in 1851. Edited, with Introduction and Notes, by EDMUND GARDNER, M.A. Collotype Frontispiece in two colours.

10. **Ancient English Christmas Carols, 1400-1700.** Collected and arranged by EDITH RICKERT. With 8 Photogravures. Special price of this volume, boards, 7s. 6d. net; pigskin with clasps, 10s. 6d. net.

11. **Trobador Poets:** Selections. Translated from the Provençal, with Introduction and Notes, by BARBARA SMYTHE. With Coloured Frontispiece and Decorative Initials.

12. **Cligés:** A Romance. Translated with an Introduction by L. J. GARDINER, M.A.Lond., from the Old French of CHRÉTIEN DE TROYES. With a Frontisp.

**MELBA: A Biography.** By AGNES M. MURPHY. With Chapters by MADAME MELBA on THE ART OF SINGING and on MUSIC AS A PROFESSION. Illustrated. Demy 8vo, cloth, 16s. net.

**MERRICK (HOPE). — When a Girl's Engaged.** Cr. 8vo. cloth, 3s. 6d.

**MERRICK (LEONARD), by. The Man who was Good.** Crown 8vo, cl., 3s. 6d.; post 8vo, illust. bds., 2s.

Crown 8vo, cloth, 3s. 6d. each.
**Cynthia.** | **This Stage of Fools.**

**MERWIN (HENRY CHARLES). The Life of Bret Harte.** With Photogravure Portrait and 10 Plates. Demy 8vo, cl, 10s.6d. net.

**METHVEN (PAUL), Novels by.** Crown 8vo, cloth, 6s. each.
**Influences.** | **Billy.**

**MEYNELL (ALICE).—The Flower of the Mind:** a Choice among the Best Poems. In 16mo, cloth, gilt, 2s. net; leather, 3s. net.

**MITCHELL (EDM.), Novels by.** Crown 8vo, cloth, 3s. 6d. each.
**The Lone Star Rush.** With 8 Illusts.
**The Belforts of Culben.**

Crown 8vo, picture cloth, flat backs, 2s. each.
**Plotters of Paris.**
**The Temple of Death.**
**Towards the Eternal Snows.**

**Only a Nigger.** Crown 8vo, cloth 3s. 6d.; CHEAP EDITION, cloth, 1s. net.

**MINTO (WM.).—Was She Good or Bad?** Crown 8vo, cloth, 1s. 6d.

**MITFORD (BERTRAM), Novels by.** Crown 8vo. cloth. 3s. 6d. each.
**Renshaw Fanning's Quest.**
**Triumph of Hilary Blachland.**
**Haviland's Chum.**
**Harley Greenoak's Charge.**
Crown 8vo, cloth, 3s. 6d. each; picture cloth, flat back, 2s. each.
**The Luck of Gerard Ridgeley.**
**The King's Assegai.** With 6 Illusts.
**The Gun-Runner.** Cr. 8vo, cl., 3s. 6d.
POPULAR EDITIONS, medium 8vo, 6d. each.
**The Gun-Runner.**
**The Luck of Gerard Ridgeley.**

**MOLESWORTH (Mrs.). — Hathercourt Rectory.** Crown 8vo, cloth, 3s. 6d.; post 8vo, illust. boards. 2s.

**MONCRIEFF (W. D. SCOTT-),— The Abdication: A Drama.** With 7 Etchings. Imperial 4to, buckram, 21s.

**MORROW (W. C.).—Bohemian Paris of To-Day.** With 106 Illusts. by EDOUARD CUCUEL. Small demy 8vo, cl., 6s.

**MOZART'S OPERAS: a Critical Study.** By J. DENT. Illustrated. Demy 8vo, cloth, 12s. 6d. net.

**MUDDOCK (J. E.), Stories by.** Crown 8vo, cloth, 3s. 6d. each.
**Basile the Jester.**
**The Golden Idol.**
Post 8vo, illustrated boards, 2s. each.
**The Dead Man's Secret.**
**From the Bosom of the Deep.**
**Stories Weird and Wonderful.** Post 8vo. illust. boards, 2s.; cloth, 2s. 6d.

**MURRAY (D. CHRISTIE), Novels by.** Crown 8vo, cloth, 3s. 6d. each; post 8vo, illustrated boards, 2s. each.
**A Life's Atonement.**
**Joseph's Coat.** With 12 Illustrations.
**Coals of Fire.** With 3 Illustrations.
**Val Strange.** | **A Wasted Crime.**
**A Capful o' Nails.** | **Hearts.**
**The Way of the World.**
**Mount Despair.** | **A Model Father.**
**Old Blazer's Hero.**
**By the Gate of the Sea.**
**A Bit of Human Nature.**
**First Person Singular.**
**Bob Martin's Little Girl.**
**Time's Revenges.**
**Cynic Fortune.** | **In Direst Peril.**
Crown 8vo, cloth, 3s. 6d. each.
**This Little World.**
**A Race for Millions.**
**The Church of Humanity.**
**Tales in Prose and Verse.**
**Despair's Last Journey.**
**V.C.** | **Verona's Father.**
**His Own Ghost.** Crown 8vo, cloth, 3s. 6d.; picture cloth, flat back, 2s.
**Old Blazer's Hero.** Cr. 8vo, cl., 1s. net.
**Joseph's Coat.** POPULAR EDITION, 6d.

**MURRAY (D. CHRISTIE) and HENRY HERMAN, Novels by.** Crown 8vo, cloth, 3s. 6d. each ; post 8vo, illustrated boards, 2s. each.
**One Traveller Returns.**
**The Bishops' Bible.**
**Paul Jones's Alias.** With Illustrations.

**NEVILL (RALPH), Books by.**
**London Clubs: their History and Treasures.** With 9 Plates (one Coloured). Demy 8vo, cloth, 7s. 6d. net.
**The Man of Pleasure.** With 28 Illustrations, Coloured and plain. Demy 8vo, cloth, 12s. 6d. net.

**NEWBOLT (HENRY). — Taken from the Enemy.** With 8 Coloured Illusts. by GERALD LEAKE. Cr. 8vo, cl., 3s. 6d. net ; fcap. 8vo, no Illusts., 1s.

**NEWTE (H. W. C.), Novels by.** Crown 8vo, cloth, 6s. each.
**Pansy Meares.** [Also Cheap Ed. 1s. net.
**A 'Young Lady':** A Study in Selectness.
**The Home of the Seven Devils.**
**The Cuckoo Lamb.**
**A Pillar of Salt.**
CHEAPER EDITIONS. Crown 8vo, picture boards, 1s. net. each.
**Pansy Meares.** | **A 'Young Lady.**

**NIJINSKY, THE ART OF.** By GEOFFREY WHITWORTH. Illustrated in Colour by DOROTHY MULLOCK. Post 8vo. cloth, 3s. 6d. net.

**NISBET (HUME), Books by.**
**'Bail Up!'** Crown 8vo, cloth, 3s. 6d. ; post 8vo, boards, 2s. ; medium 8vo, 6d.
**Dr. Bernard St. Vincent.** Post 8vo, illustrated boards, 2s.

**NOGUCHI (YONE), The Story of.** Told by Himself. With 8 Illustrations by YOSHIO MARKINO. Cr. 8vo, cl., 6s. net.

**NORDAU (MAX).—Morganatic.** Trans. by ELIZABETH LEE. Cr. 8vo, cl. 6s.

**NORRIS (W. E.), Novels by.** Cr. 8vo, cl., 3s. 6d. each ; bds., 2s. each.
**Saint Ann's.** | **Billy Bellew.**
**Miss Wentworth's Idea.** Cr. 8vo, 3s. 6d.

**OHNET (GEORGES), Novels by.** Post 8vo, illustrated boards, 2s. each.
**Dr. Rameau.** | **A Last Love.**
**A Weird Gift.** Crown 8vo, cloth, 3s. 6d ; post 8vo, illustrated boards, 2s.
Crown 8vo, cloth, 3s. 6d. each.
**The Path of Glory.**
**Love's Depths.**
**The Money-maker.**
**The Woman of Mystery.**
**The Conqueress.**
**Doctor Rameau.** Cr. 8vo, cloth, 1s. net.

**OLIPHANT (Mrs.), Novels by.** Post 8vo, illustrated boards, 2s. each.
**The Primrose Path.**
**The Greatest Heiress in England**
**Whiteladies.** Crown 8vo, cloth, with 12 Illustrations, 3s. 6d. ; post 8vo, bds., 2s.
**The Sorceress.** Crown 8vo, cloth, 3s. 6d.

**OLYMPIA : the Latin Text of Boccaccio's Fourteenth Eclogue.** with an English rendering and other Supplementary Matter by ISRAEL GOLLANCZ, Litt.D., and Photogravure Frontispiece. Printed in the Florence Press Type upon hand-made paper. Edition limited to 500 copies. Fcap. 4to, boards, 6s. net ; vellum, 12s. 6d. net.

**O'SHAUGHNESSY (ARTHUR).**
**Music & Moonlight.** Fcp. 8vo. cl., 7s. 6d.

**OUIDA, Novels by.** Crown 8vo, cloth, 3s. 6d. each ; post 8vo, illustrated boards, 2s. each.

| | |
|---|---|
| Tricotrin. | A Dog of Flanders. |
| Ruffino. | Cecil Castlemaine's |
| Othmar. | Gage. |
| Frescoes. | Princess Napraxine. |
| Wanda. | Held in Bondage. |
| Ariadne. | Under Two Flags. |
| Pascarel. | Folle-Farine. |
| Chandos. | Two Wooden Shoes. |
| Moths. | A Village Commune. |
| Puck. | In a Winter City. |
| Idalia. | Santa Barbara. |
| Bimbi. | In Maremma. |
| Signa. | Strathmore. |
| Friendship. | Pipistrello. |
| Guilderoy. | Two Offenders. |
| | Syrlin. |

Crown 8vo, cloth, 3s. 6d. each.
**A Rainy June.** | **The Massarenes.**
**The Waters of Edera.**

CHEAPER EDITIONS, crown 8vo, cloth, flat backs, 2s. each.
**Syrlin.** | **The Waters of Edera.**

POPULAR EDITIONS, medium 8vo, 6d. each.

| | |
|---|---|
| Under Two Flags. | Moths. |
| Held in Bondage. | Puck. |
| Strathmore. | Tricotrin. |
| The Massarenes. | Chandos. |
| Friendship. | Ariadne. |

Two Little Wooden Shoes.
**Idalia.** | **Othmar.** | **Pascarel.**
**A Village Commune.** (Crown 8vo.)
**Folle-Farine.** | **Princess Napraxine**
**Wanda.** In Maremma.

**Two Little Wooden Shoes.** LARGE TYPE EDITION. Fcap. 8vo, cloth, 1s. net.

CHEAP EDITIONS. Cr. 8vo, cloth, 1s. net.
**Ruffino.** | **Syrlin.**

Demy 8vo, cloth, 5s. net each.
**A Dog of Flanders, The Nürnberg Stove, &c.** With 8 Illustrations in Colour by MARIA L. KIRK.
**Bimbi:** Stories for Children. With 8 Illustrations in Colour by MARIA L. KIRK.

**Wisdom, Wit, and Pathos,** selected from the Works of OUIDA by F. SYDNEY MORRIS. Pott. 8vo, cloth, gilt top, 2s. net; leather, gilt edges, 3s. net.

**OSBOURNE (LLOYD), Stories by.** Crown 8vo, cloth, 3s. 6d. each.
**The Motormaniacs.**
**Three Speeds Forward.** With Illusts.

**OXFORD FROM WITHIN.** By HUGH DE SÉLINCOURT. With a Note and 12 Illustrations in Colour and 8 in Sepia by YOSHIO MARKINO. Demy 8vo, cloth, 7s. 6d. net. ; parchment, 15s. net.

**PAGE (THOMAS NELSON).—** Santa Claus's Partner. With 8 Coloured Illustrations by OLGA MORGAN. Crown 8vo, cloth, 3s. 6d. net.

**PAIN (BARRY).—Eliza's Husband.** Fcap., 8vo, 1s. ; cloth, 1s. 6d.

**PANDURANG HARI; or,** Memoirs of a Hindoo. Post 8vo, illustrated boards, 2s.

**PARIS.—Bohemian Paris of To-day.** By W. C. MORROW. With 106 Illustrations by E. CUCUEL. Small demy 8vo, cloth, 6s.

The Illustrated Catalogue of the Paris Salon. With about 300 illustrations. Published annually. Dy. 8vo, 3s.

**PATTERSON (MARJORIE).—** The Dust of the Road: A Novel. Crown 8vo, cloth, 6s.

**PAUL (MARGARET A.).—Gentle** and Simple. Crown 8vo, cloth, 3s. 6d. ; post 8vo, illustrated boards, 2s.

**PAYN (JAMES), Novels by.** Crown 8vo, cloth, 3s. 6d. each ; post 8vo, illustrated boards, 2s. each.
Lost Sir Massingberd.
The Clyffards of Clyffe.
A County Family.
Less Black than We're Painted.
By Proxy. | For Cash Only.
High Spirits. | Sunny Stories.
A Confidential Agent.
A Grape from a Thorn. 12 Illusts.
The Family Scapegrace.
Holiday Tasks. | At Her Mercy.
The Talk of the Town. 12 Illusts.
The Mystery of Mirbridge.
The Word and the Will.
The Burnt Million.
A Trying Patient.
Gwendoline's Harvest.

Post 8vo, illustrated boards, 2s. each.
Humorous Stories. | From Exile.
The Foster Brothers.
Married Beneath Him.
Bentinck's Tutor.
Walter's Word. | Fallen Fortunes.
A Perfect Treasure.
Like Father, Like Son.
A Woman's Vengeance.
Carlyon's Year. | Cecil's Tryst.
Murphy's Master.
Some Private Views.
Found Dead. | Mirk Abbey.
A Marine Residence.
The Canon's Ward.
Not Wooed, But Won.
Two Hundred Pounds Reward.
The Best of Husbands.
Halves. | What He Cost Her.
Kit: A Memory. | Under One Roof.
Glow-Worm Tales.
A Prince of the Blood.

**PAYN (JAMES)—continued.**
A Modern Dick Whittington. Crown 8vo, cloth, with Portrait of Author, 3s. 6d. ; picture cloth, flat back, 2s.
Notes from the 'News.' Crown 8vo, cloth, 1s. 6d.

Crown 8vo, cloth, 1s. net.
A Confidential Agent.
The Word and the Will.

POPULAR EDITIONS, medium 8vo, 6d. each.
Lost Sir Massingberd.
Walter's Word. | By Proxy.

**PAYNE (WILL). — Jerry the** Dreamer. Crown 8vo, cloth, 3s. 6d.

**PEARS (CHARLES).—From the** Thames to the Netherlands. Illustrated by the Author. Large crown 8vo, cloth, 6s. net.

**PENNY (F. E.), Novels by.** Crown 8vo, cloth, 3s. 6d. each.
The Sanyasi. | The Tea-Planter.
Caste and Creed. | Inevitable Law.
Dilys. | The Rajah.

Crown 8vo, cloth, 6s. each.
The Unlucky Mark. | Sacrifice.
Dark Corners. | Love in the Hills.
The Malabar Magician.
The Outcaste. | Love in a Palace.

POPULAR EDITIONS, medium 8vo, 6d. each.
The Tea-Planter. | Caste and Creed
Inevitable Law. | The Sanyasi.

**PERRIN (ALICE), Novels by.** Crown 8vo, cloth, 3s. 6d. each.
A Free Solitude. | East of Suez.
The Waters of Destruction.
Red Records.
The Stronger Claim.
Idolatry. Cr. 8vo, cloth, 6s.; also 2s. net.

POPULAR EDITIONS, medium 8vo, 6d. each.
The Stronger Claim.
The Waters of Destruction.
Idolatry. | A Free Solitude.

**PETIT HOMME ROUGE (Le),** Books by. Demy 8vo, cl., 7s. 6d. net each.
My Days of Adventure : The Fall of France, 1870-71. With Frontisp.
The Favourites of Louis XIV. With 4 Portraits.
My Adventures in the Commune. With numerous Illustrations, 12s. 6d. net.
The Court of the Tuileries, 1852-1870. With a Frontispiece. Cl., 5s. net.

**PETRARCH'S SECRET ; or,** The Soul's Conflict with Passion. Three Dialogues. Translated from the Latin by W. H. DRAPER. With 2 Illustrations. Crown 8vo, cloth, 6s. net.

**PHELPS (E. S.).—Jack the** Fisherman. Crown 8vo, cloth, 1s. 6d.

**PHIL MAY'S Sketch-Book :** 54 Cartoons. Crown folio, cloth, 2s. 6d.

**PHIPSON (Dr. T. L.).—Famous** Violinists and Fine Violins. Crown 8vo, cloth, 5s.

22

**PICKTHALL (MARMADUKE).—**
Larkmeadow : A Novel of the Country Districts. Crown 8vo. cloth, 6s.

**PLANCHÉ (J. R.).—Songs and Poems.** Crown 8vo, cloth, 6s.

**PLAYS OF OUR FORE-FATHERS.** By C. M. GAYLEY. Roy. 8vo, cl., 12s. 6d. net.

**PLUTARCH'S Lives of Illustrious Men.** With Life of PLUTARCH by J. and W. LANGHORNE, and Portraits. Two Vols., 8vo, half-cloth. 10s. 6d.

**POEMS OF THE GREAT WAR.** Fcap. 4to. 1s. net.

**POE'S (EDGAR ALLAN) Choice Works.** With an Introduction by CHAS. BAUDELAIRE. Cr. 8vo, cl., 3s. 6d.

**POLLOCK (W. H.).—The Charm, and Other Drawing-Room Plays.** By Sir WALTER BESANT and WALTER H. POLLOCK. With 50 Illustrations. Crown 8vo, cloth, 3s. 6d.

**POUGIN (ARTHUR).—A Short History of Russian Music.** Translated by LAWRENCE HAWARD. Crown 8vo, cloth, 5s. net.

**PRAED (Mrs. CAMPBELL),**
Novels by. Post 8vo, illus. boards, 2s. ea.
**The Romance of a Station.**
**The Soul of Countess Adrian.**
Crown 8vo, cloth, 3s. 6d. each ; post 8vo, illustrated boards, 2s. each.
**Outlaw and Lawmaker.**
**Christina Chard.**
**Mrs. Tregaskiss.** With 8 Illustrations.
Crown 8vo, cloth, 3s. 6d. each.
**Nulma.** | **Madame Izan.**
**'As a Watch in the Night.'**
**The Lost Earl of Ellan.**
**Our Book of Memories.** Letters from JUSTIN MCCARTHY. With Ports. and Views. Demy 8vo, cl., 12s. 6d. net.
See also under JUSTIN MCCARTHY.

**PRESLAND (JOHN), Dramas**
by. Fcap. 4to, cloth, 5s. net each.
**Mary Queen of Scots.**
**Manin and the Defence of Venice.**
**Marcus Aurelius.**
**Belisarius, General of the East.**

Small crown 8vo, cloth, 3s. 6d. net each.
**The Deluge, and other Poems.**
**Songs of Changing Skies.**

**PROCTOR (RICHARD A.),**
Books by. Crown 8vo, cloth, 3s. 6d. each.
**Easy Star Lessons.** With Star Maps.
**Flowers of the Sky.** With 55 Illusts.
**Familiar Science Studies.**

**Saturn and its System.** With 13 Steel Plates. Demy 8vo, cloth. 6s.
**Wages and Wants of Science Workers.** Crown 8vo, 1s. 6d.

**PRICE (E. C.). — Valentina.**
Crown 8vo. cloth, 3s. 6d.

**PRYCE (RICHARD). — Miss Maxwell's Affections.** Crown 8vo, cloth. 3s. 6d. : post 8vo, illust. boards, 2s.

**RAB AND HIS FRIENDS.** By Dr. JOHN BROWN. Square 16mo, with Frontispiece, cloth, 1s. net.

**READE'S (CHARLES) Novels.**
Collected LIBRARY EDITION, in Seventeen Volumes, crown 8vo, cloth, 3s. 6d each.
**Peg Woffington ; and Christie Johnstone.**
**Hard Cash.**
**The Cloister and the Hearth.** With a Preface by Sir WALTER BESANT.
**'It is Never Too Late to Mend.'**
**The Course of True Love Never Did Run Smooth ; and Singleheart and Doubleface.**
**The Autobiography of a Thief ; Jack of all Trades ; A Hero and a Martyr; The Wandering Heir.**
**Love Me Little, Love Me Long.**
**The Double Marriage.**
**Put Yourself in His Place.**
**A Terrible Temptation.**
**Griffith Gaunt.** | **A Woman-Hater.**
**Foul Play.** | **A Simpleton.**
**The Jilt ; and Good Stories of Man and other Animals.**
**A Perilous Secret.**
**Readiana ; and Bible Characters.**

Also in Twenty-one Volumes, post 8vo, illustrated boards, 2s. each.
**Peg Woffington.** | **A Simpleton.**
**Christie Johnstone.**
**'It is Never Too Late to Mend.'**
**The Course of True Love Never Did Run Smooth.**
**Autobiography of a Thief; Jack of all Trades; James Lambert.**
**Love Me Little, Love Me Long.**
**The Double Marriage.**
**The Cloister and the Hearth.**
**A Terrible Temptation.**
**Hard Cash.** | **Readiana.**
**Foul Play.** | **Griffith Gaunt.**
**Put Yourself in His Place.**
**The Wandering Heir.**
**A Woman-Hater.**
**Singleheart and Doubleface.**
**Good Stories of Man,** &c.
**The Jilt ; and other Stories.**
**A Perilous Secret.**

LARGE TYPE, FINE PAPER EDITIONS.
Pott 8vo, cloth, gilt top, 2s. net each ; leather, gilt edges, 3s. net each.
**The Cloister and the Hearth.** With 32 Illustrations by M. B. HEWERDINE.
**'It is Never Too Late to Mend.'**

POPULAR EDITIONS, medium 8vo, 6d. each.
**The Cloister and the Hearth.**
**'It is Never Too Late to Mend.'**
**Foul Play.** | **Hard Cash.**
**Peg Woffington ; and Christie Johnstone.**
**Griffith Gaunt.**
**Put Yourself in His Place.**

23

READE (CHARLES)—*continued*.
POPULAR EDITIONS, medium 8vo, 6d. each.
**A Terrible Temptation.**
**The Double Marriage.**
**Love Me Little, Love Me Long.**
**A Perilous Secret.**
**A Woman-hater.**
**The Course of True Love.**
**The Wandering Heir.** LARGE TYPE
EDITION, fcap. 8vo, cloth. 1s. net.
**A Perilous Secret.** Crown 8vo, cloth,
1s. net.
**The Cloister and the Hearth.**
With 16 Photogravure and 84 half-tone
Illustrations by MATT B. HEWERDINE
Small 4to, cloth, 6s. net.—Also the
ST. MARTIN'S ILLUSTRATED EDITION,
with 20 Illustrations in 4 Colours and
10 in Black and White by BYAM SHAW,
R.I. Demy 8vo, cloth, 7s. 6d. net ;
parchment, 10s. 6d. net.

REITLINGER (FRÉDÉRIC).—A
**Diplomat's Memoir of 1870.** Trans-
lated from the French by HENRY REIT-
LINGER. Crown 8vo, cloth, 2s. net.

RICHARDSON (Frank), Novels by.
**The Man who Lost his Past.** With
50 Illustrations by TOM BROWNE, R.I.
Crown 8vo, cloth, 3s. 6d. ; POPULAR
EDITION, picture cover, 1s. net.
**The Bayswater Miracle.** Crown
8vo, cloth, 3s. 6d.
Crown 8vo, cloth, 6s. each.
**The King's Counsel.**
**There and Back.**

RIDDELL (Mrs.), Novels by.
**A Rich Man's Daughter.** Crown
8vo, cloth, 3s. 6d.
**Weird Stories.** Crown 8vo, cloth,
3s. 6d.; post 8vo, picture boards, 2s.
Post 8vo, illustrated boards, 2s. each.
**The Uninhabited House.**
**Prince of Wales's Garden Party.**
**The Mystery in Palace Gardens.**
**Fairy Water.** | **Idle Tales.**
**Her Mother's Darling.**

RIVES (AMELIE), Stories by.
Crown 8vo, cloth, 3s. 6d. each.
**Barbara Dering.**
**Meriel:** A Love Story.

ROBINSON (F. W.), Novels by.
**Women are Strange.** Post 8vo,
illustrated boards, 2s.
Crown 8vo, cloth, 3s. 6d. each; post 8vo,
illustrated boards, 2s. each.
**The Hands of Justice.**
**The Woman in the Dark.**

ROLFE (FR.), Novels by.
Crown 8vo, cloth, 6s. each.
**Hadrian the Seventh.**
**Don Tarquinio.**

ROLL OF BATTLE ABBEY,
THE: List of the Principal Warriors who
came from Normandy with William the
Conqueror, 1066. In Gold and Colours, 5s.

ROMAUNT (THE) OF THE
ROSE. With 20 Illustrations in
Coloured Collotype by KEITH HENDER-
SON and NORMAN WILKINSON. Crown
4to, cloth, 21s. net.

ROSENGARTEN (A.).—A Hand-
book of Architectural Styles. Translated by W. COLLETT-SANDARS. With
630 Illustrations. Cr. 8vo, cloth, 5s. net.

ROSS (ALBERT).—A Sugar
Princess. Crown 8vo, cloth, 3s. 6d.

ROWLANDS (EFFIE ADE-
LAIDE), Novels by. Crown 8vo,
cloth, 6s. each.
**The Price Paid.** | **Her Husband.**

ROWSELL (MARY C.).—Mon-
sieur de Paris. Cr. 8vo, cl., 3s. 6d.

RUNCIMAN (JAS.).—Skippers
and Shellbacks. Cr. 8vo, cloth, 3s. 6d.

RUSKIN SERIES (The). Square
16mo, cl., with Frontispieces, 1s. net ea.
**The King of the Golden River.**
By JOHN RUSKIN. Illustrated by DOYLE.
**Ruskin as a Religious Teacher.**
By F. W. FARRAR, D.D.
**Rab and his Friends.** By Dr. JOHN
BROWN.
**Old Christmas.** WASHINGTON IRVING.
**Fairy Tales from Tuscany.** By I.
M. ANDERTON.
**The Pocket Ruskin.** 16mo, cloth gilt.
2s. net. ; leather gilt, 3s. net.

RUSSELL (W. CLARK), Novels
by. Cr. 8vo, cl., 3s. 6d. each ; post 8vo,
boards, 2s. each ; cloth limp, 2s. 6d. each.
**Round the Galley-Fire.**
**In the Middle Watch.**
**On the Fo'k'sle Head.**
**A Voyage to the Cape.**
**A Book for the Hammock.**
**The Mystery of the 'Ocean Star.**
**The Romance of Jenny Harlowe.**
**The Tale of the Ten.**
**An Ocean Tragedy.**
**My Shipmate Louise.**
**Alone on a Wide Wide Sea**
**The Good Ship 'Mohock.'**
**The Phantom Death.**
**Is He the Man? | The Last Entry**
**The Convict Ship. | Heart of Oak.**
Crown 8vo, cloth, 3s. 6d. each.
**A Tale of Two Tunnels.**
**The Death Ship.**
**Overdue.** | **Wrong Side Out.**
POPULAR EDITIONS, medium 8vo, 6d. each.
**The Convict Ship.**
**Is He the Man?**
**My Shipmate Louise.**

RUSSELL (DORA), Novels by
Cr. 8vo. cl., 3s. 6d., ea. : pict. cl. 2s. each.
**A Country Sweetheart.**
**The Drift of Fate.**

24

**RUSSELL (HERBERT).—True Blue.** Crown 8vo, cloth, 3s. 6d.

**RUSSIAN BASTILLE, THE** (The Fortress of Schluesselburg). By I. P. YOUVATSHEV. Translated by A. S. RAPPOPORT, M.A. With 16 Plates. Demy 8vo, cloth, 7s. 6d. net.

**SAINT AUBYN (ALAN), Novels by.** Crown 8vo, cloth, 3s. 6d. each ; post 8vo, illustrated boards, 2s. each.
**A Fellow of Trinity.** With a Note by OLIVER WENDELL HOLMES.
**The Junior Dean.**
**Orchard Dameral.**
**The Master of St. Benedict's.**
**In the Face of the World.**
**To His Own Master.**
**The Tremlett Diamonds.**
        Crown 8vo, cloth, 3s. 6d. each.
**The Wooing of May.**
**Fortune's Gate.**
**A Tragic Honeymoon.**
**Gallantry Bower.**
**A Proctor's Wooing.**
**Bonnie Maggie Lauder.**
**Mrs. Dunbar's Secret.**
**Mary Unwin.** With 8 Illustrations.
**To His Own Master.** Cr. 8vo, cloth, 1s. net.

**SAINT JOHN (BAYLE). — A Levantine Family.** Cr. 8vo, cl., 3s. 6d.

**SALA (G. A.).—Gaslight and Daylight.** Post 8vo illustrated boards. 2s.

**SANDEMAN (GEORGE).— Agnes.** Crown 8vo, cloth, 6s.

**SÉLINCOURT (HUGH DE), Books by.**
**Oxford from Within.** With a Note and 20 Illustrations in Colour and Monochrome by YOSHIO MARKINO. Demy 8vo, cloth, 7s. 6d. net ; parchment. 15s. net.
**A Daughter of the Morning.** Crown 8vo, cloth, 6s.

**SERGEANT (ADELINE), Novels by.** Crown 8vo, cloth, 3s. 6d. each.
**Under False Pretences.**
**Dr. Endicott's Experiment.**
**The Missing Elizabeth.**

**SERMON ON THE MOUNT (The).** Illuminated in Gold and Colours by ALBERTO SANGORSKI. Fcap. 4to. Jap. vellum. 6s. net ; parchment, full gilt, with silk ties, 8s. 6d. net.

**ST. MARTIN'S LIBRARY (The).** In pocket size, cloth, gilt top, 2s. net per Vol. ; leather, gilt edges. 3s. net per Vol.
        By WALTER BESANT.
**London.**      |     **Westminster.**
**Jerusalem.** By BESANT and PALMER.
**All Sorts and Conditions of Men.**
**Sir Richard Whittington.**
**Gaspard de Coligny.**
        By GIOVANNI BOCCACCIO.
**The Decameron.**

ST. MARTIN'S LIBRARY—continued.
        By ROBERT BROWNING.
Illustrated in Colours by E. F. BRICKDALE.
**Pippa Passes : and Men and Women.**
**Dramatis Personæ : and Dramatic Romances and Lyrics.**
        By ROBERT BUCHANAN.
**The Shadow of the Sword.**
        By HALL CAINE.
**The Deemster.**
        By WILKIE COLLINS.
**The Woman in White.**
        By DANIEL DEFOE.
**Robinson Crusoe.** With 37 Illustrations by G. CRUIKSHANK.
        By CHARLES DICKENS.
**Speeches.** With Portrait.
        By AUSTIN DOBSON.
**Eighteenth Century Vignettes.** In Three Series, each Illustrated.
        By W. S. GILBERT.
**Original Plays.** In Four Series, the Fourth Series with a Portrait.
        By THOMAS HARDY.
**Under the Greenwood Tree.**
        By BRET HARTE.
**Condensed Novels.**
**Mliss, The Luck of Roaring Camp,** and other Stories. With Portrait.
**Poetical Works.**
        By OLIVER WENDELL HOLMES
**The Autocrat of the Breakfast-Table.** Illustrated by J. G. THOMSON
Compiled by A. H. HYATT.
**The Charm of London:** An Anthology.
**The Charm of Edinburgh.**
**The Charm of Venice.**
**The Charm of Paris.**
        By RICHARD JEFFERIES.
**The Life of the Fields.**
**The Open Air.**
**Nature near London.**
        By CHARLES LAMB.
**The Essays of Elia.**
        By LORD MACAULAY.
**History of England,** in 5 Volumes.
        By JUSTIN McCARTHY.
**The Reign of Queen Anne,** in 1 Vol.
**A History of the Four Georges and of William IV.,** in 2 Vols.
**A History of Our Own Times** from Accession of Q. Victoria to 1901. in 4 Vols.
        By GEORGE MacDONALD.
**Poetical Works.** In 2 vols.
**Works of Fancy and Imagination,** in 10 Vols. 16mo. (For List, see p. 18.)
        By W. H. MALLOCK.
**The New Republic.**
        By OUIDA.
**Wisdom, Wit, and Pathos.**
        By CHARLES READE.
**The Cloister and the Hearth.** With 32 Illustrations by M. B. HEWERDINE.
**'It is Never Too Late to Mend.'**
        By PERCY BYSSHE SHELLEY.
**Prose Works.** 2 vols. with 2 Ports.
**Poetical Works.** 2 vols., with 2 Plates.
Selected by FRANK SIDGWICK, and Illustrated in Colours by BYAM SHAW.
**Ballads and Lyrics of Love.**
**Historical and Legendary Ballads.**

25

# CHATTO & WINDUS, 111 ST. MARTIN'S LANE, LONDON, W.C.

**ST. MARTIN'S LIBRARY**—*continued.*
In pocket size, cloth, gilt top, 2s. net per Vol. ; leather, gilt edges, 3s. net per Vol.

By ROBERT LOUIS STEVENSON.
**An Inland Voyage.**
**Travels with a Donkey.**
**The Silverado Squatters.**
**Memories and Portraits.**
**Virginibus Puerisque.**
**Men and Books.**
**New Arabian Nights.**
**Across the Plains.**
**The Merry Men.**
**Prince Otto.**
**In the South Seas.**
**Essays of Travel.**
**Weir of Hermiston.**
**Tales and Fantasies.**
**The Art of Writing.**
**Lay Morals, etc.** | **Poems.**

By H. A. TAINE.
**History of English Literature,** in 4 Vols. With 32 Portraits.

By MARK TWAIN.—**Sketches.**
By WALTON and COTTON.
**The Complete Angler.**

By WALT WHITMAN.
**Poems.** Selected and Edited by W. M. ROSSETTI. With Portrait.

## SANGORSKI (ALBERTO),
**Books Illuminated by.** Fcap. 4to, Jap. vellum, 6s. net each : parchment gilt, with silk ties, 8s. 6d. net each.
**Prayers Written at Vailima** by ROBERT LOUIS STEVENSON.
**The Sermon on the Mount.**
**Morte d'Arthur,** by LORD TENNYSON.

## SCOTT (CYRIL).—The Celestial
**Aftermath.** Pott 4to, cloth, 5s. net. LARGE PAPER EDITION. limited to 50 copies, signed by the Author, 21s. net.

## SHADOWLESS MAN (THE):
**Peter Schlemihl.** By A. VON CHAMISSO. Illustrated by GORDON BROWNE. Demy 8vo, cloth, 3s. 6d. net.

## SHAKESPEARE LIBRARY.
**PART I.**
The **Old-Spelling SHAKESPEARE.**
With the spelling of the Quarto or the Folio as the basis of the Text, and all changes marked in heavy type. Edited by F. J. FURNIVALL, M.A., D.Litt., and F. W. CLARKE, M.A. Demy 8vo, cloth, 2s. 6d. net each Play. Of some of the plays a Library Edition may be had at 5s. net each. A list of volumes on application.

**PART II.**
The **SHAKESPEARE CLASSICS.**
Small crown 8vo, quarter-bound antique grey boards, 2s. 6d. net per vol. ; those marked † may also be had in velvet persian at 4s. net : and those marked ⁑ on large paper, half parchment, 5s. net, per vol. Each volume with Frontispiece.

⁑†1. **Lodge's 'Rosalynde': the original of Shakespeare's 'As You Like It.'** Edited by W. W. GREG, M.A. · [*Ready.*

**SHAKESPEARE LIBRARY**—*cont.*
**SHAKESPEARE CLASSICS**—*cont.*
*Volumes published or in preparation.*

⁑†2. **Greene's 'Pandosto,' or 'Dorastus and Fawnia': the original of Shakespeare's 'Winter's Tale.'** Ed. by P. G. THOMAS. [*Ready.*

⁑†3. **Brooke's Poem of 'Romeus and Juliet': the original of Shakespeare's 'Romeo and Juliet.'** Edited by P. A. DANIEL. Modernised and re-edited by J. J. MUNRO. [*Ready.*

4. **'The Troublesome Reign of King John': the Play rewritten by Shakespeare as 'King John.'** Edited by Dr. F. J. FURNIVALL and JOHN MUNRO, M.A. [*Ready.*

5, 6. **'The History of Hamlet':** With other Documents illustrative of the sources of Shakspeare's Play, and an Introductory Study of the LEGEND OF HAMLET by Prof. I. GOLLANCZ.

⁑†7. **'The Play of King Leir and His Three Daughters': the old play on the subject of King Lear.** Edited by SIDNEY LEE, D.Litt. [*Ready.*

⁑†8. **'The Taming of a Shrew':** Being the old play used by Shakespeare in 'The Taming of the Shrew.' Edited by Professor F. S. BOAS, M.A. [*Ready.*

⁑†9. **The Sources and Analogues of 'A Midsummer Night's Dream.'** Edited by FRANK SIDGWICK. [*Ready.*

10. **'The Famous Victories of Henry V.'**

11. **'The Menaechmi': the original of Shakespeare's 'Comedy of Errors.'** Latin text, with the Elizabethan Translation. Edited by W. H. D. ROUSE, Litt.D. [*Ready.*

12. **'Promos and Cassandra': the source of 'Measure for Measure.'**

13. **'Apolonius and Silla': the** source of 'Twelfth Night.' Edited by MORTON LUCE. [*Ready.*

14. **'The First Part of the Contention betwixt the two famous Houses of York and Lancaster,' and 'The True Tragedy of Richard, Duke of York': the** originals of the second and third parts of 'King Henry VI.'

15. **The Sources of 'The Tempest.'**

16. **The Sources of 'Cymbeline.'**

17. **The Sources and Analogues of 'The Merchant of Venice.'** Edited by Professor I. GOLLANCZ.

18. **Romantic Tales :** the sources of 'The Two Gentlemen of Verona,' 'Merry Wives,' 'Much Ado about Nothing,' 'All's Well that Ends Well.'

⁑†19, 20. **Shakespeare's Plutarch:** the sources of 'Julius Cæsar,' 'Antony and Cleopatra,' 'Coriolanus,' and 'Timon.' Ed. C. F. TUCKER BROOKE, M.A. [*Ready.*

## SHAKESPEARE LIBRARY—*cont.*

### PART III.

**THE LAMB SHAKESPEARE FOR YOUNG PEOPLE.**

With Illustrations and Music. Based on MARY AND CHARLES LAMB'S TALES FROM SHAKESPEARE, and edited by Professor I. GOLLANCZ, who has inserted within the prose setting those scenes and passages from the Plays with which the young reader should early become acquainted. The Music arranged by T. MASKELL HARDY. Imperial 16mo, cloth, 1s. 6d. net per vol. ; leather, 2s. 6d. net per vol. ; School Edit, linen, 8d. net per vol.

I. **The Tempest.**
II. **As You Like It.**
III. **A Midsummer Night's Dream.**
IV. **The Merchant of Venice.**
V. **The Winter's Tale.**
VI. **Twelfth Night.**
VII. **Cymbeline.**
VIII. **Romeo and Juliet.**
IX. **Macbeth.**
X. **Much Ado About Nothing.**

XI. **Life of Shakespeare for the Young.** By Prof. I. GOLLANCZ.
[*Preparing.*

XII, **An Evening with Shakespeare:** 10 Dramatic Tableaux for Young People, with Music by T. MASKELL HARDY, and Illustrations. Cloth, 2s. net ; leather, 3s. 6d. net ; linen, 1s. 6d. net.

### PART IV.

**SHAKESPEARE'S ENGLAND.**
A series of volumes illustrative of the life, thought, and letters of England in the time of Shakespeare.

**Robert Laneham's Letter,** describing part of the Entertainment given to Queen Elizabeth at Kenilworth Castle in 1575. With Introduction by Dr. FURNIVALL, and Illustrations. Demy 8vo, cloth, 5s. net.

**The Rogues and Vagabonds of Shakespeare's Youth:** reprints of Awdeley's 'Fraternitye of Vacabondes,' Harman's 'Caveat for Common Cursetors,' Parson Haben's or Hyberdyne's 'Sermon in Praise of Thieves and Thievery,' &c. With many woodcuts. Edited, with Introduction, by EDWARD VILES and Dr. FURNIVALL. Demy 8vo, cloth, 5s, net.

**Shakespeare's Holinshed:** a reprint of all the passages in Holinshed's 'Chronicle' of which use was made in Shakespeare's Historical Plays, with Notes. Edited by W. G. BOSWELL STONE. Royal 8vo, cloth, 10s. 6d. net.

**The Shakespeare Allusion Book.** Reprints of all references to Shakespeare and his Works before the close of the 17th century, collected by Dr. INGLEBY, Miss L. TOULMIN SMITH, Dr. FURNIVALL, and J. J. MUNRO. Two vols., royal 8vo, cloth, 21s. net.

## SHAKESPEARE LIBRARY—*cont.*

**SHAKESPEARE'S ENGLAND—*cont.***

**Harrison's Description of England.** Part IV. Uniform with Parts I.-III. as issued by the New Shakspere Society. Edited by Dr. FURNIVALL. With additions by Mrs. C. C. STOPES. (250 copies only.) 17s. 6d. net.

**The Book of Elizabethan Verse.** Edited with Notes by WILLIAM STANLEY BRAITHWAITE. With Frontispiece and Vignette. Small crown 8vo, cloth, 3s. 6d. net ; vellum gilt, 7s. 6d. net.

**A Study of Shakespeare.** By A. C. SWINBURNE. Crown 8vo, cloth, 8s.

**The Age of Shakespeare.** By A. C. SWINBURNE. Cr. 8vo, buckram, 6s. net.

**Shakespeare's Sweetheart:** a Romance. By SARAH H. STERLING. With 6 Coloured Illustrations by C. E. PECK. Square 8vo, cloth, 6s.

**SHARP (WILLIAM).—Children of To-morrow.** Crown 8vo, cloth, 3s. 6d.

**SHELLEY'S (PERCY BYSSHE)** Complete Works in VERSE (2 Vols.) and PROSE (2 Vols.), each with Frontispiece. Edited by RICHARD HERNE SHEPHERD. ST. MARTIN'S LIBRARY Edition. Pott 8vo, cloth, 2s. net per vol. ; leather gilt, 3s. net per vol.
*** Also an Edition in 5 vols. cr. 8vo, cloth, 3s. 6d. per vol., in which the POETICAL WORKS form 3 vols. and the PROSE WORKS 2 vols.

**SHERARD (R. H.).—Rogues.** Crown 8vo, cloth, 1s. 6d.

**SHERIDAN'S (RICHARD BRINSLEY) Complete Works.** Edited by F. STAINFORTH. With Portrait and Memoir. Cr. 8vo, cloth, 3s. 6d.

**SHERWOOD (MARGARET).— DAPHNE:** a Pastoral. With Coloured Frontispiece. Crown 8vo, cloth, 3s. 6d.

**SHIEL (M. P.), Novels by.**
**The Purple Cloud.** Cr. 8vo, cloth, 3s. 6d.
**Unto the Third Generation.** Cr. 8vo, cloth, 6s.

**SIGNBOARDS:** The History of, from the Earliest Times: including Famous Taverns and Remarkable Characters. By JACOB LARWOOD and J. C. HOTTEN. With 95 Illustrations. Crown 8vo, cloth, 3s. 6d. net.

**SISTER DORA: a Biography.** By M. LONSDALE. Demy 8vo, 4d. ; cl. 6d.

**SIMS (GEORGE R.), Books by.** Post 8vo, illustrated boards, 2s. each ; cloth limp, 2s. 6d. each.
**The Ring o' Bells.**
**Tinkletop's Crime.** | **Zeph.**
**Dramas of Life.** With 60 Illustrations.
**My Two Wives.** | **Tales of To-day.**
**Memoirs of a Landlady.**
**Scenes from the Show.**
**The Ten Commandments.**

27

**SIMS (GEORGE R.), Books by**—*cont.*
Crown 8vo, picture cover, 1s. each; cloth, 1s 6d. each.
**The Dagonet Reciter and Reader.**
**Dagonet Ditties.** | **Life We Live.**
**Young Mrs. Caudle.**
**Li Ting of London.**
Crown 8vo, cloth, 3s. 6d. each; post 8vo, boards, 2s. each; cloth limp, 2s. 6d. each.
**Mary Jane's Memoirs.**
**Mary Jane Married.**
**Rogues and Vagabonds.**
Crown 8vo, cloth, 3s. 6d. each.
**Joyce Pleasantry.** With a Frontispiece by HUGH THOMSON.
**For Life—and After.**
**Once upon a Christmas Time.** With 8 Illustrations by CHAS. GREEN, R.I.
**In London's Heart.**
**A Blind Marriage.**
**Without the Limelight.**
**The Small-part Lady.**
**Biographs of Babylon.**
**The Mystery of Mary Anne.**
Picture cloth, flat back, 2s. each.
**Rogues and Vagabonds.**
**In London's Heart.**
POPULAR EDITIONS, medium 8vo, 6d. each.
**Mary Jane's Memoirs.**
**Mary Jane Married.**
**Rogues and Vagabonds.**
**How the Poor Live; and Horrible London.** Crown 8vo, leatherette, 1s.
**Dagonet Dramas.** Crown 8vo, 1s.
**Dagonet Abroad.** Crown 8vo, cloth, 3s. 6d.; post 8vo, picture cover, 2s.
**His Wife's Revenge.** Cr. 8vo, cloth 3s. 6d.; CHEAP EDITION, 1s. net.
**Memoirs of a Landlady.** Crown 8vo, cloth, 1s net.

**SLADEN (DOUGLAS).—A Japanese Marriage.** Medium 8vo, 6d.

**SLANG DICTIONARY (The): His-**torical and Anecdotal. Cr. 8vo, cl., 6s. 6d.

**SMEDLEY (CONSTANCE: Mrs. Maxwell Armfield), Novels by.**
**The June Princess.** Cr. 8vo, cl., 3s. 6d.
Crown 8vo, cloth. 6s. each.
**Service.** With Frontispiece.
**Mothers and Fathers.** Frontispiece.
**Commoners' Rights.** With 8 Illustrations by MAXWELL ARMFIELD.
**Una and the Lions.**
See also **The Flower Book**, p. 11.

**SOCIETY IN LONDON.** Crown 8vo, 1s.; cloth, 1s 6d.

**SOMERSET (Lord HENRY).—**
Songs of Adieu. 4to. Jap. vellum, 6s.

**SPALDING (Kenneth J.). — A**
Pilgrim's Way. Fcap. 4to, 3s. 6d. net.

**SPANISH ISLAM: A History of**
the Moslems in Spain. By REINHART DOZY. Translated, with Biographical Introduction and additional Notes, by F. G. STOKES. With Frontispiece and Map. Royal 8vo, buckram, 21s. net.

**SPEIGHT (E. E.).—The Galleon**
of Torbay. Crown 8vo, cloth, 6s.

**SPEIGHT (T. W.), Novels by.**
Post 8vo, illustrated boards. 2s. each.
**The Mysteries of Heron Dyke.**
**By Devious Ways.**
**Hoodwinked;** & Sandycroft Mystery. | **The Golden Hoop.**
**Back to Life.** | **Quittance in Full.**
**The Loudwater Tragedy.**
**Burgo's Romance.**
**A Husband from the Sea.**
Crown 8vo, cloth. 3s. 6d. each
**Her Ladyship.** | **The Grey Monk;**
**The Master of Trenance.**
**The Secret of Wyvern Towers.**
**Doom of Siva.** | **As it was Written**
**The Web of Fate.**
**Experiences of Mr. Verschoyle.**
**Stepping Blindfold:**
**Wife or No Wife.** Post 8vo, cloth. 1s. 6d.

**SPIELMANN (MRS. M. H.), Books by.**
**Margery Redford and her Friends.** With Illustrations by GORDON BROWNE. Large crown 8vo, cloth, 5s. net.
**The Rainbow Book: Sixteen Tales of Fun and Fancy.** With 37 Illustrations by ARTHUR RACKHAM, HUGH THOMSON and other artists. Large crown 8vo. cloth, 2s. 6d. net; also the FINE PAPER EDITION, cloth ilt, 5s. net.

**SPRIGGE (S. SQUIRE).—An Industrious Chevalier.** Cr. 8vo, cl. 3s. 6d.

**'SPY' (FORTY YEARS OF), by**
LESLIE WARD. With over 150 Illustrations after Portraits and Caricatures by the Author. Demy 8vo, cloth. 16s. net.

**STAFFORD (JOHN).—Doris and**
I. Crown 8vo, cloth. 3s. 6d.

**STATHAM (H. HEATHCOTE).**
—What is Music? With Frontispiece. Crown 8vo, cloth, 3s. 6d. net.

**STEDMAN (E. C.).—Victorian**
Poets. Crown 8vo, cloth, 9s.

**STEPHENS (RICCARDO).—The**
Cruciform Mark. Cr. 8vo, cl., 3s. 6d.

**STEPHENS (R. NEILSON).—**
Philip Winwood. Cr. 8vo, cl., 3s. 6d.

**STERLING (S.).—Shakespeare's**
Sweetheart. With 6 Coloured Illustrations by C. E. PECK. Sq. 8vo, cloth, 6s.

**STERNBERG (COUNT). — The**
Barbarians of Morocco. With 12 Illusts. in Colour by DOUGLAS FOX-PITT, R.B.A. Large crown 8vo, cloth, 6s. net.

**STERNDALE (R. ARMITAGE).**
—The Afghan Knife. Post 8vo, cloth, 3s. 6d.; illustrated boards. 2s.

**STERNE (LAURENCE).—**
A Sentimental Journey. With 89 Illustrations by T. H. ROBINSON, and Portrait. Cr. 8vo, cloth, 3s. 6d.; post 8vo, cloth, 2s. net; leather, 3s. net.

**STEVENSON (BURTON E.).—** Affairs of State. Cr. 8vo, cl. 3s. 6d.

**STEVENSON (R. LOUIS),** Works by.

**Virginibus Puerisque, and other Papers.** FLORENCE PRESS EDITION. With 12 Illustrations in Coloured Collotype by NORMAN WILKINSON. Crown 4to, hand-made paper, bds., £2 12s. 6d. net ; vellum, £3 3s. net.

**Stevenson's Poems:** Underwoods, Ballads, Songs of Travel, A Child's Garden of Verses. Printed in the Florence Type. Small fcao. 4to, cloth, 12s. 6d. net ; velvet calf, 18s. net.

Crown 8vo, buckram, 6s. each.

**Travels with a Donkey.** With a Frontispiece by WALTER CRANE.
**An Inland Voyage.** With a Frontispiece by WALTER CRANE.
**Familiar Studies of Men & Books.**
**The Silverado Squatters.** With Frontispiece by J. D. STRONG.
**New Arabian Nights.**
**The Merry Men. | Lay Morals, &c.**
**Underwoods:** Poems.
**Memories and Portraits.**
**Virginibus Puerisque. | Ballads.**
**Prince Otto. | Across the Plains.**
**Weir of Hermiston.**
**In the South Seas.**
**Essays of Travel.**
**Tales and Fantasies.**
**Essays in the Art of Writing.**
**Records of a Family of Engineers**

The above books are also issued in a FINE PAPER EDITION, pott 8vo, cloth, 2s. net each ; leather, 3s. net, with the exception of 'Underwoods' and ' Ballads,' which are printed in 1 vol. together with 'Songs of Travel,' under the title of 'Poems.' 'Records of a Family of Engineers' is also published at 6s. only.

**Songs of Travel.** Cr. 8vo, buckram, 5s.
**A Lowden Sabbath Morn.** With Coloured Front. and numerous Illus. by A. S. BOYD. Crown 8vo, buckram, 6s.

Large crown 8vo, cloth, 5s. net each ; parchment, 7s. 6d. net each ; or, LARGE PAPER EDITIONS, vel., 12s. 6d. net each.

**An Inland Voyage.** With 12 Illustrations in Colour, 12 in Black and White, and other Decorations, by NOEL ROOKE.
**Travels with a Donkey in the Cevennes.** With 12 Illustrations in Colour, 12 in Black and White, and other Decorations, by NOEL ROOKE.
**A Child's Garden of Verses.** With 12 Illustrations in Colour and numerous Black and White Drawings by MILLICENT SOWERBY. Large crown 8vo, cloth, 5s. net ; LARGE PAPER ED., parchment, 7s. 6d. net ; velvet calf, 10s. 6d. net.

Long fcap. 8vo, quarter-cloth, 1s. net each.
**Father Damien.**
**Talk and Talkers.**
**A Christmas Sermon.** Post 8vo, bds., 1s. net ; leather, 2s. net. Also a MINIATURE EDITION in velvet ca'f, 1s. 6d. net.

**STEVENSON (R. L.)—**continued.

**Prayers Written at Vailima.** Post 8vo, bds., 1s. net ; leather, 2s. net. Also a MINIATURE EDITION in velvet c lf yapp, 1s. 6d. net. ; and the EDITION DE LUXE, illum. by A. SANGORSKI in gold and colours, fcap. 4to. Jap. vel., gilt top, 6s. net. ; parch. gilt. with ties, 8s. 6d. net.
**New Arabian Nights.** CHEAPER EDITION, post 8vo, illust. boards. 2s. ; POPULAR EDITION, medium 8vo, 6d.
**The Suicide Club; and The Rajah's Diamond.** (From NEW ARABIAN NIGHTS.) With 8 Illustrations by W. J. HENNESSY. Crown 8vo, cloth, 3s. 6d. 16mo, decorated cloth, 1s. net each.
**The Sire de Malétroit's Door.**
**A Lodging for the Night.**
**The Pavilion on the Links.** With Coloured Frontispiece and numerous Illustrations by GORDON BROWNE, R.I. Demy 8vo, cloth, 3s. 6d. net.
**The Stevenson Reader.** Post 8vo, cloth, 2s. 6d. ; buckram, gilt top, 3s. 6d.; SCHOOL EDITION, cloth, 1s. 6d.
**The Pocket R.L.S.;** Favourite Passages. 16mo. cl., 2s. net ; leather, 3s. net.
**R.L. Stevenson:** A Study. By H. B. BAILDON. With 2 Portraits. Cr. 8vo, buckram, 6s.
**Recollections of R. L. Stevenson in the Pacific.** By ARTHUR JOHNSTONE. Cr. 8vo, buckram, 6s. net.

**STOCKTON (FRANK R.).—The** Young Master of Hyson Hall. With 36 Illusts. Cr. 8vo. cl., 3s. 6d. ; pic. cl., 2 .

**STOKES (FRANCIS GRIFFIN).** Translated and Edited by :
**Epistolæ Obscurorum Virorum (1515-1517).** The Latin text of the Editiones Principes, with English Rendering, Introduction, Notes, and two Plates. Royal 8vo, buckram, 25s. net.
**Spanish Islam : a History of the Moslems in Spain.** By REINHART DOZY. With Introduction and additional Notes by the Translator. Frontispiece and Map. Royal 8vo, buckram, 21s. net.

**STONE (CHRISTOPHER),** Novels by. Crown 8vo, cloth, 6s. each.
**They also Serve.**
**The Noise of Life.**
**The Shoe of a Horse.**

**STRAUS (RALPH), Novels by.** Crown 8vo, cloth, 6s. each.
**The Man Apart.**
**The Little God's Drum.**

**STRUTT (JOSEPH). — The** Sports and Pastimes of the People of England. With 140 Illustrations. Crown 8vo, cloth, 3s. 6d.

**STUART (H. LONGAN), Novels** by. Crown 8vo, cloth, 6s. each.
**Weeping Cross. | Fenella.**

**SUNDOWNER, Stories by.**
**Told by the Taffrail.** Cr. 8vo, 3s. 6d.
**Tale of the Serpent.** Cr. 8vo, cl., 2s.

29

**SUTRO (ALFRED). — The**
Foolish Virgins. Fcp. 8vo. 1s.; cl., 1s.6d.

**SWIFT'S (Dean) Choice Works,**
in Prose and Verse. Cr. 8vo. cl., 3s. 6d.
**Jonathan Swift**: A Study. By J. CHURTON COLLINS. Cr. 8vo. cl., 3s. 6d.

**SWINBURNE'S (ALGERNON CHARLES) Works.**
**Mr. Swinburne's Collected Poems.** In 6 Vols., crown 8vo, 36s. net the set.
**Mr. Swinburne's Collected Tragedies.** In 5Vols., cr.8vo, 30s. net the set.
**Songs before Sunrise.** FLORENCE PRESS EDITION. Crown 4to. hand-made paper, boards, 26s. net ; vellum, 36s. net.
**Selections from Mr. Swinburne's Works.** To which is appended a Sketch of the Poet's Life by Himself, and a Preface. With Portrait and View. Fcap. 8vo, cloth. 6s.

**The Queen-Mother; and Rosamond.** Crown 8vo, 7s. 6d. net.
**Atalanta in Calydon.** Crown 8vo, 6s.
**Chastelard**: A Tragedy. Crown 8vo, 7s
**Poems and Ballads.** FIRST SERIES. Crown 8vo, 9s.
**Poems and Ballads.** SECOND SERIES. Crown 8vo, 9s.
**Poems and Ballads.** THIRD SERIES Crown 8vo, 7s.
**Songs before Sunrise.** Cr. 8vo, 10s. 6d.
**Bothwell**: A Tragedy. Crown 8vo, 12s.6d.
**Songs of Two Nations.** Crown 8vo, 6s.
**George Chapman** (in Vol. II. of G CHAPMAN'S Works.) Crown 8vo, 3s. 6d.
**Essays and Studies.** Crown 8vo, 12s.
**Erechtheus**: A Tragedy. Crown 8vo 6s.
**A Note on Charlotte Bronte.** Crown 8vo, 6s.
**A Study of Shakespeare.** Cr. 8vo, 8s.
**Songs of the Springtides.** Cr. 8vo, 6s.
**Studies in Song.** Crown 8vo, 7s.
**Mary Stuart**: A Tragedy. Crown 8vo, 8s.
**Tristram of Lyonesse.** Crown 8vo, 9s.
**A Century of Roundels.** Cr. 8vo, 6s.
**A Midsummer Holiday.** Cr. 8vo, 7s.
**Marino Faliero**: A Tragedy. Cr. 8vo, 6s.
**A Study of Victor Hugo.** Cr. 8vo, 6s
**Miscellanies.** Crown 8vo, 12s.
**Locrine**: A Tragedy. Crown 8vo, 6s.
**A Study of Ben Jonson.** Cr. 8vo, 7s.
**The Sisters**: A Tragedy. Crown 8vo, 6s.
**Astrophel, &c.** Crown 8vo, 7s.
**Studies in Prose and Poetry.** Crown 8vo, 9s.
**The Tale of Balen.** Crown 8vo, 7s.
**Rosamund,** Queen of the Lombards**: A Tragedy. Crown 8vo, 6s.
**A Channel Passage.** Crown 8vo, 7s.
**Love's Cross-Currents**: A Year's Letters. Crown 8vo, 6s. net.
**William Blake.** Crown 8vo, 6s. net
**The Duke of Gandia.** Crown 8vo, 5s.
**The Age of Shakespeare.** Crown 8vo, 6s. net.
**Charles Dickens.** Cr. 8vo, 3s. 6d. net.

**The Pilgrimage of Pleasure.** See p. 17 for Mrs. DISNEY-LEITH'S **Children of the Chapel.** Cr. 8vo, 6s. net.

**SWINNERTON (FRANK),**
Novels by. Crown 8vo, cloth, 6s. each.
**The Merry Heart.**
**The Young Idea.** | **The Casement.**

**SYRETT (NETTA), Novels by.**
Crown 8vo, cloth, 3s. 6d. each.
**Anne Page.**
**A Castle of Dreams.**
Crown 8vo, cloth, 6s. each.
**Olivia L. Carew.**
**Drender's Daughter.**
**The Endless Journey, &c.**
**Three Women.**
**Barbara of the Thorn.**
POPULAR EDITIONS, medium 8vo, 6d.
**Anne Page.** | **Olivia L. Carew.**
**Three Women.**

**TAINE'S History of English**
Literature. Trans. by HENRY VAN LAUN.
Four Vols., with 32 Portraits, pott 8vo.
cloth, 2s. net each ; leather gilt., 3s. net ea.

**TAYLOR (TOM). — Historical**
Dramas: JEANNE DARC. 'TWIXT AXE AND CROWN. THE FOOL'S REVENGE. ARKWRIGHT'S WIFE. ANNE BOLEYN. PLOT AND PASSION. Cr. 8vo, 1s. each.

**TENNYSON (CHARLES). —**
Cambridge from Within. With 12 Illustrations in Colour and 8 in Sepia by HARRY MORLEY. Dy. 8vo. cl., 7s.6d. net.

**THACKERAY(W. M.).—The Rose**
and The Ring. With Coloured Frontispiece and 44 Illustrations by GORDON BROWNE. Demy 8vo, cloth, 3s. 6d. net.
**The Pocket Thackeray.** Arranged by A. H. HYATT. 16mo, cloth, gilt top, 2s. net ; leather, gilt top. 3s. net.

**THOMAS (ANNIE). — The**
Siren's Web. Crown 8vo, cloth. 3s. 6d.

**THOMPSON (FRANCIS). The**
Hound of Heaven. Ten Drawings Illustrating by FRIDESWITH HUDDART. Royal 4to, boards, 7s. 6d. net. Also 50 copies on parchment, signed by the Artist. 12s. 6d net.

**THOREAU: His Life and Aims.**
By H. A. PAGE. Post 8vo, buckr. 3s. 6d.

**THORNBURY (WALTER). —**
Tales for the Marines. Post 8vo, illustrated boards 2s.

**TIMBS (JOHN), Works by.**
Crown 8vo, cloth, 3s. 6d. each.
**Clubs and Club Life in London.** With 41 Illustrations.
**English Eccentrics and Eccentricities.** With 48 Illustrations.

**TOLSTOY: What he Taught.**
Edited by BOLTON HALL. Crown 8vo, cloth, 6s. net.

**TROLLOPE (FRANCES E.)**
Novels by. Crown 8vo, cloth, 3s. 6d. each; post 8vo, illustrated boards, 2s. each.
**Like Ships upon the Sea.**
**Mabel's Progress.** | **Anne Furness.**

30

**TROLLOPE (ANTHONY), Novels by.** Crown 8vo, cloth, 3s. 6d. each; post 8vo, illustrated boards, 2s. each.
**The Way We Live Now.**
**Frau Frohmann.** | **Marion Fay.**
**The Land-Leaguers.**
**Mr. Scarborough's Family.**
Post 8vo, illustrated boards, 2s. each.
**Kept in the Dark.**
**The American Senator.**
**The Golden Lion of Granpere.**
**John Caldigate.** Crown 8vo, cloth, 3s. 6d.

**TROLLOPE (T. A.).—Diamond Cut Diamond.** Post 8vo, illus. bds., 2s.

**TWAIN'S (MARK) Books.**
UNIFORM LIBRARY EDITION. Crown 8vo, cloth, 3s. 6d. each.
**Mark Twain's Library of Humour** With 197 Illustrations by E. W. KEMBLE.
**Roughing It: and The Innocents at Home.** With 200 Illustrations by F. A. FRASER.
**The American Claimant.** With 81 Illustrations by HAL HURST and others.
**Pudd'nhead Wilson.** With Portrait and Six Illustrations by LOUIS LOEB.
\* **The Adventures of Tom Sawyer.** With 111 Illustrations.
**Tom Sawyer Abroad.** With 26 Illustrations by DAN BEARD.
**Tom Sawyer, Detective.** With Port.
⁹ **A Tramp Abroad.** With 314 Illusts.
\* **The Innocents Abroad; and The New Pilgrim's Progress.** With 234 Illusts. (The 2s. edition is also known as MARK TWAIN'S PLEASURE TRIP.)
⁹ **The Gilded Age.** By MARK TWAIN and C. D. WARNER. With 212 Illusts.
\* **The Prince and the Pauper.** With 190 Illustrations.
\* **Life on the Mississippi.** 300 Illusts.
\* **The Adventures of Huckleberry Finn.** 174 Illusts. by E. W. KEMBLE.
\* **A Yankee at the Court of King Arthur.** 220 Illusts. by DAN BEARD.
\* **The Stolen White Elephant.**
\* **The £1,000,000 Bank-Note.**
**A Double-barrelled Detective Story.** With 7 Illustrations.
**Personal Recollections of Joan of Arc.** With 12 Illusts. by F. V. DU MOND.
**More Tramps Abroad.**
**The Man that Corrupted Hadleyburg.** With Frontispiece.
**The Choice Works of Mark Twain.** With Life, Portrait, and Illustrations.
\*\*\* The Books marked \* may be had in post 8vo, cloth, without Illustrations, at 2s. each.
POPULAR EDITIONS, medium 8vo, 6d. each.
**Tom Sawyer.** | **A Tramp Abroad.**
**The Prince and the Pauper.**
**Huckleberry Finn.**
**Mark Twain's Sketches.** Pott 8vo, cloth, gilt top, 2s. net ; leather, gilt edges, 3s. net ; post 8vo, cloth, 2s.
**The Adventures of Tom Sawyer.** Illustrated by WORTH BREHM. Royal 8vo, cloth, 6s. net.

**TYTLER (C. C. FRASER-).—Mistress Judith.** Post 8vo. boards, 2s.

**TYTLER (SARAH), Novels by.** Crown 8vo, cloth, 3s. 6d. each ; post 8vo, illustrated boards, 2s. each.
**Buried Diamonds.**
**The Blackhall Ghosts.**
**What She Came Through.**
Post 8vo, illustrated boards, 2s. each.
**Saint Mungo's City.** | **Lady Bell.**
**The Huguenot Family.**
**Disappeared.** | **Noblesse Oblige.**
**The Bride's Pass.**
**Beauty and the Beast.**
Crown 8vo, cloth, 3s. 6d. each.
**The Macdonald Lass.**
**The Witch-Wife.**
**Rachel Langton.** | **Sapphira.**
**Mrs. Carmichael's Goddesses.**
**A Honeymoon's Eclipse.**
**A Young Dragon.**
**Three Men of Mark.**
**In Clarissa's Day.**
**Sir David's Visitors.**
**The Poet and His Guardian Angel.**
**Citoyenne Jacqueline.** Crown 8vo, picture cloth, flat back, 2s.

**UPWARD (ALLEN), Novels by.**
**The Queen against Owen.** Crown 8vo, cloth, 3s. 6d. ; picture cloth, flat back, 2s. ; post 8vo, picture boards, 2s.
**The Phantom Torpedo-Boats.** Crown 8vo, cloth, 6s.

**VANDAM (ALBERT D.).—A Court Tragedy.** With 6 Illustrations by J. B. DAVIS. Crown 8vo, cloth, 3s. 6d.

**VAN VORST (MARIE).—Fairfax and his Pride.** Crown 8vo, cloth, 6s.

**VASHTI and ESTHER.** By ' Belle ' of The World. Cr. 8vo, cl., 3s. 6d.

**VICENZA (The PAINTERS of).** By TANCRED BORENIUS. Demy 8vo, cloth, 7s. 6d. net, full-page Plates.

**VIZETELLY (ERNEST A.) Books by.** Crown 8vo, cloth, 3s. 6d. each.
**The Scorpion.**
**The Lover's Progress.**
Crown 8vo, cloth, 6s. each.
**A Path of Thorns.**
**The Wild Marquis:** Life and Adventures of Armand Guerry de Maubreuil. Demy 8vo, cloth, 7s. 6d. net each.
**The Favourites of Louis XIV.** With 4 Portraits.
**My Days of Adventure: the Fall of France, 1870-71.** With a Frontispiece.
**The Court of the Tuileries, 1852-1870.** With a Frontispiece. Demy 8vo, cloth, 5s. net.
**My Adventures in the Commune.** Illustrated. Demy 8vo, cl., 12s. 6d. net.

**WALTON and COTTON'S Complete Angler.** Pott 8vo, cloth, gilt, 2s. net ; leather, gilt edges, 3s. net.

**WARDEN (FLORENCE), by.**
**Joan, the Curate.** Crown 8vo, cloth,
3s. 6d.; picture cloth, flat back, 2s.

Crown 8vo, cloth, 3s. 6d. each.
**The Heart of a Girl.** With 8 Illusts.
**Tom Dawson.**
**The Youngest Miss Brown.**
**A Fight to a Finish.**
**The Old House at the Corner.**
**Love and Lordship.**
**What Ought She to Do?**
**My Lady of Whims.**

**Tom Dawson.** POPULAR EDITION.
Medium 8vo, 6d.

**WARMAN (CY).—The Express**
**Messenger.** Crown 8vo, cloth, 3s. 6d.

**WARRANT to Execute Charles I.**
With the 59 Signatures and Seals. 2s.
**Warrant to Execute Mary Queen**
**of Scots.** Including Queen Elizabeth's
Signature and the Great Seal. 2s.

**WASSERMANN (LILLIAS).—**
The Daffodils. Crown 8vo, cloth, 1s. 6d.

**WERNER (A.). — Chapenga's**
**White Man.** Crown 8vo, cloth, 3s. 6d.

**WESTALL (WILL.), Novels by.**
**Trust-Money.** Crown 8vo, cloth, 3s. 6d.;
post 8vo, illustrated boards, 2s.
**With the Red Eagle** POPULAR
EDITION, medium 8vo, 6d.

Crown 8vo, cloth, 3s. 6d. each.
**A Woman Tempted Him.**
**For Honour and Life.**
**Her Two Millions.**
**Two Pinches of Snuff.**
**With the Red Eagle.**
**A Red Bridal.** | **Nigel Fortescue.**
**Ben Clough.** | **Birch Dene.**
**The Old Factory.**
**Sons of Belial.** | **Strange Crimes.**
**Her Ladyship's Secret.**
**The Phantom City.**
**Ralph Norbreck's Trust.**
**A Queer Race.** | **Red Ryvington.**
**Roy of Roy's Court.**
**As Luck would have it.**
**As a Man Sows.**
**The Old Bank.**
**Dr. Wynne's Revenge.**
**The Sacred Crescents.**
**A Very Queer Business.**

**WESTBURY (ATHA). — The**
Shadow of Hilton Fernbrook. Crown
8vo, cloth, 3s. 6d.

**WHISHAW (FRED.), Novels**
by. Crown 8vo, cloth, 3s. 6d. each.

**A Forbidden Name.** | **Mazeppa.**
**Many Ways of Love.** With 8 Illusts.
**Near the Tsar, near Death.**

**WHITMAN (WALT), Poems by.**
Selected and Edited, with Introduction
by W. M. ROSSETTI. With Portrait.
Crown 8vo, buckram, 6s.; pott 8vo, cloth,
2s. net; leather, 3s. net.

**WILDE (LADY).—The Ancient**
**Legends, Charms, and Superstitions**
**of Ireland.** Crown 8vo, cloth, 3s. 6d.

**WILLIAMS (W. MATTIEU).—**
**The Chemistry of Cookery.** Crown
8vo. cloth, 6s.

**WILLIAMSON (Mrs. F. H.).—A**
**Child Widow.** Post 8vo, illust. bds., 2s.

**WILLS (C. J.).—An Easy-going**
**Fellow.** Crown 8vo, cloth 3s. 6d.

**WILSON (Dr. ANDREW), by.**
**Leisure-Time Studies.** With Illustra-
tions. Crown 8vo, cloth. 6s.
**Common Accidents, and how to**
**Treat Them.** Cr. 8vo, cloth, 1s. net;
paper cover, 6d. net.

**WINTER (JOHN STRANGE), by.**
**Regimental Legends.** Post 8vo,
Illustrated boards, 2s.; cloth, 2s. 6d.
**Cavalry Life; and Regimental**
**Legends.** Crown 8vo, cloth, 3s. 6d.;
picture cloth, flat back, 2s.

**WOOD (H. F.), Detective Stories**
by. Post 8vo, illustrated boards 2s. each.
**Passenger from Scotland Yard.**
**The Englishman of the Rue Cain.**

**WORDSWORTHSHIRE: An In-**
**troduction to the Poet's Country.**
By ERIC ROBERTSON, M.A. With 47 Illustrations by ARTHUR TUCKER, R.B.A., Portrait and Map. Dy. 8vo, cloth, 7s. 6d. net.

**WRAGGE (CLEMENT L.).—**
**The Romance of the South Seas.**
With 84 Illusts. Cr. 8vo, cl., 7s. 6d. net

**ZANGWILL (LOUIS).—A Nine-**
**teenth Century Miracle.** Crown 8vo,
cloth, 3s. 6d.; picture cloth, flat back, 2s.

**ZOLA (EMILE), Novels by.**
UNIFORM EDITION. Mostly Translated or
Edited, with Introductions, by ERNEST
A. VIZETELLY. Cr. 8vo. cloth, 3s. 6d. each.
**His Masterpiece.** | **The Joy of Life.**
**Germinal.** | **Thérèse Raquin.**
**The Honour of the Army.**
**Abbe Mouret's Transgression.**
**The Fortune of the Rougons.**
**The Conquest of Plassans.**
**The Dram-Shop.**
**The Fat and the Thin.** | **Money.**
**His Excellency.** | **The Dream.**
**The Downfall.** | **Doctor Pascal.**
**Lourdes.** | **Fruitfulness.**
**Rome.** | **Work.**
**Paris.** | **Truth.**

**The Downfall.** WAR EDITION. Cr. 8vo,
cloth, 2s. net.
POPULAR EDITIONS, medium 8vo, 6d. each.
**Abbe Mouret's Transgression.**
**The Fortune of the Rougons.**
**Lourdes.** | **Rome.** | **The Downfall.**
**Paris.** | **Money.** | **The Dram-**
**The Joy of Life.** | shop.
**Germinal.** | **Thérèse Raquin.**
**Dr. Pascal.**

UNWIN BROTHERS, Ltd., Printers, 27, Pilgrim Street, Ludgate Hill, London, E.C.

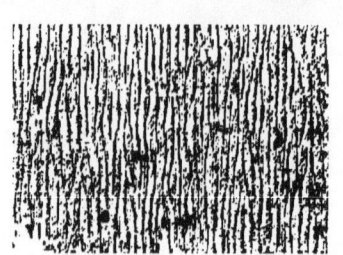

www.ingramcontent.com/pod-product-compliance
Lightning Source LLC
Chambersburg PA
CBHW060512030726
47498CB00004B/915